Love is
a time of enchantment:
in it all days are fair and all fields
green. Youth is blest by it,
old age made benign:
the eyes of love see
roses blooming in December,
and sunshine through rain. Verily
is the time of true-love
a time of enchantment — and
Oh! how eager is woman
to be bewitched!

THE PEACOCK RIDER

Robert Reid and his wife Laura are living in the beautiful valley of Lambagh with their four-year-old son, James. On his father's recent demise, Robert has become Sir Robert Reid, and the new owner of the family estate, Moxton Park in England. But Robert's heart is in India. Laura, however, is desperately homesick, and, expecting their second child, implores him to return to England with her. Meanwhile, trouble is brewing in the neighbouring states, and Kassim Khan, Ruler of Lambagh, enlists Robert's help.

KATHARINE GORDON

THE PEACOCK RIDER

Complete and Unabridged

ULVERSCROFT
Leicester

First published in Great Britain in 1994 by
Severn House Publishers Limited
Surrey

First Large Print Edition
published 1996
by arrangement with
Severn House Publishing Limited
Surrey

British Library CIP Data

Gordon, Katharine
    The peacock rider.—Large print ed.—
Ulverscroft large print series: romance
1. English fiction—20th century
I. Title
823.9′14 [F]

ISBN 0–7089–3604–0

Published by
F. A. Thorpe (Publishing) Ltd.
Anstey, Leicestershire

Set by Words & Graphics Ltd.
Anstey, Leicestershire
Printed and bound in Great Britain by
T. J. Press (Padstow) Ltd., Padstow, Cornwall

This book is printed on acid-free paper

1

AUTUMN had come to the valley. The herds had been brought down from the high pastures; the village houses had roofs of gold where the maize cobs and the pumpkin slices had been put out to dry before storage, and chillies strung on cord hung like chains of uncut rubies from every balcony. Winter was still a few months away, but each morning the snow that lay in fresh glitter on the far peaks was a little further down the slopes. At night the wind had a bite in it that spoke of the cold to come, and the swifts had all gone from their nests under the temple eaves.

It was in the cold dark hour before dawn that the messenger came to Lambagh, his coat blowing in the chill wind, his horse clattering over the frost-hard cobbles of the road outside the old Lambagh Palace. The noise brought the guard out, and the messenger, dismounting stiffly, as exhausted as his horse, found himself surrounded by watchful faces. Lamplight gleamed on curved swords, and he spoke quickly.

He carried a message he said, from the Raja of Jungdah, and it was to be delivered from his hand to the Ruler's hand. He produced the message, carefully wrapped and tied into yellow silk. He was well dressed, though the lanterns they held up showed that his clothes had suffered on the journey, as had his horse.

"You came in great haste, man of Jungdah."

It came out as a question more than a statement, but the messenger was not talkative.

"When may I go before the Lord of the Hills?"

"When he wakes."

The messenger glanced over his shoulder at the darkness outside the circle of lamplight, and then back to the guard commander.

"He wakes soon?"

"With dawn. He rides early."

Once again the messenger looked over his shoulder into the darkness, and the guard commander frowned.

"What is it, man? What follows you? Is there war in your hills?"

The messenger shook his head.

"Nay — nothing. I am but the carrier. How do I know what passes between the lords of the valleys? But I was told to return as I came — with speed."

"Do not be a fool then. You die on your feet in front of us, and have you taken stock of your animal? We will be lucky to walk him as far as the stables. You will be taken to the Ruler when he wakes. Until then, come in and sleep for an hour."

The messenger did not sleep. He sat in disarray, visibly exhausted, on the string bed they had given him in the guard room. He stared at the window with red-rimmed eyes, watching for the morning or perhaps for something else, for his free hand rested on the hilt of his dagger.

They took the dagger from him before they led him into the room where the Ruler of Lambagh stood. Through the window of the room the messenger could see the red streaked sky, and two horses that waited, stamping and blowing in the cold of the morning.

The letter, divested of its yellow silk, was read quickly. The Ruler looked at the man standing in a shaft of early sunlight.

"Your name?"

The messenger tried to hold himself erect.

"Shivnath, Lord."

"You rode hard. The guard told me that your horse was almost foundered."

"My master so ordered, Lord — that I was to come with speed."

"How many days?"

"A day and a night, Lord."

"Without drawing rein from the look of you. You did well. Now go and sleep. The letter is in my hand. You will have your answer soon."

"Lord, it was also ordered that I return as swiftly as I came."

"You heard me, Shivnath. You will have your answer, and a fresh horse to take you back. Go now, and sleep." No one in the hill countries argued with Kassim Khan. The message safely delivered, there seemed to be nothing to hold the messenger upright. He raised his hands, palm to palm and bowed over them, and staggered from the room, almost falling in the process. In minutes he was asleep in the quarter allotted to him.

But before he would even lie down, he asked for his dagger, and it was clenched in his hand as he fell asleep.

The Ruler was re-reading the letter when his name was called and he looked up smiling as his wife came into the room. She lifted a willing mouth to his kiss, as if she had not lain close against his side all the night, but had just returned from a journey. The Begum Sara had adored her husband as a child. Now, the mother of a grown son, she still loved her husband with a passion that was returned.

"The horses are getting cold. Do we ride today, or shall I have them sent back to the stables? Is it bad news that came this morning? Or some news that will change the day in other ways?"

"The news, I regret, will not affect the Chotamahal. But I do not know if it is bad news or not. As I read

5

it, it is a perfectly ordinary letter from one ruler to another, making a request that is not difficult to grant. But the messenger nearly killed himself and his horse getting here, and had the shadow of a great fear about him. He was ordered to come swiftly by his master of Jungdah, and wishes to return at once — and yet there is no haste written in the letter. Well, we will ride, and I will speak to the messenger again later."

He took his wife's hand and walked out with her, reflecting that another hour or two would make little difference according to the words written in the letter. It was the words that were not there to be read that interested him, and by the time they had enjoyed their morning ride the messenger would be rested and better able to answer questions.

They rode beside the blue, reed-bordered lake, letting their horses go until they began to slow of their own accord. Then they reined to a stop and stayed to look at the lake, and in it the reflections of the white peaks broken by the busy forays of the water birds.

Sara said softly, her eyes full of tears,

and her voice breaking, "Poor Robert. On such a morning . . . "

She was looking at the small white palace that stood on a hill on the other side of the lake, its domed roof pearly in the light.

The Chotamahal, the place that had been the home of so much happiness. The Ruler shook his head with a grimace.

"It would not matter if there was a blizzard — today could be no worse for him."

"When I heard that there had been a message from outside the valley, I hoped that it would be news that would somehow stop this tragedy."

"Nothing would have stopped it. She is determined to go." He turned, and leaning over, took his wife's hand and raised it to his lips. As always she turned her hand so that he kissed her palm, and she folded her hand over, closing it as if she held something precious.

"If you ever left me . . . " His voice was a growl, his eyes slitted in ferocity that was only half assumed.

"I never will, while life lasts. You know that, my dear Lord."

They looked at each other, each seeing the most precious and beloved creature in the world. Their love did not need to be told, and yet, like all lovers, they told it. He kissed her hand again, and then pulled her half out of the saddle to kiss the tears away from her eyes. "Do not weep for anyone, my darling. I cannot bear to see you weep. I promise you I will help Robert in every way I can. Be happy."

They stayed beside the lake, talking softly together, until, faint on the morning air they heard the bleating of sheep and goats being taken down to the river meadows. It was time to go back, and take up the business of the day, and they turned their horses for home.

On the other side of the lake men rode up the twisting path to the white palace, followed by other men leading pack mules. A day that Robert Reid had dreaded had dawned, and must be lived through.

Robert had not slept that night. He had not wished to sleep. He wanted the night to last forever, so that he could lie beside his wife, and hear her soft breathing, and pretend that nothing had changed in his life. Lying like that, it was easy to think that all was well, that nothing could change, nothing go wrong in his life.

It was a bird, suddenly starting to sing, that broke his false dream. Hearing the first tentative notes of the bird's song, he knew that the night was almost over, this precious last night.

In spite of the darkness, the bird grew confident, and began to sing loudly, a throbbing, bubbling song that ran like water into the room. Sweet and silver, gentle as moonlight, the song swelled, reminding Robert of many other nights, filling his heart with pain. It was a bulbul singing, the nightingale of India, singing its autumn song.

Robert listened and recalled the nightingales that sang in the woods of Moxton Park, his father's home in England. He did not think of England with nostalgia. All that he wanted was here, in the beautiful valley of Lambagh. Still here, although soon he would be lying alone in this great bed, and Laura, his beloved, and, as he had thought, loving, wife, would be in England.

The pain that seized him as he thought about it was half made up of a burning anger, a stinging fury of pride. He did not any longer hear the bird, although it was still singing. He lay, remembering with an astonished rage, how quietly determined Laura had been in her decision to take their four-year-old son James and return to England.

The letter from Lady Reid, his grandmother, giving them the news of his father's sudden death, had, no doubt about it, provided Laura with the excuse she must have been looking for for some time. That was what hurt him. That she had wanted to go.

She had said nothing for a month, while the Lambagh family, and the people of the valley, had mourned with Robert. They had all known his father, Alan Reid, and he had been held in great respect in the valley where he had been as a young man, and where he had met Muna, his beautiful wife, Robert's mother.

When the month had passed, Laura had announced that she thought it was time Robert returned to England.

"You have inherited the place, and the title now, Robert. You are Sir Robert Reid, and you have responsibilities and duties in Moxton Park, which is, after all, your real home. We must go back, and be with your grandmother. She must be so lonely with both your grandfather and your father gone." She had avoided Robert's amazed stare. He had answered her in a tone of voice that he had never used with her before.

"I am Dil Bahadur, Nawab of Lambagh. This is our home, Laura. As for my grandmother, she will be lonely now until she dies. No one is ever going to take the place of my grandfather in her life, least of all I. And she would be the very last person to expect me to uproot my life and go back to England. Look at me, Laura — look at me, and tell me that you did not know, when you married me, where my life was set!"

"Of course I knew that you love this valley, and enjoy your life here. But it is different now! This title of Nawab is a courtesy title, given to you by Kassim Khan. This Dil Bahadur business is a masquerade, Robert! A dream! Your real life, your real home, is in England. The estate cannot run itself, and you have a son to think of now. Is his future of no importance to you? Do you mean to bring him up as — as an *Indian* boy?"

Under the sudden flare of anger in Robert's eyes she had become silent. His voice was very cold.

"The *courtesy* title was given to me by the Ruler of Lambagh when he adopted me as his son. The estate in England is remarkably well run by the man my grandfather engaged when my father rejoined his regiment after my mother's death. As for James — he can very well stay here until he is eleven, when he will go to school in England."

"Like all the Lambagh Princes!" said Laura, furious suddenly.

"Yes. Is that so terrible?"

"No. Except that he is *not* a Lambagh prince. He is my son, an English boy, and he will, in due course, be Sir James Reid."

"When I am dead, you mean? You speak as if you are looking forward to his inheritance!"

"Robert!"

"Well, so it sounds to me. He is my son too, Laura. You appear to have forgotten that my mother was Indian, so I must remind you that Robert has my blood in him too. As far as I am concerned this is his home. And yours, Laura. Unless you can think of any other good excuses for leaving the valley, where you are, as you know, much loved. Do you hate Lambagh so much that you search for excuses to get away?"

There was pain as well as anger in his voice, but Laura heard only the anger, and had reacted swiftly with a rage of her own.

"Yes!" she flung at him. "Yes. I hate it. Hate India as a whole. Loathe it. Have I not reason enough, with my memories?" It was as if she had taken a dagger and stabbed him. Robert had gone white, and when he next spoke his voice was shaking with pain.

"Your memories — yes, I agree, you had a terrible experience when you were kidnapped. But your memories are twisted, Laura. You were taken by a European, not an Indian. It was an Indian girl who saved you,

13

almost losing her life to do it. Had you forgotten Meeta, and all that she did?"

"I forget nothing about Meeta. Nothing, Robert. I love the Ruler, and the Begum Sara, and the family in Madore — of course I do. I am not ungrateful for all the kindnesses and the love; I love in return — but — "

"In all this list of love and remembrance, I notice one omission." Laura, tears on her face, stared at him, and he moved closer to her.

"Have you forgotten me, Laura, in this welter of sudden hate and love? Where do I stand? You once said that you would love me forever — and now . . . ?" She was caught in his arms, her sobs muffled against his shoulder.

"Oh Robert, I do love you — with all my heart, you know I do. If I did not love you, do you think I would have been able to stay here so long, in a place where every sound that I do not recognise makes me afraid, where I fear not only for myself, but for you and for James — what do you think I feel when you go off on border fights, when I am

14

alone here, waiting for news?"

"But the other wives — you are not alone in this."

"Do you imagine that makes it any better? And they do not have the same fears. They are born here, are of this country. Oh Robert, I want to go home — please, I want to go home. I am homesick, Robert, don't you see? And there is something else — "

"Oh yes? What else can there be?"

"Robert, please listen to me — dear love, don't be so angry with what I cannot help. You remember James's birth was not an easy one. I should like to bear my next child in my own country."

The words had dropped like stones into the pool of Robert's silence. He had not known that she was pregnant, and was bitterly hurt that she had chosen such a way to tell him. He remembered the night that she had told him she was carrying their first child. Then they had sat, talking and dreaming over the future, sharing the same goblet of wine, passing it from her hand to his, with a kiss before every sip, watching the new moon rise, pale in the evening sky above

15

the lake. She had been glowing with joy and with love.

Now she was using her pregnancy as a weapon. To say that she wished to bear *her* child in *her* country! There could only be one ending to all this. He loved her with all that he was, heart and body and soul. To see her unhappy was more than he could bear. He gave her two years. No more. She could go back to England for two years. Then, if she wished, she could return, or she could stay. But in either event, the children were to come back. He told her this, with a face that was set like granite, to disguise his pain and anger. She thanked him with a radiant happiness, a wild gratitude that showed him the intensity of her desire to go, and hurt his pride still more. She did not seem to remember that he was not going with her.

2

THE pain of these memories became too much to bear. Robert's mind blocked them off. He heard the bird's song again, gentle and tender, seeming to hold in its soft cadences all the heartbreak in the world.

Robert was only hours away from a parting from his wife which might be a permanent break, and Laura was so deeply asleep that it was as if she had already gone from him, although he could feel her hair spilling over his arm like warm silk, and hear her even breathing.

The room grew lighter, the high arched window glimmering silver with dawn. He turned to look down at his wife lying asleep, her face half veiled by her tossed hair. Her shadowed eyelids, her mouth red with the night's kisses; the dawn discovered one thing after another, touching at last the white shoulders and the gentle curving breasts. He leaned over and kissed her, pulling her close.

"My dear love . . . "

She turned in his arms, her eyes opening, her body ready for him before she was properly awake. Her cry as he took her to the heights of love — was he never to hear it again? Lost, forgetting everything but each other, they burned with a fire brighter than the rising sun. She fell back at last, his name whispering on her lips and he watched as the tides of sleep overwhelmed her again. He lay, looking at the light grow in the room and wondered how she could sleep. By the time this sunlight had moved, and grown brighter, had faded and gone down into darkness they would be apart; and she wasted precious time in sleep.

A child's voice called outside, and he heard the stamp and clatter of horses. His grief lost itself in a wave of fury. Laura was taking two years of his son's life from him. He would lose two years of watching the boy grow. This was hard to forgive. But she sighed in her sleep, and he saw that there had been tears on her face. She was, after all, not going easily, whatever she might say. He put his lips lightly on her outstretched arm, and got out of bed. It was time to start this terrible day . . . by having a farewell ride with his son.

He watched the boy riding, and set himself to avoid any signs of grief. At last the ride was over, and with it, one of the ordeals of the day. The worst was yet to come. The final goodbye.

Laura was meeting English friends, the Lees, at Faridkote, a town in the foothills. Lady Lees was coming down from Pakodi, a neighbouring state, where her husband was Agent, and was travelling to England herself, so Laura and James would be well escorted.

Robert said goodbye to Laura at the Lungri Pass. Their farewell was brief because it was unbearable. Robert held his little son in his arms, feeling the child's body wriggling with excitement. Why not? He could have no conception of the length of time that would pass before he saw his father again. He was setting off on an adventure, a journey. Robert would not have wished him to be sad. He put his son down, and it was time to say goodbye to Laura.

He took her shoulders between his hands, and saw that she was in great trouble. This going from him was as hard a thing for her as it was for him. She clung to him at the last, uncaring about the escort, and wept.

"Laura! For God's sake! Come home, dearest heart, this is stupidity. Come *home*," said Robert, half out of his mind with pain, forgetting all pride. "Please Laura, come back with me now — *please*."

"I have to go," said Laura, and sobbed as she saw the grief on his face change to anger. She pulled herself out of his arms, and ran to her horse.

He said no more. He helped her to mount, and she leaned down to him, giving him her hand, the hand on which he had put the Peacock Ring, the great emerald that was a perfect copy of the ring he wore on a chain round his neck. Her ring burned with fires of its own as her hand moved.

"Remember me, Robert? Remember me, darling," said Laura, as if she were being sent away for ever, and Robert could only look, and kiss the beringed little hand, and step back.

They rode away then, James turning to wave before the escort closed in around them. But Laura did not turn. She rode on, without looking back once.

Robert stayed where he was, his horse cropping at the thin grass. He sat, unmindful of time, looking at the mist that had drifted over the pass. There was always a moving, swirling mist at this pass. Against this moving curtain, he saw a picture of Laura, always the same picture. Laura, riding away from him without a backward look. Time lost itself in pain, did not exist. He sat, totally without coherent thought, as still and cold as the rocks about him.

When his horse stamped and whinnied, he came back to the present, and found that the high peaks had turned from white to flame. The sun he had seen moving the shadows on his bedroom floor that morning had almost set.

The day was over.

Live pain stabbed him into action. He stood up and looked down the track. The mist had cleared, but the path was empty, there was nothing to see. Laura had gone.

Robert could never be sure, afterwards, what he intended to do when he turned towards his horse. He might have lost all pride and raced down the track to Faridkote to find Laura and force her to come back. But when he turned, he found that he was not alone.

Kassim Khan, the Ruler himself, was sitting quietly in the shadows, holding his horse, and Robert had no way of knowing that he had been there for at least two hours.

"Kassim Khan — " The Ruler smiled, and stood up, stretching.

"At last! I was afraid that you would have moss growing on you if you did not move soon. I know that you wanted to be alone for your farewells, but there is a time for being alone and a time for the family to be close to help you. You have had your time alone. Now, in the name of all that is good let us get home. We are both cold, and we both need a drink. Also — while you have been out of our world, a message has come, and I want you to look at it. Come?"

They mounted and turned their horses and rode down into Lambagh, down the long, twisting road they both knew so well, and into the narrow streets, where now light spilled from open doors and women's voices called to their children as the night settled in.

In the old Palace there was light and warmth and welcome. Robert's face was cold and set as he entered the big lamplit room where the Begum Sara held out her hand to him. When he bent over her, she looked up and saw his eyes, and pulled his head down to kiss him, saying nothing. She had not seen him for three days and in that time what had happened to him? Even the timbre of his voice had changed. His voice was harsh as he greeted her, in spite of its control, and his face looked older, with a sort of bitter pride, a cold arrogance that she had never seen there before, though Kassim Khan had once or twice remarked that Robert in a rage was a difficult man to handle. She saw that the rage was there, behind that controlled, bitter face. What on earth had Laura done to him? Sara had, in her life with Kassim Khan, seen rage on his face, though never directed at her. Now she saw that same dangerous look on Robert's face. He could never look anything but handsome but now he looked remarkably hard and almost cruel. She kissed him again and told him to get himself a drink. She decided that she would make no reference to Laura. That subject would be left until it could be approached with safety.

Robert was grateful for her silence. He could not trust himself to discuss an event that had struck so cruelly at his self esteem and confidence.

As they ate and drank Robert heard of the messenger from Jungdah.

"Jungdah. Pakodi's wife came from there."

"Yes. She is there, with her father and mother, and with her son, born after Pakodi's death. I am Regent for Pakodi State, as you know, until the boy is of age. Now — well, read this." Robert read the letter and agreed that there did not seem to be any reason for undue haste in sending an answer.

"The old Raja wants you to send for the boy and bring him up here. He wants him to be sent to England in due course and then he wants him to do a year with our forces before he comes of age and ascends the guddee of Pakodi. All very sensible and suitable. How old is the boy?"

The Ruler raised his eyebrows.

"You do not remember? He was born about eight months after his father was murdered in Bombay. He must be a year older than your James."

Sara looked at her husband, but Robert's voice was even when he replied.

"So he is about five. I really do not understand what all the haste is about. *Five?* His mother and his grandmother will have something to say about it if the old Raja decides to take the boy away from them now."

"His mother — didn't you read the letter? His mother comes too."

Robert returned, frowning, to the letter.

"Oh yes, I see. But even so — less need for a scurrying messenger and a hasty answer, I should have thought. What did the messenger say? Did you ask *him* what all the speed means?"

"I did, and he said he knew nothing, and stood there looking like a frightened mule and repeating that all he knew was that when the Raja put the letter into his hand he told him to make all haste and to return with my reply at once. He is sitting in the guard room now, with everything girded up, waiting to go, and he is terrified. But even the men can get nothing out of him. I told the guard to soften him up with a drink or two, but he would not drink. Then they thought of the House of Many Pleasures, and would have taken him down there, but he struck them all dumb by saying that he had taken a strong vow against women until he had given my answer to his Raja in Jungdah. He holds the hilt of his dagger in his hand all the time, and will not turn his back on a window or a door. Very strange."

Robert started to read the letter through again, and the Ruler laughed, watching him.

"You will have it by heart, boy, as I have. There is nothing of haste in that letter. But all the same . . ."

Robert nodded. "Yes. A feeling."

"A feeling. Well, I have sent for Jiwan Khan. He should be here tomorrow. Then we can all study the letter again. I cannot send an answer to a question that I have not been asked, until I know what the question is. All this about the boy is so straightforward, it is nothing. It could easily take two or three months to make the arrangements at that end, what with the young Begum shifting her household, and all the farewells to the heir — for that boy is the only heir, not only to Pakodi but to Jungdah as well. Pakodi was no fool. Rich as he was himself, he married money as well. No. There is something here I do not understand, and until I do see what it is, the messenger will have to sit and be patient. Jiwan Khan might have heard something that will explain a bit of this puzzle, which should not be a puzzle."

Jiwan Khan, Kassim Khan's only son, and his heir, was acting as his father's representative in Pakodi State. He arrived late the following evening, with a two-man escort, all three of them on lathered horses. Robert rode out to meet him. The two men were close friends, and

Jiwan Khan had long stopped thinking of Robert as an adopted brother. It seemed that they *were* brothers as well as friends. They clattered back into the fort, where Robert had decided to live, unable to face the ringing silence of the Chotamahal.

Jiwan Khan gave Robert a quick, comprehensive look, asked one question and thereafter did not mention Laura's name. He bathed and changed in Robert's quarters and they rode together to the old Palace, racing each other over the Maidan and through the narrow streets to draw up with a flourish at the Palace gates. Then, turbans correctly slanted, they strode in to find the Ruler and Sara, who welcomed Jiwan Khan no more warmly than they greeted Robert; one was their only son, the other the adopted son of their hearts.

Jiwan Khan had heard nothing in Pakodi of any happenings in Jungdah. He read the letter twice, and shook his head over it.

"I smell fear. Why?"

"Allah alone knows. If there had been danger of fighting between two states, I would have heard."

This was true. The Ruler had an information service that was envied not only by his fellow rajas. Jiwan Khan and Robert exchanged glances and the Ruler nodded, as if they had spoken.

"Yes. I would have heard of anything serious. But Jungdah is only four days' easy riding from here, and the messenger did it in a day and a night, nearly killing himself and his horse."

"Haste indeed!"

The yellow silk that had been wrapped about the letter was lying on a little ivory table beside Sara. As she watched the three men, and listened, she picked the silk up and ran it through her fingers. Beautiful silk, soft and fine, and embroidered with little flowers and scrolls.

"Kassim! Kassim, look at this — "

"What?"

Sarah was holding the silk out to him.

"Kassim, look, there are words embroidered on this silk. Some of these scrolls are words. Here, and here. See?"

"Yes — I see. What do they say?"

"'Come soon'," read Sara.

" 'Come like the wind, the North Wind, for the birds of the South are flying and the summer is almost gone. Come soon my love, come soon, or who will hear my song?' "

"Well, it is an old love-song," said Jiwan Khan, and hummed a few bars. "The kerchief must have been a love gift from some girl to the messenger and he kept it and used it to wrap about the letter. What else? Perhaps that explains his haste. He wishes to return to the girl."

"Yes. But does a love gift inspire fear? Also, that is beautiful silk. A princely gift for a messenger."

The Ruler looked at the yellow silk, frowning.

"If that old fool in Jungdah needs help, why does he not ask for it?" Jiwan Khan was getting irritable.

"He is no fool, that old man," said his father. "Perhaps he *is* asking for it."

"What! Embroideries on yellow silk? Wah! We live in an old story, with love tokens and hidden messages."

"Jungdah is a small state, a poor state with a very rich raja. The people are backward, the living hard. It is not a fertile valley. The Raja is good to his people, bringing in food, paying from his own pocket when times are bad. But he is very old, and his only heir is the son of his daughter, a child." The Ruler was thinking aloud, and both Jiwan Khan and Robert were silent. Kassim Khan poured himself a goblet of wine and drinking it, gave them his plan. He would send an answer to the Raja. Robert, who had not seen the messenger, was to travel with him, as an ordinary trooper of the Lambagh State Forces, as far as Jungdah.

"Look, and listen, and be very wary. If you have any suspicions, when you have reached Jungdah, then return at once, and fast. I will wait for seven days, for news. If there is none, I shall send you, Jiwan Khan, with an escort of fifty men. Dil Bahadur, you will remain hidden and join Jiwan Khan before he makes his official entry into the palace — Dhalli Palace. It is built some distance away from the principal town of Jungdah. You will join Jiwan Khan as yourself, my adopted son, Nawabzaida Sahib of

Lambagh, Dil Bahadur. Then, with as little delay as possible you will escort the Begum and her son back here."

The plan seemed a good one to two young men, both anxious for action; Jiwan Khan because he had spent a long, boring summer learning statecraft from Sir Richard Lees in Pakodi, Robert because anything that promised to keep his thoughts from Laura was welcome.

The messenger, called in and told he could leave the following day with a fresh horse and a guard, expressed gratitude but disclaimed any need for the guard.

"I am sending a man with you, nevertheless," said the Ruler firmly. "It is a gesture of courtesy to your Raja."

Against this, there was nothing the messenger could say. He salaamed and left. Robert, standing out of sight, studying his face, agreed with the Ruler when he said, "That man is terrified of something — what?"

"Yes. Terrified. Perhaps I shall find out on the journey," said Robert.

Shortly afterwards, the two young men left, their horses rousing echoes in the narrow, sleeping streets.

After they had gone, Sara, looking at the flowers and the scrolls that made words on the yellow silk, was full of thought.

"Sara, beloved, what is it?"

"I am afraid we send our sons into danger — I do not like this 'Come like the wind' . . . "

"Bird of my heart, be still. I would not send them there if I thought they would be in danger. Dil Bahadur is not a fool. If there is bad trouble he will get word back here before Jiwan Khan leaves."

Sara said, "Dil Bahadur — Robert — has changed. Did you notice how changed he is? When he came in with Jiwan Khan tonight he was like a stranger coming in."

"Yes. I think the name Robert is no longer suitable for him. He is now entirely Dil Bahadur and a very reckless man. He looks for trouble to enable him to forget something that he thinks has made him less of a man. Laura's departure."

"And yet you think it good to send him on this journey? I think that if he does not find trouble, he may make it."

"No. Not if it might touch Jiwan Khan or Lambagh State. He will be cautious for us, where he would be reckless for himself. My love. Come to bed. Kiss me and take that look of worry from your eyes. I promise you, our sons are not going into harm. They are grown men, beloved."

Sara's lovely eyes closed under his kisses, and her mouth smiled, but behind her closed eyes it seemed to her that she could see the beautiful face of Muna, the dancer who had been Robert's mother, and now the words she could hear sounded like a warning.

"Come soon, come like the wind . . . "

3

ROBERT and the messenger, Shivnath, rode fast, and in silence. Shivnath, once he discovered that his companion could ride well and was willing to ride without stopping for as long as Shivnath wished, looked happier. Robert let him lead. When narrow paths, or slippery slopes forced them to slow down, he saw how Shivnath turned his head constantly, looking at every rock or fold of country that might provide cover for an ambush. This was interesting. The foe that Shivnath feared was not in Lambagh, but travelled with them, or waited for them. Robert became very watchful thereafter, but there was nothing. They stopped only when they had to, to rest their animals. Finally, tired men on tired horses, they arrived at a high, windy pass and Shivnath at last drew rein. When Robert came up beside him, he saw that the man was smiling. This must be the end of the journey. The relief of a task accomplished showed in every line of Shivnath's body.

"We have arrived? Or we rest here?"

"We have arrived. We rest, and wait. The Raja will take the message from me here."

"Here? The Raja comes here himself?"

"Yes. He thinks it best. My village is there. See? Beyond the old fort." Robert followed the line of his pointing hand, and saw a walled fort, so old that it was hard to distinguish it from the rocks that matched its walls, and beyond, a village perched in a patchwork of small fields. The village looked poor, and no smoke hung over it although the morning was well advanced.

"Your village rises late, friend."

"Aye. There is little to do in the fields at this time." A shadow had fallen over Shivnath's face and he turned away to open his saddlebag and throw a blanket over his sweating horse. Robert followed his example. They left the horses free. The animals were too tired to wander far, and in any case, here on the lip of a precipice there was nowhere for them to go. Robert flung himself down beside

Shivnath, who was looking out over the misty depths of the ravine beneath them to a bare range of black mountains opposite.

"There is Jungdah town — and behind that saddle between the peaks of Lah and Shinwe is Dhalli Palace. A full day's journey from here." He stretched widely, gulping at the fresh cold air as a thirsty man drinks water. He sighed deeply then and said, on the sigh, "Oh it will be good to be in my village again. So very good. I am not a man for palaces."

Robert looked at him and decided to risk a question.

"Shivnath, speak to me of something. What did you fear when you brought your message to Lambagh? Indeed you were afraid every mile of the way back also. We came here like men pursued by devils. What was it?"

Under his eyes he saw terror come back to Shivnath's face. When he spoke he was almost whispering.

"There was need for haste. Indeed, we were pursued by evil spirits. This message that I took to your Ruler was the fourth message that has been sent from Jungdah to Lambagh. I was protected. I took the message, I delivered it, and I have returned with the answer. The others, sent before me — no one has seen them since, and it was plain they had never reached Lambagh. Even the birds that carry messages from Dhalli Palace to Lambagh, or to Pakodi State, even the pigeons were found, days later, dead — untouched but dead, the messages still on their legs. The sacred birds of Shiva! The priests themselves could find no reason for any of this!"

His voice was so low that Robert had to lean close to hear him, his eyes were wide with superstitious fear.

"So that when you asked all the time for leave to go, and spoke of haste, it was devils you feared?"

Shivnath nodded. "Indeed, friend, what else snatches men and horses from the earth, leaving no trace? Who but demons would dare to harm the sacred birds?"

"Well, you have outwitted the demons — you are safely back — "

"In the name of Shiva the Protector! Do not speak yet. I was fortunate. The priests consulted and chose a time when the devils could be outwitted — in the time when the moon is waning, they said. Thus, I have fulfilled my mission. Tomorrow I will make a rich gift to the Temple. My brother serves in the Temple of the Goddess, he will make the offering for me."

The hoofbeats coming up behind them had been muffled by the thick turf on which they sat. It was their horses' lifted heads that warned them. Robert looked over his shoulder to see three men reining in to stand their beasts in a semi-circle. Shivnath scrambled to his feet.

"The Raja comes," he said. "These be his men. Palace guards."

Palace guards indeed. Richly dressed, their saddles embroidered and gilded, their sword hilts carved and jewelled. Not hill men. Two were men of the plains, men from central India. The third, who was in the centre and looked to be the leader, was different. Shivnath was smiling, looking beyond them, waiting for his Raja to appear.

The slender man in the centre of the semi-circle raised himself in his stirrups and leaned forward. Like a man, making a good shot at polo he lifted his sword and swinging it, struck Shivnath's head from his shoulders with a swift, clean cut. Robert had seen such expertise at the Dasera festival in Nepal, when the scented incense smoke rolled across the crushed grass outside the temple and the sacrificial buffalo waited with uplifted, frightened head.

Shivnath's body stayed upright, spouting blood like a terrible fountain. His head jumped and fell and rolled, only a little way, to lie, still with an expectant smile on the face, close to where Robert had been sitting.

As Shivnath's head was severed Robert flung himself down, away from the scything sword that had in turn struck at him. He went over the precipice, his head pressed against his knees, clasping his shins, making his body as like a ball as he could.

Like a ball he fell, bounding and rebounding from rock to tree to rock again. His turban no longer protected his head, it had gone, falling before him. The breath left his body, but for a moment he retained enough thought to be grateful that he was rolling and not falling directly into the depths. Presently there was no thought left, only pain and then dark silence.

He did not know how long he was unconscious, but there were voices sounding faintly above him. He was lying on a very narrow ledge, so narrow that he was terrified to find that his shoulders were barely supported by it. Above him was a bush, scrubby, bare of leaves, but equipped with long hooked thorns and very thick branches. His arm and one leg were tangled in the thorny branches. As he could see nothing through the bush, he trusted that he could not be seen from above.

There was a sudden slither of earth and shale and Shivnath's body hurtled past him. Robert shuddered; the body fell so straight. Beneath him there must be terrible depths. He heard the men speaking, and a great deal of trampling, and wondered if they had begun to search for him. The sound he heard next was terrible. The agonised cry of a terrified horse. The animal was still struggling as they forced it over the edge. No saving

41

ledge for the poor beast — it followed Shivnath's body and this time Robert heard, far below, the final crash. The second horse was his own. His well-loved Shasti, the horse he had ridden so often. At least they had cut Shasti's throat before they pushed him over. Robert imagined that Shasti would have fought the strangers who were trying to take his life. His blood spattered on Robert as he hurtled past and the thorn bush jerked and shuddered, almost causing Robert to lose his hold. Now, he thought, now they will come to search.

But no one came. It began to grow dusk, and there was no sound from above.

It was very cold on the ledge. The grief he felt for Shivnath and for his beautiful horses had taken his mind off his own situation. It had been quiet for some time, no voices sounded. He had no idea of how he could ever get off the ledge, but would have to try before it grew dark. He moved a little and felt his sleeve tear free and his body slip. With a gasp he grabbed the bush, horrified to discover that it was not his arms that had been securely held but only the fabric of his clothes, and that at any moment the cloth could rip away. He lay, shaking with cold and fear, all courage gone. He held the thorny branches tightly, not feeling the thorns that were so sharp.

The soft whisper of falling shale beside him was almost a relief. He heard firm, determined movements. Whoever was looking for him was quite unafraid. Robert, at this extremity, was glad to find that he had lost his fear. There was no point in struggling. The strange compulsion of the depths had taken him. He decided to let go of the bush and fall into the purple shadows he had glimpsed when he had been sitting beside Shivnath. He would fall, and be at peace. Cramped, cold, bruised and in pain, Robert thought of Laura and his son and prayed for their happiness in the years that he would not share. Then he opened his hands.

He did not fall. The bush was holding him with thorns and branches. He could not get free, and the searcher was on him. He closed his eyes against the triumph he did not want to see on the enemy's face.

The cry of discovery was so loud, so harsh that it surprised him into opening his eyes to look death in the face after all.

Instead he looked, at very close quarters, into the face of an astonished goat who was pulling at the branches of Robert's bush. The goat was considerably startled and jumped aside — and while Robert watched, totally bemused, the animal continued nimbly along the ledge and vanished in an upward direction.

Robert lay for a few more moments, getting his breath back. He found that to be snatched from death was as unnerving as to face it. Then, with infinitely more caution than had been shown by the goat, backed, writhing like a snake along the ledge and through some more bushes and found himself on a gentle slope that led up to an easily negotiable rocky outcrop, not very far from where he had been sitting with Shivnath that afternoon. He lay down and tried to stop trembling and took stock of his wounds. A bad cut on his forehead, a splitting headache, severe bruising, and judging by the pain he suffered if he tried to breathe deeply, perhaps ribs broken before had been damaged again. Otherwise nothing. Robert could not believe his luck. He reckoned he had fallen at least three hundred feet, rolling and hitting himself all the way. He got up. Where there was a goat, there must be a goatherd. Presumably from Shivnath's village, where he might find safe shelter.

First he investigated the goat track. It was difficult to see in the last of the light, but from what he could make out the path would have been hidden from anyone standing where they had all been earlier. Unless a man knew the country well, he would have no idea that there was a path down into the ravine. Robert could not explore very much, the sun had gone and it was getting very dark. The goat had vanished and there was no sound of a herd anywhere. Perhaps the goat had been a straggler, strayed from the herd.

Robert decided to find a sheltered spot for the night. He did not fancy investigating the fort, until he was sure of who Shivnath's friends were. He found a big rock, jutting out from a slope, and crawled into the undergrowth beside it. Under the bushes the ground was thick with fallen leaves and he was sheltered from the cold wind that had risen as darkness fell. There, in spite of his pain and bruises he fell asleep, and slept soundly all through the cold night, to wake stiff and shivering in the early dawn, with the sound of goat bells ringing in his ears.

With caution he crawled from a place the dawn revealed as a most inadequate hiding place. Anyone coming up on the path from the ravine that he had followed the evening before would have seen him easily. When he saw the drop that was on one side of the path he felt ill. The ravine fell away to nothing, a straight clean cut of smooth rock. Had he fallen there . . . he turned away, shuddering.

Stiff, and still suffering from a vile headache, he looked around and found the herd — a small mixed herd of sheep and goats, and unattended. Robert had hoped for a goatherd from the village. The growing light revealed the sheep and goats, their bells ringing as they moved, but nothing else. No movement from the fort, no sound of voices that would have carried easily, the air was so still.

From where he stood, Robert could see the fort plainly. It occurred to him that if there was anyone in the fort, they could see him too. He ducked back behind his rock, and followed it round, further into the thick bushes, feeling his way with one hand against the rock. His hand encountered a space. He felt about, for the light had not penetrated the thicket, and discovered a small cave which he crawled into. It went back quite far enough for him to lie full-length, and it was dry and a shelter from the cold morning air. Here he might lie hidden when the searchers came. He was sure they would come, to be certain that he had fallen and was dead; he had seen them kill Shivnath and they would want to be sure of his permanent silence. He was thirsty and hungry and cold, his clothing reduced to rags, most of his quilted waistcoat left on the long thorns of the bush that had saved him. His poshteen, the long fur-lined coat of the valley people, had been rolled behind his

47

saddle, his sword, the sword given to him years ago by the Nawab of Pakodi, had been on the ground beside him — that had gone too, no doubt, into the depths. He felt for his dagger — no, gone, shaken from its scabbard in his fall. He was unarmed, and unhorsed. Poor Shasti, poor beautiful beast . . .

Robert's mind suddenly came out of a fog of shock and pain and he realised just how serious his position was. Ordinary animal fear had sent him searching for somewhere to shelter. Now, thinking properly again, he knew that shelter was not enough. Somehow he had to get back to Lambagh with his news, for the trouble in Jungdah State was very serious. Leaning his aching head in his hands he thought about what he had seen and what it meant.

Shivnath's death, and the quick disposal of his body and of both the horses explained why no messages had been getting out of Jungdah. The Raja was not part of the conspiracy, whatever it was. Possibly the priests were also loyal. But the army! Shivnath had known the men who had come to kill him, known them well and trusted them. They must have been officers, for surely the ordinary soldiers of even a rich raja were not dressed and accoutred as they had been. Something about the man who had killed Shivnath bothered Robert.

A familiarity, strong but fugitive tormented him, making his headache worse. He stopped thinking about the man, he had too many other things to worry about. The men were officers in Jungdah's State Forces. Therefore it must be a mutiny and a plot to get rid of the old Raja. But in that case why not just kill the old man in an unobtrusive way? The heir was a child, and whoever wanted the power could rule as regent. But of course — there was Lambagh.

The Ruler was Regent for Pakodi State, until Jungdah's grandson came of age. He would not meddle in the affairs of Jungdah but he would certainly take an interest in anyone who became Regent for the young Raja, who was already the Nawab of Pakodi. It was, Robert saw, utterly imperative for him to get news to Lambagh and stop Jiwan Khan coming to

49

Jungdah. He would be riding into deadly danger.

His thoughts were suddenly scattered. He heard voices close by, and froze. Many voices, and the sound of bushes being brushed aside, of sticks beating among the branches. He had taken part in many hunts. Now he knew how the hunted felt. The beaters were being directed and hectored by commanding voices. Nearer and nearer they came. There was no chance for him he knew. He heard a dog barking, deep and fierce. How well he knew the hill dogs, huge woolly beasts, ferocious and brave, with spiked metal collars round their throats to protect them from bears and panthers. One of the dogs would find him even if the men missed his cave. He was going to be caught like a beast in hiding, and dragged out and killed. He had no longing to die with dignity.

All he wished was that the cave was a passage so that he could run from the hunters, get away, and get back to Lambagh. He pressed as far into the cave as he could and then, with his back against the earth wall he waited.

He saw the bushes round the opening of the cave quiver, and then a dog barked sharply. Robert saw the gleam of a curved sword, and then a dog pushed into the cave, its lips lifted in a terrible silent snarl. A chain attached to its spiked collar dragged it back. A man's face peered into the cave.

The slit eyes above high cheek bones looked straight at him. The wide mouth curved into a smile, and he winked. Then he backed out, dragging his dog with him, shouting in answer to an angry query,

"No. Nothing. No one. Some old rags used by the goatherd, that is all."

Robert leaned back against the wall of the cave with all the blood in his body thundering in his head. The hunt moved on. It was very thorough, but no one came his way. At last there was silence and only the sound of birds settling about their business after the disturbance. Even the goats appeared to have gone. He waited in his cave, afraid to come out, and finally saw daylight begin to decline into the grey of a mountain twilight. The birds had been silent. Now one flew out close by, crying in alarm, and there was a brushing noise in the bushes, and a voice spoke softly.

"Friend — can you hear me?" It was a hill man who spoke, but Robert waited, afraid to answer. He heard the man move, and then the bushes were parted, and the man came to the mouth of the cave.

"Friend, you saw my face this morning. Come out now, it is safe for the present. The searchers have gone."

There was no alternative. If the man was ill-disposed he could easily kill Robert as he sat there. He had to trust him.

The long day crouching in the cave had been hard. Robert could barely move, and when he was finally out, and through the bushes, he could not stand because he was so dizzy, and the pain in his head was so severe. In the grey light his companion peered at him, and softly clicked his tongue.

"Eh, brother. They caught you once and you got away! The Gods have smiled on you. They were hot with rage, those Palace men. Can you walk?"

Robert, sitting on ground that appeared

to sway every time he moved, said carefully, "In a moment," and tried to focus his eyes. The man looked round him anxiously.

"We must go before it is full dark, or the gate will be shut against us. We will go with the herd. The boy has been out for a day and a night, and the goats with him. We will take the herd in; he will have to shift for himself. Can you move now?"

Robert did not answer. All his energies were concentrated on getting to his feet. He managed it, and the man, frowning, gave him a tall stick on which to lean.

"Follow," he said urgently. "Follow, leaning on the stick. You are my old father if any ask. If we are quick there will be no questions."

It was not possible for Robert to be quick. The man and the herd of goats went ahead, and he reeled after them, falling twice because of his inability to see properly. The pain in his head had now become a separate thing, something that was living and moving inside his skull.

The fort was not very far, but it seemed to Robert that it was a day's journey. There were lights in the fort, but the gate was not manned, and they passed it safely. Then there was a long, dreary interval of time until they came to the walls of the village, just as the gatekeeper was dragging the gates across to close the village for the night. He waited in silence for the goats, and Robert and his companion to go through. Robert could no longer stand alone, he leaned on the man, his head too heavy to hold up.

"He was caught after all," said the gateman, dragging the heavy wooden gates shut, and then pushing thorn bushes against them.

"Nay. He must have been caught yesterday and escaped."

"Where will you take him?"

"To the widow Lalaini. Where else? He will have to lie up for several days."

"Yea. He can no longer walk. Wait till I secure the gate and I will aid you."

Robert heard none of this. The pain in his head had swelled, mushrooming until his skull could not contain it and he felt his head burst. The grey twilight had filled his empty eyes. The two men,

54

the goats, the single narrow street, all vanished into the misty grey light that was slowly flooding through him, like an evening tide coming in. He sank gratefully into the encroaching tide, and into peace at last.

4

THE woman sitting beside the lamp, grinding something with a small pestle and mortar, did not know the moment when Robert became conscious again. She was concentrating on her work. He had time to lie, watching her, and looking at as much of the room as he could see without moving. There was a lamp on one side of the woman, throwing her shadow huge on the wall. On the other side of her was a chula, a clay basket containing glowing charcoal. Robert was lying on a pile of quilts on a platform raised about two feet above the floor. He was, he discovered, naked, and covered with thick padded quilts. He could see a wooden door that was so strongly barred and bolted that it must be the main entrance to the house. He was warm and comfortable, and in no pain. As to *where* he was, this Robert lay dreamily pondering.

The woman was just as strange to

him as his surroundings. He lay quietly,
watching her shadow on the wall. He
wondered what would happen if he held
his own arm up. Would it cast a shadow?
Possibly not. Perhaps he was only a
spirit.

One thing was certain. Spirit, or
person, he had no idea who he was.

In his state of warmth and comfort,
this did not bother him at all. Robert
decided that perhaps he was asleep and
dreaming. He lifted one hand and looked
at it. A hard, sinewy hand, long-fingered,
a hand that looked strong. So. A soldier
perhaps? Robert was not distressed in any
way. He felt light-headed and unworried
by all this strangeness. He looked at the
woman again. Not very young, not very
old. His mother, perhaps? Something
deep within him denied this. His wife
then? She wore a long woollen robe,
very plain, with an overdress banded
with embroidery. Her hair had turquoises
twisted into its glossy plaits, and she had
a necklace of gold and silver coins. Her
hands were slim and brown and moved
quickly at their task. Her downcast eyes
were long and tilted, her cheek bones

very high, and she was singing very softly as she worked. Watching her, he wanted to see more of her, and moved his head, and pain came, pain like a flash of lightning that made him groan, and then was gone again.

The woman was on her feet at once, putting aside her pestle and mortar.

"Lord," she said, bending over him, "Lord, you are with the world again. Three days you have lain between the earth and the stars."

"Not my mother," said Robert, "and I think not my wife." She frowned, puzzled.

"Wife, Lord? Mother? We only found you; Derva said, you alone. Now, I will give you broth, and then I will call Derva." Robert drank the strong chicken broth she gave him, a mouthful at a time, and wondered who Derva would be. His mind was an empty room. All he had was a vague memory of severe pain.

Derva came, a man in duffle tunic and trousers, with an anxious expression on his slant-eyed face.

"Lord! How is your spirit now that it has returned to you? We were afraid it would not return but you have been fortunate. Three days you have lain in the hand of Yama, so still we could not tell if you breathed. But the God of Death was merciful; he did not close his hand and you have returned."

Robert found that he knew what the man meant. Yama was the God of Death who caught men's souls in a noose. There were other gods he could remember. Perhaps he was a priest? He tried some names.

"Shiva, the Creator," he said softly; and then, as if someone had put the words into his mouth he said, "Kali, the Beloved." Derva bowed his head over hands placed palm to palm.

"Lord, you do well to give thanks."

"Why do you call me 'Lord'?"

"But what else should we call you, Heavenborn?"

"Should I be given such a title? How do you know?"

"But — by your ring, Lord!"

"*Ring?*" asked Robert, holding up bare hands. "Ring?"

"The ring you wear on a chain about your neck, Lord." Robert put up a fumbling hand, and found the ring on a long chain. He raised it so that he could see it.

Like green fire, like the fire in the eyes of an animal deep in the shadows of the jungle, the jewel burned. A fierce pain attacked Robert. Derva was babbling, afraid of the look on Robert's face.

"Heavenborn, if it is secret, if we did wrong to take your clothes from you, forgive us. But we have told no one, Lalaini and I, we only said you were a man hunted by the Palace guards and therefore worthy of help." He broke off, and called frantically for the woman. When she came running in Robert had fallen unconscious again.

After another day it became obvious to Lalaini and Derva that he did not know who he was.

"It must have been the blow on his head, and the deep wound. Another finger's breadth down and he would have lost his eye. What can we do? He cannot stay here. It is a wonder that they have not searched the village for him already. He is a great lord, Derva, perhaps even a prince."

"They have not searched the village because they think he is dead. Some of his clothing was found on a bush on the side of the khud. The men searching for the goatherd found it and took it to the fort. So the palace guard have gone. I must speak with this one, but you stay nearby, woman, lest he leaves his body again."

Lalaini sat on the floor at the foot of the bed, and Derva stood, and they talked to Robert and Robert's head ached fiercely, but nothing helped him to remember who he was. Even the ring told him nothing except that looking at it hurt his head.

"What clothes was I wearing?"

"Rags, Lord. They must have beaten you with knotted whips, those sons of Eblis."

"*Who* beat me?"

"Men from Dhalli Palace. Officers of the Raja's new guard. Truly, nothing has been good since these men came up from the plains. They are that upstart Nephew's men. Nephew! The child of a bazaar woman and a syce, he struts in the Palace claiming relationship with the little Begum's dead husband. Who is to say he lies? But we of the villages know — " Lalaini put up her hand.

"Derva. You confuse the Lord. Tell him of the men who searched for him."

"Ay, I grow old and talk too much. Men of the plains as I said, men of rank. I have seen them about here before. Pillage and rape follow in their steps and the Raja does nothing. The Raja is a good man, but too old. Much troubled by his lack of an heir. He had several sons, but none of them lived. Now he has only the girl, she that was wife to Pakodi, and bore a son to him. Pakodi was killed, and now there is only the child."

A flash of pain made Robert wince. Something was stirring in the blankness of his mind.

"Could I have been a visitor to the Court?"

"By your clothes, no — and you had neither sword nor dagger. But your voice, your looks — truly Lord, we think you are from some princely family. We would take you to the Palace to see if any know you there, but we would be taking you to your death.

The men who searched for you are there."

"Do you know them?"

"Indeed, Lord. One is second to the Chief of the Raja's army. His name is Swaraj. Then there was Sham Dass and Govind. They are high in the Raja's army too. What can you have done, Lord, to make them beat you as they must have done, and then search for you, offering much gold to the one who found you?"

"The Gods alone know." Robert's forehead was creased with pain. After a silence, Lalaini spoke.

"It comes to my mind that perhaps you were too much the Raja's friend. I have heard it said that he is not content with his new army. So his friends could offend the officers of it."

"Lalaini! Woman of great wisdom! That could be true. Now, if I am the Raja's friend, I should be safe if you take me to him. Can you help me into the Palace without those others seeing me? Then if I am blessed with good fortune, the Raja may give me back the man I am."

The others sat discussing this, while

Robert lay still, trying to master the headache that was again threatening to take away his senses. Presently Lalaini saw the trouble he had and brought him an earthenware cup of a bitter tasting drink. He drank it, and was grateful for the oblivion it gave him.

This was the pattern of the next few days. He woke and talked, mustered enough strength to walk about the house, and after dark up and down the walled, cobbled courtyard at the back. He asked many questions, hoping to find something that would rouse his memory. But nothing found an echo in his mind. Derva told him of the sorrow in the village. The headman's only son, a servant of the Raja, had vanished, going off into the hills with a message and never returning. Another had gone missing when the goatherd had taken his goats out one morning. The goats had been found, but the boy had vanished. The village lay silent under a pall of grief and superstitious fear. No lights showed at night, no children played outside the houses.

"It is good only for you, Lord. You

64

were saved when these others were lost. Shivnath was seen, riding fast, early in the morning of the day before I brought you here. Also, that was the morning when the boy was lost."

A dreadful tragedy. Robert felt pity, and was glad to feel it. It was getting difficult to live with an empty mind. He asked for a description of the three who had been so anxious to find him. Derva gave it to him, in detail. It told Robert nothing. Lalaini brought him the rags he had been wearing when he was carried into her house. They were shreds of cloth, nothing more.

"But the ring, Lord — you must remember the ring!"

"No. Perhaps I stole it."

"Nay. You must have worn it a long time. See, it has kept your skin from the sun, where the chain circled your neck. Also, your boots. I have hidden them. No common man wears such boots, embroidered and made of the finest skin. Lord, you are no common soldier. Your looks tell me that."

Any prolonged thought still brought headaches. Lalaini would drive them away with her bitter draught.

After a week, she came to him to say that Derva had a plan to get him into the Palace safely. He was to go with Derva to the Temple of the Goddess to make offerings for the village. The Temple was within the Palace wall. He would go as a man of the village. Derva came then, before Robert had had his morning bowl of tea, thick with butter, and spiced with some of Lalaini's bitter herbs.

"We leave tonight, Lord. It is a good time. The army is on exercise in the further ranges. There will be few of the plainsmen in the Palace. If we move fast, by night, I can take you safely in by moon-rise tomorrow night."

Robert felt a strong reluctance to leave the shelter of Lalaini's house. But there was no hope that he would find his past by staying there. He agreed to Derva's plan, and the man hurried away to arrange for ponies.

Lalaini came to Robert with trousers and a tunic of duffle, and put them on the bed with a brightly embroidered cap and a long bit of woollen cord to coil round and round his waist. She brought warm water, heated as Robert knew over a small fire of dried dung and a little precious charcoal. She put aside his protests, and washed him and shaved him. She looked at the wound on his head.

"Does your head pain you, Lord? The wound is healing cleanly, but your eyes seem clouded."

"They are clouded with grief at leaving you, Woman of Gentle Heart."

"Eh, Lord! A woman could be beguiled by such a sweet speaker."

"Beguiled, Lalaini? Then, come, let us be beguiled together. I am a man with nothing but the present. When I go from here I will be nothing, except in your memory. Let me at least know that you will remember me!"

"Ah, Lord, do you think I will forget your grey eyes so quickly?"

"I will have the memory of your gentle hands and your kindness, and the curve of your lips — ah, Lalaini, I have so few memories. Increase my store, give me something that as a man I should remember — will you, Lalaini?"

When the shadows had lengthened into

the darkness of night, Derva came to the door, leading two hill ponies. He found Robert ready for him, dressed, his scar hidden under the tilt of his embroidered cap. A curved dagger with a silver handle was tucked into his rope girdle. Derva approved his appearance. He looked like a young hill man in his best clothes.

Lalaini put a small packet into Robert's hands.

"If your head gives you pain, Lord, mix the powder with milk and drink it. Go, Lord, in the protection of the great Goddess."

"I thank you — for my strength which you have given back to me, and for the things you have given me to remember. Remember me well, for you will see me again."

He saw her eyes fill with tears and turned away, and swung himself up easily on the back of the pony to ride after Derva who had already started up the narrow street.

The gateman was waiting, a smoking torch in his hand.

"Go in safety, and return." He said the ritual words hurriedly, anxious to close the gates. Robert heard it creak shut behind him; there was finality in the thud of the bar falling into place. Derva muttered an invocation half under his breath and took the lead, thanking all his Gods that whatever else this stranger had forgotten, he had not forgotten how to ride.

The moon was young, and gave very little light. Rain fell, a fine rain that made the night obscure even though Robert's eyes had grown used to the darkness. The going was treacherous, he could tell his pony had to pick its way, and he was content to leave the reins loose on its neck.

As the night wore on, Robert wondered if this was a road known to him, if he had ever travelled it before. At least, he thought, I can ride. The feeling of being on horseback was as familiar to him as walking.

Dawn showed bare country, a vast expanse of rolling green steppe stretching to the wall of black mountains — still distant, though it seemed they had ridden towards them all night.

As the sun rose they began to

meet people on their way. High-cheeked nomads with everything they possessed loaded onto a string of dromedaries swayed past; fierce dogs ran beside them. Robert wondered how the beasts would negotiate the paths he had ridden over during the night. Eagles hung overhead and looking up, he had a sudden picture of a lake . . . Which? Where? The memory was gone before he could get hold of it and he was left with the beginning of a violent headache. He knew his state well enough now to hurriedly make his mind blank to stop the pain. Instead of thinking, he looked, studying the country, absorbing sights and sounds and trying to avoid using his brain for anything more important than showing interest in the marmots scuttling from the path or the sight of a party of nomads putting up their tents of felt stretched over wooden frameworks, the women working with the men to make their camp.

Derva stopped and talked with one family, grouped about their tent. A girl, her cheeks glowing, her silver ornamented cap perched rakishly over her eyes, brought them bowls of mares' milk, slightly fizzy, as it fermented into airag, their favourite drink. Robert pulled out his packet of herbs but the girl exclaimed and brought him a separate bowl of plain goat's milk to mix his powdered herbs into. She looked like a younger Lalaini, and Robert smiled at her as he drank his two drinks, a sip of the herbal mixture and a sip of the airag.

Derva came over and said that the nomads had offered the hospitality of their tent until the evening. Robert was glad to accept, he felt giddy and exhausted. Lying in the tent, on a clean quilt, he began to feel better. He told Derva that the girl had reminded him of Lalaini.

"Well she might," said Derva, settling himself on the other side of the tent. "Lalaini is of that tribe. She married a man of our village and came to live in his house. It was hard for her at first, being used to moving with the seasons, but she settled well. She made a good place for herself in our lives, being skilled with herbs and drugs. Talli, her man, went to do his service in the Palace — "

"Service?"

"Yea, Lord. Every two years, each village in the valley sends as many young men as it can to serve in Dhalli Palace. Some are gardeners, some syces, some are soldiers. Talli was a strong man and rode as if he had been born in the saddle. He never returned. He has never been seen again."

"What!"

"I speak the truth, Lord. I tell you, there is talk of devils in these hills, who take men and horses together. We of the villages know that there were no devils here until the men from the plains came. But no one listens to us."

"How long ago did this happen?"

"Over twelve full months have passed. Lalaini has finished her mourning. She will go into the house of her husband's brother at the time of the next full moon."

He looked over at Robert and saw that he was no longer listening. He had fallen asleep. Derva looked at Robert's sleeping face, with the deep frown of pain not smoothed even in sleep, and the half-healed scar in plain view now that his cap was off. Derva did not sleep. He sat and bit his fingers, working out how best to get this young man safely into the Dhalli Palace.

The mountains were closer now, a solid black wall against the horizon. When they started again, they should reach Dhalli Palace within four hours' riding.

Four hours from sunset, to moon-rise and moon set. Then there would be the guards on the main gate to pass.

Derva sat and made plans. His nomad friends had given him bad news. There were still many men from the plains in Dhalli Palace, and the army was not on training exercises. It was recruiting men again, as it had before.

5

THE frail moon rose. Robert and Derva said grateful farewells to their hosts and rode away. The girl, standing in the doorway of the felt tent, watched them until her mother called to her sharply to close and fasten the tent flap; the wind was cold.

They rode fast. The black bar of mountains at the end of the plateau grew closer and towered above them. They climbed away from the grassland of the plateau, up a rocky path between stunted trees that grew leaning sideways, away from the bitter wind.

Robert, blinking his eyes against the wind, saw that they had come to a village. There was no gate. The flat-roofed houses were dark, the doors closed. They rode down the narrow street which was soft with mud. There was nothing to see, nothing moved — nothing; but the silence around them lived and listened. There were people in these dark, quiet huts.

Robert felt a sort of shuddering fear as the ponies' unshod hoofs raised muffled echoes; this was a dreadful place. He slowed his animal and Derva looked over his shoulder at once and beckoned him on. Presently they stopped in front of a house that seemed larger than the others.

"Here," said Derva in a whisper, dismounting. "Follow me. Do not speak."

Leading his horse, Robert followed him, wondering if in his buried memories there was an event that would explain his horror of this place, where so early in the evening the houses were closed and dark, no dogs barked, no children laughed. Even in Derva's poor village he had seen dogs, and there had been the voices of children. Here, there was nothing but dark silence and a horrible creeping fear that made him shudder inwardly.

Derva was knocking at a door, knocking with the flat of his hand so that the sound was muffled. There was a faint voice inside, and Derva put his mouth close to the door and spoke, barely louder than a whisper. Bolts were drawn, and Derva went in, pulling his pony after him, and Robert, after a second's hesitation, followed him.

He found that he had entered a small courtyard, but he could see nothing. Someone brushed past him and the door was closed and the bolts rammed home. Derva came up beside him, and put his mouth to Robert's ear.

"Leave your animal, it will be taken care of. Come with me, Lord."

Robert dropped his reins and followed the dim bulk that was Derva. Another door was unbolted after a brief whispering pause, and Robert followed Derva into warmth. He heard the door close behind him, the bolts shoot home, and then the scratch and rattle of flint and steel. The welcome yellow glow of lamplight came at last.

He was standing in a large room with Derva and three others. A very old woman who stood with her back to the door, and a young man with the shaven head of a monk. The room was warm and stuffy as if it had never had a fresh breeze blow into it. The monk bent and moved something and a charcoal stove's red eyes made a brighter glow. Robert saw that it had been covered with a flat iron dish, presumably so that no light would show when the door was opened.

The third stranger in the room moved then and began to be busy with dishes and bowls. A girl, slight and small. She passed round bowls of tea. Derva was talking quietly to the monk. The girl brought Robert a bowl of tea, offering it to him on the flat palms of her hands, her head bowed. He thanked her, speaking in a whisper as silence seemed so important to these people. She looked up and he was horrified at what he saw. One of her eyes appeared to be gone, leaving a dark socket. Her hair hung in filthy rats' tails and there was dirt ingrained round her mouth and nose. The smell that Robert had noticed when he had first entered the room was very strong, and as she moved he realised where it came from. Her body must be dirtier than her face. He found it hard to drink the tea she had brought him, though the bowl he held appeared to be clean. He was cold, and presently, gulping the hot liquid, forgot how filthy was the hand that had brought it to him.

Derva finished talking with the monk, and came over to him.

"When you are ready, Lord, we go. Nathu, a novice at the Temple, will take us in, as pilgrims who are benighted. There are more of the plainsmen in the Palace than usual. He does not know if the men who searched for you are among them."

Robert recognised the desire for haste in Derva's eyes and swallowed the scalding tea as quickly as he could. Any action would be better than hiding in this stinking room.

The old woman had dropped beside the charcoal stove, spreading her fingers round it to warm them. She beckoned to Robert suddenly, and with reluctance he obeyed her gesture and bent over to hear what she wanted to say. He looked into a seamed brown face and saw laughter in wise old eyes. Immediately the feeling of horror left him. If this woman, so old and poor, could smile in such a place, there was still hope in the world, and a warmth came into his empty heart. A thin claw turned his face round to the light.

"Eh, son of beauty! A breaker of hearts, and a leader of men, used to command. Go in safety, my son, and fear nothing. You will find again all that you have lost."

Her whisper was so low that no one outside could have heard it, yet every syllable was clear in the room. Robert smiled at her and turned away. The girl held out his cap, and Robert noticed the shape and delicacy of her hand under the dirt and wondered what she would look like if she were clean. He joined his hands and bowed over them as he saw Derva doing, and knew that this was a gesture he would not naturally make. He listened to his instinct, and, leaning forward, took the old woman's hand and raised it to his forehead and then to his lips. She smiled and said softly, "Go under the protection of the great Goddess, my son." Robert turned back to the girl. Her face, fearful in its dirt and mutilation, looked at him without expression. Her arms hung by her side. She looked vacant as well as hideous and filthy. He reached for one of her hands and looked down at it. The hand of a beauty, long-fingered, small and slender — and revoltingly dirty. He kissed it, and wondered if he would finish his days as a leper. Her face did not change, her one good eye stared past him as if she had not seen him.

Derva was at the door. The stove was already covered, the lamp was turned out. The door was unbarred and opened; the dark chill courtyard received them. It seemed they were to go on foot. The girl came out and unbarred the door into the street. They filed through, the monk leading the way. The door shut silently behind them. Robert imagined the poor slut of a girl fumbling the bolts into place and then creeping back to the gloomy room. The old woman's smile now seemed an impossible miracle. No one could smile living like that.

They left the village and in single file began to walk along a path that turned steep almost at once. Looking up, Robert saw walls black against the night sky, far above, like part of the mountains themselves. *Was* it a wall? Then he saw lights. They were approaching the Palace.

A monumental curtain-walled gate, well-lit, suddenly came into view as they rounded a sharp curve. The path twisted to run along beside the wall. They came to a low gate, so low that the monk, standing under the single oil lamp that hung above it, had to bow his head. He knocked loudly and firmly, like a man without fear, a man in his rightful place. Robert heard a voice call and almost at once the gate was opened. Another young monk stood there holding a lantern. He stood aside for the monk Nathan, but frowned when he saw Derva and Robert.

"Nathu! What is this? You cannot bring strangers in at this gate!"

"I bring my uncle and my older sister's son. They come to make offerings to the Goddess for favours received. They were late leaving, and if they stay in the village you know how it will be. My sister's son is young and strong. He will never see his home again if the guards see him before he enters the Temple. They have been taking recruits from every village in the valley." The other monk shook his head, but stepped back. He looked hard at Robert in the lantern's light, and said, "It will be hard for him to escape service — he is made for it. And what about your uncle?"

"He came to guide my sister's son here. He goes back."

The monk looked at Derva who, turning to Robert, said his farewells and walked quickly back down the path. Then the monk, turning back to Robert and Nathu, nodded and let them through. He barred the gate behind them and they began to walk quickly through the main courtyard. They entered a passage that ended in a long flight of steps. The steps led up to a long, narrow verandah.

The room they went to opened off a great hall. It was small and warm, with thick carpets on the floor, and a charcoal stove with a twisted chimney that went across the angle of the wall and out through the top pane of a window. Robert realised how high up they were when he saw that the window was filled with sky. He went over and looked out. The room was above the gate and looked out towards the village. It was dawn, but there were no lights showing in the village, no smoke came from the houses. Nathu pulled him back from the window.

"If any raise their eyes and see a face they will come up here. No one uses this room. It is kept for one who seldom comes."

"Why is it so dangerous for me to be seen by the ordinary people of the Palace? Did Derva not explain to you that I only have, as far as I know, three enemies?"

"Lord, it is because you are a young man and strong. Derva was foolish to bring you here. Even we who are monks and sworn to peace are not safe. They are taking men for their armies! That is what they do now in the valley. They say they fight mock battles to keep their soldiers ready. They lie. They are taking every young man they can find."

"And the Raja?"

"He can do nothing. His army is no longer loyal. His own officers have gone — God knows where — and now he is surrounded by these people from far off who only pay him lip service. He has sent out many requests for help but none comes, and his messengers never return.

Lord, you should not have come here. Even if the Raja is willing to help you, he will not dare to do anything if you are taken by the army. You will vanish like the rest."

"*Vanish?*"

"Yea, Lord. The young men are taken, and are not seen again." Robert felt the monk's fear as if it were tangible, like a cold wind blowing in the warm room. There was something that Robert should do. Something was crying to be released from his locked mind, but he could not open his memory's door. Sweat burst out on his forehead and was clammy under his clothes. As if he was engaged in physical combat, he found himself straining and gasping for breath. Then the struggle was over and he was left, limp and exhausted, with a blinding pain in his head, and nothing else. He felt in the pouch at his waist for the packet Lalaini had given him and pulled it out. Nathu brought him water from a flask that stood on a carved and inlaid table. As the monk helped him to mix the powder and the water, Robert told him that he would sleep deeply when he drank it.

"Lord, it is safe enough here. No one uses this room any more. Only habit keeps it in readiness. I will keep watch outside. Sleep in peace."

There was nothing else that Robert could do. He was almost blind with pain. He swallowed the draught and lay down on the floor in the window embrasure, and with the gradual easing of pain and the onset of sleep, he saw a clear picture of the lake he had seen before. This time a girl was standing on the lake shore, her face turned away from him, her long dark hair blowing in a wind that he could not feel. He was still trying to see her face when he fell asleep.

6

WHEN he woke, Nathu was in the room. He beckoned, and Robert followed.

A short, quick walk and they were in an open court, the sky full of stars above them. There were roses planted in the octagonal brick-edged flower beds between which they walked. The air was full of the scent of the flowers; warm, reminiscent, sweet. The scent halted Robert like a hand laid on his arm, like a voice calling him. Something moved in his empty mind, a ghost that almost took flesh. A name formed on his lips, but the sound would not come.

Far away in the silence a dog howled and the moment was broken. He leaned down and picked a white rose and held it to his face, and then walked after Nathu, feeling a terrible loneliness. Roses, the white rose . . . his mind full of fragments, bits of a life that would not come together. He followed Nathu into a long, narrow passage.

There were latticed windows spilling light on the way ahead. Nathu pinched out his lamp. Robert heard a girl's laugh, and the sound of a flute trickled out from behind one of the lattices.

"The Bibikhana, the Place of the Women," said Nathu, and knocked on a door deeply set in the wall. The door opened at once.

"In the hands of the Gods, friend," said Nathu, and on these whispered words he had gone, leaving Robert to walk alone through the doorway.

There were only two people in the room, two old menservants. Under their eyes, with their willing, experienced help, Robert washed the sweat of the journey and of the troubled day from his body.

The clothes laid out for him were known to him. Were the shadows in his mind parting? He knew that he was used to this service, to this apparel. The emerald ring on the chain round his neck gleamed, and he wished that he could catch the words that seemed to sound in his head and in his heart when he looked at it. If the servants knew the ring they did not say so. Indeed they did not say very much, but helped him dress, finally kneeling to put boots of soft leather on his feet. Such small memories . . . Robert saw another room for a moment, felt other hands on his feet . . . then the vision was gone, and he was back, back to this room and this time. He refused to put on the kulla with its carefully tied turban; his head was still too tender for that. They brought him a small cap of close-curled black fur. The dagger at his waist was not the one Lalaini had given him. This one had a golden hilt, and the scabbard was splendid with jewels. He drew it and looked at the blade with pleasure. It was not a toy. His hands seemed to remember skills his mind had forgotten. He shot the blade home into its scabbard and knew that the two old men watched him. He was ready.

A heavy curtain was drawn aside, and the door behind it was opened. He walked into the next room, bracing himself. Now he would see the Raja, and would meet either recognition or a blank stare.

The servant following Robert carried a tray with goblets and a long-necked jug. He began pouring wine. When the servant lifted the goblet to his lips and drank, before passing the wine to an old man who was in the room, Robert knew that this was the Raja.

He took his own drink when it was given to him, and when the servant had gone, he bowed to the Raja.

"I am Jain Singh, Raja of Jungdah."

Robert waited, but the old man said nothing more. Finally Robert said quietly, "My hope was in vain. You have never seen me before."

"No, my son. You have never been to this court before, and I have never seen you."

Robert had hoped so much. He felt like a man who had been pushed back into darkness from the edge of light. He could not speak for a few minutes. He drank, he sat down motionless, desolate. The Raja put his goblet down.

"Listen to me, my son. It is true. I have never seen you, but I am sure that I know who you are. You are Dil Bahadur, the son of the Ruler of Lambagh."

Dil Bahadur — Robert waited for a moment, and then looked into the Raja's attentive eyes.

"Am I? Are you sure? Because the name says nothing to me. Surely my own name would rouse something in this dead memory of mine!"

"The blow on your head must have been very severe. Also, I think the powder you were given to dull the pain may have caused the confusion in your head to grow worse. Later tonight a hakim will examine your wound and give you more suitable medicine. But have no doubts, I am sure: you are his mirror image. Also there are other reasons why I am so certain."

There had been no sound, but suddenly Robert was sure they were no longer alone. He saw the Raja look over his shoulder, and immediately Robert put up his hand to his dagger and began to draw it. As he turned though, he stopped, staring, and the dagger fell from his hand to the floor.

A girl was standing just inside the door, looking at him. She was veiled to the eyes. Her long robe of heavy white silk fell straight, unbroken by any curves. Her eyes, wide and dark, stared at Robert, and he read recognition in them. At last there was someone who knew him.

She gave no sign; said nothing, showed nothing. After that one look, her eyes turned from his face to the Raja. She came in, closing the door behind her. She put her hands palm to palm and bowed over them, first to the Raja and then to Robert.

"This is my only child, my daughter, the widow of Pakodi," said the Raja, and Robert automatically stepped forward and, taking her hand, kissed it. The Raja laughed a little.

"If I needed any other proof, I have it now. The first Ruler of Lambagh married a European. You kiss a woman's hand, Dil Bahadur, as your father would. His father was an Englishman, and he spent the first sixteen years of his life in England. You too. You were schooled there, as was his other son, the heir Jiwan Khan."

None of the names helped the broken pattern in his mind, but Robert was full of hope again. The Raja was speaking to his daughter, telling her that this was the Nawab from Lambagh, that he had been attacked on the way.

"He is injured and his mind is confused, his memory of the past having gone from him."

The heavy-lidded tawny eyes above the white veil flicked a look at Robert and were lowered again. She murmured her regret at the Nawab's misfortune, but nothing else. Robert tried to catch her eye but she did not look directly at him again. Her arrival was the signal for food to be brought. Heaped on silver trays and platters, the evening meal was carried in. Seeing the quantities, Robert looked for other guests, but there were none.

A woman servant came to stand behind the Begum; the men who brought the food in went, and only the Begum's woman and the two men who had helped Robert to dress remained.

Robert waited, but with impatience. The Begum surely could not eat veiled. As he had hoped, the woman began to remove the scarf that covered her head and face.

She was very young. Her face was all that her beautiful eyes had promised. Her hair was pulled back from her brow and knotted to hang in loops and curls to below her waist. She wore no jewels and Robert remembered then that her father had said, "My daughter, the widow of Pakodi." So young, and yet widowed?

The Begum moved, and Robert saw that she had flushed above the high-fastened collar of her robe. He realised that he was staring at her, and quickly looked away. What he then saw amazed him.

Every dish, before it was presented to the Raja, was tasted by one or the other of the two servants. The woman tasted the Begum's food. His own food was also tasted before he was allowed to eat anything. The Raja saw his astonishment.

"There have been many attempts at poisoning," said the Raja, without any emotion. Robert recalled then that the wine they were drinking had also been tasted. But why so much food? There were so many questions that were unanswered, but one was paramount. When would the Begum speak? Or had

93

he imagined that she knew him?

There was music playing somewhere, flutes and sitars and a tabla, a hand drum that beat time softly, beating like a pulse. The Begum did not raise her eyes, nor did she speak. The smell of the rose garden seemed to have come in with her, but in spite of her white robe, it was of crimson roses that Robert thought, roses heavy and sweet and darkly red like the Begum's mouth. He found it hard not to look at her. He saw that her feet were slender and high-arched, and bare. He had been hungry, the food was delicious, but his appetite seemed to have left him. He drank wine thirstily and his goblet was refilled. As he raised it, he saw that the Begum had lifted hers. He looked at her and saw her eyes over the silver rim of her goblet before she drank, and looked away. But she did not speak, and he did not dare to ask her directly: "Do you know me?" A hand seemed to be laid in warning on his lips.

The food was removed, and more wine poured.

The Begum did not withdraw when her servant went. She settled herself comfortably among the big cushions below the dais where Robert sat with the Raja and listened to her father talking to Robert. It was at first hard for Robert to listen to the old man, the girl's very stillness a distraction, but what the Raja was saying was not to be ignored. Presently Robert had forgotten everything but the Raja.

The girl, who knew the story well, sat among her cushions and remembered a moonlit night in a garden in Bombay when this young man who now did not know her had taken her body with no great skill or gentleness and had left her with a love and a desire for him that five long years had not blurred.

Outside, the musicians still played, and her heart seemed to beat with the swift pulsing throb of the drum that sounded so softly, a background for the music, a companion for her heart.

7

SEATED in luxury, the Raja spoke of disaster. He told of the slow death of his power in Jungdah State and of the defection of his army.

All that Robert had been told by Derva and Nathu was true. The Palace of Dhalli had become a prison for the Raja and his family.

"I still have some friends in my army, and I have loyal servants, but I fear for them. I speak with a man one morning perhaps, and by sunset he has gone, never to return. We are like men marooned in a flood and the ground we stand upon grows smaller every day. I hear stories of devils and demons in the hills, and of a curse that has fallen on this valley."

"Not all your people think your state is in the power of devils, unless they are human devils," said Robert. "When I was with the woman Lalaini in the village of the Fort, I heard it said that all the trouble came to your valley with a man they called the 'Nephew'."

The Raja repeated the name as if it was a curse.

"Ay. Truth, terrible truth. A serpent, and I let him enter my household. The Nephew."

As the Raja repeated the name, a sort of shutter opened for a second in Robert's mind and he frowned, trying to catch the thought that the name roused, but without success. The sound of music seemed louder, the beat of the small drum more insistent. The beat filled the empty spaces of Robert's mind and he wished that it would stop. It made it so hard for him to think.

"Derva said he claimed kinship with the Begum's husband, but that he claimed it with no rights. How did he enter your household?"

"We were in great grief. Ali of Pakodi had been murdered, my daughter, so young, was with child, and a widow. I thought of nothing but her sorrow. This man who came claiming kinship was not important to me. He was a man who rode well and could use a sword. He asked to serve in my army. Why not? He began to train the young men in horsemanship, though we were always foot soldiers here: this is mountain country. But with his own money he brought in good horses, horses from the high plateaus of the North, bred for use in mountain fighting."

"So he was rich, this man."

"No. When he came, I told you, he had a horse, a good horse, and a sword."

"But he bought horses from the North? Where did he get the gold?"

"The Gods only know. But it began to flow from his fingers like water. He kept great state in the quarters I had given him. Friends began to come up from the plains, and they stayed. They too brought good horses, and men with them. Now they are here, everywhere — his cavalry, he calls them. With truth, for he now commands my army. My officers are either dead or in hiding. The Nephew commands the army, as I say — and therefore, he rules my State."

Once again there was a long silence, filled by the sound of music outside. The

Raja saw Robert glance at the door, and nodded his head.

"My musicians are my guards. As long as they are playing, no one can hear what we say, and if the music changes and there is a singer we know danger approaches. They can give me warning in many ways, and also let us know when it is safe for us to go about in the Palace. They guard me with flutes and sitars and drums — I who had swordsmen standing before my door to guard me once."

"You sent for help, Derva said."

"I sent for help. Very early, when the trouble first showed itself. I do not think my messengers ever got as far as my own borders. Even the pigeons, my little swift carriers, were poisoned before I could send them out. Shiva's sacred birds. There must be a curse on the man who would do that."

The Begum got up and, picking up the wine jug, poured wine for her father, and then came to Robert.

"Lord?"

Robert looked at her.

"I bring you fresh wine, Lord — "

Her voice was soft, with an odd break

in it. There was a look in her eyes — a question; the wide dark eyes above the full-lipped mouth were asking him something. But he could not understand her look and she said nothing more. He accepted more wine and she turned away and went back to her cushions. Robert held up his goblet to the Raja.

"It is safe for you?"

"They tasted it before they left."

The Raja saw nothing strange in Robert's question. To have a constant fear of poison had become natural to him.

The Begum looked at Robert's hand holding his wine cup, and her breath caught as she remembered the touch of that hand. But neither of the men noticed her.

"But I am now hopeful," the Raja went on. "The last message must have got to your father. You are the proof. He sent you to help me. Alas that you rode into danger and were wounded. What your father wanted me to know is locked in your mind. Until we find the key we must wait, and waiting is very hard." The Begum lifted her head.

"Waiting is dangerous," she said softly. "There were more sweets today." The Raja swore violently, his old voice cracking.

"Father, keep your strength. We got them away from him in time. But no one knows where they came from. This time he had them in his hands. We cannot wait until they ensure that the poison reaches his mouth. He is too little to learn that gifts can contain death!"

She looked across at Robert, her eyes full of tears.

"They try to poison my son — "

"Yes," said the Raja. "Devils in human form. A little beloved boy, brought up to love and trust everyone, and they try to kill him. He is the Nawab of Pakodi — or will be if — no, *when* he comes of age. In due course he will have my State also, even if my daughter were captured — oh yes, they have tried that too. But even if she were taken and forced into another marriage, the child is still the heir. You can understand the danger in which he lies."

Robert saw the picture clearly. The child dead, the girl seized and forced into marriage; her husband would then have two rich states within his grasp. In spite of the squalor of the villages he had seen, Jungdah was obviously a rich state; everything around him spoke of wealth.

The other state they spoke of, Pakodi, he did not know. Or did he? The name tapped at his mind like the hand of the drummer tapping the drum. He was tormented by a wisp of memory that drifted away before he could catch it. These people needed his help and he could find nothing but a patchwork of memories and odd words that rattled in his mind and made no sense.

"You are sure that I am Dil Bahadur?"

Why did the girl not speak, say that she knew him? Or had he been mistaken when he thought he saw recognition in her eyes? It was the Raja who answered him.

"I am sure. Your looks — you could not more closely resemble Kassim Khan as a young man than you do. Your speech and your manner — you were bred to rule. Also, there is something else. Round your neck, on a chain, you wear the Peacock Ring."

So the old servants had told the Raja. Robert unbuttoned his coat and pulled the ring out, and looked down on it.

"So the ring has a name. And a meaning?"

"Yes. It belonged to Kassim Khan. The story goes that it was given to your mother, who in turn gave it to you. Why do you wear it hidden?"

"I have always worn it on a chain round my neck when I travel . . . "

The words seemed to come from some echoing place in Robert's mind. A door had opened, and a whole world was there for him to see.

"I am Dil Bahadur," said Robert loudly.

The Begum stood up quickly, and the Raja leaned forward.

"I am — I know who I am!" He stood up. The drumbeats roared in his ears and for a few minutes he could hear nothing else. Then the noise quietened. The Begum's hand on his arm, the Raja's anxious voice — Robert took the water the Begum gave him and drank it, and at their joint urging, sat down. He looked at them and saw behind their anxiety for him the hope that was in their eyes, and knew that he would kill that hope with his first words.

Although he was sure of his name and he could remember a great deal of his past, it was still blurred, and worst of all, he knew nothing of what he was supposed to be doing in Dhalli Palace.

He told them quickly, and saw the lines on the Raja's face deepen. The Begum said quietly, "What is the last thing you can remember of Lambagh?"

"Riding fast through a dark street with someone — but I do not know who. It is as if my head is full of memories shouting to be recognised."

Pain flickered like lightning in his head. The Begum, looking into his drawn face, said firmly, "He must sleep, Father. I will take him to the tower room, he will be safe there. The music is quiet. It is time for us to move. Tomorrow we will hear more."

The two old servants were waiting. Staggering like a drunken man, Robert walked supported between them through quiet empty courtyards and along a colonnaded hall. The room they entered was large and had windows on all sides. The tower room . . . it sounded for some reason he could not place, like a prison. But the whole Palace is a prison, he thought dizzily. A younger man was in the room and he helped Robert to undress. Dazed, he was glad to lie down on a wide couch. He felt a quilt being put over him, heard some whispering, questions and answers, but without attempting to see who the newcomer was, unable to stop himself from doing so, he fell asleep.

The Begum, an elderly woman beside her, stood by Robert's couch and looked down at him.

"Is it indeed the Prince, Amara?"

"It is he. It is the prince that I saw in the garden of Pakodi's palace in Bombay. He spoke then of Lambagh Valley. The ring that he wears on the chain was on his finger then. I remember the ring."

She remembered every moment of that brief encounter, she thought sadly. Robert's bare long-fingered hand lay outside the quilt. She imagined herself kneeling to lay her cheek against his hand, to waken him with kisses. "Oh love, if I could but stay with you and

sleep beside you it would be enough . . . "
The words were so clear in her mind she was afraid she had spoken them aloud. But the servants were making the room tidy, the old woman had heard nothing. The words had not left her heart.

She gave some whispered directions to the servants, looked again at Robert and went quietly away, Saida behind her. She passed through empty courts where shadows were deep in unlit corners, where water whispered along channels and dripped into pools, and made the air sweet. Like shadows themselves, on bare feet, the young woman and the old woman walked swiftly, until they came to a guarded door, where men in the uniform of the palace guard lounged, drawn swords across their arms. They did not straighten or salute as she stopped at the door, but these were loyal men, the Begum knew. Because of watching eyes, she made no sign, but she heard the thread-like whisper.

"All is well, Lady. Go laughing." The man who spoke had not altered his casual, disrespectful stance. He saw her lovely eyes lift briefly to his face, then, her head high, she stood to one side. Saida opened the door, the two women swept in, and the door was shut.

On the other side of the barred door the Begum stood for a moment looking round the small walled garden that divided her rooms from the rest of the Bibikhana.

This part of the Palace was very old, the walls thick and high, ensuring privacy. These had been the rooms of the Ranis of Jungdah for as long as Dhalli Palace had been the royal residence. Here the Begum's mother had come as a bride and here the Begum had been born. She had left these quarters, a frightened little girl of twelve, to marry a rich elderly man of another religion, and after two years had returned a widow, carrying a child in her body. In these rooms she had gone through her terrible labour and her son had been born.

All her life, this corner of Dhalli Palace, the palace that was built like a fort among black threatening mountains, this court and these rooms, had seemed a haven, a place to which she had longed to return, a place where she would find the carefree happiness of childhood.

Now her son's laughter raised echoes in this court as hers had once done. Her precious boy played here; endless games of imagination that lonely children play. Her son, who did not know that he lived in danger and that this was his prison, this place that had once been his mother's home.

In an inner room, the child slept, while guards watched. He lay on his back, one arm flung over his head, his black curling hair tumbled, his cheeks flushed in sleep. Beside his bed was a wooden model of a horse, carved and painted, with a wonderful harness of silver and scarlet leather, and a sheepskin saddle. The boy did not stir as the Begum disentangled his fingers from the reins of his toy, and pulled his arm down to cover it. His hand lay limp in hers. So small, and yet a perfect miniature of a man's hand already. She pressed her lips to the tough little hand, drew the quilt closer round him and went back to her own room. She went out and across the courtyard to kneel at the shrine of the Goddess. Her prayer was wordless, but desperate.

"Let me have his love, Great One. You who know the hearts of men, turn his heart to me!" She crouched before the figure, looking up at the calm carved face, the far-seeing eyes. She heard the whisper of the falling water behind her but she did not hear the words that breathed on the night wind, the wind that rose and blew her hair about her face and caught at her robe.

"You may have his body," said the voice in the wind, the cold crystal ringing voice, "but his mind and his heart are taken. Those you cannot have — and the body is nothing unless you have the mind and the heart as well."

She remembered Robert's eyes, and his hand holding the goblet and the sound of his voice. She remembered their meeting, five years previously. Then she went to her room and sought sleep.

8

SILENCE and sleep lay over the Palace as the night brooded over the mountains.

In the tower room Robert woke from a deep sleep. He lay very still, his eyes closed, and slowly, as if the pages of a book were being turned before him by a loving hand, his past life came back to him, clear and entire.

He knew who was helping him, whose hand was showing him his past. The scent of sandalwood seemed to linger around him, and he tried to hear her voice and see her face against his closed eyelids. Muna the Dancer, the Rose, his beloved mother.

Another page turned. He saw clearly the face of Laura, the dear companion of his heart. Her memory flooded into his heart and his mind and his body, blocking out everything else for a few minutes. He thought of her with longing, and with pain and anger. Laura who had gone from him in sorrow. His dear love . . . his body ached as his mind had done, ached and burned with the fever of love-desire. He was not strong enough yet to stand this longing, he pushed her memory away. But he could hear her voice clearly. "Remember me, Robert. Remember me . . . " She had said those words as she left him. In grief he opened his eyes and found that dawn was golden on the windows.

Laura's pleading voice faded. He sat up, and at once a man stepped forward, salaaming.

"Lord, I am Alam Beg, your servant."

Robert asked for tea and watched the man taste it before giving it to him and was sharply reminded of all he must do that day. No time now to think of Laura, no time to dream. Thinking of a dozen different things he bathed and dressed quickly. He was appalled to hear that he could not leave his room during the daylight hours.

He asked questions of Alam Beg.

The village — was it derelict? There was no smoke coming from the houses, and no movement.

"No," said Alam Beg. "It is the closed time. There is one hour yet, before the horn will blow at mid-morning and they can open their houses and go about their work. Those that are left."

"What do you mean?"

"The village was the largest in the valley. Now perhaps forty men and women live there."

"What happened? Pestilence?"

"Yea, Allah! You could call it thus, Lord. The village is too close to the Palace, and most of the men there were of the Raja's army or men who had finished their service and had returned to live out their old age in their own houses while their sons and grandsons became soldiers in their stead. When the Nephew — may Allah visit him with dishonour and death! — began to change the army and inch, like a snake, into power, these villagers tried to rise against him.

"Well, Lord, the village is as you see it now, and even the bodies of brave men cannot make those burned fields fertile; the old men died, the young men went . . . Allah knows where."

The sun was high. Robert heard a horn blown harshly somewhere outside and watched the village come to slow life. A small herd of goats, released from a stone-walled fold, leapt up the slopes and scattered, foraging, while the girl who had let them loose followed slowly, to sit on a rock in the sun. Smoke spiralled and blew above a few of the houses, and there was the sound of a cock, free at last to yell his fury to the sky.

"From noon to sunset," said Alam Beg, bringing Robert a tray of food. "Only from noon to sunset can they move and have fires and go about their work."

He tasted the bowl of sour milk, and the vegetable stew and the chapattis. Robert insisted that they eat together. He asked where the food came from, remembering the enormous amount that had been carried into the Raja's room the night before.

"He feeds us all," said Alam Beg. "The food is prepared in the household kitchens, and after he and his family — those that are still here — have eaten,

113

it is brought out and distributed among us. We all eat the same food."

But Robert wasn't listening. He was thinking of something Alam Beg had said earlier.

"How many of the Raja's family *are* here?" The answer was surprising.

"Only his daughter, the Begum, and her son, Lord."

"His Rani?"

"He sent her out with the other girl, while it was still easy for them to move about."

"What other girl?"

"Roshanara, the daughter of the Ruler of Seldang. She is a relative. Her mother was the Raja's sister. Her mother died soon after she was born, and Roshanara was brought up here, a younger sister for the Begum."

"Why in Allah's name did the Raja keep the Begum and her child here? Why didn't he send her out with the others?"

"The boy was ill with a high fever and pains in his chest. The hakims said that he was too ill to move and she would not go without him, and when he recovered it was too late, the monks could no longer come and go so easily and had become afraid. The Begum is a prisoner now and her child is in terrible danger. One day, do what we will, they will get to that child."

He spoke with despair, and Robert saw that although he was a brave and resolute young man, he was totally without hope for the future. Robert, who had himself so lately been without hope, understood, and became determined that somehow he would save these people. He wondered if he was perhaps still suffering from his head wound because, in the face of all the despair around him, he was so full of hope and plans. Then, as Alam Beg took away the used dishes, and Robert looked at the bright sky and the glitter on the far peaks, he understood where his feeling of confidence came from. He had been lost and without a name. Now he knew himself and his past, and was strong again. There was always hope.

The day slipped into afternoon, the sun no longer lay warm on the divan in the window and Alam Beg lit a charcoal fire in the round chula, puffing out his cheeks as he blew the blackness into red and glowing heat.

Robert found a pen case and a block of black ink and a flat pile of coarse paper. He sat and made notes and drew maps from memory, and as he worked his mind was busy with plans. Alam Beg did not interrupt him. Robert had suddenly withdrawn. Men who knew him well would have told Alam Beg that a plan was being formed that would be almost flawless. As it was, Alam Beg looked with respect at the busy hands and thoughtful face, and was quiet.

When the sun had dropped below the high peaks and it was growing too dark for Robert to see, he put the pens and the paper on a table, and stood looking out into the evening, glad to see the day gone.

"When can I see the Raja?" His desire for action was urgent in his voice.

"Patience, Lord. They will send a signal as soon as it is safe."

As his servant spoke they heard the liquid notes of a flute. Someone was playing softly, trying out a tune as they walked past the tower room. The sound faded, and Alam Beg stood up.

"Saida, the old woman servant, has sent her sign," he said. "All is well."

"Then let us go to the Raja, quickly," said Robert.

9

THEY walked quickly through empty courts, and down long ill-lit passages that were full of wavering shadows. Alam Beg was barefooted; Robert wore soft leather boots. They made no sound as they hurried.

The clear notes of the flute, growing louder, came to them as they entered the last passage.

At the Begum's door, two guards in gaudy yellow turbans and loose shirts and trousers lounged, one on each side of the door, drawn swords held in negligent hands. Robert reached for his dagger, startled to see them there, but Alam Beg said quickly, "Nay, Lord, it is well. These be of the brotherhood." Brothers of loyalty he had called the men who were loyal to the Raja. Robert's glance met two pairs of watchful eyes, their alert stare belying their owners' casual pose.

The flute was joined by a sweep of

notes from a sitar plucked by a skilled hand, and all the time there was the steady beat of the tabla. The music makers were three young men, sitting on a carpet beyond the light that shone on the Begum's closed door. The man playing the flute was Nathu.

As the music rose the door opened and Alam Beg went in. Then he came out and stood aside for Robert. Saida was there to swing the door shut, and the two old men, Alam Beg's grandfather and uncle, shot the bolts home.

The scented Persian roses, the last of the year, blooming in spite of autumn frosts, were sweet on the air. The fountain seemed to dance to the music outside, tossing its white plumes in the light of many oil lamps. A figure of the Goddess, incense burning at her feet, flowers about her shoulders, stood with stone eyes and a smile on her full, carved lips, her peacock beside her, its jewelled eyes glinting.

Robert saw none of this. He walked through the beautiful little court as if it was an empty street. The long day's inactivity was over. Now he was impatient to talk with the Raja about his urgent plans.

But the room he entered was empty. He saw silver lamps and silk cushions and comfortable divans; small, delicate tables inlaid with ivory; embroidered hangings; painted screens; and marble, cut and carved into delicate tracery over the windows. This was a woman's room. There was a domed cane cage in one corner, where a bulbul sat, fluffing its feathers. Beside the cage stood the Begum. Robert looked about him and turned to her.

"The Raja? Where is he?"

"He comes. Sit, Dil Bahadur, and drink some wine. In a little while he comes."

The Begum had removed her veil, her head cloth and her high-necked coat. Her hair hung heavy and gleaming in a thick plait. As she leaned to offer him wine the loose neck of her thin robe fell forward and he could not help but see the upper part of her breasts, curved as perfectly as the goblet she was handing him. He could smell the mingled scents of sandalwood and jasmine breathing from her body, sweet nostalgic scents, taking him back, reminding him of his beautiful mother, and of his youth. He took the goblet from her and sat down and she settled herself beside him, watching him, her eyes wide and soft, the smoothly drawn black brows above them as delicate as a butterfly's antennae. Her mouth was unpainted, soft-lipped, richly curved.

Robert drank his wine and felt the attraction that came from her slowly stealing into his mind. Where was the urgency he had felt to tell the Raja of the plan he had made? It had been suddenly transmuted into an urgency of another kind. It seemed that he had been unhappy and worried for too long. His young manhood spoke to him with a clear commanding voice. He lifted his goblet and drank to the dark eyes that watched him so intently. He became enchanted by the way her lashes hid her eyes when she looked down, by her shadowed eyelids, and by the curve of her mouth. He enjoyed the taste of the wine, and at the same time enjoyed looking at the girl.

When she leaned to refill his goblet,

he found that he could not look away from her. He looked at the curve of the half-seen breasts, he looked at her eyes, and then at her mouth, and she met his look without shame and answered it with the warmth of her gaze. Robert put his goblet down, and took her hand to raise it to his lips, and as she moved closer to him, a whisper of sound came from the closed door behind them. The moment was broken, he saw the Begum's expression change, and she sighed, half glad and half sorry that they had been disturbed. She stood up and beckoned to him, and he followed her to the door that had been opened. As they entered the room he expected to see the Raja waiting for him, but the room was a bedroom, and on the bed was a child, half asleep, with an elderly man sitting beside the bed, a drawn sword across his knees.

Robert watched as the Begum bent over the child, her face alight with love and pride. He said softly, "Is this your son?"

"My son. My father's precious heir, and also — this is the heir to Pakodi State."

The child's dark hair was tousled over his forehead. He looked thin and pale, as if he had been ill at some time. The Begum bent to put her lips to his forehead, and the child sighed, turned and smiled at his mother, and then looked in surprise at her companion.

"Mother! I was dreaming. I will tell you about my dream — but who is this? Is he a friend of ours? Hamid — "

As he spoke the name he had turned to look at the elderly man now standing beside his bed, the sword still in his hand, and Robert thought he could see fear on his face. But the man, an old soldier from his bearing, smiled and began to put his sword into its scabbard, and the child relaxed.

So this was the child, a child of great importance, born after his father's death. The Begum had been Ali of Pakodi's favourite wife. Robert remembered Ali speaking of the young girl from the hills, the only girl of all his women that he had married. "Sweeter than honey, and as gentle as a dove," he had said; and that he hoped for a son from her.

Well, here was the son, but Ali lay

in an ornate tomb. He had never seen his wish fulfilled, never held his heir in his arms.

For this boy, the Ruler of Lambagh guarded Pakodi State. This grave-faced child, with a hint of fear in his eyes, would one day sit on the guddees of Pakodi and of Jungdah, and would inherit great wealth. This little boy, with bright watchful eyes, in a face that was too thin and pale.

The child spoke, breaking into Robert's thoughts.

"Are you a prince of Lambagh? I was told by my grandfather that one would come."

Smiling, Robert bowed.

"I am Dil Bahadur from Lambagh. What is your name, Highness?"

"I am called Atlar Khan, son of Ali Khan of Pakodi. Have you come with an army and horses?"

"Nay, Highness, I came alone. But horses and men will come, be sure of that."

The boy nodded, and flinging back the coverlet got out of bed and came to stand close to Robert, holding up a toy he held in his hand, a small model of a horse, beautifully carved and with a leather saddle and bridle enriched with precious stones that glittered in the light.

"See my horse. This is such a good horse! His name is Sultan. He is a magic horse and never grows tired."

Standing, the child showed himself as a well grown, sturdy little boy, although he was thin, too thin, and very colourless. Robert turned to the Begum.

"Has he been ill? He looks so pale . . . "

"He is pale because he needs to be out in the open, to see the sun, and to ride in the fresh air. He longs for freedom, and to ride."

"But of course — and why not, at his age?"

The Begum looked at him in astonishment, almost angered.

"How can you ask? Do you think we could let him go outside these walls for even a minute? What do you think would happen?"

The child was listening to them, and interrupted.

"I must never leave these rooms. I

must never go outside. People who go outside never come in again. Devils take them away." The child was almost whispering, his eyes round with fear. Robert could not bear to see this child, who reminded him so much of his own son, in so much fear. He swung the boy up into his arms, saying, "Come, my Prince. No devils shall take you. A Prince who owns a magic horse! That is wonderful indeed!"

The boy smiled into his eyes, his fear forgotten.

"Wah, you are strong, Prince of Lambagh. No devils would take me if you were here. One day, I shall be tall and strong like you. Will you stay with me, until I am strong?"

Robert thought of James, sturdy and independent, full of energy and able to go where he pleased in perfect safety. This poor child, a prisoner, and living in fear — he could not bear to think of it. He answered the boy gently, telling him that he would have to return to Lambagh soon. "I must go back to my son," he said, with pain in his heart, thinking of the distance that now separated him from his wife and child. The boy clung round his neck for a moment, then, distracted by the heavy gold chain he wore, pulled at it, and the emerald ring came into his hand.

"What is this ring? It is very bright, like green fire. Look Mother, such a ring . . . "

Robert took the ring and dropped it back into its hiding place. "My son cut his teeth on that ring."

"Your son — yes, I remember news of his birth," said the Begum. "He is about three years less in age than Atlar Khan. He will have nine years soon — if Allah wills . . . " The last few words were spoken in a whisper, but Robert heard them. He was still holding the boy in his arms, and his grip tightened as he said, "If Allah wills — he will grow to be a fine strong man — is that not so, Atlar Khan?"

The boy had pulled the ring from its hiding place again, and his mother chided him and took his hand, and for a moment the three were joined together, with the ring and the chain linking the boy, the woman and the man. A silence fell in that moment as Robert and the Begum looked at each other, the boy between them — a silence so deep that the caged bird in the room behind them heard the notes of a free bird in the garden outside and essayed a few notes of its own liquid song. Then it fell silent again as the door opened and Saida the old maidservant came in. She stared at the three standing together, and for a moment her hand went to her mouth. She slid her eyes towards the old man standing beside the bed in a glance full of meaning. Then she said quickly, "It is time, Lady. Time for his draught. Come, Highness, and I will give it to you." The boy clung to Robert, protesting, but the Begum took him from Robert's arms, saying firmly, "You heard what Saida said, my son. It is time for you to rest now. Say farewell to Dil Bahadur — only for a short time — say farewell. You will see him again, if Allah so wills . . . "

"What draught is this that he takes?" It was the child who answered Robert, pulling a face as he spoke.

"It is to make me sleep. It gives me many dreams, and sometimes they make me afraid, but not always. Sometimes I dream that I am riding over the mountains on my magic horse, and that is very good." The Begum walked out of the room, and Robert bent to kiss the boy, saying his farewells and promising to see him later after his rest, and followed her.

"What medicine is this, Begum Sahiba, that you give your son? Is it a drug?" She looked at him in silence for a moment, then turned to seat herself before she spoke.

"My son has the heart of a lion. He is a strong child, and is interested in everything, and very active. He speaks of his future as a ruler, and of horses and riding — and he is a prisoner within two rooms and has not been outside these rooms for nearly four years. It is hard for him, and for us. How do you think we could keep him here, under our eyes, and guard him, if we did not use a drug? Used with care, it helps to make his imprisonment easier. He bears it well. I am proud of my son. Indeed, I am very proud. His life is terrible but he does not often rail against it, or weep."

129

Dry eyed, head high, she looked proud and cool, until Robert saw the torment in her eyes. He was horrified by the knowledge that they had to regularly drug such a fine, strong boy, in order to keep him in this unnatural imprisonment. But he could think of nothing to say to her. This to him was the heart of the tragedy in this ill-omened place. Apart from anything else, the boy was ill; Robert had felt the fever that burned in his body as he held the child in his arms.

"What do you think about, Dil Bahadur?" Looking down at her face he could not say, "I think that your child is living a terrible life and I think he is ill with fever." It was not possible to say that to her. So he gathered his will, and said firmly, "I think of all that I must do, and of how little time I have. When will your father come?"

"Soon. Do you hunger? No? Then more wine?"

Her tone was persuasive but he refused. He needed a clear head to think, and the combination of wine, the child, the Begum's attractions were not helping him. Such a fine child — no wonder that when she could have gone to reach safety with her mother and her friend, she would not go, but decided to risk everything for him.

She was moving about the room, searching for something — her grace and her appeal drove everything else out of his mind as he watched her. Her head veil had fallen back, revealing her shining coils of hair, and her small ears, ornamented with gold earrings which were studded with diamonds that glittered no more brightly than did her eyes that she turned to look at him, feeling his gaze on her. He was startled by the warmth of her look and by his own reaction to the message her eyes gave him. They stood in silence, staring at each other, a breath away from being in each other's arms.

The silence was broken by music. Someone was singing a love song. The flute was silent, only the hand drum played, and the voice sounded, each word clear, the tune plaintive.

"Oh wind," sang the voice,
"Oh wind blow down the blossom
Before the fruit can form,
My false love gathers other blooms
And leaves for me a thorn,
Oh wind, kind wind — "

The Begum's face drained of colour; she pointed frantically at a door on the other side of the room. Alam Beg came running, and snatched up Robert's goblet.

"Lord, follow me — quickly, for all our sakes . . . "

Robert turned to the Begum. "Not without you."

"Ssh — I cannot come. They expect me to be here. If I were not here they would search, and all our plans would be for nothing."

Plans? What plans? For all Robert could see, apart from a warning system, they had no plans. But he had, and it was urgent that he should carry out the first stage before it was too late. She was pushing at him, her whisper vehement.

"Do you wish them to kill you here, in front of my eyes? They are close, listen

to the music. Alam Beg, take him — "
Take him? Like a child dragged to safety!
Robert grew furious. On the point of
flat refusal, he saw the terror in her
eyes, shrugged, and turned to follow
Alam Beg.

The flute had joined the voice; singer
and player made music that should have
been heard with pleasure; lovers should
have been listening, dreaming in each
other's arms. Instead the music had been
turned into an alarm.

"I will lie on the fallen petals, as on
   my bed.
I will hold the thorn.
I will wait in my empty rooms
Until my false love comes.
While the lamp burns late
Shamed by red dawn.
And I wait — and I wait . . . "

The song faded into silence behind them
as Robert and Alam Beg ran swiftly,
quietly. There were voices now in the
room beneath them. Alam Beg raised a
hand to halt Robert. They were directly
above the Begum's room. Alam Beg lay

down and put his ear to the floor, and
Robert did the same.

The voices were so clear that it was as
if they were in the same room. Women's
voices.

10

THE Begum and Saida were still alone. They were talking together. Now that he could not see her face, he was aware of a wistful upward inflexion in the Begum's voice, a husky break that was very charming.

He heard them with shame and admiration. Their bravery was astounding. These women were holding fear at bay with small talk so that he could get safely away. He wondered how often the conversations he had heard in the past between Laura and her friends or her women servants had helped her to bridge gaps between fear and courage, had given comfort or covered pain; he thought of how often he could have given help or comfort in turn, if he had bothered to try and understand instead of smiling indulgently and closing his mind to what he had thought of as 'chatter'. Now, far from his wife, he admired the courage of the two women below, and was ashamed of his intolerance in the past.

A noise, a jingle of spurs in the garden court, a man's voice calling. A rich, laughing voice. Then the Begum's answer.

"Who is it? Do not enter, we be two women alone, and I am not veiled. What do you want?"

There was a pause, the sound of a determined step, and the Begum spoke again.

"Ismail Mohammed! I regret you find me in disarray. My father is not here, if you are seeking him."

"No. I do not seek him. As for disarray — do not veil your face, Lady of the Rose Court. It was to rest my eyes on your beauty that I came."

"It is not for me to sit unveiled before you, Ismail Mohammed."

"Modesty is sweet in a woman, but I am the loser. Like a man who sees the moon vanish behind clouds. May I beg a cup of wine?"

"If you wish. It is there, on the table at your elbow."

"Saida — pour and taste for me."

"I will pour, but I do not need to taste,

Ismail Mohammed. The venom of the cobra does not harm the creature itself, they say."

Saida's voice was steady, bitter with hatred. Robert felt Alam Beg stiffen. There was silence in the room below for a moment that grew in the listeners' minds into eternity.

The man's laughter broke the dangerous silence.

"Woman, you are brave. Ten like you in my bodyguard and I would need no more. Well, I drink the wine in faith, untasted by your servant, Lady. I drink to your eyes. In such twin lakes a man could lose himself, to drown in pleasure."

"In both eyes, Ismail Mohammed, or only one?"

"I do not understand you, Lady."

"Do you not? I have heard that there are girls in this valley who have lost an eye because they declined a little more than allowing a man to drown his sorrows in their eyes."

"Perhaps they refused an honour they would have been wiser to accept."

"The honour of rape? I see. Am I being threatened, Ismail Mohammed?"

No fear in the Begum's voice, it rang with authentic rage. There was a sharp click. The man had put down his wine cup.

"Who threatens you, Lady? Tell me, and I will tear his entrails from his body and make him eat them . . . "

"How charming you are, Ismail Mohammed. Such a delightful picture you paint for me. One can see you were trained for the camps, not the court."

"Rose of the Palace, you stab deep with your tongue. But you cannot wound me. Your words fall like music, in your voice a curse sounds like a blessing. However . . . "

"Yes?"

"I repeat. If anyone threatens you, tell me. For your peace of mind and safety and your continued presence, there is nothing I would not do."

"My peace of mind, my safety, and what was the third thing you mentioned? My liberty?"

"What is this talk of liberty? You are as free as a bird."

"As free as my bulbul in his cage there."

"You keep him there because his song pleases you, and also because, having always been sheltered, if he flew free he would be in danger. There are cats in the Palace and hawks in the sky . . . "

"And so, I, like my bulbul, am kept in a cage which is never opened, but for what reason? I, Ismail Mohammed, the daughter of your benefactor the Raja of Jungdah, and widow of Ali of Pakodi, I am no singing bird. So why?"

Her voice was a lash and at last the man's poise was shaken. He answered in a different tone, his rich voice rougher, as if the lash of her words had bitten deep.

"You are here for your safety."

"What cats stalk me in my father's Palace, what hawks search for me in the skies above Jungdah where I was born?"

"I know the dangers you are in, Begum Amara. When they are removed, you will be free."

"I know my enemies, Ismail Mohammed — do you want to hear their names?" Robert heard the man move suddenly, and the voice was wooing again, persuasive, charming.

"How we do waste these few minutes together speaking of dangers and enemies! You speak truly when you say that I was not trained for the court, Lady. How can I speak to your heart as I would when you burn me with your eyes . . . "

"Burn you? A few minutes ago I think you spoke of drowning in my eyes. Perhaps I am a danger, fire and water — "

"No: fire and ice. But my heart is lost to you, Lady of the Rose Court. Burned or drowned, it does not matter. I love you and I have only one desire in life."

"Oh?" The word sounded like a stifled yawn.

"Marry me, Amara. Let me show you what love can be, you who were married to an old man. What do you know of the fire and ice of love? Come, clear your eyes. Do not see me as an enemy. See me at your feet, a man enthralled by your beauty, wild with love . . . "

Robert, listening, frowned. For the first time the man was showing his true self and one thing sounded an authentic note. When he spoke of love, he was obviously speaking the truth. Ismail Mohammed was passionately in love with the girl who now answered him in a quiet, bitter voice.

"Do not speak to me as you speak to your bazaar women, Ismail Mohammed! I am here without my father, unprotected, and you dare to behave thus? Be ashamed. Be ashamed, and know one thing. I will never marry with you. Never."

"Flower of the heart! Never is a very short word. Think before you use it. There is time to think before the full moon. I will see you then. Remember that never is not a word to use with me. Never can be a very short way leading to nothing, to darkness. Next time I speak with you, your father will be with me."

★ ★ ★

They heard his spurs ringing as he walked out, then silence as the door shut behind him.

No idle chatter in the room below now. Robert heard the Begum say quietly, "The moon is full in fourteen days," and her voice broke into sobbing. He began to get to his feet, but Alam Beg pressed him down and whispered, "Not yet, Lord. Wait for the flute player . . . "

It was not long, the waiting. The notes of the flute, single, spaced, clear, came softly into the room and they both moved together. Robert had expected to go back the way they had come, but Alam Beg shook his head. He spoke in his normal voice.

"Never the same way twice. Now we use the safe way, because tonight the danger is great. We go through the shrine and no one will trouble us. *This* shrine those sons of pigs fear. With reason. I also . . . " He turned, and led the way.

Three empty, dusty rooms, opening one into another. Then a dark, dank stone passage. The whole atmosphere of this part of the Palace was different and spoke of great age, of building done by hands centuries before, now turned to dust. Silence, a rough cold stone passage, and then light, and a familiar smell containing nothing but happy memories as Alam Beg pushed on a heavy door.

The room was small and the smell of incense was strong. It was joined by another smell, also familiar to Robert, but not nostalgic. A robed priest with a shaven head except for a tail of hair hanging from the crown; a low altar, and towering over it a great, many-armed figure.

Kali the Black One, the fierce, the terrible. The One before whose image blood must never be dry. Her eyes glared down at Robert, her scarlet tongue protruding from her fang-toothed mouth, a necklace of skulls hung round her neck like a garland. Her steed, a tiger with open, snarling mouth, stood beside her, lest she should wish to mount and ride out to wreak destruction on mankind. On the slab of stained stone that was her altar, a white bird trembled, bleeding and dying.

Robert had seen many images of Kali, but never one that lived and breathed such malevolence. He averted his eyes and felt a shudder of horror.

"Wah, this is an evil place, this shrine. But safe. The priest is dumb. Someone tore his tongue out many years ago. Now he serves that — that One in there, and provides safety for us. But I am always glad when I am away from this place. His eyes are almost as terrible as the eyes of the One he serves. Idolators!" said Alam Beg, and looked with fear over his shoulder. Then he beckoned, and they walked through the narrow passage into what seemed to be an empty, dark courtyard where a fountain was silent and no flowers grew. A man rose in the shadows before a low door, and Robert saw the glint of a drawn sword as he opened it for them and closed it again.

They were in a room where a great pillowed bed stood against a wall that was painted with flowers and birds, and gilded, so that it gleamed richly in the light of a hanging lamp. The scent of sandalwood and jasmine was everywhere. This was the Begum's sleeping chamber. The further door led straight into the room where he had left her.

She was alone, sitting cross-legged among her cushions. Her black hair was loose on her shoulders; her veil discarded and her face was almost as white as her robe.

Something about her, some fine, stretched feeling, as if a strand of silk were pulled to breaking point, stopped Robert in mid-stride. Her eyes were so wide and so fixed that he grew afraid. Then he realised that she was listening, her ears straining to hear something; what? Alam Beg had stopped just inside the door. Now he walked over and pulled aside a hanging that hid another door, and opened it. Nothing but darkness; and then, as Robert looked and his eyes adjusted he saw a short flight of stairs leading down from the door. Held by the Begum's concentration, they stood, looking at the stairs, and waited with her, straining their own ears.

A whisper of sound, the creak of a door — Saida appeared, coming up the steps quickly, her veil blowing about her. The Begum stood up and looked at her.

"Safe, Amara. He was delivered into the hands you sent him to. You did well, and bravely."

The Begum put her hands over her face but not before Robert had seen the contortion of grief that twisted her mouth and closed her eyes.

"What is it? May I know?"

He felt as if he was living in a

madman's dream and would wake and find himself either on a bare hillside by some camp fire with his men sleeping round him, or else back in his own bed with Laura breathing quietly beside him.

It was Alam Beg who explained. While the Begum and Saida had talked with Ismail Mohammed, a carefully laid plan had been successfully carried out. The child was safely outside the Palace and in a secure place from which he would be taken over the mountains to Panchghar. Robert thought of his own plans and admired the neatness of the child's escape. The Begum had conceived the plan, and had made sure it was successful. Robert thought of her voice and the way she had kept Ismail Mohammed inside, and gave her unstinted praise.

"Yes, thank you, Dil Bahadur. As long as they do not discover his absence, all will be well. The Nephew will not come back for fourteen days — "

"And in that time, you must go. There is no reason now why you should not."

But of course there was. The reason came in, smiling, apologising for delay, very old and very much beloved by

146

his daughter, and very important to his state.

The Raja, his red silk cap a little askew, was looking strained, and was obviously glad to sit and be given wine. There was a fine tremble in his hand, and although his eyes were as bright and wise as they had been the day before, Robert saw with despair that he did not look well.

The Begum noticed too, but at first said nothing, merely making her father as comfortable as she could, sending for food, and busying himself when it came over the choosing of dishes, keeping all strain and distress from her face. Robert's admiration for her grew. The Raja relaxed; he ate a little and drank, and looked better. The food was cleared away, more wine was poured, and then the Begum looked at her father and said quietly, "Bapu-ji-tell. What did that monster do?"

"Nothing, daughter, nothing to disturb yourself about."

"Nothing. So you came to my court nearly three hours late, and you are trembling with fatigue. *Nothing*, Father?"

The old man moved his hands, one over the other, and frowned a little and looked at Robert as if to ask for help, but got none, for Robert wanted to hear his answer. He could guess in fact what the Nephew had done.

The Begum waited and then the Raja meeting her eyes shrugged suddenly.

"It *was* nothing, Amara. He asked me for something I value, and I refused to give it to him, and he went away. But he was determined, and so — being also determined — I was late. I ask your forgiveness. He has gone now. Back to his camp."

"And he returns within fourteen days. He comes with the full moon, to ask again. No?" The Raja's eyes fell before hers.

"My child, I am tired. Ask me no more. I can tell you no more."

The Begum stood up, her shining hair falling about her like a cloak.

"Father. My dear and honoured father. My son is safe. He went out this evening." Robert saw the worry and the distress drain away from the Raja's face.

"I will not ask you how, Amara, lest I

be asked by another in some hard way, and disclose from weakness what I would keep safe. But I am very happy."

"Also, now, he can put no pressure on you to give him my hand — can he Bapu-ji?"

"Once you have gone, Amara, all will be well."

"I do not go without you."

She turned away and sat, regal, a young cheetah, head erect, tawny eyes steady, one arched foot showing beneath her robe. Robert watched her, fascinated. He had known and admired many women, loved his wife with his whole heart, but he thought that he had never met a woman like this, whose every move held his eye, reminding him of youth and the delights and treasures of the body; at a time when they were all in danger, and he had a perilous task ahead of him.

The Raja appeared to have regained strength and authority. He spoke sharply, and his voice had the sound of command in it.

"My daughter, you will, at last, do what you are told. Do not make a show of disobedience because you have an audience. You will go when I tell you, Amara, and then I will not have to spend three hours being bullied and shouted at by a man who is determined to take you, in marriage. If you do not go he will take you without marriage, and do it knowing that you will marry him afterwards to save my name. So — you will go before he returns."

"And when I am gone, he will not spend three hours shouting at you, my lord father. He will take you into those rooms from which the smell of blood comes under the doors even now. How long before you die under his hands — or the hands of his servants? Or how long before your servants run to tell him where I am, tell him *anything*, to save you? Father, we go together."

The Raja and his daughter sat glaring at each other. The Raja was the first to turn away. He looked at Robert, and as if he were a man lost in a wilderness, seeing at last a known path, he spoke with pleasure.

"Oh, Dil Bahadur! Give me pardon that I have not told you of my pleasure that you have found your mind again. We wrangle like children and all the time you sit here patiently, knowing the answer to all our problems. Speak, my friend. You have remembered everything?"

The moment had come on Robert too suddenly; he had so easily forgotten his own worries, watching the girl and listening to her. His mind cleared and he looked away from the Begum.

Now he had to tell this brave old man, her father, that his message had reached Lambagh but that it had brought no sense of danger within the words of the message. Only the messenger's fear and haste had spoken of trouble, and that had not been understood. Because of the wording of the Raja's letter there had been no haste. Because of the feeling of unease the messenger had brought, he, Dil Bahadur, had been sent to be sure that all was well, and to send news. He had sent none, and now Jiwan Khan, and fifty Lambaghi men, were riding into danger.

Jiwan Khan! If it were anyone else he would not take their hope from these brave people. But he could not allow Jiwan Khan to fall into the Nephew's hands. He set his mind on what he had to say, and began to speak.

When he had finished, there was silence. Amara sat looking down into her hands, lying palm up in her lap. The Raja looked at Robert, and his eyes were despairing. Robert could not be silent under such a look.

"But you understand! Your message was not clear! If you had only said something — anything. Why did Shivnath not speak?"

"Because he was afraid. Do not forget no one knew what had happened to the earlier messages I sent. The men never came back, there was no answer to my requests for help. So this time I was careful, and I swore him to secrecy. Not very difficult. He was sure demons pursued him. Well. It is done."

"Yes. But I must get warning to Jiwan Khan. He must not fall into the Nephew's hands. If Ismail Mohammed knew what a rich prize was coming — with only fifty men — !"

Robert's voice was wild with impatience. The old man was too calm; was it the calmness of shock, or the tranquil acceptance of the inevitable?

"If Ismail Mohammed knows?" said the Raja quietly, "*If* he knows? Of course he knows. I think my message got through for that reason only. All his plans were laid; he had followed instructions, and the trap was laid."

"Followed instructions? What do you mean?"

"Ismail Mohammed was not a rich young man when he came asking for permission to live here and join my army. I told you that he spent money freely, and always had more. Jiwan Khan — and you yourself — are in worse danger than you know. Ismail Mohammed has a master. The master comes here, entering Jungdah in time for the night of the full moon. Dil Bahadur, the master comes up from the South."

The master. *The Master!* Robert recalled another man, now dead, who had spoken of the Master, and had taken money from him to do Lambagh harm.

"Sagpurna. Oh my *God*!"

The old Raja nodded. "Yes. Sagpurna."

11

IT was very late. The two old servants stood by the door and Alam Beg lay sleeping against the wall. He had, after all, watched all the previous night beside Robert. Saida had gone through into the Begum's bedchamber, where she could be heard moving about, readying the room for when it pleased Amara to come to bed.

The three who had sat together had repeated their arguments until they were angry and exhausted. Robert was determined to leave the Palace by any means so that he could get to Jiwan Khan, who would be well on his way.

"If I leave at dawn I can stop him at the first pass, where Shivnath was killed."

"The Bab-i-margh."

"The Gate of the Dead? What a name for the entrance to your state! Yes, I can stop him there if I go at dawn."

"If you leave — or try to leave at

dawn, you will be taken, Dil Bahadur. The Nephew was here today, and has left the guards humming like disturbed wasps. By tomorrow night, with suitable aid from some of my men, they will be drunk, and careless. They are a rabble, those who are left to guard us. The Nephew has no fears that an old man, a girl, and a sick child will get away easily from this place. His real troops are with him. So wait, wait until darkness tomorrow night."

"Tomorrow night will be too late."

"If you are taken, we will be taken too. Do you wish that? If you do, Dil Bahadur, it is understood. Jiwan Khan is your friend and the heir to your state. So — you must decide. I can talk no more. If you will pardon me, I, who am very old, must retire."

The Raja did indeed appear on the point of utter exhaustion. He looked at his daughter for a moment and her wide eyes seemed to give him strength, for he smiled suddenly and stood. Robert jumped up and steadied him as he walked to the door. The Raja leaned heavily on him as he said good night to

155

his daughter, and Robert went through the court with him. There the old man said quietly, " If you must go, then tell Alam Beg. He will get you away. But oh, Dil Bahadur, do not fall into their hands. They will not kill you because the Nephew will see your likeness to Kassim Khan. But I fear what they will do to you. You may very well uncover to them all our secrets . . . "

Robert set his lips.

"I will not be caught."

The Raja looked at his hard, determined face, sighed, and said his farewells.

Robert stood for a minute in the courtyard and felt the cold wind that was blowing drifts of clouds over the starry sky. He shivered and went back to the lighted warm room, meaning to wake Alam Beg and tell him that he must help him to get out as soon as possible.

But Alam Beg no longer slept against the wall. Only the Begum was there, sitting twirling an empty goblet between her long fingers. She turned her velvet stare on Robert and held out the goblet. As he poured her wine, Robert asked for Alam Beg.

"He has gone to make a room ready for you."

"Here? In the women's court?"

"In *my* court. You cannot go through the Palace tonight to the tower room, it would be foolish."

"I thank you, Begum. In any case, I am going soon — it is necessary that I tell Alam Beg."

The Begum lifted her glass and looked into it as if she might see something in it. The goblet was unusual, in that it was of fine glass. She seemed to be holding a great ruby, and her fingers were so fine, her hand so slim that Robert imagined he could see the wine through it. He stopped looking at her hand with difficulty and said firmly that he would like to speak to Alam Beg as soon as possible.

"He will come soon. I have told him that you wish to leave at dawn. He will be making ready."

She looked up from her study of the wine and added, "Do you remember the way you came into the Palace? Do you remember the house where you stopped?"

"I do — very well. But how do you know?"

157

"It is our sanctuary. We use that house for many things. My son is there now."

That charming, feverish child in that filthy place, perhaps cared for by that girl . . . Robert could not hide his expression of distaste.

The Begum smiled.

"You saw only one room; there are many. You will see more when you go. My Lord Dil Bahadur, will you see my little son for me? He will not understand why I have sent him away. Will you tell him something of comfort? Even Hamid is not with him. He stands guard here, over an empty bed with a bundle of quilts in it."

The voice with the husky break in it was choked with tears. Robert did not know how to comfort her. His departure was going to put her, and her father and her precious son, into danger. He looked at her averted face and saw her put a hand up to catch the tears that were falling down her cheeks.

"I will tell him that you are coming soon, and that he must ride among the stars every night to become prepared for the horse he will ride after he crosses the mountains." She turned and smiled at him, and lifted her glass to drink.

"Will you not have a glass of wine, Lord? There is wine there . . . "

Wine? The breaking voice, the velvet, tawny eyes! Robert sat, staring, unable to speak, and she looked back at him, and he suddenly knew why he had seen recognition in her eyes when she had come into her father's room three nights before. This was his first girl. Not his first love, but the first girl he had ever taken. The last shreds of his memory had returned.

For a moment he saw her as she had been, remembering her standing naked under the shivering shadows of the trees, offering him wine, the sifted moonlight shining on the silver jug in her hands and on her face. He recalled with perfect memory the feeling of her skin under his hands, the pliant reply of her body to his. In the silence of the room he heard again her broken cry as he took her, and heat filled his body at the memory.

"*Why* did you not tell me? You knew me at once!"

"How could I tell you? You had forgotten me."

"I had forgotten everything."

"But you remembered the rest. All your life that you had forgotten, you remembered, but not me. You had never thought of me after that night."

Robert looked away from her eyes. How could he tell her that for months afterwards he had thought of her every time he took a woman, but that Laura had driven every memory of every other woman from his head?

Amara said softly, "Yes. You forgot me. But I, Lord, never forgot you. How well they named you. You have been lord of my heart and of my body since that night."

"Oh come — a fumbling boy, throwing you on the ground! I was a virgin and knew nothing. You were my first."

"I know." Her voice had laughter in it. "I knew it then. But — it did not matter to me, your lack of skill. I reached paradise with you. Even to reach it once is good. One remembers the pleasure, however short." She smiled without bitterness, drank from her glass

160

and held it out to him.

"Share my wine before you go, Dil Bahadur. Take wine with me. I have spent so many nights alone with thoughts and dreams. Now sit with me a little. It lacks some hours to dawn. Is it too much to ask?"

"No," said Robert, "it is not too much." He took her glass and drained it and poured it full again and handed it to her. She had not moved, made no effort to lean closer to him, or entice him to come closer to her. She only turned the goblet in long slender fingers, turned it slowly until she could set her lips where his had been.

Robert, watching her, knew that unless he walked out of the room immediately, he was committed. Indeed, even if he walked away, she would by her stillness, her pride, pull him back. He was lost. He knew her now as if he had been her lover for years. Her robe disguised the tender body he remembered, but he knew the beauty that the cloth covered. He leaned towards her to take back the glass and her warm musky smell enveloped him. This time he did not refill the glass; he put it down and, turning, took her in his arms.

Once, in a shadowed garden, he had taken her quickly, clumsily, without tenderness. Now he held her closely and felt the shiver that ran through her body repeated in his own.

"Could we perhaps get rid of this garment?"

She heard the tremor in his voice that might have been laughter, though there was no smile on the face so close above hers. She undid the clasp of the robe and let it fall, glad that she could please him, and saw his face and his eyes, and put her arms up about his neck to pull his head down to hers.

The night burned away from starlight to dawn. Robert explored an enthralling country where he had travelled before and now discovered again, valleys and mountain peaks of delight, where nothing lived or moved but his fellow traveller and himself.

Alam Beg waited in the room that he had prepared for Robert, and finally slept.

Robert woke in the Begum's bed

chamber. Tangled in the silk of her hair, he turned to look at her. She lay, felled by sleep, her eyelashes crescents of black on the shadows beneath them. Her naked body could face the broadening light proudly, it was perfection. He longed to let his lips move up her arm to set his teeth in the creamy flesh and leave his mark, a mark that would remain, to say, "This is mine, set aside for me alone."

As he leaned closer she woke. She did not smile or speak. Her arm rose and circled his neck, her hands, one on his shoulder to pull him down, the other searching his body as her mouth searched for his. As the sun rose in splendour over the black mountains, their passion blazed until at last they slept in each other's arms.

At midday Saida scratched at the door and came in with tea in glasses enclosed in silver holders. Midday! The sun was high as Robert pulled on a loose robe and walked to the window, cursing himself silently. He suspected that he had been beguiled into staying, but could only be angry with himself.

It appeared that he could not have

gone in any case. He would not have got away, Saida said firmly, the guard had been rated by the Nephew and his bodyguard and none of them had dared to sleep through the night or leave their posts as they usually did.

"They did as they are supposed to do every night, going through the Palace every hour and shouting to each other. Did you not hear them? No, well it is seen that you did not. But tonight — it will be easy tonight. A skin of Persian wine will be found by chance in the store. By sunset they will be busy with other things. Girls from a caravan have come, eager to earn silver for their dancing. Goats will be allowed to stray and will certainly be slaughtered. Tonight you can go out easily."

The Begum, sitting up to drink her tea half-naked and deliciously relaxed and happy; her eyes smiled at him over the rim of her glass. She was a sight to take anxiety from any man, let alone a young man who had lived a lonely and distressed life for over a month. Saida left the room quietly, having put all in order. There was fruit on a table, and wine. She spoke to Alam Beg, standing beside the fountain.

"It is well. He will go out tonight. If we had a little longer, I think she would go with him. This is the answer to a long dream for her."

"And for him?"

Saida shrugged in answer.

"For him — not a dream. He is hungry, he eats. His dream, from all I have heard and remember, is elsewhere. Amara Begum knows this well. I trust she remembers that dreams are momentary things, and that one wakes."

She walked out of the court into her room and Alam Beg salaamed low as she passed him, looking after her with a curious mixture of admiration and pity on his face. Then he too went away, and the fountain was left to whisper to itself while the Goddess stared with tranquil, stony gaze through the flying spray.

12

THERE was time for talk in the big room while the sunlight moved from one side of the painted gilded walls to another, picking out flowers and birds and golden pavilions, and the Begum rested creamy shoulders and tossed black hair against her pillows.

Robert asked a great many questions, and she answered all that she could, her eyes never leaving his face, as if she were learning every line of it by heart.

She told him of the hidden escape route from Kali's shrine, unknown to anyone but members of the family; a secret way, passed down from generation to generation, from the time lost in history when the first stones of the Palace were laid.

"Should you tell me this?"

"You are from the family of Lambagh who are our overlords. We do not tell our servants lest they be tortured past their strength and give it away. My boy went out that way."

"Then whoever took him out knows the way and could be made to talk . . . "

"The one who took him out will never talk."

"Do you also send news out that way?" She shook her head.

"No. It is for escape only. We hope to get our people out that way, before the end."

There was one question that touched him deeply, but he found it hard to ask.

"Amara — touching the matter of the boy — "

Her voice was alarmed and she said quickly, "The boy? My son? What of him?"

"You know what I would ask. Is he *my* son?"

"He is Atlar Khan, heir to the nawabdom of Pakodi State, and also heir to my father, the future ruler of Jungdah. What else? Does that answer your question, Lord?"

Indeed, it was the answer he had expected. To claim the boy as his son would leave the states of Pakodi and

Jungdah without heirs. The boy was of importance to this family — and he himself had nothing to offer the boy in place of this rich inheritance. He bowed his head and was silent, remembering a night of shadows in a garden, a night of brief, sweet passion. The boy was his, he was sure; the child's eyes, the grey eyes that had seemed so familiar — they were familiar because they were so like his own grey eyes and so like the eyes of his son James. But he could prove nothing and indeed he did not wish to. The boy had a different background and he had no place in his life — except to try to see him into safety.

The Begum sat silent beside him, studying his downcast face, and her expression was very sad. Presently he turned to her and smiled.

"Amara, you have answered my question. May Atlar Khan grow in health and live in safety and happiness. Now there is another matter I must speak of. You must know that Ismail Mohammed is in love with you. No, listen to me. He loves you beyond sense, and therefore you must be careful of him. Do not provoke him. Because of this love — "

The Begum interrupted him with an angry gesture, and turned away.

"You speak of love in connection with that man? He who has tried to poison my son, who has killed so many of my father's faithful servants? He knows nothing of love. He is a monster."

"Even so, he loves you. Call it desire, lust, what you will — but be careful. Truly, Amara, you must leave here before the moon is full. You must."

"Ach — I do not fear him. He will not harm me. I am sure of that at least. He wants to get Pakodi State through me — that is how much his love is worth. I do not fear him." She saw Robert's frown, and asked softly, "Do you care then, Lord of my Heart?"

"How can you ask such a foolish question. If I did not care, would I urge you to leave?"

If she found something lacking in his answer, she made no sign. She smiled and took his hand and laid her cheek against it, and said, "Do not be angered.

I cannot leave my father."

"First the boy, now your father. You will never leave."

"Perhaps."

"And your son — is he to make the long and dangerous journey over the hills without your care? Is that wise?"

Her face contorted with pain and then was smooth again.

"Amara. Listen to me. Come out with me tonight." Her sigh breathed against his cheek as he bent over her.

"And then? I sit, waiting for news of my father, of you? I would die of that waiting. I know the boy is in safe hands and will soon be doubly safe. I go out with my father, or as you say, not at all. And Lord — do not imagine that death holds any fears for me, I who must face your departure tonight."

He almost told her, then, what his plans were — almost. But he kissed her instead, and her arms pulling him close, and her waiting, hungry body, drove his thoughts in another direction.

★ ★ ★

Sunset ornamented the room still more with beams of red and gold, and Saida scratched at the door.

Alam Beg, a changed man, with a shaved upper lip, wearing a duffle tunic girdled up short with a rope belt, was waiting. Swiftly he helped Robert into the same kind of clothing. There was a plain serviceable dagger and tinderbox. Dressed, Robert turned for the Begum's room.

She was standing by her window, looking out towards the black mountains.

"Say no farewells, Lord of my Heart. If the Gods are willing, I will see you again. Go in safety, go laughing."

She turned away firmly, and Robert, glad to be spared a tearful farewell, admired her greatly as he went to join Alam Beg.

Going through the outer court, Robert heard the flute playing softly. On impulse he plucked a small red rose and dropped it before the image of the Goddess. Saida opened the door and stood back. He looked into her eyes as he said farewell to her and was surprised and touched to see tears in them.

171

"Saida — take care of her . . . "

"As always, with my life. Go laughing, Dil Bahadur."

The traditional words sounded strangely inappropriate, thought Robert, following Alam Beg down the colonnade, with the music of the flute growing faint behind him.

They walked fast, two paharis with kiltas, conical baskets, strapped to their backs, empty, their goods delivered. The Hall of the Many Gods was on their left; Robert saw the gleam of lamps, smelled incense and blood, and caught a glimpse of the priests moving about their evening tasks. They entered a long dark passage and Alam Beg paused, looking about him. Then he nodded to Robert, and moving more purposefully led him to a door which he opened. Once they were through, he shot home the iron bolts and turned a key that worked so easily and so quietly that Robert guessed it had been oiled in preparation for their coming. Now they were going through rooms that were unlit except for a faint light that came through small, barred windows.

Their walk ended in a big room, where the smell of dust and damp and age was strong. Alam Beg lit the oil lamp he carried, and revealed a room furnished but unused for centuries it seemed. Spiders had spun webs across the marble filigree that screened the high windows. The lamplight showed shadowed, cushioned divans and carpets, richly embroidered hangings and the eyes of a household god seated brooding in an alcove.

He looked into the main courtyard, into a blaze of torch-light and understood the source of the constant roaring of many voices that he had been conscious of ever since he had entered this room.

He looked down at chaos. As a commander of men he recognised the disorder caused by a total breakdown of discipline. The men of the guard were there in force, but not for duty. Fires had been lit, and the smell of roasting meat came from the carcasses of the goats that were cooking, whole, on makeshift spits. Girls carrying earthenware jugs of wine were threading their way among the shouting, laughing men, and a group of musicians with drums and flutes were standing against the far wall, tuning up, though no one could hear anything but the beat of the drum through the din. Some men were kicking and stamping through a drunken, disorderly version of a Khattock dance. Robert watched the confusion in astonishment.

"The Nephew allows his men this liberty? To become drunk on duty?"

"He has gone, a day's journey towards the Chotagalli Pass, to see the arrival of some of his horses. He would go mad if he could see this. The moment was well chosen."

"Indeed. Surely we can go now. We could take the whole household out, these sots would not even notice an army leaving."

"You do not know, Lord. There are others here, who guard unseen. It pleases them to see the Nephew's men thus, but they would know if the Raja tried to escape. We must wait, Lord, even we, unknown and unimportant as we seem, until we are told it is safe to leave; not only because of our safety but because if they take us the links in our fragile chain of defence will be broken."

To have to wait, to waste precious time, thought Robert, time when I should be trying to get warning back to Lambagh. And my plan! Jiwan Khan must be stopped before he came up to Dhalli Palace. Well, he must use this waiting time usefully. There was much he did not yet know.

Robert began to ask questions, and learned much. Alam Beg was intelligent and observant and no longer thought of Jungdah as anything but his own valley. Also, his grandfather, the elder of the two guards who served the Raja, was high in his master's confidence.

The question of the disappearance of the young men recruited from the villages of the valley was one of the mysteries that Robert wished to unravel.

"It is said that they are taken by devils — do you believe that, Alam Beg?"

Alam Beg laughed.

"Nay, Lord. I did, at first, but my grandfather told me not to be a fool. He says that they were taken over the Lang-su Pass, to the Khand Plateau, and went willingly, sworn to secrecy and promised much reward. There, on that plateau, my grandfather Shamdan thinks that they are trained as horsemen. Fighting horsemen."

"How does your grandfather know this — if he is right?"

"At first there was less secrecy, and he watched some of them go. One was my cousin, and he broke his hip, and came back lame. He is here, he was brought in to be with us, the brothers of loyalty."

"And these fighting horsemen — what does Ismail Mohammed want with them? They will cost him much gold to keep."

"They *bring* gold, Lord. There are many warlords in the far North, over those passes, who would pay much gold for a trained, well-led army. They rise all the time against their Chinese conquerors. My grandfather thinks that the Nephew is building a mercenary army. He says also that the Nephew was foolish to accept as officers so many of these men from the South. They brought gold with them, which he needed at first, and because he accepted it he was ordered by their master to do this and that — which to his shame be it said, he did. But he did not do *all* that he was told, and my grandfather says that there were spies here watching what the Nephew did and that his private army of well-armed horsemen was not in the Master's plan."

"Did that matter? The Nephew had surely used the gold as he was told. He had suborned the army, and killed a good many of the Raja's loyal friends, and has taken away his freedom. What more was he meant to do?"

"My grandfather thinks that the plan was for trouble to spread further afield than just this valley. Also — well, the Raja and his daughter — and the heir — still live. My grandfather is sure that some part of the plan meant death for the family. He said that the other night, when the Nephew returned unexpectedly — before he visited the Begum - that he quarrelled with one of the senior men of the southerners, and that the man shouted that the Master was coming, and that then the Nephew had better look out for himself for he had misused the gold, and his day would be over when the Master came."

The Master!

"Do you know who the Master is?" asked Robert.

"No. But it is said that he is a Raja of great riches from the South."

"He is a man of great riches and great evil. He is the Raja of Sagpur."

"Well, he comes with the full moon as a companion! Fourteen days from now the moon will be full. It is a time of high festival for the idolators of this valley, and for a week at least the people have more freedom than is usual. They take the gods about the Palace and out into the fields and pray for an easy passage through the winter and a fertile spring. Fertility for these untilled fields! I can remember when these fields were rich with grain, when there was peach blossom blowing like snow on the spring winds. But now — there are so few men to work the fields, and so little time when they are free to come and go . . . "

Alam Beg suddenly stopped speaking, staring over his shoulder with fear in his eyes.

"What was that? I heard something — Allah! I turn coward in this place . . . "

"Nay, Alam Beg. You are no coward.

This place is strange. One waits for someone to return, one catches sight of movement in shadows. I would be glad to have you at my back, sword in hand. Here we fight shadows and whispers."

Alam Beg at that moment, in his heart, swore eternal fealty to Robert and did not know that many men had already done so. Robert had always been a leader, even when he had been very young, an untried boy of nineteen, joining Lambagh's forces, and determined to command one day.

Silence fell between them, only the noises from the courtyard below sounded in the room. Robert sat and thought of Sagpurna and his machinations, and Alam Beg watched the expression on his face and became afraid.

"What do you think of, Lord?"

"I think of the Raja of the South and his plans."

"Do you know what his plans are, Lord? For we cannot see what a rich southerner wishes to do here . . ."

I know what he wants, thought Robert. Sagpurna's plans were plain to him. Very clever. A year to frighten an old man into

179

sending out messages for aid, and then making sure that the messages do not get through. Then one message *is* allowed to get through — but tampered with so that it makes little sense; so that no great force would be sent in reply. Spies, clever spies, up in Pakodi State, reporting on Jiwan Khan's restless boredom. Who better for the Ruler of Lambagh to send to Jungdah than his heir, who knew Pakodi State; who better to send than Jiwan Khan to collect Pakodi's widow and his son? Something for a bored young man to do — not dangerous, just a courtesy to a fellow Raja; and the bastard's plan had worked — Jiwan Khan was, at this moment, riding into a trap. And I, thought Robert, I could have got away last night, I am sure I could, and I allowed a woman to delay me for nearly twenty-four hours! He cursed himself, burning with rage and shame, and stood up, wild with impatience to get out.

"What is it, Lord?"

Alam Beg looked with fear at the deep cleft between Robert's brows, thinking that his wound was troubling him again.

"I am angered at my own foolishness."

Allah forfend that he should ever be angered with me, thought Alam Beg, looking at the furious face.

"Alam Beg, I am going. I can afford no more time, I have wasted too much already."

"Lord, I beg of you. If you are taken you will have no time at all . . . "

A sound from the shadows where the lamplight did not reach, a sound — a whisper. They turned, staring, their daggers in their hands.

A footfall, light as a falling leaf, a whisper, a drift of scent.

A girl, her face paint smeared, her silks awry, came forward into the light.

"Come now, Alam Beg. Come to the guard post at the small gate in the Western wall . . . "

"And the guard . . . ?"

"One we had to kill. A new man; he walked about too much, and would not drink. The other was already occupied with one of the girls. It is safe, the gate is unguarded."

"If there was one killed, what of the body? If he was from the South, he will be missed."

"They will find that he was killed in a fight over a girl. He will have liquor poured over him and there will be another killing. Do not fret, we know our business. Are you coming, or do you wish to waste all that we have done in picking holes?"

Robert was already at the door. Alam Beg joined him and in a few minutes they were out and into the seething, red-lit courtyard. The girl screeched with laughter and hung on Robert's arm; Alam Beg, suddenly drunk, reeled on her other side and roared a song.

No one paid them any attention. A short, stumbling walk, and the girl broke away and vanished, singing, into the press of shouting, laughing men. Robert and Alam Beg were in darkness now, following the wall, the noise fading a little behind them.

"Now," said Alam Beg.

Sounds from an alcove, a man's voice, a girl's high-pitched giggle, indicated where the guard was. There was no sign of a body or a struggle. Alam Beg looked round carefully, then opened the gate, and they were through, outside the

Palace wall, leaning against the closed gate and listening.

But there was nothing but the sound of distant roistering to disturb the quiet night. The path down to the village was the scrambling, twisting goat path that Robert remembered. He felt that centuries had passed since he had last stood outside the high windowless wall, and he remembered the stinking darkness of the court where they waited while unseen hands closed the outer door and admitted them into the house.

The smell was, if possible, worse than he remembered. The old woman was not there, only the girl, an old man in duffle robes and an eared fur hat and a young man in travel-worn clothes. Robert waited impatiently while Alam Beg talked aside to the two men in hurried undertones. The girl stood by the fire, her stringy hair over her face, her hands folded inside her wide sleeves.

At last Alam Beg came over to Robert with the young man.

"Your people have been seen, Lord. This man is from the old fort at the Bab-i-margh."

"How far have my men come?"

The young man spoke, looking warily at Robert.

"They will be here perhaps in two days. They are camped for the night. We tried to delay them."

"You tried to delay the Lambaghi men? How, in Allah's name?"

"We fired on them, Lord. Only a little, and without taking aim."

"I see!"

Robert thought of the Lambaghi troopers, and Jiwan Khan, being fired on 'only a little' by a fort that they would have imagined to be friendly.

"Hm. Well, what happened?"

"They became angered, Lord. They took the fort and have tied up the guard commander and the guard. I ran away as soon as I saw what was happening, to bring news. They were very angry, Lord, your men, and the young Lord with them."

"Yes," said Robert. "Yes, it is seen that they might be angered. Alam Beg, you have a horse for me?"

"Lord, it is arranged. It is waiting in a safe place. But I am in distress, Lord.

I cannot come with you."

This was very bad news. Robert did not feel sure of the way he had come, confused as he had been then by his head wound and drugs. Alam Beg saw the worry on his face.

"You know, Lord, I would come if it meant losing my life. But it is not my life. It is the life of Atlar Khan, the heir. I think — I know I will have to go back and bring him out. The boy pines and the hakim here is afraid for his life."

The old man had been standing silent. Now he stepped forward, bowing to Robert, his hands crossed on his breast.

"Lord, the boy will neither eat nor drink. He has asked for his mother and his servant, and having been told that they were still within the Palace he has turned his face to the wall. It seems they lied to him, bringing him out, saying that all the family was coming. I fear that he may die very soon, there is no strength in his body."

How much better if he does die, thought Robert, thinking of the drugs the child was taking — and the danger he was in. Then he remembered the

185

Begum's face when she looked at the child and heard the pain in her voice when she spoke of him. He remembered something else too. "This is your son," said a voice insistently in his heart, "this is your eldest son — will you let him die?"

"But I have no time," said Robert angrily to himself, "I must go and stop Jiwan Khan!" But deep within himself knew that he could not do anything until he had seen the boy.

Robert looked at Alam Beg.

"Where is he?"

It was the girl who, after a pause, said, "We can take you to him — "

"I will see him now, before I go — but make haste . . . "

Alam Beg stepped forward.

"I will guide you, Lord, before I go."

It was a crazy journey, up through a hole in the roof and over tilting, slippery-tiled roofs, down onto crumbling walls that spilt earth and stones under their feet. How, wondered Robert, had they got the boy over these obstacles? Finally they dropped off a high wall into an open court, where a lantern burned, turned so low it was a mere glimmer. There were stables along one wall. The court was malodorous with goats, who rolled their strange devils' eyes in the dim light of the lantern. There was a door, closed and bolted after them, and they emerged into a clean, warm room, with a stove burning in one corner and a woman's voice crooning in the room above.

Their entry caused silence. Slippered feet sounded on the ladder, and, looking up, Robert met wise old eyes he remembered. The old woman he had seen on his arrival in the village nodded at him. "The Gods be thanked. Come up, Lord, and welcome." The boy was there, propped against cushions, and Robert saw what two nights had done to him. He had shrunk, it seemed; his eyes were enormous in a face that looked as if it was made of paper. The eyes — the eyes that reminded him with pain of James's bright eyes — were ringed with dark shadows. The boy looked at him, and looked behind him hopefully, and then looked away. But he remembered Robert's name.

"Dil Bahadur? What do you here?

Have you left them too?"

"I am on a mission. I had to leave them. Your mother is well, and greatly relieved to know that you are safe."

"I am not safe without my mother. I wish to return. This is not my place — I know that they will hurt my mother now that I am not there — they will hurt her to find me. I heard them talking, my mother and Saida. It is better if I die, and then no one will hurt my mother to find me."

Was that why he was refusing to eat? This was a gallant child if that was the reason. Robert thought of what his short life must have been like to make him think of such things. He seated himself on the bed beside the boy.

"Prince, your mother will be with you soon. I, who speak to you, do not lie. And do not speak of dying: you are a future Ruler, you have a duty to your people. For their sake, and your mother's sake, you must stay alive. If you die — what do you think your mother will do? Grieve herself to death, that is what she will do. And your enemies — they will force her to marry someone, because they will want to get the right to the two thrones — the guddees of Pakodi, and of Jungdah. I tell you again — you must fight to stay alive."

The child sighed, a deep and heartfelt sigh. The old woman beside him put her hands over her eyes, as if Robert's words had shown her how far the boy had travelled along the road to death. Atlar Khan stared up at Robert out of his shadowed, grey eyes, eyes that were so familiar to Robert, though he had never seen such a look of desperate exhaustion in James's eyes.

"They will make her marry again, you think? Yes, I know that. It has already been spoken of. Often. Ismail Mohammed, he wishes to marry with my mother. But Saida says it is not because of the guddee. She says it is because he has love for my mother. Saida is strange. When Ismail Mohammed is with my mother, Saida speaks of him as if he were a dog. And yet, I think she does not hate him. No one has spoken to me as you have. As if I was a man. I like to hear you. Do you speak the truth about the people needing me? Yes, I see that you do. You are also a prince, and princes do not lie to each other. Not princes of the blood. You said you were my father's friend. I wish my father were here now. I need a father to help me to be strong."

The old woman was wiping her eyes. Robert felt his throat thicken as he met the child's gaze. The boy smiled, and with an effort leaned to touch Robert's hand.

"Do you be my father? I take you as my father, because you are a strong man as my father was. Will you marry with my mother?"

Robert's voice was steady as he answered. "I cannot marry your mother, Atlar Khan. I have a wife already, and I do not take another. But I will gladly take you as my son — my brave child, I am proud to have you as my son. One day you will meet James, my other son, and be friends as well as brothers. I look forward to that meeting. Now I must go, Atlar Khan Bahadur, to warn my men that they ride into danger. While I am gone, eat and drink well, and grow strong. I shall think of you and feel proud that I have a son of such courage, who chose me as his father."

He leaned over and put his lips to the tumbled black hair and turned to go.

The boy watched the tall figure as Robert bent his head before the low door to the ladder.

"He is my father now," he said to the old woman who was also watching Robert go from their view. There was such pride in the boy's weak voice that the woman's eyes overflowed as she turned to him.

"Oh indeed, he is your father, and a fine man. Now, for his sake, and your mother's sake, and for mine, Prince of Bravery, eat a little, take a small swallow of this soup now . . . "

The child smiled, and entered the lists of his battle to live, once again.

13

WHEN Robert entered the room downstairs he found the girl from the first house waiting there.

"Alam Beg has gone back into the Palace. He will bring Hamid, he says. I am to guide you to the village of the Bab-i-margh."

"You? I cannot take a girl on this journey. There may be fighting, and it will certainly be dangerous for you."

"Nevertheless, I guide you, and as there is no goat path between here and the Bab-i-margh that is unknown to me, you will reach your destination with speed, but not if we stay here to argue. Your horse is concealed in a place known to me. Do I lead you?"

As she spoke she turned to the door, and Robert had to follow. He had no idea where the horse would be, and was unsure of the way.

The girl led him through the house and

out into a wide courtyard. As he reached for the latch of the door in the wall she stopped him.

"You must wait, counting fifty. Then you should hear the horn blown for sunrise. Then you open the gate and take the path to your left, keeping close to the walls, until the path leaves the village. Then keep straight on until you reach the river. There you follow the river to the right, through rocks. I will join you at a place where the path turns away from the river, with the animals."

Once again she had moved before she had finished speaking, and with a flash of dirty but remarkably well-shaped long legs, she had climbed on to a horse block and was up on the wall. He heard her whisper, "Put out the lantern," and then she was gone.

He put the lantern out and stood in darkness. The sunrise horn! So another night had gone; time that he needed was flashing by. He gritted his teeth, heard the horn sounding from the Palace, and opening the gate slipped through and closed it.

He had barely gone three steps before

he heard a stealthy movement behind him, and a slither of loose rubble, and knew that someone was following him. He stopped and listened. He could see nothing for the horn had been blown at the first sight of dawn, a mere thread of light was in the night sky. Between the walls of the village it was pitch dark.

The man who grappled with him, coming suddenly out of the dark, was not a trained wrestler; his inexperience showed very early in the fight. Soon Robert, breathing heavily, was standing over a fallen assailant, who was clearly not going to move or speak again. He could not leave him there, outside the house where Atlar Khan was hidden. He picked the man up and put him over his shoulder and set off quickly, listening for the sounds of any other attackers.

His burden was growing heavy when he came to a fork in the path, and heard a sound like rain on leaves, and in the cold light saw the girl, surrounded by a small herd of goats, a long peeled willow switch in her hands. She looked at the stiffening bundle on Robert's shoulders, lifting the flap of the coat that covered it to examine the dead face.

"He is a watcher. One of the Palace men who spies around the village. Was he the only one?"

"I saw no one else — but it was black dark."

"We pass the Place of the Dead. This one's resting place will be the crop of a vulture or the stomach of a wolf. Eh, you have done well, Lord of Courage."

Robert met the vacant, one-eyed stare, and wondered. Her words were so sharp and venomous, her face so blank. Poor thing; what a tragedy to visit on a girl whose face, had it matched what he could see of her legs and feet and hands, filthy though they were, would have made her a beauty. Now, small and slender, one-eyed, filthy, with a tangle of lank hair streaming from beneath her embroidered cap, she made a nightmarish figure.

He could not understand how she could allow herself to be so revoltingly dirty; water at least was plentiful . . . and realised that all his life he had been used to women who were fastidious and immaculate. Laura's body was like a flower, as clean and fresh as the white roses that she loved so much. Laura! So far away, so loved and so missed that even her name was enough to set him dreaming, so that he rode without looking, letting his horse have its head.

The girl had to call twice, her voice shrilling like the cry of the carrion kites that circled in the sky. When he finally heard her and drew rein, he saw that they were close to a great outcrop of rock.

"This that we carry goes from us here, Lord. You will see where to leave the body when you come to the right place. It is not fitting that I take it the rest of the way. I will wait with your horse."

The path went round a large boulder, and became lost in broken rocks and shale. The pony stood, shivering, having no more need to pull and sidle, for Robert had stopped walking, and stood staring.

He saw the slow shrugging movements of the vultures first, their bare necks and beaks stained and dripping, then the lift and slither of black wings as the croaking ravens rose and dipped in angry disturbance, and he heard the shrill protest of a kite, flying up from the bloated belly of a corpse.

The bodies were new. All around were the dead. Where the birds flapped and quarrelled, ignoring him because he stood so still, the bodies were perhaps only a few days dead. Further out were the picked over remains of corpses that were older; then, drying into the rocks and the soil, dark and ragged, the innumerable dead of many months and years.

The stench, the silence — Robert had seen some bloody fights, and the resulting corpses, but this place was like a dream of hell. He quieted the white-eyed pulling pony, and fumbled with the ropes that held the body in place, eager to get away. He saw that the corpses had been left naked, and forced himself to tear the clothes from the body and then tumbled it down unceremoniously and led the pony away. As he went he heard the clamour break out behind him, the flutter and thump of heavy bodies landing and imagined the hooked beaks dipping to their feast.

The girl was waiting where he had left her, leaning against his horse. She took the lead rope of the pack pony and looking at his white, sickened face, she told him that there was a flask of clean water in his saddle bag. Robert who was afraid that he might vomit, found the flask and was grateful for the clear, cold taste of the water. He mounted, and kicked his horse into a fast canter, anxious to put as much distance as he could between himself and that accursed place.

"That place. Is that the work of the man they call the Nephew?"

"The Nephew — or some of his friends — killed some of those who lie there, no doubt. But not all. That is the Place of the Dead. We do not burn or bury our dead in this valley. The soil is too sparse and too hard, and there is little wood to spare for pyres. So — the dead find a resting place in the stomachs of the birds of the air and the wolves and leopards."

She had spoken truly when she said it would be a short, hard ride. The going became very rough and the path narrowed. They began to climb steeply, and the ravine fell away beneath them so that a slip or a stumble could mean a long fall with death at the end of it. But the horses were surefooted and Robert was used to this kind of terrain, and so apparently was the girl, for she showed no fear.

"It is in my mind that you will reach your friends just after they leave the fort if you take this short, quick way. Go in safety, Dil Bahadur Khan. I will give your horse back to you when you want it, do not fear."

He had climbed the first slope before he thought to be surprised at her words, "I will give your horse back to you." How did she guess that he had no intention of leaving Jungdah? He had kept his plan to himself. Perhaps, to make up for her hideous appearance, she had been given the gift of foresight. It was too late to go back and ask questions; looking back he saw that she was already out of sight, hidden in a fold of the hills.

He was glad to find that he had fallen back into the loping walk of a hill man, the pace that had carried him so easily over so many miles and up so many steep hillsides. The days of his sickness were as if they had never been. He breathed the clear, cold air with ease, and watched the skies and the mountain ridges with an accustomed eye. And all the time, while below him the forest fell away into the blue distance, his thoughts were busy with his plan.

It would work, he knew it would — provided he could make Jiwan Khan listen to him and do what he suggested. He could find no fault in his plan. He was sure that no member of the Nephew's people in the Palace had seen him — and none of the southerners. Only the man he had killed that morning, and he was not going to carry any tales back.

It was an easy plan, he reflected. He would take over the men that Jiwan Khan had brought, he would return to the Palace as Jiwan Khan, the son of the Ruler of Lambagh, come in answer to the old Raja's message, and Jiwan Khan would return immediately to Lambagh and gather enough men to deal with the enemies of Jungdah. There was no danger for Jiwan Khan, because he was certain that the Ruler would stop him coming back with army. Jiwan Khan would be furious, but his father was a wise man, he would not send him back into the kind of danger that waited for him in Jungdah, with Sagpurna's men swarming about the Palace — everything hinged on Jiwan Khan listening to him, and going back to Lambagh.

An eagle's scream in the heights above him brought him out of his thoughts and back to the present. He could no longer hear the river, which was far beneath him as he climbed, but the girl had told him, when he had crossed two high windy ridges, that the path began to curve down, and presently he saw the village of the fort, and beyond it, the fort itself. Seeing smoke rising from it, he realised with a great lift of the heart that Jiwan Khan must still be in the fort. He was in time. Breathing a prayer of thankfulness, he stopped to rest and plan how he would descend to the fort.

He leaned back against a convenient rock, and looked across the ridge and down to where the river foamed, small as a thread in the distance. He was glad to rest and look around him, knowing that he could get to Jiwan Khan with ease.

At first the men moving near the river were like ants. Then his mind focussed and he began to watch, breathless.

This must be part of the Nephew's army. This was the enemy, and there were more of them than he had guessed. This looked to be an army readying itself for attack. Here was danger, and possible defeat, capture and death for his men, and for Jiwan Khan. Then, as he watched, the gate of the fort swung open, tiny, but clear in the distance, and he saw the horses and men ride out. The Lambagh troops and their leader were on their way.

Robert did not know when he had started to move. He was on a lower path, winding down the mountain slope as fast as he could, trying to watch the road beneath him, and the river beyond at the same time.

Now he could see his men clearly, riding at ease, tired after a disturbed night and a long trip. He heard Jiwan Khan's laugh and cringed — then realised that the men by the river, being well below the path on which Jiwan Khan and his men were riding, could not see them — and thanks to the noise of the river close beside them, they could hear nothing. The noise of that rushing water would blank out all sound.

If he could only get near enough, he could throw stones across Jiwan Khan's path, and that would at least make him stop and look at him. If only he had his pistol!

Robert set himself to climbing diagonally across the side of the mountain, where every bit of shale, every stone that his foot displaced, could give him away; but speed was more important than silence to him now.

He reached a lower crest and flung himself down. The path that Jiwan Khan must use was below him, to the left. On the right was the river, and there, on the bank, he saw a flash of movement. He stared, blinking to keep the moisture of strain from clouding his sight, but saw nothing more, and had no idea if the enemy were moving closer.

Jiwan Khan and two of his men almost shot him as they came up behind him. Jiwan Khan knocked up the rifle of the man taking aim and opened his mouth, obviously about to shout with astonished rage, but Robert's gesture silenced him and he dropped soundlessly to lie full length beside Robert, his two men beside him.

"What in the name of ten thousand devils are you doing? You sounded like an army, so I came up with Dost Mohammed and Jan Abdel to see what was happening. What in the devil's name are you doing here?"

"Send to halt the men," was the only reply Dil Bahadur gave. With no argument Jan Abdel wriggled back the way he had come.

"Well? Do you tell me what all this means? You have never been nearer death. We thought you were an ambush. What is it, Dil Bahadur?"

"I have come to warn you — oh God, I do not know where to begin. But you must go back. At once."

"Go back? Why? And what happened to your head? . . . I am not going back," said Jiwan Khan, the light of understanding beginning to shine in his eyes. "I am certainly not going back. I know you. That feeling of fear, the haste, the strange urgency over what is apparently nothing — there is trouble here, and you are trying to get me out of it. Come on, we will return to the fort. We can talk better there than lying with stones denting our bellies. I think you watch the river for a reason. Enemies?" At Robert's nod, he sighed with pleasure, and Dost Mohammed left them silently, and when Robert and Jiwan Khan reached the fort, the horses and men were once more within the walls.

Dost Mohammed came up to shake Robert's hand and make his report to Jiwan Khan.

"There are many men, down by the river. No one has seen us. I sent two men up the hill to look down on the river. The men there are moving along the bank, away from here. We can catch them easily when we are ready," said Dost Mohammed with the perfect confidence of a well-armed and well-trained hill soldier.

"Good," said Jiwan Khan, and turned to Robert. "Now, Brother of my Heart — you have been fighting with the panthers of the mountains? This time you have really damaged that handsome face of yours. Sit, drink, and let us hear your story."

Robert looked round at smiling, familiar faces, and then back at Jiwan Khan's eager eyes. His story would be joyfully received; but how was he going to persuade Jiwan Khan to fall in with his carefully thought-out plan? He could not imagine that Jiwan would go back to Lambagh unless he was tied up and taken back by force.

Sighing at the thought of the argument ahead, Robert began to tell the story of his days in Jungdah.

14

FAR from the mountain passes that surrounded the country of Jungdah, Laura was riding on the road to Faridkote. Every mile of the way was familiar to her, and spoke to her of her first months in India, and of her life with Robert.

She had travelled up to Lambagh on this road in a magnificent palanquin carried by four men, going to her marriage with Robert riding alongside. They had stopped very often, ostensibly so that she could rest, but in reality so that, leaning in through the curtains, Robert could kiss her and tell her over and over again how much he loved her. Now all she could hear in memory was his voice saying desperately, "Laura! Come home with me now — Laura . . . " It was as if she could hear the words being spoken beside her they were so clear.

Oh Robert! How could she leave him? If only he had agreed to come with her, if only she did not have this growing horror of India and this feeling of disaster. She did not know what to do, how to explain that every time she saw a sheepskin coat, or a tall burly hill man in duffle clothes, her heart almost suffocated her with its frightened beating.

The first year of their marriage had been one of perfect happiness and she had not been conscious then of fear. But her pregnancy had brought strange nightmares and her labour had been terrible, for as well as the normal pains she had discovered a terror that had lain dormant since her rescue from the hands of Stepan, her abductor. Her screams in labour had been more through fear than because of the difficult birth of her baby.

The horror had stayed. She had found pleasure in her beautiful son, and her adoration of Robert had never altered. But now, always, there was fear. When James began to walk and then to ride, she had hidden her terror lest she should, by her fear, spoil his splendid courage. Every time Robert left her to go with his troops, in her heart she said goodbye to him for ever, convinced that he would be killed. It was a dreadful shadow on her life, and she could not tell anyone about it, she felt that if she spoke of this fear, of all the horrors that she saw in her mind's eye, it would all come true.

Then, as time passed, she began to find things to dislike in her life in India. She resented what she thought of as the proprietary airs of the Lambagh family — calling James "Jamshyd" and Robert "Dil Bahadur". It seemed to her that they were forcing the Indian side of Robert forward, when she wanted to remember the boy, Rob, with whom she had fallen in love. Those wonderful days, the rides in the woods and fields of Moxton Park, the beautiful old house and the roses in Robert's grandmother's garden . . . The Chotomahal with its white dome and marble walls, the fountains and the blue lake with the ramparts of the mountains no longer meant "home" to Laura, dreaming of Kentish woods and bluebells in spring.

Now, on her way to those woods in Kent, she saw nothing but Robert's hurt and angry face, heard nothing but his voice. She wept as she rode and her servants and the men of the escort looked at each other and shook their heads. What was it with the white Begum of Dil Bahadur that she should first decide to leave the valley and take her son over the plains to the black water and beyond to Belait, and now wept like an outcast thrown from her home? None of them could understand, nor cared to intrude on this strange grief.

At the half way stage of Chenar they stopped and made camp. Moti, the ayah, put James to bed. He was so tired that he fell asleep without noticing that his mother had not heard his prayers, nor had she kissed him good night. Laura sat with the bustle of the camp going on around her and saw none of it. Only when they lit a big fire did she look into its red depths and find there the face for which she searched. As if she was the same age as James she allowed herself to be led away by Moti and bathed in a galvanized iron tub that had clattered down the tracks on the back of a pack pony. She remembered how she had laughed with Robert about what they called "the travelling tub". There was no one to laugh with now. She went like an obedient child, silently to her bed, but no child would have endured the pain she felt when, having slept for a short time, she woke, and stretching out her hand, still half asleep, found that she was alone.

The days passed, and the nearer she got to Faridkote, the worse her behaviour seemed to her. If only she could have talked to someone! She had always felt that Kassim and Sara had welcomed her because of Robert's love for her, not for herself. She could not let herself get close to them for some reason, in spite of their loving care of her. She remembered always that they despised her mother and father, and although she also found her parents tiresome and uncongenial, the Lambagh family's attitude put her at a disadvantage.

On the fourth day she came to the North Gate of Faridkote, and riding through the narrow streets, she wondered how she was going to bear her first sight of the House of Paradise, where she was to meet Honor Lees. She could not talk to Lady Lees about her present trouble, because she knew that Honor had not been at all sure that Laura would be happy married to Robert, and she could not bear to see even a shadow of an "I told you so" in Honor's kind eyes.

And Meeta? How was she going to explain to Meeta that she was leaving Robert alone and going so far away. Nothing, Laura was convinced, would make Meeta understand.

Meeta was the girl who had saved Laura's life when she had been kidnapped by the man Stepan, a servant of a man Robert had eventually killed. Meeta had risked her life over and over again to save Laura. She had been very young, been sold by her father to a fat money lender to pay his debts. "A little plain girl with a lion's heart," was how Robert had described her.

But there had been many changes since the little plain fourteen-year-old had nearly died saving Robert's girl for him, having lost her own heart to Robert at first sight.

Oh, thought Laura, how shall I face Meeta, my dear Indian friend. How shall

I tell her that I want to go away from India and live in my own country; that I am sick of mountains and eternal snows and sunlight on blue lakes and the smells of sandalwood and jasmine and roses and spices, and open drains, and — and I don't want my son brought up as a prince of an Indian state, I want him to be an English schoolboy and learn the English way of life. It is no good, said Laura, to some unseen listener, it is no good telling me that all the Lambagh princes except Sher Khan were brought up in England and went to Harrow and indeed in two cases, had English fathers. I don't care. It isn't the same. The House of Paradise had belonged to Robert's mother Muna. She had given it to the Lambagh family when she married Robert's father, and it was used by the family as a place to stay whenever they travelled from Lambagh to Madore. Meeta and her lover, Yar Khan, lived there as guardians and Yar Khan commanded the small body of troops that the Ruler kept based in Faridkote.

The high walls of the house were now in sight, and the carved wooden gates were open. Tall and handsome in a long fitted achkhan and an emerald green turban, Yar Khan came forward to meet her, laughing with pleasure at seeing her. Oh, that emerald turban, worn at the identical angle that Robert wore his! He had set a fashion and every man in the Lambagh army tried to copy that rakish tilt.

Laura let Yar Khan lift her from her saddle and while he turned to receive loud greetings from James, Laura walked through to the inner court where she knew that Meeta waited for her.

"Laura-jan! You make my heart very glad! Come, come in. Is Dil Bahadur with you? No? Oh — then he comes later. Let us go and talk. I want to hear all your news, and why you are making this journey to Madore . . . "

It was worse than Laura had feared. Meeta did know that she was going to England. When Laura explained, she was horrified.

"But Belait! England! Across the black waters and so far from us all, and alone! Why?"

"Not alone, Meeta. I am travelling with Lady Lees. She is meeting me here — you know that surely?"

"Of course. Her rooms are ready. But you go without your husband? I do not understand. Come with me, Laura pyari, come to your room . . . "

Laura followed her, her heart sinking. She knew the room where she would sleep. A beautiful room, with a big window overlooking the garden. She had spent many days in this room recovering from her kidnapping experiences, and here she had been reunited with Robert, on just such an evening, with sunset gilding the painted walls and turning the fountain's spray into a glitter of golden drops against the green trees. There was the bed, heaped with pillows, a bed for lovers. How was she going to lie in that bed alone? What have I done? thought Laura, and Meeta saw her eyes fill with tears.

"Sit, pyari. I go to get us wine, and we will talk afterwards. You are tired from your journey. Rest and think of nothing until I come."

Alone, Laura turned her back on the bed and sat in the window seat, looking out into the green garden where the fountain still played and the parrots flew, emerald and noisy, to settle in the trees as the evening began to take the colour from the sky.

When Meeta came back she brought wine and also Laura's ayah, and together they took Laura's riding clothes from her and bathed the dust of the road from her tired limbs. When she was dressed in one of the beautiful loose robes she had become used to wearing, the ayah dressed her hair, coiling it up as Robert liked her to wear it, caught into a thick knot with one large jewelled pin. Smoothed, scented, and beautiful, Laura stood in front of her mirror and heard Meeta's compliments and longed for Robert to come and put his arms round her and pull out the jewelled pin and tell her he loved her.

But Robert was in Lambagh, and she sat in the window in the last of the light and drank wine with Meeta, and as she lifted her glass she saw the embroidered cuff of her robe and remembered who had first given her one of these garments.

The Begum Bianca: Robert's adopted

grandmother. Bianca, the beautiful Irish woman who had married Sher Khan, and had loved him so much and suffered so deeply because of her love. She would understand all that Laura felt. If she could get to Madore quickly, and talk with Bianca, perhaps this horrible feeling of loss and insecurity would leave her. Bianca of all people would understand why she had to go. Bianca had lived with her own nightmares and had conquered them.

Laura drank her wine in the golden light of the setting sun, but burned inwardly with impatience. If Honor Lees would only come, they could perhaps set off the following morning and have an extra few days in Madore. She scarcely heard what Meeta was saying, answered at random and Meeta finally left her, very worried and distressed about her beloved Laura.

Laura, alone in the beautiful, silent room, did not know how to stay there; it spoke to her of such different times. Robert was so close; a mere three days and she could be in his arms. But — but something in the way he had looked at her when he had asked her to return with him and she had refused — in retrospect his expression frightened her, he had looked so proud, and hard and angry. She lifted her left hand and looked at her ring. She no longer had the original ring, the Peacock Ring, given to Robert by his mother. The Ruler of Lambagh had given the ring to Robert's mother, and he wished Robert to wear it, and took it from Laura. In its place he had an exact replica made, and put it on Laura's finger himself.

Now, looking into the green stone, it was like looking into a pool of clear green water, where pictures formed and faded as she looked. What would Muna the Beautiful, who had worn the Peacock Ring, think of the way Laura was behaving, the girl her son had loved so much, and who was now running away from him, and away from the beloved valley that Muna had loved so much.

But it wasn't the same ring. It was as if one link had already been broken. "They even took my ring," said Laura, childishly, to herself.

Downstairs, Meeta sat on a pile of

cushions at Yar Khan's feet. They heard the soft, impatient footfalls in the room above.

"What is it with her, Meeta? Has the marriage broken?"

"I do not think so. Whatever it is that is wrong, she is in great sorrow. I think she remembers Stepan and the bad time of her capture, and it has grown big and hidden the good part of her life."

"Eh, what a foolish girl! As if lives were not lost to rescue her — and your life above all! I thought you were lost to me, my fire and my flower."

"But I was not lost, Yar Khan."

They sat in silence, while the noises of the fountain splashing, and the settling birds came into the room from the garden court. Then Yar Khan sighed and took Meeta's face between his hands and turned it up to his, looking into her eyes.

"Do you remember old pains, old longings, dear love?"

"Nay. I remember only a tall man who came to me as he had promised, and took from me all memories except the memory of his desire for me, and the sweetness of his love. How can you ask, you who are the master of my life?"

"How can I ask? I can ask forever because I love you and therefore can never be sure — I love you as if I had just seen you but had not yet tasted the honey of your love."

Meeta stretched up and closed his mouth with her kiss, and took his hand to her breast, and he said nothing more. Into their sweet silence came the sound of pacing footsteps, but they were no longer listening.

Later that night, as the three of them sat over their food, a messenger rode up to the gate.

Lady Lees was delayed, and would not arrive for another day and a night.

"It does not matter, Laura-jan!" said Meeta to Laura's desperate face. "It does not matter at all! You have plenty of time to get to Madore for the rail-carriage. It only means that we have the joy of your company and that of James for a little longer. Do not look as if you cannot bear to stay with us, Laura!"

"But I cannot," said Laura, and wept

in Meeta's arms, and Yar Khan went quietly away.

Meeta took Laura up to her room, and after a while came down to look for Yar Khan.

"She wishes to go to Madore at once, Yar Khan. I think her mind is disturbed. She is with child as well, and afraid of so many things — she is living in a nightmare. But she says she must speak with the Begum Bianca, that she will understand. I think it is necessary that we make everything easy for her, and let her go. And Jamshyd . . . she has not even asked after him since they arrived . . . things are very bad with her."

Yar Khan made arrangements, and told Meeta of them. She went up to Laura's room, where Laura sat in the window seat, her hands in her lap, staring out at the dark garden.

"In the morning, at dawn if you wish, you may go to Madore. We send Zaman Beg, and Rabindra with you. Jamshyd will stay here with us, so that you can make more speed on the road, and we will send him down to you with Lady

Lees when she comes. Is this as you would wish?"

At dawn the following morning Laura was on her way. James had made no trouble over being left. He adored Yar Khan, and also the son of the head groom was a friend of his. Laura was shocked to find how little she minded leaving him. Her love for her son did not seem to fill the great void that was in her heart.

The little party made good speed, and by evening Laura was riding through the dust and barred shadows of the Grand Trunk Road.

15

THE sun was setting as they began to look for a suitable place to camp. Laura declined to stop at two of the suggested camping places, the paraos, because they were crowded, and when they found one that she liked it was growing dark.

The parao was empty. No one had stopped here for the night; there were no other camp fires twinkling among the dark trees. But Laura liked the place. The thick grove of mango trees made it very private and peaceful. She was stiff after her long ride and walked about while the men unsaddled and fed and watered the horses, and then hobbled them. Laura watched the fire being lit, and the lanterns, mellow islands of light in the dark grove. It was so quiet — even the birds seemed to have settled early for the night. She looked up into the interlacing branches of the trees and decided that it would be a waste of time to pitch a tent for her, the trees were thick enough to give all the shelter necessary, and the skies were clear.

The men lit an extra fire, and put down a rug and a thick quilt for her. Their own fire they lit a little distance away, far enough to give her privacy. She settled beside her fire, sipping a glass of tea, while across the clearing the men prepared the evening meal.

Presently Rabindra brought her a spiced dish, cooked that morning in Faridkote and carefully heated up for her, and she made an effort to eat some of it. Rabindra, who knew her well, shook his head at her when he came to collect her dishes, she had eaten so little. He brought her a basin of hot water, and after stamping his booted feet on the far side of a big tree, put the basin down with a lantern beside it, and left Laura in perfect privacy to prepare for the night. She knew why he had stamped and walked about before he put the water down. He was making sure that there were no snakes. She washed hurriedly, and was glad to come back to her fire, where, rolled in one thick quilt and lying on another, she lay looking into the red embers and waited for sleep.

★ ★ ★

Laura slept dreamlessly until just before dawn, when Rabindra saw her wake and lean up on her elbow. He had just finished brewing tea, and took a glass over to her. He found that she was still half in a dream, looking about her as if she had never seen the clearing before.

"Rabindra! Where is the child?"

"Child, Lady? There is no child here . . . "

"Yes — I heard a child crying. Is it lost? Crying for its mother? Are there others camping here?"

"Nay, Lady, we are alone. There is no child here; I have heard nothing."

Laura took the proffered tea. "Perhaps I dreamed," she said, and Rabindra went away and heated water for her, and she was washed and dressed.

A scarlet dawn glowed through the trees, and before the sun had begun to send horizontal rays deep into the grove, she rode out with the three men.

She looked back once, and thought she saw a boy standing under the trees, but it was a trick of the shadows, she decided, or the men would have seen it too, and they had not paid any attention to the grove once they had stamped out the fires and buried the ashes. Laura kicked her horse into a fast trot that turned to a canter, and tried to think of nothing but the day's journey that would end in Bianca's house outside the red walls of Madore.

It was a blue day, clear and cold and as fresh as spring water. Northern Indian autumnal weather. A brisk wind kept the dust off the road and sent the shadows of the trees scudding like ripples on the stream of humanity that wandered at various speeds in both directions, a shouting, laughing, busy crowd, full of their own concerns but always able to be interested in everybody else's business.

Laura was fascinated, as always, by the travellers. She smiled to herself as a little group of English ladies went past her in the opposite direction, memsahibs returning to the plains after a summer spent in the hill stations: Simla, or

Dalhousie, or Missouri. They looked so uncomfortable in their high-necked, tight-waisted dresses, and their hideous solar topis perched like white mushrooms on top of carefully curled and pinned coiffures. They sat in dhoolies, carrying chairs, parasols held aloft in gloved hands, veils over their faces . . . Laura stopped feeling amused by them when she remembered that very soon she would look as they did. She could scarcely take her journey to England dressed in the beautiful robes of a high-born hill woman. No, it would be whalebone-stiffened necks and tight sleeves and gripping waists for her too.

The little group of silently enduring English memsahibs went out of sight and a chattering, laughing party of women in a domed, scarlet-curtained cart drawn by reluctant bullocks crawled by, like an animated bird cage, the women supposedly in purdah, but all taking advantage of the journey to let their boorkahs stay folded back from their faces so that they could see everything. After them, a band of armed soldiers on splendid horses, a local raja's escort, the raja himself sitting, fat and bleary-eyed in a palanquin, so dull-faced that Laura wondered how he could command soldiers at all.

She began to grow impatient at having to rein in her restive horse, and finally pulled over to the side of the road close to the trees and set a better pace there. Most of the travellers walked or rode on the crown of the road. Away from the crowd, Laura was able to let her horse go. Zaman Beg was forced to set his heels to his horse, muttering about the speed Laura was choosing. He was supposed to ride ahead of her, and found himself riding abreast at first, and then, lighter and on a very lively horse, she was past him and he was pounding at her heels. Well, he thought, there is a long day ahead — at this rate the horses would be tired long before they came in sight of the turn off for Madore City.

He saw then the bobbing heads high above the crowd, and heard through the general babble the swinging double ring of camel bells. Cursing, he tried to see Laura, but his beast was already shying and bucking half across the road, and he turned his head to bellow at Rabindra.

"She is mad," he panted as Rabindra rocketed up. "Try to make her go more slowly, that horse of hers is a devil when camels are in sight — oh, son of ten thousand ill-bred goats, get out of my way or you break my horse's legs on your accursed cart. This road was not made for bullock carts to slumber on. Move!"

Rabindra fled on, leaving the row of carts to swell behind him. He saw Laura going fast ahead, and she appeared to be in control of her beast. The camels, three of them, were on the far side of the road going north, and he saw who was walking by the leading animal and raised a hand in greeting as he went by. His own horse was not excited by camels; only snakes caused him distress.

Laura was safely past the camels and was going faster still, and Rabindra only had time to think that the Begum was a very good rider before he buckled down to catching up with her.

Laura had not even seen the camels. The sound of their bells had reminded her of the bells that rang in the temple on the other side of the lake in Lambagh. She heard them clearly across the water every day. She rode now with her mind turned to this strange change in her feelings. No memories of Kent and the green lanes and the soft rain she had longed for came to comfort her. All she could think of was the man she had left, and the home they had made together. She would tell Bianca the whole story, but now she did not have to ask for advice. All she wanted to do now was to return to Lambagh, and beg Robert's forgiveness for being so ridiculous, and feel his arms around her again. There was her safety and happiness; how could she ever have imagined that she wanted to leave him even for a short time. However angry he was, he would forgive her, Robert: her dear love.

Dreaming, smiling, Laura rode carelessly with a slack rein, the horse going as he wished.

The wind was freakish. It dropped to nothing, and dust swirled up at once in a blinding cloud, white and smothering. Out of the dust rose a woman, only vaguely seen, one corner of her sari caught in her mouth, a basket balanced on her head and a black dog running at her heels. She appeared right in front of Laura's horse, seemed to hesitate, and was gone as the wind rose and whirled the dust away.

It was enough for Laura's nervous horse. The camels had unsettled him, there was no firm hand on his reins, and no grip on his body. The shadowy figure, the dust and the wind and the running dog, unnerved him. The horse reared and danced and reared again, and Laura fell off heavily and rolled, turning over to lie face down in the white dust of the road.

The three men in her escort were there in minutes, winnowing through the crowd on their horses, oblivious of angry shouts and swaying palanquins and scattering men and women.

Rabindra, on his knees, turned Laura gently so that he could slide his hand under her head. Her face was as white as the dust that covered it. Her veil had fallen off, her long hair was powdered with dust. He wiped her face clean with his other hand and was terrified because she lay so still, and did not open her eyes. He looked up at Zaman and saw the dawning fear on his face.

"She is alive?"

"Yes, may the Gods be thanked. But I am afraid. She is with child, you know that. We need a woman. Are there no women here?"

"Harlots, going to Nucklao. In the red cart," said Jamal, and, turning his horse, went back down the road until he found the red, tinselled cart and the chattering, laughing girls. A few words with the oldest woman there, obviously in charge of the rest, and the cart was turned and came lumbering, creaking and rocking back to where Rabindra knelt on the ground. Zaman was using his voice and his rearing, kicking horse to keep the curious away.

The women in the cart were as big-hearted as all their kind. Space was made, quilts were unfolded, and Laura was lifted and put in the cart, and the creaking journey began, up the long dusty road; but very slowly now.

Laura opened her eyes and found herself surrounded by kind, anxious faces,

and searching enquiries as to how she felt.
Did her back trouble her; could she move
her limbs? A slender henna-tipped hand
felt about her stomach and abdomen, and
a voice said urgently, "Lady, how many
months have you carried this child?"

"Three and two weeks," said Laura,
her eyes on the woman's worried face.
"There is nothing wrong? I have no
pain . . . "

"There is bleeding, Lady, your robe is
stained. Aiee, why were you riding? A
palanquin is what you should have had.
Now we must do as best we can — "

She did not finish her sentence as
Laura's face contorted and she drew her
knees up with a groan.

"I have pain . . . "

"Yes," said the woman grimly, and
shrilled a command to the driver of the
cart. The man pulled his bullocks off
the road. All but the woman in charge,
and one other, dismounted. Laura, with
kind hands and encouragement, fought
with pains that led to no triumphant
conclusion, only an agonising interlude
. . . and the life that had been in her
womb was lost and gone for ever.

233

"Eh, Lady, do not weep. You will have other children, you are young. Be still, habibi, and let us make all clean, and take you to your destination. Leila, take that out now, it is not for her to see . . ."

Laura spoke out of the mists of pain and exhaustion that were creeping over her. "He is to be buried," she said. "Tell my men, he must be properly buried — "

The woman looked at her sharply. "Hush, we will do all that is necessary as you wish, Lady. Do not trouble yourself, he will go into the ground with honour, as is fitting."

Laura was bathed and made as comfortable as was possible. The kindly, gentle-handed women did everything they could, wrapped her in clean linen from her bedding roll and combed back the tangled hair from her white face. She lay unheeding of their kindness. It seemed to her that she was in another place, in a dark grove, hearing a child cry for its mother. Grief enveloped Laura, grief and guilt, and the woman tending her saw the shadow on her face, and grew afraid. She climbed down from the cart and went looking for Rabindra. Then she saw he was talking to a tall woman in black trousers and shirt and black head cloth. One of the people of the camel caravans had come, her beast was kneeling on the ground nearby, making the horses of the Lady's escort snort and struggle with their halters. The woman from the cart waited, not wishing to have any dealings with the tall woman, who was a frightening figure in the twilight. The woman from the cart made the sign against the evil eye, and felt for her blue beads as she waited.

Presently the woman in black strode away, her camel padding after her, the bell at its neck still audible after she and her beast had vanished into the shadows. Then Rabindra turned to the waiting woman. "How is the Lady?"

"She is not well; she grows fevered, and there has been much blood. It is better that we move on at once, and take her to Madore. It is of no matter to us when we reach Nucklao — and I fear for the Lady if we delay to get to some place where she will be among her own people."

"It means crossing the plain after dark."

"Yes, but with you three splendid men to guard us, why should we fear the dark plain?" She had not forgotten how to smile and flatter a man, thought Rabindra, even if she is not in the flower of youth . . .

"Very well, Woman of Great Heart. Let us go."

The bullocks were yoked to the cart and the slow journey began, the lanterns inside the red curtains making the cart glow like a ruby. The women sat round Laura, and whispered of her beauty, and smoothed her hand comfortingly, and watched her wince as the cart bumped and rattled over the rough road across the great plain, wincing themselves in sympathy.

The cart came to a stop at last. There was shouted enquiry from the guard at the gate, and startled voices, and then Laura heard the voices she was longing to hear and was lifted from the cart and laid on a bed, with Bella and Bianca walking beside her, into the house and into the hands of kindness and love.

The red-curtained cart, its occupants well-rewarded and praised, set off on its interrupted journey at dawn the next day. The women had plenty to chatter about, all the way to Nucklao. Only the oldest of them was quiet, still wondering how Laura had known that the child she had lost had been a son.

16

IT was far into the night by the time Robert had finished his story. Wine had been poured and food laid out, and they had all eaten while they listened. When Robert stopped, his voice hoarse, the men began to discuss his story among themselves.

He had given them the complete sequence of events, and the present conditions in Jungdah, making no suggestions about what should be done. But now, islanded in privacy in the midst of all the ensuing talk, he turned to speak quietly with Jiwan Khan.

It had been a long day for both of them. Robert propped his head on his hands and looked at Jiwan Khan with tired, bloodshot eyes.

"I trust we are not going to argue, Jiwan."

"How argue? You command this troop. I shall, of course, as always, do what you tell me. All I ask is that you sleep now for a few hours. You look like one returned from the grave. We can still leave before dawn, even if you sleep for three hours — "

"*We* are not leaving together at all. I am returning to Dhalli Palace. You, brother, are going back to Lambagh, to collect as many well-armed men as the Ruler thinks will be sufficient against the forces of which I have told you. Make it clear to him that it is not only the men in the Palace we are to meet, but also what appears to be a strong and well-armed force from outside. Return before the full moon if the Ruler is agreeable."

"Are you mad, Dil Bahadur? Listen to me. You cannot go back to the Palace; you will never get out alive. Another thing, do you think that the men will allow you to return alone, and then follow me tamely like sheep to Lambagh, knowing the danger you will be in? Also — touching the matter of the Ruler allowing me to return — my father will not be pleased with a son who ran away, leaving you in danger. I am not a child to be sent out of trouble. If there is to be fighting here, then here I stay."

Robert set his goblet down hard on the board that served them as a table.

"Jiwan Khan, you have just said that I command this troop. Why are you refusing to obey my orders? Does this set a good example to the men? You haven't understood my plan. *I* take the men with me. I shall need them. *You* return to Lambagh with one man only. If it is danger you want, you will have enough of it on your return journey. As to what your father will think — he will know that I am doing my duty in trying to keep his hot-headed son out of Sagpurna's reach. Sagpurna would use you as a pawn to force your family into doing whatever he wants — for God's sake, Jiwan! Think of what I am saying! I know my duty, and you know yours."

The men looked over their shoulders in surprise and curiosity, hearing the raised voices of their leaders. Jiwan Khan leaned to glare into Dil Bahadur's eyes.

"You are run mad like a dog in the sun! What are you trying to do? Make a present of fifty of our best men to that popinjay Ismail Mohammed, the Nephew? For what reason? He will take your head to play polo with! I can see that the scar has spoiled your looks, but I did not know that your brains had spilled. This plan of yours ... what is it? It makes no sense to me — ”

"Softly, brother! I am indeed going to make a present of these men to the Nephew — in return for his services. And believe me, he is no popinjay, though I think he has been a fool. Tell me, what was said of him in Subbur? You were there with him for a while, were you not?”

"He was there for only a very short time: he had offended so many of the older men of the court that Sir Richard sent him out almost at once. He is arrogant, and pays great attention to his dress — and he spoke always of being the rightful heir, which of course was his downfall. Pakodi's son was healthy, his mother was the wife of Pakodi, and the child was therefore declared the rightful heir at his birth. Ismail Mohammed, the Nephew, had no hope of that throne. He left vowing all sorts of disaster. He swore that he had the right to the guddee through his father,

Pakodi's brother — but he was not born in wedlock. You know all this. Why are you asking questions about this man who has, by your own account, caused disaster in Jungdah?"

"Because I want to make sure I am right about him — and your description of him fits my picture. A man who was probably assured of being adopted as the heir . . . Pakodi was not a young man, and he had not produced a legitimate son. Who had a better right to the guddee than Pakodi's own brother's son, with only one stroke against him: his mother was not married to his father. He would think that was nothing. How many of the rulers in the hill states around us have taken as heir their brother's son? And not all of them were legitimate. No, he has a right to be disappointed and angry — "

"And vengeful. He left the state swearing that he would return with an army. You say he is building an army secretly; why do you think he is doing that if he is not going to attack Jungdah, and take back what he considers his own? And you appear to be about to assist him, by presenting him with our men. Dil Bahadur, what kind of a story am I to take back to my father?"

"The Nephew has raised an army of mounted soldiers, men trained for war and mounted on fine horses. He spent a fortune buying mares from Khokund, and stallions from down the Rann of Cutch. He is not a fool. He will use his men as mercenaries, fighting for warlords on the borders between India and China. Those men will pay much gold to keep their borders safe. They rise all the time against their Chinese conquerors. You remember what we saw when we went up beyond Baradhurri Pass. That khan would have given much to have had such an army as Ismail Mohammed has raised.

"But he has been a fool. He needed money to buy the horses, he needed money to pay the men — and he borrowed from the devil. He has put himself into the hands of Sagpurna, and I think that he is now discovering how foolish he has been. He is being ordered to perform acts that are against his nature.

"Listen. If I can open his eyes to the

243

danger he has put himself in, and get him to come over to us, we can turn that army of his, officered by our men, against Sagpurna, and drive the Master from the hills forever . . . "

Jiwan Khan was listening now, without argument. He knew Dil Bahadur as a fighter, and as a commander of men, and trusted him. He stifled his feelings of rebellion against being sent away from the action, and began to ask questions.

Lamps were guttering out. The men began to roll themselves into their padded resais round a central fire, to sleep the last of the night away while their two nawabs argued. Robert, exhausted, had to fight hard for patience as he continued to outline his plans.

"I need more of our men. Ismail Mohammed's men are trained fighters, but they are untried. Our men, scattered among them, will lead them."

"But Ismail Mohammed — *is* he going to hand over his army to you? Why should he wish to do so?"

"When I have shown him the coil he is in, he will hand over to me — because he will need my help. I will not have to persuade him — I can show him proof of the events that have taken place in the Palace that he has known nothing about. There is the small matter of the poisoning of the heir — the son of the woman he loves to madness. He would never try to poison anyone, of that I am sure — but there is poison, there are deaths . . . "

"Then why does he not know? And who is this woman he loves — there are too many questions, brother — "

"And all of them are easy to answer. He knows very little of what is taking place in Dhalli Palace, because he is seldom there. He spends most of his time with his army, beyond the Lang-su Pass. He comes back every two or three months, and receives a falsified report from a suborned man, who has been well bribed. As to the woman he loves — who but the Begum Amara, Pakodi's widow?"

"Wah! This reads like a winter tale told round the fires on a cold night. So. You are about to do what?"

"I am going to show him proof of what has happened in his many absences, and I shall also warn him of the extreme danger the Begum and her father are in — if he has not already guessed that. I shall insist that he gets the family away from Dhalli Palace and out of Jungdah at once. Then we can speak of the action that we can take against the men of the South who are slowly taking over the Dhalli Palace and fort."

Jiwan Khan flung up his hands.

"Acha. You know what your plans are; they seem like a spider's web of hopes to me, but then I am not inside your mind. But you have won. I will go — but I consider that is not a good thing. You could explain more fully to my father what you mean to do than I can. *I* could go to Dhalli Palace and persuade the Nephew to listen to you when you return — and I could guard the family until he is ready to move — "

"Jiwan Khan, you are arguing like a spoiled woman cheated of an outing. I beg of you to remember who you are, and the promise I made when I came to your State — the promise I gave to your father. Please, argue no more." His intense weariness husked in his voice; his eyes were half closed and swollen with lack of sleep. Jiwan Khan gave in.

"As you say then. I will try to get back with a strong force as soon as possible. Before the full moon, you say. Allah! What if the weather breaks? Have you thought of that?" There was no answer; Robert had fallen asleep where he sat, his arms stretched out on the board, his head pillowed on the hard wood. Jiwan Khan saw Osman, his risaldar major, sitting up watching them, and beckoned him over, and together they picked Robert up and rolled him into a quilt beside the fire. He did not stir.

Jiwan Khan saw Osman's questioning eyes and told him of Robert's plan. Osman listened and nodded but doubtfully. After a moment's thought he said, "It is a good plan — if Dil Bahadur can bend the Nephew to his will and is sure that he can be trusted. I know the Nephew well. He was not a bad man until he was disinherited."

"Disinherited? He was not adopted, was he? I did not hear of that?"

"Nay, huzoor, it had not been done with paper and seals. But I was about the courts of Ali of Pakodi — you know that my father was in the Pakodi State Forces — and I heard from very early days that the brother's natural son was Ali's heir. From one minute to the next, it was taken from him, and he was given nothing in exchange. His father being dead, there was no one to speak for him, and then Ali was killed, by treachery some say, and Ismail Mohammed no longer even had a name — he became the 'Nephew' and his hand turned against everyone. But he is a strong man, and a good fighter. Dil Bahadur maybe sees further than most; he picks his men well."

"Well, if anyone can make him turn, I think Dil Bahadur can. Let us hope so — and let us also hope for good weather, there is much to do before the passes close."

"Aye, Lord. Also, there is another small matter — the men we captured this morning in this fort. They are men of the hills, and they swear that they are loyal to the Raja of Jungdah. What is in your mind for them?"

"What do you think of them?"

"We have listened to them, and hear

them speaking together. We think that they are loyal and honest men, but we will do as you say, Lord."

"Then let us keep them until Dil Bahadur wakes. Now, in the name of Allah, let us sleep before the dawn . . . "

Two hours later, Robert woke, rested and fully in command of his senses. Jiwan Khan had always admired his ability to be so totally awake after deep sleep. As they splashed their faces with cold water from the well in the centre court of the fort, Jiwan Khan spoke to Robert of the prisoners, and Robert agreed that they should be released.

"They will be useful. They have no love for the Palace people as they call the men that Ismail Mohammed has foolishly recruited from the southern plains. Let me speak with them."

The prisoners were released, and after a few words with them, Robert was satisfied that he could use them as watchers and informers, if not as fighters.

"It is as the boy I spoke with in Dhalli said. They are men of the hills. They will watch and bring news. Now, Jiwan Khan, it is time for you to go. I hope for your reinforcements as soon as possible."

"Who comes with me? I cannot go alone, and you need every man you have . . ."

"Take one of your choice. And two horses each. And make haste, brother."

"My choice is one of these hill men." He turned and pointed. "You there. What are you called?"

"I am Darshan, Lord."

"Darshan. Very well. Can you ride?"

"I can."

The horses were led up, and mounted. Jiwan Khan looked down at Robert.

"I go, under protest, brother. May Allah guard you. If possible, stay alive and keep some of the fighting for me." He wheeled his horse and clattered off into the darkness, and Robert winced and cursed under his breath. Did Jiwan Khan have to advertise the fact that someone was riding out of a fort that was supposedly empty? But nothing happened and Robert remembered the noisy river. No one down near that water would hear anything. He sent up for the scout posted on the hillside to be relieved. The man came down and reported that the soldiers by the river had made camp at last light, had lit fires and were showing no signs of movement.

"*If* they are soldiers. They have not even set outposts," he said with contempt.

It was still dark, although dawn was touching the fresh snows far above. It was time to prepare to leave for Dhalli.

Robert gave his orders quietly, and while the men made ready, he changed his clothes, glad that Jiwan Khan had remembered to bring his baggage. When he mounted the horse they brought up for him, one of Sher Khan's splendid animals, he recalled his slaughtered horse Shasti, and his resolve hardened. The murdering ruffians who had infiltrated Jungdah would die if he could succeed in his plans.

His men looked at him, surprised when he rode forward in front of them. He wore a splendid high-necked tunic, a green turban and his dress sword belt, glittering with jewels.

"Dil Bahadur Khan, you look very fine, but you make a good target! At least take your old sword belt and scabbard.

Those jewels at your waist ask for a marksman's winning shot."

"Osman, I do not think anyone will shoot. I shall get safely to Dhalli Palace. They are hoping for important game. I am hoping that my fine feathers will mislead them into thinking they have it. So. Are we ready? Let us go."

The cavalcade, Robert leading, moved out and fell into the position of a march. Presently he dropped back and rode beside Osman, an old friend and trusted commander. He was full of enthusiasm for Robert's plan, and repeated all that he had told Jiwan Khan about Ismail Mohammed. As they rode, and dawn blazed into day, Robert began to feel unaccountably depressed.

The valley, once they were past the village where the gate had not yet been opened, had narrowed. The hills rose on each side of them like walls, throwing back the echo of the horses' hoof beats so that it was as if they rode with drums beating. It was a bright morning, but to Robert it seemed overcast and dull. He had an urgent desire to order his troop to halt and turn back; his plan seemed madness indeed, and their lives were in his hands. He half turned in his saddle to shout the order to halt. The sight of his men riding calmly behind him made his apprehension seem ridiculous. They had ridden together on other dangerous missions, it was their life, accepted by them, and enjoyed.

Far above, perched on a steep ridge, the girl who had guided Robert the day before watched him pass with his men. As the last man went round a curve in the hill path and out of her sight, she went back to the hobbled ponies, unloaded fodder and water, and having fed and watered the animals, began to reload the provisions and prepare to follow Robert.

Faintly, from the misty distance behind her, she heard the high scream of an eagle. She stopped what she was doing, and stood, waiting, eyeing the skies and calculating how long it was before midday. Then she placed her hand round her mouth, and answered the eagle's cry, a perfect copy of the bird. She sat down, her back against a rock, and settled to wait for the messenger she knew was on his way, while the sun rose higher and the shadows round the rocks that sheltered her grew small as the day advanced.

17

JIWAN KHAN had been riding hard for an hour when he signalled to Darshan and reined up to rest his animals. He was unhappy about leaving Robert, and annoyed because his conscience told him that Robert was right to send him back, out of Sagpurna's reach.

Jiwan Khan heard the high shrill scream of an eagle, and looked up. His gaze fixed on the skies above. Like smoke, a collection of birds was flying above the higher ridge ahead of them, disturbed birds, circling.

Something, someone? — was moving on the path ahead. He watched, frowning. The birds were not settling, so whoever, or whatever, was on the path that he was using himself, was still moving. Jiwan Khan felt sweat prickling on his neck.

"There are horses, Lord," said Darshan beside him.

"Horses, and they come fast this way."

Jiwan Khan could feel, rather than hear, horses coming, and his own — restive, ears pricked — were watching the path ahead.

"Take the beasts back, Darshan, and get into cover; and keep them quiet."

He kept his own horse with him in case he had to make a quick escape, and then wished that he had not. There was so little cover on this cursed path. A large boulder, grey and splotched with lichen, half blocked the pathway. He led his horse, sliding and reluctant, up a little way, and sheltered in the shadow of the rock. He put his hand tight on the animal's nose, saying under his breath, "One sound, only one snort, my fine friend, and we are lost."

Now he could hear the horses coming clearly. He needed both hands free, and was forced to release his animal, praying that it would be silent. Rifle in position, he lay on the boulder looking along the narrow path. The riders were making no effort to be quiet; speed appeared to be their main objective.

They came into view, three of them. Jiwan Khan, sighting along his rifle barrel, grew rigid for a second, sighed words that were both a prayer and a curse and stood up, his heart beating heavily, his mind a wild mixture of relief and fear.

The foremost rider came to a slithering halt and the two behind him, unwary, did their best to avoid slipping over the edge of the khud. When the cursing men and the dancing horses had been brought under control, Jiwan Khan remembered Darshan. "Friends, Darshan!" he shouted, and then turned to the three in front of him.

"Rabindra — " His father's most trusted man, with Jemal and Zaman Beg . . .

Had something happened to his father? He asked the oh-so-important question at once, and could only find two words.

"My father — ?"

Rabindra dismounted and came forward to where Jiwan Khan was waiting, his body stiff with apprehension.

"Nay, Lord, be at peace. Your father and mother are both well, al hamdu li llahi. The bad news I carry concerns Dil Bahadur. Where is he?"

"On his way back to Dhalli Palace.

What is the news that is bad enough to send you hurrying here?"

"Bad enough, Lord. His Begum has miscarried and lies very sick in Madore. It is thought that he should go to her at once. Also, I have a message for you from the Ruler."

"What does my father say?"

"You are to return to Lambagh at once. There is some trouble in Jungdah, and he wants you away from it. He told me to give you this — "

He held out a scrap of orange silk to Jiwan Khan who laughed as he took it.

"The silk with the love song worked on it — the song that is a warning, that only a woman could read. Come, sit, and I will tell you what has been taking place in Jungdah."

They sat on the lee-side of the great boulder and he told them all he knew. Then he heard their news. After that Jiwan Khan sat thinking, while Rabindra watched him, knowing that Jiwan Khan was going to refuse to return with him.

Jiwan Khan came to a decision that seemed sensible to him — and also pleasing.

"This is what we do, Rabindra. You and I go after Dil Bahadur and tell him this news. Then you go with him, to Madore. I will go into Dhalli Palace in his place. You, Zaman, and Jemal, and my man here, Darshan, will go back to Lambagh — Darshan can shown you the shortest way through these hills. Tell my father what I have told you of events here. We need as many well-armed men as he can spare. Tell my father that it is not possible for both myself and Dil Bahadur to leave Jungdah, because it is necessary that we take the family from Dhalli Palace before — " He hesitated. To say that Sagpurna was expected in Jungdah Valley with the full moon was to make his father and mother wild with anxiety. He said quickly, "Before the passes are closed by bad weather. I am staying here to see to their escape, and we will return together."

Rabindra said quietly, "The first thing the Ruler will ask is why, if you are only going to assist the family to leave Jungdah before the bad weather, why do you need a large body of armed men? Jiwan Khan, I think you should obey

259

your father and return."

"I cannot return. The old Raja needs help. He and his daughter will be taken if no one assists them. Why do you think Dil Bahadur went back? I know what his plan is, and I will carry it out. The armed men we need to help us get away. There is not time to talk about this now — we must get to Dil Bahadur so that he can leave at once."

Rabindra did not argue any more. He felt sure that as soon as they reached Dil Bahadur, Jiwan Khan would be sent out of harm's way. In fact, Jiwan Khan could ride to Madore with Dil Bahadur, and he, Rabindra, could stay to help the Jungdah family. Better to let Jiwan Khan have his head now.

Minutes later Jiwan Khan and Rabindra were on their way back to the Bab-i-margh and the other three men were beating forward against a rising wind with sleet in its teeth, towards Lambagh.

Jiwan Khan reached the Bab-i-margh in the early afternoon. The place lay quiet and deserted, but something made Rabindra signal to Jiwan Khan and they stopped.

"I smell something, Jiwan Khan. Food smoke? Could some of the Lambagh men have remained here?"

"Unlikely. I do not think that Dil Bahadur would divide his force. Perhaps some of the local men remained behind, though I heard Dil Bahadur sending them off to check on the movements of men down by the river. Could it be the camel caravan — the powindahs?"

"Not possible, unless they grew wings. They were up beyond Faridkote when I saw them. I go, Lord, and see."

Jiwan Khan accepted the hard fact that if a life had to be risked at that moment, it must not be his. Bad enough to have disobeyed a direct order from the Ruler, he must not run his head into unnecessary danger. His future had never pressed so hard on him before, and the love and admiration he had always felt for his father increased as he realised that Kassim Khan's life must be as circumscribed by duty as he now found his own to be.

He watched with admiration as Rabindra moved towards the fort, taking advantage of every bit of cover and indeed seeming

261

to vanish in front of his eyes. He could see nothing of Rabindra's movements, did not see him go up to the fort, or enter it, although the place was so close.

Presently he heard the soft croon of a dove, and riding his own horse and leading Rabindra's mount, he went up to the gates of the fort without taking any precautions at all. There were no doves in the winter weather of these barren valleys.

Rabindra was not alone. A small boy, dressed in the rags of a duffle tunic and as thin as a bone, was kneeling in the middle of the courtyard, blowing on a fire of sticks. Rabindra was watching him with folded arms.

"What is this?" asked Jiwan Khan The boy looked up, bright-eyed, and answered for himself.

"I am Halim the Goatherd, Lord. I watch for any danger that might come up from the pass below the Bab-i-margh. My father did the watching before me, and in those days I watched the herd. But one night my father took a message to the Palace, and has not returned, and I — I saw three men from the palace guard kill Shivnath and I was afraid, so I left the herd, and have been in hiding. My village knows that I am not dead, but they will not talk. I heard the three plainsmen asking where the herd boy was, they must have guessed that I saw them. So it is better that I stay dead. But I would not be afraid to be with you. This one" — he gestured at Rabindra — "your man — he says that you wish to speak with the nawab who went by earlier today with armed men. I can take you by a quick way if you will trust me. Also, I have news for the Palace and with you I can take it safely."

"You can tell us the news."

The boy looked at Jiwan Khan for a moment, reluctant. Then, making up his mind to trust them, he nodded.

"Yes. Listen then, Lord. There are many men in the river valley, and from the main body some are moving up towards Dhalli Palace, but very slowly. They seem to me to be following the nawab, keeping out of sight as if they were herders driving a nervous flock ahead of them."

Jiwan Khan looked at Rabindra. "So.

Dil Bahadur's plan is working. He is pulling them after him — "

"Because they think he is you," said Rabindra suddenly. "Heavenborn, if they take you, they will have such a grip on your father — "

"I know that. Say no more, I have heard all of that talk that I need to hear. At this moment I am in no danger, because they are convinced that I am there, leading the Lambaghi men. Tell me boy, how was the leader dressed?"

"He was very fine, Lord, with a rich tunic and a jewelled belt, and his turban was green — "

"As I thought. Dil Bahadur is letting them all think that the heir rides with his men. Well, let us take our news forward, Rabindra. What of this boy?" he added. "His eyes look likely to fall back in his head with fright and — " He was interrupted.

"I fear nothing, Lord," said the child firmly, "but I am very hungry."

"Then wait, we will find you some food before we go."

Jiwan Khan turned to his saddle bags and when they started on their way the

264

boy was devouring a leg of chicken, another clutched in his other hand. He rode perched behind Rabindra like a monkey, shrilling his directions. They rode up steep slopes and slithered down into dips where the snow had already set in a hard crust, ankle deep. Presently it was necessary for them to dismount and lead their horses, the going was so rough. The boy scrambled agilely in front of them.

Jiwan Khan, turning to watch his horse's footing, saw pricked ears and called a halt.

"There are horses ahead. Our beasts have sensed them. Rustom never tells me a lie. Boy, get behind lest we shoot you in error."

"Lord, Dil Bahadur will think you have plotted with me to join him if he sees you without warning. He will be very angered," said Rabindra.

"Yes. This is what we do. We join the rear ranks and go in behind him. I will tell those near me of what has happened, and you do the same with those near you. Then I will work my way up through the men until I come to him. Once we are within the Palace, I will take his place and he can leave at once. Rabindra, they come. Look there . . . "

They made a brave showing, riding slowly like men with a perfect right to be where they were, riding at ease, talking and laughing. The heir to Lambagh had arrived with an escort to call on the Raja of Jungdah in answer to a letter of invitation. Robert's plan, so carefully thought out. Jiwan Khan nodded to himself. Robert's plan had been a good one. Robert himself rode as if he had no cares, his green turban set rakishly on his head, his attention entirely given to something Osman was saying.

"Now," said Jiwan Khan and stepped out, just as the rear ranks of mounted men came abreast of them, the riderless extra horses being led by the last men, as Jiwan Khan had known they would be.

Jiwan Khan's hissed, "Be silent!" stopped an immediate outcry. Within minutes they were both mounted and were leading other horses. Each did as they had agreed, and shortly every man except those nearest to Osman and Dil Bahadur knew that Jiwan Khan and

266

Rabindra had appeared out of nowhere and that they had brought bad news for Dil Bahadur.

The river was left behind and they rode through the quiet, apparently deserted village, and over the empty fields where Robert had seen goats grazing; in single file they started up to the great gate, and still they had not been challenged, nor had they seen anyone. Robert was no longer smiling. He held his arm up, and the long cavalcade of men and horses halted. Then he turned to Osman.

"Call for entry, Osman," he said, using the stilted, conventional phrase that applied, and then said quietly over his shoulder, "Pass the order. Swords out." He heard the rattle as the order was obeyed, and then Osman lifted his great voice.

"Open the gates for the Nawabzaida Sahib of Lambagh and his men!"

Heads appeared above the wall, where the sentries should have been on guard, and a sound of astonished voices drifted down.

"Dil Bahadur! Do you hear that? They did not know we were here! We have come unnoticed. What manner of guards are these?" asked Osman, and as the sound of angry shouting rose on the other side of the high wall, he drew his sword and took a firm grip of the reins. Robert already had his sword in his hand, and he returned Osman's astonished glance and began to move forward towards the gate.

18

THE shouting inside the walls was silenced by the shrill scream of a trumpet. An authoritative voice shouted a question, and was answered by the voices of the men on the wall.

Rabindra leaned towards Jiwan Khan.

"Nawabzaida Sahib!"

Jiwan Khan turned to him in astonishment. Among his own men, his title was never used. Either his own name was title enough for them, or they called him "Lord" at the most. At this moment, the title was like a command; it contained as much authority as if his father spoke it, yet this was Rabindra, a faithful and trusted friend, younger by some years than most of the other men, only a year older than Jiwan himself. The title on *his* lips was startling.

"Nawabzaida Sahib — " Rabindra repeated the words as if they vested him with authority and gave him strength. Then he put out his hand and gripped

Jiwan Khan's arm, and began to speak quickly and quietly.

"Nawabzaida Sahib, you who will, with the help of all the gods of the world, both your single God with his prophet and my many gods, will one day rule our lives. For all our sakes, and for the sake of the future, you must tell Dil Bahadur now that you are here. Do not let him enter the Palace unknowing of your presence and of the news we bring. Go up to him now, Lord, and make yourself known. We can cover him if he wishes to go away now; he can drop back and ride away, but only if you give him the opportunity. Tell him you are here, and tell him of his Begum — now, Nawabzaida Sahib."

He spoke with extraordinary power; his voice was strange, as if another voice spoke through him, a voice that had to be heard, and obeyed. Jiwan Khan saw sweat starting out on his forehead and felt the tremble of the hand that gripped his arm. He looked at Rabindra's eyes and saw that they were wide and sightless; or did they see something far down the years that no one else could see? Jiwan Khan said nothing to him, but freed his arm and began to make his way to the front, moving his horse at a walk between the other men who sat waiting on their horses, drawn swords in their hands.

Behind him, Rabindra looked about him like a man waking from a dream, and then kicked his own horse into a walk and followed Jiwan Khan.

Jiwan Khan had reached the front rank. Robert, who had been listening to the shouting voices inside the walls, turned to speak to Osman, and saw Jiwan Khan.

His rage was obvious but controlled. Jiwan, who knew him so well, could imagine what he thought. After all his careful planning, Jiwan Khan, for what must appear a selfish whim, was putting everything into jeopardy. Jiwan Khan had seen that cold murderous rage on Robert's face before, but never directed at him. He spoke quickly, unable to bear the pain of betrayal that he knew Robert must be feeling behind the rage that was making his eyes burn.

"Dil Bahadur, I had to return. I have bad news of Laura."

The rage left Robert's face, which

became totally without expression.

"Where is she? I know she is not dead."

"She is with Bianca in Madore. She — " Oh Allah! Did he know that Laura had been pregnant when she left him to go to England? Looking at Robert's cold, set face, Jiwan Khan did not know how to break this news to him. He said slowly, "She is not well. She had a bad fall from her horse . . . "

"She has lost our child?" A dead, cold voice.

"Yes. She asks for you."

"I cannot go. Not now. Not with you here."

It was said with total finality, as if there could be no argument.

"Do not be a fool, Dil Bahadur! You could not go if I was *not* here. I am the next in line of command of these men! Do me the honour of remembering that at least!"

"I forget nothing, Jiwan Khan. But I cannot go. You have sent a message to your father? How? Ah, by the messenger he sent to you, I presume."

"Bianca sent Rabindra to Lambagh to

ask you to come in haste. I met him on the way here, with Zaman and Jemal. They have gone back to tell my father that we need men and arms. Rabindra came with me, he wishes to speak with you." Robert's cold gaze swept the ranks, focussed, and he nodded.

"I see him. Now, with no more words, go. You are in great danger here and your presence ensures that I am unable to do what I told you I was going to do. So, Jiwan, swiftly."

"No. You go. My danger is no more than yours, and I have no sick wife asking for me."

A hot, angry blue stare was met by a cold grey glare.

"Do you not hear what those men are shouting, and whose orders they obey, Jiwan? Things have gone wrong. I do not know who those men gathering by the river below the fort were, but they were not Ismail Mohammed's men, and he was not leading them. He is here, within the Palace. Jiwan Khan, must I speak of duty to you? Remember your oath. My life for yours, now and always."

"And Laura's life?"

"Set against that oath? Do not be foolish Jiwan Khan. Laura married me knowing that I had taken an unbreakable oath to the Lambagh family. Oh, I have no time to talk, curse it! Will you get back into the ranks of the men and slip away? It is an order from me, Dil Bahadur, and I command you while you wear that uniform and while I am here."

Jiwan Khan saw the high gate open behind Robert, and saw who was standing in the opening.

"I regret, Dil Bahadur," he said quietly, "it is too late: I have been seen. You get back. I took the oath also. As your future Ruler, I speak. Go. Do not turn around. The Nephew does not know you, he will not miss you. He has seen me. Go, I tell you!"

The voice that called from the gate was deep and full, a strong man's voice.

"Welcome Jiwan Khan, son of the Ruler of the Three States! Had I had notice of your coming I would have met you at the frontier. Is all well? You have come a long way in bad weather. I trust nothing unfortunate brings you here at this time of year!"

"No, Ismail Mohammed, thanks be to Allah, nothing unfortunate. I come at the invitation of the Raja, to spend a few days before returning to Lambagh."

As Jiwan Khan spoke, he saw Robert move back into the second rank of the Lambagh men, and drew a breath of relief. Robert was, after all, going to Laura. Jiwan Khan now gave his full attention to the man who was standing in the gateway.

Jiwan walked his horse forward, feeling all the pleasure of a mounted man who automatically has an advantage when he is speaking to a man on the ground. Ismail Mohammed looked up at him, and smiled slightly, a smile that could have been a snarl.

"You are invited by our Raja? He neglected to tell me — but then, I have been away from Dhalli for some days."

"The Raja, in fact, invited my father — but he is occupied with state business, so sent me instead to carry out the Raja's wishes."

The snarling smile faded from Ismail

275

Mohammed's face.

"The Raja's wishes? And what are they? I am in darkness. I know nothing."

"Then take me to the Raja, if you will, or am I to sit out here talking to you in the gate for the rest of the evening?"

Ismail Mohammed looked past Jiwan Khan to the ranks of men, the horses, the drawn swords.

"Wah! Jiwan Khan, you have an armed guard fit for the Ruler himself. Do you always travel in such state? But come in, of course, come in and be welcome. Songhur, show the risaldar of the men of Lambagh to the stables and to the guest court. See that they have everything for their comfort. Jiwan Khan, you have made a tiresome journey, this is the beginning of winter here. Nothing but matters of the greatest importance brings people through those high passes once this weather sets in. But come — let us go and talk about this invitation from my master, the old Raja of Jungdah. You know that I command the Raja's forces?"

"No, I did not know. My felicitations, Ismail Mohammed. I have not seen you since you left Pakodi State." He saw a flash of rage in the man's eyes, and turned away to speak to Osman.

"Osman, you will call on me when the men are in their quarters. Someone will no doubt guide you to where my quarters are."

"*I* am here, Jiwan. I will call you to inspection. Osman will stay with the men, with your permission," said a voice behind him.

Jiwan Khan looked into the dispassionate grey eyes beneath a defiantly cocked turban.

"Very well, Dil Bahadur," he said quietly, his curses only in his mind, nothing showing on his face of his rage and disappointment that Robert had not gone. He rode into the courtyard where Ismail Mohammed waited, as the commands began to crack out briskly behind him, and the Lambaghi men rode in like kings, their swords at the carry.

Dismounted, Jiwan Khan and Ismail Mohammed were of a height, and Ismail Mohammed gave the sweeping hand on forehead and then on the heart bow that is suitable for a prince, but succeeded in infusing insolence into it. Jiwan Khan tipped one finger from his forehead with a negligent flick in reply, and Ismail Mohammed set his lips.

The Nephew led the way to an inner court and through that to a room of such comfort and luxury that Jiwan Khan's eyebrows rose as he looked about him. This was a rise for a man who had lived from hand to mouth in rather seedy conditions during his stay in Pakodi after the death of the Nawab. Now — Ismail Mohammed caught his glance as Jiwan Khan looked about the room, and through an arched opening into more luxury beyond, and nodded.

"You think that I have done well for myself? It is true, but I have been useful also, and I have earned my comfort. There is need for me here: the old man is losing control. But with me here, he has a good army, and his state is under guard for him." Perhaps he saw the thoughts that moved behind Jiwan Khan's schooled expression, for he stopped speaking, turned away, and, picking up a jug, poured two silver cups full of wine.

"Choose," he said carelessly, and Jiwan Khan picked up the cup nearest to him and waited while his host raised his cup.

"Good fortune and long life? Shall that be our toast?"

Smiling, Ismail looked the perfect welcoming host. Jiwan Khan raised the cup and repeated, "Good fortune and long life." He heard a door open behind him and turned, the cup still at his mouth. Dil Bahadur walked into the room. "Do not drink, Jiwan Khan!" He spoke in English, and as he spoke he leaned to pluck the cup from Jiwan Khan's hand. Then he turned to Ismail Mohammed.

"You drink the toast, Nephew. From this cup."

Jiwan Khan's hand fell to his sword hilt at the tone of Robert's voice. No man could accept an order in that tone of voice, not in his own place, having poured out wine with his own hand. Jiwan Khan was expecting the instant clash of swords and moved instinctively to find a position where he could cover Robert's back and have space round himself as well.

Ismail Mohammed stared at Robert and burst out laughing. He took the cup of wine and, raising it, drained it, and handed it back to him.

"What stories has your man been told?" He picked up the jug and refilled the cups. "There are many in the Palace who are jealous of my success and who put it about that I am a dangerous man. But I did not know that they said I used poison to gain my ends, or that I stepped on dead men to gain this height." He shrugged, and looked at Robert. His eyes grew intent.

"This face I have seen before. Who are you?"

In fact, he had never seen Robert, but he had seen the Ruler, frequently, and Robert's likeness to Kassim Khan was uncanny.

"I am Dil Bahadur Khan. No doubt you have heard of me?"

"No doubt," said Ismail Mohammed, "no doubt. But refresh my memory. What should I have heard?"

"That Dil Bahadur commands my father's forces." Jiwan Khan lifted his cup and drank. Watching Robert's face, he was thankful to see the murderous look leave it. For a moment he had expected Robert to strike Ismail Mohammed down. The man appeared to be quite unconscious of the danger in which he had been.

"You have certainly come in force in answer to the Raja's invitation — or was it a message of another sort?"

"If you think that an escort of fifty men is coming in force — and what other sort of message might the Raja have felt he should send?"

"Who knows? The Raja is a very old man. Old men have strange ideas sometimes — but no matter. Fifty men as an escort, led by the Commander of the State Forces? Yes, I call that coming in force."

Robert moved forward.

"The heir was *sent*. I came of my own wish," he said. Jiwan Khan felt like a man crossing a marsh in darkness, with no knowledge of where he would put his foot for the next step forward. Robert's tone had changed, first murderous, now dripping with charm. Ismail Mohammed looked puzzled and suspicious.

"Of your own wish? Why?"

"To see the man who took foot soldiers and made horsemen of them, building a force that is already becoming known outside these valleys. Not every man could do this." Robert's voice was rich with admiration. Watching, Jiwan Khan saw that Ismail Mohammed was still suspicious.

"Oh? You yourself have a force, cavalry and foot, which is very well known, and not only in the mountain states. Why should my horsemen become of interest so suddenly?"

"Our men are, as they say, born on horseback. You took farmers and goatherds and mounted them on horses — not simple. Also — and more important than anything else — the horses. Your horses. I hear that you have brought stallions from Khokund, and that you breed them with mares from the plains — you hope for bone, stamina, and sure-footedness. Yes?"

The conversation took a different turn. Jiwan Khan saw Ismail Mohammed change from a wary, dangerous man into a man speaking of something close to his heart. In five minutes Jiwan Khan himself was involved, and a good hour later, Ismail Mohammed climbed to his feet, wine cup in hand, to lead the way to the stables and display with justifiable pride, his stallions and his breeding mares.

Jiwan Khan watched and wondered what Robert had in mind. Robert? The English name no longer seemed to fit the man he saw in front of him. It was impossible to think of him now as anybody but Dil Bahadur. He was a hill prince in every way. The Englishman appeared to have vanished forever.

The Nephew was expounding on training and breeding, food grains, green fodder and the difficulties of growing it in this area. He had drunk a great deal, but was still in command of himself. Whatever Dil Bahadur's new plan was, it was going to take time if the Nephew was to be rendered incapable by wine before it could be carried out. Dil Bahadur appeared to be totally engrossed, a man as lost as Ismail Mohammed in his favourite subject. But there was a glint in his eye as he glanced at Jiwan Khan, and he had been drinking very sparingly. Jiwan Khan made a decision as to his next best move and when he told a waiting servant to take him to his men's quarters, he saw from Dil Bahadur's face, fleeting though the change of expression was, that he had done the right thing.

The court where the Lambaghi men had been accommodated was large. Here the fort aspect of Dhalli Palace showed plainly. Round three sides of the open court were the sleeping quarters and storerooms, and a cook house. The fourth side was stables, a farrier's shop and an arms store. The sentries on duty were taken from his Lambaghi men, he was pleased to see; in fact there was no-one there that he did not know. The walls around the court were high, and stoutly built of stone.

Osman appeared and they inspected the sleeping quarters together. The images and the pictures were representations of hill gods and goddesses, luridly coloured, but nothing worse than they had seen before. Then they went to the stables where the horses now seemed peaceful. Even rations had arrived and the cook house was full of savoury smells.

All was as it should be, but Jiwan Khan was nonetheless conscious of feeling an acute anxiety. He heard a shout from the courtyard and found his hand had dropped to his sword hilt, and his sword was half drawn. The Lambaghi guard came up to salute and say that a man waited to take him to his quarters.

Jiwan Khan was loathe to go. He told Osman to double the guard, and agreed that the men should sleep in the stables; saying he would return later. He reluctantly went out of the stables to find a servant waiting with a lantern. He had already noted that all the servants about the Palace appeared to be men with two occupations. They were dressed in plain white trousers and loose woollen overshirts, with embroidered velvet waistcoats, but they all carried arms, and looked like men who were trained in the arts of fighting. With his mind full of worried conjectures, Jiwan Khan followed the man with the lantern, and looking over his shoulder at the sound of footsteps, saw that another armed man walked behind him down the dusky passage.

19

THE rooms to which Jiwan Khan was taken were as luxurious as Ismail Mohammed's own quarters. His guides — or were they guards? — left him at the door. Inside he found an elderly manservant waiting; his baggage had been brought in.

In the dressing room there were some new garments, a long green robe made of fine wool, and soft leather boots. There was also a cap of white astrakhan, and a heavily jewelled sword belt.

"A gift of respect from the Nephew," said the old man and began to help Jiwan Khan out of his riding clothes. He brought a tray on which stood a silver cup and a jug of wine. Jiwan Khan would care to drink before he bathed? Jiwan nodded, and watched, astonished, as the old man poured the wine, took a drink, threw the first into a bowl, wiped the cup and, filling it again, presented it to him.

Jiwan Khan drank, and wondered what he would have done if the old man had fallen to the floor. How long did poison take to work? It did not seem to be a question that he could ask. He bathed, and was assisted to dress, watching again as each garment he put on was shaken and searched. The embroidered leather boots were turned upside down and a stick padded like a drumstick was pushed into each boot. He could not keep silent watching this performance.

"For what do you search?"

The man was squatting on the floor, holding the boots for Jiwan to pull on.

"I look for poison, Lord, or a sharp nail or a small knife set in the sole — or even a thorn or a snake — a krait. Any one of these things can take a man's life."

"And the clothes?"

"The same. Powder in the seams and a thorn, or a rock scorpion — there are so many ways to send a man to meet the face of his God."

"But we were here — and no one came in!"

"Lord, we were in the bathroom. As I

poured water, would you have heard one who came with feet bare?"

"With a guard on the door?"

"Who knows what they guard? While you are here, Lord, I beg you to treat each shadow as your enemy, and eat nothing, drink nothing, that has not been tasted."

Jiwan Khan stared at him. This was like listening to tales of the long ago days, told to frighten children. Before he could express his unbelief, a voice spoke from the doorway between the dressing room and the bathroom.

"Jiwan Khan, this is good talk. You are in the dangerous land of treachery, and this man is a good and trusted friend who serves the Raja. Your own people cannot guard you here."

It was Rabindra who spoke, Rabindra dressed as a hill coolie in a short duffle tunic and trousers, a rope girdle tight about his waist, into which was stuck a thin-bladed knife and a leather tinder box. He did not look like Rabindra, he looked exactly as he should and if he had not spoken Jiwan Khan would have taken a few minutes to recognise him.

"Rabindra! How did you get here?"

"As usual. Through the privy door; the one door that is almost always forgotten."

He grinned at Jiwan with a flash of white teeth, an infectious young man's grin that reminded Jiwan Khan of the many escapades they had shared together in their very early youth — and spoke of all the various privy doors that Rabindra had found unguarded. Not all of them had led to danger or duty, thought Jiwan Khan, remembering Rabindra's reputation with the women of many places. He smiled back at his clever, brave friend.

"Well, now I imagine this one at least will be guarded. Should you be here?"

"I cannot reach Dil Bahadur, and I have yet to deliver to him the Pahareen's message. She would send no message that was not of importance. Dressed thus, I can come and go easily. I think Dil Bahadur will come to escort you to Ismail Mohammed's quarters. So I came here to wait. The load of wood I carried is stacked in the bathroom."

Newly born caution made Jiwan Khan turn to the old servant.

"It is safe to talk?"

"Yea. These walls defeat eavesdroppers. I will watch at the door. As your servant says — they forget the privy door, and the unclean ones who come to empty the night soil cannot speak."

Dil Bahadur came into the room. Behind him was a man with a drawn sword in his hand, but he did not enter, merely looked in and then closed the door. Rabindra stood to one side.

"I come to take you to Ismail Mohammed's rooms," said Dil Bahadur. "Are you ready to come?"

"I am. But there are one or two things I wish to speak about. Have we time?"

"Is this wine safe? Was it tasted?"

On Jiwan Khan's nod, Dil Bahadur poured himself a cup of wine and sat down. He wore a long woollen robe like Jiwan Khan's robe, belted tightly about the waist with his own jewelled sword belt, and his own sword hung from it too, his battle sword, not a dress sword, though the sheath was jewelled like the belt. His cap was made of embroidered wool, and was set as rakishly as possible, hiding his barely healed scar.

Watching him settle himself, Jiwan Khan marvelled at the change he had already noticed. Dil Bahadur had always been a proud and spirited person. Now, whatever he did had a hard glitter to it, a certain flair in every movement, in his voice, his eyes. He looked bitter and arrogant, and difficult to reach. Jiwan Khan found it in his heart to blame Laura, and then wondered if he was right. Perhaps this was always going to happen, this was what Robert would have become. Dil Bahadur, the Nawab of Lambagh, the son of Muna — Dil Bahadur, but his friend still, no matter how he changed.

"Well? You are staring at me as if we have never met before; we have time, Jiwan, but not so much. What is it you wished to discuss?"

"I do not think that I have *ever* met you before. What are you doing with Ismail Mohammed? You appear to be about to lie down with that hyena and make love."

"Don't be a fool! I must be a friend to him if we are to get safely out of this place and get the Raja and the Begum out as well. Are you going to help me, or are you going to stand about staring at me as if I was a jinn from hell, suddenly appeared before you?"

"Oh, I will do anything you say!" Jiwan's blue eyes began to sparkle with anger. Dil Bahadur's tone was annoying to say the least. "I will of course obey you. Who am I but one of your officers, after all?"

"If, Jiwan, you *were* one of my officers, you would now be half way to Lambagh and I would not be in the position of having your life on my hands. You will forgive me if I am angry."

"Angry? Yes, you are very angered. But I must know what you are doing if I am to play my part."

"Can you not trust me? Follow my lead a little? You used to be able to, without any trouble."

It was suddenly the Dil Bahadur he knew who was speaking, no longer the hard, embittered stranger.

"Of course I trust you. But you ask a great deal. I will do anything you want of me, but I need to understand. You seem to me to be wooing the Nephew like a lovesick old woman."

"Listen then, and see me as I want him to see me. I am full of treachery and jealousy. I am a man disappointed about my place in Lambagh, frustrated in that, a year older than you, I have no expectations of any higher place than I have already attained. So — I am looking to a man who is in much the same position as I am. What could be more natural, I ask you? As he becomes rich and important, so shall I, if I put my life beside him. Now do you understand a little more? As his friend I have freedom here . . . Are you seeing the picture clearly?"

"Yes, I am. Too clearly. You have forgotten something. Our mutual devotion which has become a byword throughout the valleys. Your often tried and tested loyalty to my father. Your love for your English wife — all these things are the talk of the valleys and the hill states. Do you imagine anyone is going to believe this tiger changing his stripes?"

"Ismail Mohammed knows very little of me. I was of no interest to him when I was first in Lambagh and he was in

Pakodi State. He was too busy trying to gild his own sword at that time. He did not know who I was — only my likeness to your father made him notice me. Must we waste time in arguing? I have work to do, and while I do it I have to be certain that by waiting long enough to get the Raja and his family out I do not place you in Sagpurna's hands. Let us waste no more time, or Ismail Mohammed will send guards to collect his guests for his welcoming feast."

"And Laura? What of her, while you wait here to rescue the Raja?"

"For God's sake, Jiwan Khan! That is my affair!"

"Well, it may be. But what *about* Laura? Rabindra was sent here to get you because she asks for you, she is ill. She must be very ill for Bianca to send in such haste."

Dil Bahadur stood up and set his goblet down. His voice was very quiet, his face showed nothing, but Jiwan Khan knew that he was fighting rage.

"Jiwan Khan, Laura is in safe hands, and until we get away from here, I must forget her. I *have* forgotten her. My life for yours, now and always. To me that vow is everything, and I made it to your family. I need say no more.

"Rabindra," he went on after a moments pause, "what will you do while he sits with the Nephew? Are you free to move about?"

"I am, Lord. And I have a message for you from the Pahareen, met outside Faridkote as I was on my way from Madore to Lambagh."

While they were speaking, Jiwan Khan waited, feeling a deep sorrow as he remembered the words Dil Bahadur had spoken. "I have forgotten her." Did love go out of mind so easily? He was glad that no girl had touched his heart. The love his father and mother shared had been the yardstick for him. Until he found someone who took his heart as they had taken each other's hearts, he laughed at love. But even so, when Dil Bahadur and Laura had married, he had envied their happiness. And now — he felt that he had been hunting a dream, the dream of one day finding perfect love and companionship. Dreams fade and die, thought Jiwan Khan, and looked then at Dil Bahadur's face and saw torment in his eyes. Dreams fade and die, but they had not died easily for Dil Bahadur after all.

Rabindra had already gone, when a double thump on the door heralded the arrival of a richly dressed man. He was a man from the plains, a low caste man with a dark, pockmarked face and a precariously high opinion of himself. His tone, bidding them to come to Ismail Mohammed, made Jiwan Khan's mouth curl with disdain. In any well-ordered household the summons would have been couched in different words: "Honoured one, Ismail Mohammed is thinking of you." But this man said, "You are to come now. The Nawab Ismail Mohammed is waiting."

"And when did Ismail Mohammed become a Nawab?" said Jiwan pleasantly to Dil Bahadur, speaking in Lambaghi and turning a dangerously pleasant smile on the pompous messenger.

"He is anything he wishes to be for the next few days, and we do well to remember it," said Dil Bahadur, standing back to let Jiwan Khan precede him, and contriving to so jostle the messenger that he almost fell. His apologies were profuse, but the man's eyes were hate-filled.

"Have a care, Dil Bahadur. You have made an enemy there."

"So, I have made an enemy of a dung beetle. I will stamp my foot and he will run. There are worse enemies to be faced than this. Lead on, Lord of wisdom, and try to keep those blue eyes of yours from expressing total contempt for everything you see. We are now actors, so let us act — for our lives."

Smiling, walking together, the two Nawabs of Lambagh strode after their guide with nothing on their faces but pleasure and amusement.

20

ISMAIL MOHAMMED waited for them, the trappings of a very rich man all about him. Bareheaded, dressed in brocade and scented with musk and rosewater, he still showed no signs of being as sybaritic as his surroundings. He looked a handsome, hard man in the full flower of his strength and was obviously determined to charm and entertain. His attentions to both his guests were fulsome.

There were, when they arrived, no other guests, but the cushions and divans were so arranged that it was plain he expected at least three more people. There was also a large, heavily carved and gilded chair set on one side. A throne? wondered Jiwan Khan.

Ismail Mohammed seated Jiwan Khan, poured wine for him, and with a wry smile at Dil Bahadur, drank a little from the goblet before handing it on.

"It is good wine, and has no additions,"

he said, and clapped his hands. Servants came in and passed platters of meat, cubed and spiced and skewered. Jiwan Khan, for the first time in his life, wondered if he would finish the meal writhing in agony.

Before he could lift the skewer to his mouth he heard music outside. Ismail Mohammed suddenly lost all interest in his guests and turned towards the door. Jiwan was able to say quickly, "Can I eat? Can I drink? In Allah's name, Dil Bahadur, is everything dripping with poison?"

Dil Bahadur, who was watching at the door, smiled.

"Tonight, brother, you eat and drink. He will not, I think, poison this banquet."

The door was flung open with ceremony, the music swelled and a man's voice swooned over the words of a love song that Jiwan Khan knew well.

"The birds of the South are flying, and the summer is almost gone — almost gone. Come soon my love . . . " crooned the voice.

The woman who entered on the words

was veiled and swathed in white robes that hid her body but could not disguise the grace of her walk. Her veil was merely a nod to modesty, for it was so fine that it hid nothing of her face. Large topaz coloured eyes turned to Jiwan Khan, passed him as if he did not exist, and fixed, with a sudden flare in their depth, on the tall man behind him.

"Alas for Laura," thought Jiwan Khan and turned to salute the old man who was following the woman into the room. He was a tall old man who bowed and smiled and spoke Jiwan Khan's name. He seated himself as of right in the throne-like chair, and turned to Jiwan.

"It was good of your honoured father to send you so quickly in answer to my message."

"And we have not yet heard the reason for such a hasty reply — nor indeed the necessity for the answer to be brought by such an important visitor as the heir himself," said Ismail Mohammed.

"I did not feel it necessary," said the Raja gently, "to tell you, Ismail Mohammed, what I wished to say to the Ruler of Lambagh. It was a personal message and had nothing to do with the army or with any of the other matters which are now in your hands." His voice was calm, his old eyes looked steadily at the Nephew. The woman had seated herself, and behind her stood an elderly woman, unveiled, her white head cloth only partly hiding her white hair, which had been dyed in streaks with henna to show that she had made the pilgrimage to Mecca. Behind the Raja's chair stood an old man, who so closely resembled the man who had assisted Jiwan Khan to dress that Jiwan guessed he must be a brother.

The door was closed, but the music still sounded, muted now to a background of gentle melody. "Come soon my love . . . " The voice faded and a flute took up the tune. The woman put up her hand and adjusted her veil, and Ismail Mohammed poured a goblet of wine and passed it to her, saying, "You are among your own household, Lady. Jiwan Khan and Dil Bahadur are as your brothers, and your father is here. Are you not going to unveil?"

"As I am going to eat and drink

with you, Ismail Mohammed, I must. So." The voice was memorable, thought Jiwan Khan, that sudden break and the upward cadence at the end of the sentence . . . he watched with interest as her veil was lifted away and her face was revealed. A voluptuous mouth, a passionate face, now schooled and quiet; but he could imagine that, if roused, a woman made for physical love would be smiling with that mouth, those burning eyes. Her eyes were the only things she did not seem able to control. As if she knew this, she looked down and the expressive eyes well hidden by heavy lids. Jiwan Khan had seen this type of face carved in friezes on temple walls, and on every image of a goddess. The face of passion and pleasure in love. A very young woman, younger than he had thought when she walked in. A strange way for a young woman of good family to behave, to attend a banquet for men, even if her father were present, though of course she was a widow. Even so . . . He glanced swiftly at Dil Bahadur, but he was feigning disinterest in everything about him, and at Ismail Mohammed . . . who was looking openly at the Begum in a way that was unmistakable. Jiwan Khan sighed, and applied himself to his wine. The evening, it seemed to him, was liable to become stormy. He wished with all his heart that he had kidnapped Dil Bahadur and sent him home to Madore, rolled in a carpet. There were more dangers than he had realised in this place. He knew Dil Bahadur's expression of disinterest well. It usually meant that he was either controlling his temper with difficulty or hiding his thoughts — or both. Also, thought Jiwan Khan, he is involved with this tigress. That I can see with ease. Let us hope that Ismail Mohammed does not see it too.

The old Raja was making use of every polite, conventional exchange possible. He asked after the health of each separate member of Jiwan's family, including Mumtaz Begum, his grandmother. On being assured that she was very well, that she still took a daily ride and enjoyed her food, the old man sighed in reminiscence.

"My father asked for her in marriage for me, from her father. The marriage would have been suitable. But your grandmother had already seen your English grandfather and had lost her heart, and we of the states — the hill states — we do not force our daughters into marriage."

The Begum looked across at him, the old woman servant stirred and turned her head, and the conversation almost foundered. Of course, thought Jiwan Khan, she must have been a child when they married her off to Ali of Pakodi. However charming he was, he must have been easily thirty years older than his bride, and that marriage had certainly not been of the bride's choosing.

The Raja was still talking, asking if Jiwan Khan had news of his English friend? Had he visited him in Madore at all, or had he gone straight to Safed? Jiwan Khan, thinking furiously, tried to make sensible answers to the questions. The Raja was not a fool, and was saying these things with a purpose.

But what English friend? Laura? No, he would not know about Laura's illness. So it must be a warning of some sort. Was he trying to tell Jiwan Khan that there were British troops near Safed? He smiled and spoke and drank, and heard Dil Bahadur speaking rather loudly to Ismail Mohammed about horse breeding on the plains, and the mares of the Deccan. He took the opportunity offered and said quietly, "My English friend?"

"Oh, I had many myself in the old days. When the Jung-i-lat first came out, Curzan, he came to me here. We had good fishing in those days. But alas, this is a hard country to reach, and also he has much work in government, so no one comes to us any more. But I have written, and with the summer, who knows, perhaps they will come . . ."

What on earth was he talking about? Jiwan risked an imploring look at Dil Bahadur. The Nephew had broken off their conversation to direct the refilling of all their goblets. The old woman servant, he had heard her called Saida, leaned forward and sipped from the Begum's goblet before putting it into her hand.

"So you think I wish to poison your mistress at my own table?" Ismail Mohammed was glaring his displeasure.

"It might be better for her if that was all you wished," said Saida looking

305

into the angry stare. Under her straight look Ismail Mohammed's rage seemed to leave him.

"I wish her nothing but good, woman," he said, and turned away. Food was carried in, and Ismail Mohammed made a great business of choosing the food from the platters for the Begum himself. Under cover of the ensuing bustle, Jiwan Khan said quickly, "Dil Bahadur, the Raja asks for news of our English friend, he thinks he is in Safed. Do you have news?" The Raja was quick-witted too, leaning over to say, "The Englishman is so anxious to see you he speaks of joining a camel caravan and coming up here. Have you heard this?" But he had not reckoned with the Nephew's hearing.

"An Englishman? Coming up here in winter?" He laughed. "Are you sure it is a man? A woman mad with love might dare the passes, for I hear that English women love greatly men of our race — but no Englishman who knows this country would come here in winter. Were you thinking of Major Windrush Sahib? For he was in Calcutta the last time I had news of him, just before the

306

first snows fell in the higher passes. Just before the passes began to close."

He leaned back among his silk covered cushions, laughing, uncaring that he had virtually admitted to them that he had messengers regularly from the plains. If he was so sure of himself, things were very bad, Jiwan Khan thought. He kept looking down at his plate, afraid of what he would see on Dil Bahadur's face after the Nephew's speech.

Without warning, the Begum took over the conversation, saying that she wished to compliment Ismail Mohammed on the food.

"It is of great excellence, Ismail Mohammed."

"Lady of perfection, if it pleases you, I am overjoyed."

"It pleases me particularly for I know who cooked it. I am glad to know that an old servant I thought lost for ever is still alive and safe."

She spoke quietly, and her voice was composed. Her words did nothing to please Ismail Mohammed, nor was his voice calm when he answered her after a pause.

"How should one of your servants not be safe, Heart of the Palace? Who would touch one of your men?"

"Come, Ismail Mohammed! Do you think I allow Saida, who has been with me all my life, to risk *her* life tasting my food and my drink for my amusement? Too many of my people have died, and too many of them have vanished for me to be allowed to eat or drink anything untasted. Death? I do not fear death, it could be better than my life, but I fear to leave my son alone. For him I must live, and so I let Saida risk her life for me. Tell me no lies, Ismail Mohammed. I know who orders the poisoning of my people." Her face was full of contempt and her voice was cool and distant as if she spoke to a lower servant, an untouchable. Jiwan Khan saw that the Nephew's attention was now fully engaged, and that this had been the Begum's intention. The Raja leaned forward and spoke, smiling, speaking just above his breath.

"You *must* get out, Jiwan Khan. Sagpurna comes within the next week, or just after. He has spies set here, I think that he watches for your coming. You are in a trap."

He leaned away and drank and said, "We have polo here that is worth the watching, but no tent-pegging. That is for the summer. Alas that I had to ask you to come in the winter."

Jiwan Khan heard the Nephew's furious voice; the Begum had coolly stoked his rage with her words. He leaned towards the Raja, saying quickly, "What more do you want to say, Raja Sahib?" conscious that Dil Bahadur had made a screen for him by half turning a broad shoulder and leaning forward over his food.

"Leave quickly, and take my daughter and the boy — " The Raja looked away from him quickly, his face changing. Then, as if making up his mind, he said in his ordinary voice, "The boy needs a change and should go before the passes close. How soon do you think?"

Jiwan Khan knew the very instant when the Nephew's attention was caught. The Raja had known too, but had not cared. Things were becoming too serious for subterfuge.

Ismail Mohammed was now leaning

forward too, trying to hear what they were saying. The Raja glanced at him, and went on speaking.

"As I said, the passes will be closed soon. When would you be prepared to leave?"

"When will the Begum and her son wish to travel? I am here at their service."

"We knew that your father would answer quickly, so we are prepared. My daughter can leave — say the day after tomorrow? That gives you a day and a night to rest your horses and your men. Let us say early the day after tomorrow?"

"Certainly. In fact they could leave tomorrow, as they are here already; most the men of them. There will of course be a strong escort going with Jiwan Khan and the Begum, and also, extra horses, but most of the men will stay. I have a great desire to study the Nawab Ismail Mohammed's method of training both horses and men."

Dil Bahadur had taken over; he was rolling the title and the compliments off his tongue, but the flattery and the honeyed voice failed. Ismail Mohammed said quietly, "It is not understood where the Begum goes. Perhaps I, the lowest of her servants, might be told?"

Jiwan Khan felt for the hilt of his dagger. The Raja pushed his plate aside, and held out his goblet to be filled.

"She goes to stay with the Ruler of Lambagh and his family for a while. Until the boy is used to his new home. It is thought by Major Windrush, who will be his guardian and his tutor, that he should live for a while in Lambagh before leaving for school in England."

Oh, clever old man, thought Jiwan, to bring the British in as well. Invoking every power he could think of to protect his precious heir against a very strong and determined usurper. Oh, clever old man.

The silence in the room drew itself out and was so intense that they could hear each other breathing. Silence pulled to a fine point, like a dagger of glass, ready to shatter at the first touch.

Then Ismail Mohammed laughed. He laughed as if the Raja had just told an excellent joke, throwing his handsome head back and enjoying his own laughter.

"Wah, old man, what dreams you

dream. You send a child to England, with Major Windrush, no less — a man among men, that one. What will he do with that boy in England? That weakling boy, child of an old man's last flare of passion. He is half asleep most of the time, I am told. The child will die in the cruel cold of England — and what will you do for an heir then?"

Dil Bahadur saw the Begum's hand rise and would have caught at it himself, but Saida was quicker. She held her mistress's wrist and the little silver-hilted dagger dropped from the Begum's fingers to lie in the white folds of her robe.

Jiwan Khan sat still, every muscle tensed. The Raja, looking at his daughter's face, was beginning to rise, trying to speak. Dil Bahadur was on his feet, but before any of them could do anything, Ismail Mohammed leaned to pick up the dagger. He looked at her, and then down at the blade. Then he lifted his hand and seemed about to drive the point of the weapon into his arm.

"No!" said the Begum suddenly. He nodded, and held out his hand.

"The sheath — "

The Begum put the thin leather case into his hand. He looked into it, and then up to her.

"Poison!" he said, with nothing on his face or in his voice but simple amazement. "Poison. You would have used a poisoned dagger on me. You!"

"You spoke evil of my son, and by implication of my dead husband." Her words were spoken sharply, in spite of her beautiful voice. "For me to use poison on you is nothing. How many times did you try to poison my child? To send poisoned sweets to a child who knows no evil!"

"I? Never, I swear!"

"You swear? On what can you swear a lie like that?"

"I do not lie. I do not use poison. Never. I will swear on what matters more than my life to me. I swear on your life. I have never used poison on any one, least of all on a child of yours."

The Begum moved suddenly, looking at him in amazement. His face blazed with emotion and honesty. It was impossible to disbelieve him. Saida cried out, "It is true — I can see truth," and they all looked at her, except

Ismail Mohammed and the Begum who were looking at each other with an intent gaze.

The Raja said quietly, "Woman, be quiet — " and Saida sank back, pulling her veil over her face. A silence held them all for a few seconds, and in that silence they heard the musicians outside clearly. The drum beat grew louder, and more insistent, and the door was opened suddenly by someone outside, so that the music was in the room. On a final throbbing note the drum stopped for a moment and flute music fitted itself to the steps of the girl who ran in, holding garlands of evergreen and paper roses.

She made a deep obeisance to Ismail Mohammed and dropped two of her garlands round his neck, and then did the same to all the others. The Begum took her garland in her hand, and for a moment the two women were joined by the ring of greenery. The dancer stared at the Begum out of khol-rimmed, slanted eyes, and murmured something. She turned and flung her next garland round Dil Bahadur, and he saw the flash of a smile, and then she was sweeping

314

her low bow to the Raja, who bowed his head to receive her decoration, and thanked her.

Jiwan Khan was the last to be garlanded. He looked up into a young face, white teeth gleaming in a smile so infectious that in spite of all that had been happening that evening he was able to smile back.

"My roses are false, Prince of Lambagh, but they are brought with respect and I have made for you a rose of gold to do you special honour!"

Her eyes, half closed by her smile, met his look, and then she was away from him, sweeping into a dance that was all curving arms and hand movements and swirling turns that sent her long hair swinging out. Then the music faded and changed and she sank down before them, hands held palm to palm, head bowed low. The dance was over.

Miraculously, so was the tension. The Raja smiled and tossed a silver coin which the girl caught, cupping slender hands. The Begum smiled at her, unhooking a jade earring and putting it into her hand. Ismail Mohammed, with a grand gesture, took off a heavy gold ring, and gave it to her. Dil Bahadur, like the Raja, threw her a coin, staring at her hands, but this time she let the coin fall and bent lithely to pick it up. Then she came back to Jiwan Khan.

"And the Prince of Lambagh? What have you for me, Lord?"

"What would you wish?"

"I will take a button from your robe, a ruby and diamond button. But later, Lord. Later, when I come to aid you to take off the robe . . . " She laughed at him and swept out, all the little bells on her skirts ringing as she went.

"Wah! Jiwan Khan, you will sleep warm tonight at least!"

The Nephew appeared to be in a very good temper suddenly. He stood up and moved to face the Begum, who was sitting with her eyes cast down and her hands folded on the garland on her lap.

"I told you, Lady of Light and Beauty, that when I next saw you it would be in your father's presence. Well, I did not know that there would be others present as well. But it makes no difference. I am a man with no family. My father is dead, my mother — " He paused and looked down for a moment and Jiwan Khan and Dil Bahadur both thought of the stories about the woman of the bazaar. Saida moved to pull her veil closer over her face, and Ismail Mohammed spoke again.

"I have no one, so I take these two, my friends, as my brothers. And before them, I speak. I offer myself to you, Raja Jain Singh of Jungdah, as a suitor for your daughter Amara. I do not mind that she is widowed. I ask for her with as much honour as if she still slept in her maiden bed, and I will give you a virgin's bride price; ask me what you will for her. Speak, Jungdah, I will make a good husband for your daughter, and a good son to you."

Standing there, he made a handsome figure, his face suddenly without guile and with an eager appeal in the eyes that he turned to the Raja.

The Raja's hands had clenched together as Ismail Mohammed was speaking, and he looked across at his daughter, his face troubled, but his voice quite steady when he spoke.

"Ismail Mohammed. You have spoken with me before on this matter. I would repeat to you what I said then. The girls of my family are never coerced into marriage. It is for my daughter to say, and she has spoken. She does not wish to marry again."

"Do you tell me that she chose, as a child, to marry Pakodi? She did not speak for herself then! I saw her come to her marriage, a frightened girl child. She did not choose then. Let her use her own tongue now; let her choose now."

The Begum had not moved. She sat cross-legged, her hands still, her face carved like one of the carved masks that Jiwan Khan had thought she resembled when he first saw her. She said, her voice very low, "You told me that you would see me with my father when the moon was full. There are yet six days, I think, to run, Ismail Mohammed."

"Love, impatient, does not reckon time correctly. Let the moon, envious of your beauty, stay behind clouds, green-sick and half-grown. I only see one moon, and she is here, within this room, richer than silver, more beautiful than gold,

318

splendid as the red roses of Persia. Give me your love, Amara! Let me take you into a land of happiness that you have never known!"

Like men held by a spell, the others sat listening. Only Dil Bahadur's jaw clenched, sending the muscles in his cheek jumping.

"You do not speak to a girl, Ismail Mohammed. I am a widow. I lay in my lord's bed, I received his seed gladly, I bore him a son. I am a widow, Ismail Mohammed, and so I wish to remain."

"You lay in your lord's bed? You lay in an old man's bed! What do you know of a young man's love? The fire that burns within you has never been fed, Amara! Turn you to me, come to me, learn what love is!"

Ismail Mohammed had forgotten everyone else in the room. His voice was vibrant; he spoke as if they were alone. Jiwan Khan saw Dil Bahadur move suddenly, his hand lifting an empty goblet. The Begum raised her head and looked at Ismail Mohammed in silence. Then she put up her hand and pulled her veil down, arranging it with care, and

319

apparently paying no more attention to anyone in the room.

Jiwan Khan heard Ismail Mohammed's breath hiss between his teeth, and dared not look at the man who had been so put down. Dil Bahadur spoke easily, softly.

"We are all friends here, all as it were one family, as Jiwan Khan has chosen us as his brothers. Therefore I can speak freely." He turned to clap Ismail Mohammed on the back.

"You are too hasty, Ismail bhai. These matters cannot be settled so simply, so speedily. Softly, Ismail my brother. Would you expect a wild mare to come to your hand at your first call? Or a falcon fly to take meat from you, untrained? Nay, then, do you not know that a girl is wilder than these wild creatures? You need to take time and trouble." Ismail Mohammed's face was a study in anger and amazement. Dil Bahadur did not appear to notice. He nodded, held his goblet out to be refilled, and waving his hand continued his speech.

"Yes. Time and trouble. You must woo, and speak sweetly, wrap your words in honey and rose petals. I, Dil Bahadur,

I who speak to you, I know." He laughed, looked at Jiwan Khan and went on.

"You remember, Jiwan bhai, that girl I had in Faridkote? Her face! And a body like a young palm tree. She set the blood pounding in a man's veins. But to get her to my bed was a task for a patient man. Patience paid. I won her in the end. Eh, Jiwan? You must remember that, Ismail Mohammed. Patience always pays, always, with women and with horses. Now, that reminds me, touching the matter of horses, which is a matter of, to me and I know to you also, a matter of very great importance — "

They were all staring at him. Jiwan wondered if he was drunk. He spoke like a man far gone in drink, turning his goblet in his hand so that the dark wine lapped at the rim and yet not a drop was spilled . . . impossible. He was not drunk.

The Begum, who had been silent throughout this last exchange, now rose in one supple movement. Without a word or a look at anyone, she bowed before her father and walked out of the room.

Ismail leapt up and would have

followed her, but was confronted by Saida. She did not speak, and they stood there, the tall old woman with one hand on the edge of the door, her eyes fierce, unblinking like the eyes of an old hawk. And Jiwan saw Ismail Mohammed's eyes beaten down before hers. Saida waited a second, then turned and went out, closing the door behind her.

21

THE room was quiet after the Begum had gone, quiet and full of thought and unspoken words. The music had gone with her, fading down the pillared hall. Only the tabla, the hand drum, sounded, a soft tapping, a pulse of sound. Ismail Mohammed stared at the closed door as if his eyes could see through it and were watching the woman who walked away from him.

Dil Bahadur looked across at the Raja, huddled in his chair, and the Raja moved as if he had heard an order. His servant gave him his stick, and he stood leaning on it as if his age had at last caught up with him and it was hard for him to bear its burden. Even his voice was faint and frail as he bowed formally and said his farewells.

"I thank you for your hospitality, Ismail Mohammed. Jiwan Khan, Dil Bahadur — you are both welcome in my State, my home is yours. Jiwan Khan, I will

323

speak with my daughter, and ask her to be ready to depart with you in two days' time. No later. The clouds were heavy with snow to the North, and in two more weeks at the most no one will get through the Bab-i-margh."

As he bowed again and turned to leave, Ismail Mohammed rose.

"No one is going from here with your daughter, Jungdah, for she is not going. Wait! Listen to me before you speak. You need a strong man for your state, a man to defend your passes. Your girl, though a widow, is only now ripe for marriage and ready for a husband who will give her strong sons for your guddee. I am the man. Accept, and be glad. She is not for all markets, widowed and with a sickly child! But I want her. Do not speak except to agree, for your words thrown against my will are as little use as husks from corn blown on the wind."

He had spoken quietly, standing to face the Raja, matching him in height and suddenly invested with dignified authority. It was easy, seeing him thus, to believe the stories about his birth, to believe that he was indeed the son of

Pakodi's brother. There was no trace of a bazaar woman's son in him as he stood before them now. He looked to be a man of good birth, and it was perfectly possible to trace the lines of Pakodi's family in his face. Jiwan Khan remembered the other stories about him. Murderer, poisoner, traitor, ingrate, a villain who was holding the ruling family of Jungdah prisoners in their own Palace. It seemed impossible that he was such a man, but where was the truth in this strange, haunted valley? Jiwan looked up to catch Dil Bahadur's eye, and saw no question on his face. He was watching the Raja with deep attention, frowning a little, waiting.

The Raja was no longer leaning on his stick: he had gathered his strength together and stood erect, holding his stick as if it was a spear, and he answered Ismail Mohammed at once, his voice firm, his eyes steady on Ismail Mohammed's face.

"You will not, Ismail Mohammed, speak of my daughter as if she was a slave to be given here or there at any man's wish. She has told you many times to my knowledge, and now again in front of witnesses, that she wishes to remain a widow. Let her be. I thank you for your offer, but it is not possible for me to give you any other answer. She is not for you."

The strong old voice held, to the listening ears, a note of regret. By Allah, thought Jiwan Khan, he would give his consent, I swear he would. It is the Begum who is refusing; but why? The man is not ill-favoured, he is strong, and full of purpose — the Begum is foolish to turn him away; and *why* is she behaving so foolishly?

The Raja and Ismail Mohammed stood facing each other for a minute longer. Then the Raja turned his head and looking at Dil Bahadur, sighed. Speaking as he turned to go, weariness beginning to show in his voice again.

"As for her departure from my State, it is arranged. She goes, with my heir, her son, to stay in Lambagh as long as she wishes."

He had reached the door, and with nothing further said on either side he walked out, his old servant following him. The door closed, and then even the sound of the tabla grew faint, for the drummer had followed the Raja.

Ismail Mohammed, left standing in the middle of the room, his face engorged with rage, flung himself down with an explosive curse.

"Old fool!"

Dil Bahadur turned his head to look at him, but said nothing. Jiwan Khan shook his head.

"Not, I think, a fool. Old, yes, and therefore perhaps worthy of respect? Also, there is another small matter. I have heard that he was generous to you when you came seeking help some few years ago?"

"You speak of the time when the Ruler of Lambagh took it into his hands to drive me from Pakodi State?"

Ismail Mohammed's eyes had suddenly the green glare of a cornered beast. Jiwan Khan looked at him, his body tightening with anger.

"My father is Regent of Pakodi State, holding it for Pakodi's son. You, Nephew, were intriguing to take the guddee."

On his lips the word "Nephew" was

an insult. Jiwan continued, his voice cold and firm.

"Also, you were accepting gold from strange quarters. My father was right to order you away, and he did not have to ask for approval from the British in Delhi. You know that is true."

"'My father'! 'My father'!" Ismail Mohammed mimicked Jiwan Khan's voice. "How proudly you say 'My father'; but I have no father to stand behind me. I have made my own way. So I took gold! You would have done the same to save your state! Pakodi was mine by right of birth. Do you tell me that you would not have done the same? Ach, a fool's question that I ask, for you, being what you are, cannot answer, you have no understanding. I could have had Pakodi State and ruled it well, a strong ally of your father, if he had helped me to my rights."

"What rights?"

"You dare ask me that? I am the true born son of Pakodi's brother, and only a small thing stood between me and the guddee — only the matter of a few words spoken by a mullah over my mother's veiled head, only a bridegroom lifting her veil instead of a lover."

"Oh yes? And the small matter of a legal son born to Pakodi's wife?"

"An ailing child, holding on to life with his finger tips. Will he hold Pakodi state steady? Or will your father keep his regency, until the state, used to his rule, becomes the fourth state of Lambagh?"

"My father will do what is right and just. He is no ill-born hill thief!"

Jiwan Khan was near to losing his temper. Dil Bahadur who had been listening and watching now joined in the conversation.

"Let there be less talk of the Ruler of Lambagh. He has proved his right to the title he bears. He is Lord of the Hills. You, Ismail, forgot that title. You listened to wild voices, took a strange and dangerous friend. You have allowed a serpent to twine about your shoulders. Do you now feel the cold coils growing tight?"

"You speak in riddles, Dil Bahadur."

"Then let me speak plainly. You are a fool, Ismail Mohammed. You took tainted gold from a killer's hand."

"You speak to me thus? You who are also a bastard? You have had good fortune, Bastard of Lambagh, rich through the Ruler's favour, man with the Ruler's face. Have a care, Jiwan Khan, guard your back! Do you trust a man who comes from nowhere and climbs into such favour?"

Jiwan Khan began to rise, but Dil Bahadur put a staying hand on his arm.

"Leave it, Jiwan."

He spoke almost in a whisper, and Ismail Mohammed, lost in rage, appeared to have noticed nothing. His voice shaking with anger, he said, "With what you call tainted gold I could have taken the guddee in Pakodi. I could have bought it, and then made it secure. But I was driven out like a dog. So I came here. My mother is a woman of these parts. Oh yes, the Raja was generous. He gave me a place in his forces, let me have the freedom of his courts and was glad when I began to build up his army. Do I have to rub his feet with my hair in gratitude like a dancing girl for these favours?"

"I have seen no gratitude."

"No, Dil Bahadur, and you will not see any. I have made him an army, and now, when I ask for my reward, he gives me the stone of a refusal. I tell you again, he is an old fool. He is beyond ruling. He needs an heir. You know what kind of wolves wait round a rich state when the ruler is old and has no heir." He paused, glaring at them, and there was authentic pain in his voice as he said, "You both saw me spurned. But I tell you, he is wrong. She feels a spark for me, that girl, and it could so easily be fanned into flame. You saw. She could not stab me, though the poisoned knife was in her hand. She could not! Aha, Amara, creature of fire and honey, virgin although widow . . . that girl Amara! Her name means immortal; they called her this when she took the Moslem faith and was married to Pakodi. An old man, and *she* a child!"

"She bore a son. She is no virgin."

"Yes, she bore a son! How Ali of Pakodi ever managed to break the hymen and impregnate her, Allah knows. He was old and finished when he took her to his bed, and she was a green bud; the

331

marriage was arranged and she obeyed. No question of choice! She was in her mother's hands, a child I tell you. Pakodi was a man of great wealth. Amara was sold for gold that they did not need."

"As was your honour." Dil Bahadur might not have spoken. Ismail Mohammed had forgotten his companions. He lifted his goblet, and drank deeply, draining it. "She knows nothing of love. A flower, a rose of fire, to be kept for one man, treasured, loved — "

"So you keep her a prisoner, poison her servants, try to kill her child — is this an endearing wooing?"

"Oho, Dil Bahadur!" Ismail Mohammed had heard what he said this time, and turned to face him. "Have you a better way of wooing? And you, Jiwan Khan, still unmarried, with your father's state to offer as a bride price? Ah! No doubt this is what the old fool wants, calling you here to escort her back to the comforts of your Lambagh Palace! No doubt he hopes that on the journey you and she may come to some agreement — no doubt that is why he sends letters in haste to your father — "

"And you were afraid of the letters that he sent and so you killed as many of the messengers as you could? But one got through your net of murder, Ismail . . . "

Ismail Mohammed's rage left him suddenly.

"I have killed no messengers, Dil Bahadur. Oh, I have heard the tales of the men and the horses who vanished and the message-carrying pigeons who fell dead — but I know nothing of this. I have had no hand in it. I swear this."

Dil Bahadur leaned to look into his face.

"You swear — is your oath one that binds? I find your words hard to trust."

"I swear it. I swear on Amara's life. Do you believe me now?"

"On that oath, yes. And the matter of the poisonings?"

"Again I swear on the life that is dearer to me than my own, on Amara's life, that I have never tried to harm the boy, or any member of the family, or her household. Am I a fool? There is no need for me to poison the boy. He will die soon enough; I hear he is very frail. But I would never try to help him on his way. Poison is not my weapon."

"Then," said Dil Bahadur, "let me ask you another question. Swear this to me, Ismail Mohammed, on that same precious life. Swear that you do not know who is bringing death and terror to this valley. Can you swear that oath on Amara's life?"

Ismail Mohammed did not answer. There was a silence in the ornate, warmly glowing room.

Into that charged silence crept a sound from outside. The gentle ringing of little bells, as soft as a fall of summer rain, muted by the closed door. Jiwan Khan heard, and turned his head. Dil Bahadur and Ismail Mohammed had not heard, each thinking about what the other had just said. They did not know, as Jiwan Khan did, that the little dancer had walked past the door; but going where? He was still holding his goblet but he did not drink. He looked into the dark wine and saw, small and perfect, the girl's face and as he looked, the pictured mouth moved and seemed to form the words, "Come soon . . . "

With an effort he pulled his thoughts back to the room, and the other two in it. Dil Bahadur was watching Ismail Mohammed like a tiger watching its prey. Presently he said quietly, "Well? Do you swear me that oath?" Ismail Mohammed lifted his head and looked up.

"This I cannot swear on her life. It does not concern her."

"No. You could not swear that oath for you would be forsworn. Now let us speak of the fears that are moving in your mind."

He leaned towards Ismail Mohammed and in a low voice began to question him. Why had he come back so suddenly from his journey into the mountains, the journey to the high passes and the plateau where the thoroughbred mares he had bought from Khokund waited? Ismail Mohammed turned to him, his hand feeling for his dagger.

"What do you know of the plateau and my mares? Are you a spy, Dil Bahadur?"

"Never mind what I know. Tell me the truth. What rumour did you hear that made you come racing back, a full

335

two weeks before you were due, leaving the mares to be brought down over those terrible paths by your men, without your watchful eyes making sure they travelled safely — those precious mares! What did you hear, Ismail?" Ismail did not answer and the silence in the room was cold and tense. Dil Bahadur sighed and stood up.

"It grows late. I will ask you again tomorrow, Ismail Mohammed. Perhaps night thoughts will bring counsel. Shall we ride tomorrow morning? Yes? Then I wish you good night and clear thinking." Jiwan Khan did not speak to Ismail Mohammed. He could think of nothing civil to say. In any case, the man did not seem to see them go, sitting lost in thought among his brocaded splendours.

Outside the door, two men waited with lanterns. The old man who had waited on Jiwan while he was dressing and the man called Alam Beg.

The night wind was blowing, whipping their robes about them and speaking coldly of the coming winter and the falling snow that would soon block the passes leading out of Jungdah valley. The splendour had been left behind the closed door. Looking about him in the lantern's flickering light, Jiwan Khan saw a ruined court with the black sky for a roof. He turned to Dil Bahadur and asked if they would be able to discuss events before they slept. With no hesitation in his voice, Dil Bahadur answered, "No. Not now. Your man will show you the way to your quarters. I will come early in the morning."

Jiwan Khan nodded, and they parted, walking away from each other briskly, the lanterns throwing their shadows darkly behind them as the servants led the way.

Jiwan Khan knew that he should be distressed that the serious happenings of the day were not to be discussed, nor any plans made until the morning. There was another thing that should be distressing him, he supposed. There was no doubt in his mind about where Dil Bahadur was going to spend the night. He recalled the flame in the velvet eyes of the Begum as they rested on Dil Bahadur. Somewhere there was an anxious query, a nagging sense of worry, but he forced it away.

His step was light and he was full of wild expectation that made him hurry, so that he almost overtook the old man lighting his way to his quarters. "Hurry!" said Jiwan Khan's heart, and he thought he heard music, a song, a faint echoing song. "Come soon, my love . . . "

The lantern steadied, the servant had stopped. Jiwan Khan drew a deep breath, and stepping forward, opened the door himself.

The room was quite empty.

22

SO much for an overheated imagination, and a dancer's promises, thought Jiwan Khan watching the old servant turning up the lamps and readying the bed. When the man had gone Jiwan Khan stood at the barred window looking out into the windy, star-scattered darkness. He could see nothing but the girl's face.

He wondered at the intensity of his feelings. There had been many girls, but this one had seemed to touch something in him that had never been touched before. As she had danced he had felt that in spite of the others in the room she was dancing for him alone. He had seen her for the first time that evening, and yet felt that he knew her, had known her all his life.

Ridiculous. Jiwan turned away from the window. What was wrong with him! A dancer from the camel caravan, a powindah woman. In daylight her clothes would be shoddy with tinsel, her face painted and common. And somewhere, no doubt, she was laughing at him and his expectations. He knew that his eyes must have shown his interest.

He put his hand up to start unhooking the high collar of his robe, and something, a movement so slight that it could have been a shadow thrown by a lamp, caught his eyes. He turned quickly, and saw a figure, out of the lamplight, standing in the dressing room door. His heart hurried its beat and he stepped forward, smiling.

At three paces the smell hit him. Unforgettable, nauseating, impossible. He stood where he was, knowing exactly who was waiting for him. What had the boy called her? Yes, he remembered.

"Devi?"

He heard a sound that could have been a gasp or a smothered laugh. Then she moved forward, lank hair, scarred face and stink, her one eye as bright as the eye of a bird.

"You remembered my name, Lord. Indeed, I am honoured. But you seem surprised. Were you expecting someone else? Did the dancer not say the words 'a rose of gold'? We thought the word 'rose' would give you warning."

Jiwan Khan cursed himself. How foolish he had been, spinning wild hopes into the words of a dancer, paid to pass a message.

"The rose of gold. Yes. Give me your message."

"It is a message from the woman they call the Pahareen. She wishes to speak with Dil Bahadur. Your man, Rabindra, would have given it to him, but it is difficult to reach Dil Bahadur. Tonight — "

"What is the message? I will get it to him somehow."

"He must be ready for one who will tell him that the woman is waiting to see him — and where he must go. An opportunity will be made to speak with him, but he must be ready. That is all, Lord."

Something in the cadence of her voice made him look at the filthy little figure before him. Mentally he put the little dancer in her place, the dancer with her flowing dark hair, her perfect face,

341

her sparkling, promising green eyes. Eyes as bright and as green as emeralds. He stared into the single eye of the girl in front of him. His gaze grew interested, and then fixed.

The girl turned away, drawing her head cloth more closely over her face.

"I go, Lord. You will warn the other nawab — "

Swiftly though she moved, Jiwan was faster. His hand gripped her arm and swung her round to face him. "Wait you — there is something — I have some questions I must ask — "

For once he did not notice her odour. He pulled her, though she was resisting, over towards one of the lamps and held her there, looking at what he could see of her face. Then he picked up one of her hands and still holding her firmly, looked at the long-fingered little hand with its perfect nails and clean palm. He said nothing in answer to her frightened questions. His face grim, he lifted her and carried her into the bathroom. There he took off her head cloth and studied her dirt encrusted face. Then, keeping his grip on her arm, he went over to the outer door and bolted it, and turned the key in the lock, and took the big brass key into his hand.

"Now, young woman. There is water and soap, and scented oils. Will you bathe, or shall I do it for you?"

"Lord! I do not bathe! Let me go, I must get back to the village before dawn, or I will be seen — "

"It lacks several hours to dawn. I have a mind to spend a little time with you. Well — will you bathe, or do I take these filthy rags and clean you myself? You have the choice."

She turned her head aside, repeating that she did not bathe, that at this time of year it was death to bathe the body. Before she had finished speaking, he put out his hands and tore the ragged robe she was wearing from neck to the ground. She made no move as it fell away, leaving her naked, but stood in front of him with her face turned away. With a set face he put his hands out, lifted her into the bathing place, and picking up a bowl, began to pour water over her head and shoulders, without saying another word. It was when he picked up the flagon of soft soap that she capitulated. She took the soap and said, her voice very low, "I will wash, Lord. Only — is there clothing for me?"

Jiwan nodded, and having checked that the door that led out of the bathroom was locked and bolted, he left her, his eyes filled with the vision of a body so delicately beautiful that her travesty of a face was a crime. He went to a chest and found a clean robe, and placed it on the step of the bathroom and then took up station in the bedroom listening to the sound of splashing water. When the splashing stopped, he unhooked his collar and took off his robe and stood by the window in shirt and trousers.

The girl came and stood in the door of the dressing room, looking at him. She did not show either fear or embarrassment. Her long hair fell dripping to below her shoulders, his clean robe swallowed her from neck to feet, lying in folds on the floor.

She was very small, very beautiful, and extremely familiar to him. She stood, the little dancer, with her perfect body and her perfect face, and looked at him out of tilted green eyes.

Jiwan Khan sighed and walked over to her. Very gently he took her face in his hands and studied it. Under his gaze she closed her eyes. He took up a strand of her hair that fronded like water weed on the shoulders of his robe. He left her and going through into the dressing room came back with a towel. He made her sit on the divan and began to rub her hair dry. Presently she took the towel from him and wrapped her hair in it, twisting it into a turban that left the pure lines of her face bare.

"Tell me how, and why, Devi."

"How is easy. Rotten eggs, oil from cooking pots, urine of goats, and soot and unwashed clothing." He shuddered. "All right. That is the smell. Now, the scar and your eye . . . "

"Chicken skin, and egg white, and ashes — and other things . . . "

"And why?"

"I do not think that I can tell you why. You are not a woman."

"No. I am not a woman. But I think I can guess why. If you did not hide all this — this beauty I see now with so much pleasure, you would have been raped. Yes?"

"Yes, Lord." She spoke seriously, and her eyes had a considering look in them as she raised them to study his face. He saw her hand gripping a corner of a cushion. The knuckles of that hand were white.

"Are you asking yourself if you should replace your chicken skin? And all the other delicacies? Be at peace, Devi. I have never raped a woman and do not intend to begin tonight." Her tongue, pointed like a cat's tongue, moistened her lips. She bowed her head, looking down at her hands, and he reached over and took one, spreading it out on his palm.

"You forgot your hands tonight, Devi. I saw them when you danced, your hands and your green eyes. You have been lucky. A discerning man could see beauty through all your disguise."

"And smell it?"

"Yes, well, that was a good barrier. But are the local soldiery so particular?"

"I do not have to fear the soldiery. The trouble for the women of the village came when the men from the plains, the men

346

dressed in silk and brocades, came up. It was then that we found that they prefer sweet perfumes and rich dresses, and fear leprosy. So we thought of this. I can go where I like when I am a leper."

"But you came in tonight as a dancer. How?"

"With the camel caravan. The Pahareen helped me. She has helped many of us, and managed to get many of us safely away. Today she brought me to the Palace and sold my time, saying I was a dancer from Madore. The street of the harlots in Madore has many such as I am — "

"Such as you are not. Tell me no lies, Devi. You have lived here, not in Madore. I know the street of the harlots well. You are a woman of the North. I saw a princess once in Panchghar who looked like you. She was not young, but you have her bearing and her clear voice. She was the sister of the Khan of Panchghar. She was very beautiful. I was a small boy, but I have never forgotten her. Tell me who you are, Devi . . . "

"Does it matter? I am Devi. Is that not enough? You were expecting a dancer tonight. Well, I am here."

"Very well. You are Devi. That is enough indeed. If you came from the street of the harlots in Madore it would still be enough and more."

"Because another, a woman who has never died in the memory of men, came from Madore?"

"The Rose? The beautiful Muna? I never saw her but she remains a story told round the fires, a song in the mind, Muna. But that is not why it would have been enough . . . "

"Then why?"

"Because you are you. You are also a song in my mind, one I will not have to forget. I will learn the song that is you."

"Learn, and sing, and forget."

"No. Learn and remember and find new words to sing every day."

He spoke very quietly, his eyes steady on her face, and she was silent then, looking up to meet his gaze. Her towel turban had slipped off and her dark hair tangled about her shoulders as it dried. He got up and found a comb and gave it to her and then returned to a seat by the window, a little way from her. She combed her hair, and he watched her as if he memorised every graceful movement, every curve of her arm and turn of her shining head. Presently he said, "What clothes can I find for you?"

"What clothes? Why, before dawn I must put on my old robe and my leprosy . . . " Her voice petered out under his steady blue gaze.

"Child of Beauty, do not speak of foolishness. You will never put on those unspeakable rags again. You are not returning to the village as Devi the one-eyed. To put yourself in danger would be to put me in danger. Now be quiet while I think."

She sat obedient, watching him, the comb forgotten in her hand. Presently he rose and went to the door and, opening it, called out. As he had guessed, the old servant was there and came at once. He heard his orders and went hurrying away. Jiwan Khan came back into the room. The girl had put up her hair into a knot on top of her head. Jiwan Khan took a goblet and poured it full of wine

349

and drank some of it. Then he sat down beside her.

"Will you drink with me, Devi?"

She took the goblet, drank, and gave it back to him.

"What did you say to the guard?"

"The guard? I saw no guard. They have given me a servant. I told him that I wanted several kinds of clothing for my girl, that what she had was not good enough."

She smiled a small, secret smile. "What did he say?"

"He said nothing. What should he say? I gave him an order, he is now doing what I told him. But I do not know where he will get women's clothing here." His eyes measured her thoughtfully, and she moved restlessly, turning her eyes down and flushing.

"Well, one thing is sure," said Jiwan Khan cheerfully, "you cannot wear the Begum's clothes. They would be a great deal too large for you."

There was a scratching at the door. When Jiwan Khan opened it, Saida, the Begum's woman, stood there with an armful of clothing. She came in and looked quickly at the girl, who stood up and walked into the dressing room, Saida following her. Jiwan Khan smiled to himself. The girl had walked straight backed, small but dignified. Her graceful slenderness was, to him, breath-takingly attractive. He knew already at least two things about her. One was that she certainly did not come from the street of the harlots in Madore. That old battle-axe of a woman, Saida, would not have followed to assist her to dress if she had been a powindah or a common whore. She was neither a whore, nor was she one of the trained temple dancers. Her dancing had been charming but amateur.

The other thing he knew with a clear, warm sureness was that he had at last found the girl with whom he would spend his life.

He could hear the soft murmur of voices in the next room, and a scent, familiar and charming, jasmine and rosewater and sandalwood oil, the smell of his mother's dressing room, came into the room. Then the girl came and stood in the doorway for a moment, as if she knew that she was stepping into a new life. She hesitated, her head half turned away from him. This touched him greatly when he thought of the dangers in which she had lived for so long — that she should stop, half afraid still of what might be going to happen to her, not knowing yet that he would gladly give his life to keep her safe.

She wore a warm woollen tunic of scarlet, over dark green trousers. Her hair was drawn tightly back and plaited to fall from the top of her head to below her waist, in a plait as thick as his wrist. She carried a scarlet scarf for her head, and she glowed and burned with colour. Jiwan Khan, that polished and detached young man, stood looking at her, unable to think of anything to say except words that he knew he must not say yet. He went forward to take the girl's hand and lead her fully into the room. He saw with enchanted surprise that she was smiling at him and that when she smiled she had dimples, and her eyes almost closed. She was perfection for him, perfection and beauty. He remembered her voice from when she was disguised, otherwise he would not have been able to believe that it was the same girl. Then the sense of what she was saying hit him.

"I am riding with you this morning?" asked the clear, charming voice.

Jiwan Khan came smartly back from his dreaming regard of her.

"Oh no, Lady, you are not. From now on, until we leave this cursed Palace, you stay guarded in this room. You eat or drink nothing that has not been tasted in front of you, and you only move from this room with a trusted guard at your side. Usually it will be me. Understood?"

"Bathing? Dressing? Other necessary things?"

"Do not be foolish. Of course you will have privacy for those things. Saida will be here with you."

"Saida will not be here. She will be with her Begum."

"Then she will bring another woman to be your maid."

"I see. So the maid and I play tric-trac in this room until the night of the full moon perhaps? Or when *do* we leave? And when the time comes to go, what then?"

"We leave. All of us."

"I see, and in the meantime, all the Palace knows by now, I imagine, that you have a girl in here — a girl from the caravan — and that you keep her locked in, a love bird for your pleasure. They will not expect you to go riding if the girl pleases you so much that you will not let her go; they will expect you to be here. One of my uncles had a girl in his quarters for ten days and she could not walk at the end of it, and he was drinking brandy and beaten eggs to get his strength back — what are you doing?"

"Getting ready to ride," said Jiwan austerely. "You may not have noticed it, but it is dawn."

"You were not listening to me . . . "

"I do not wish to hear stories about your uncles. I assure you that no hand will be laid on you, and that you *will* be able to walk when we leave here. So — enough. Sit, rest, and do whatever you like."

A furious and inelegant expletive came from the girl's beautiful mouth.

Jiwan Khan raised his eyebrows.

"Well! What delightful language. Where did you learn those words? From your uncles?"

"From the syces when I was a child, where else. Jiwan Khan, do not be foolish. If I ride with you today I can still get a message to the village. The heir must be taken from the village today. The Pahareen is the only one who can arrange it. All you have to do is to say that you want me with you . . ."

"I want you with me," said Jiwan Khan with deep feeling and was rewarded by her quick blush and upward look. All the laughter and teasing had gone from his face.

"I *must* go out, Lord. Do not stop me. We have come so far without much help, or hope. Now at a time when we have help at last, and hope of getting all the family safely away, do not, through lack of understanding, spoil our enterprise."

"I am not your gaoler, of course I cannot stop you going. But — there is one thing that I must say to you." His eyes steady on hers, he reached to take her hand.

"Your name is not Devi. You are no

dancer of the streets. Tell me who you are . . . "

"My name is Roshanara. I am the younger daughter of the Khan of Panchghar . . . "

"Jan Mohammed of Panchghar. I know him well. I have met him on the polo field often. What a jewel he has been hiding in his mountains. Why did he not send to my father and mother and speak of his daughter as a suitable wife?"

"A wife for whom, Lord?"

"My father only has one son, Roshanara Begum."

"Yes, it is known. We have heard of Jiwan Khan Bahadur. It is said that your heart is hard to touch, that you prefer to play polo or fight, or entertain dancers — "

"Play polo, yes. Fight? Yes, when necessary. But as to entertaining dancers — never before tonight did I spend so long with a dancer — who is indeed, not a dancer. Roshanara — Light of the Heart — take care. Let nothing ill befall you, for my life lives in you — remember that. My heart is touched, at last . . . "

Enchanted they stood, looking into

each other's eyes, unable to speak, held in a ring of amazed delight in each other, each touched for the first time by a love that had already become timeless.

Dil Bahadur's knock on the door broke the spell, but Jiwan Khan had already raised Roshanara's hand to his mouth and kissed it before he turned to the opening door.

23

DIL BAHADUR, when he had parted from Jiwan Khan, had not gone to the women's quarters, the Bibikhana. He went, walking swiftly, to the quarters allotted to the men of Lambagh. The door was guarded by his own men, three of them outside, and to his alarm, two guarding the door inside the court. Dil Bahadur raised his eyebrows at Osman, who came up, still fully dressed and armed, his rifle slung across his back.

"Has anything happened?" Dil Bahadur asked.

"Nothing of great import, and yet I am not at peace. We had visitors, eight dancing boys and two musicians. Sent by the Nephew to entertain us, *they* said. Painted and scented and rustling with silks like a Raja's favourite whore. But their eyes were set on the inner door and the stable court, and they were all armed with daggers — and the daggers were not playthings, nor ornaments."

"So?"

"So I thanked them for their courtesy but said that our men were tired and needed sleep more than a nautch, and told them to come and dance for us another night. They would not go and they were all over the place like sugar ants, asking questions, ogling the men, and edging their way towards the horses. I used force and threw them out."

"You did well. Be on your guard. I do not think the Nephew sent these people." Dil Bahadur left Osman and climbed the stair to the watch tower, while Alam Beg leaned against the wall at the foot of the stairs.

The night wind blew strongly but Dil Bahadur did not feel its chill. He had a rendezvous to keep and in the privacy of the little tower he sought for strength to face what lay ahead. He chose and discarded one sentence after another, knowing there was no easy way of doing what he was going to do.

He went down into the courtyard, spoke to Osman, and then left, Alam Beg going ahead of him, leading the way with no order given, until his lantern threw its light on the door of the Begum's guarded court.

The guard stood back and Dil Bahadur walked past the whispering fountain and the stone figure of the goddess and entered the room. The Begum rose from among her piled cushions to meet him.

He had armed himself as well as he could against this meeting, had come to it like a man coming to a battlefield, but even so it was hard. She would have come into his arms but that they were not stretched out to welcome her. They stood and looked at each other, suddenly adversaries in a room that had waited for a lovers' meeting.

When she spoke, he listened to her as if he had not heard her voice for a long time.

"Were you overcome with drink tonight, Dil Bahadur?"

"No."

"To me, you appeared to be far gone in drink, the way you spoke, the things you said . . . "

"I was attempting to stop you bringing Allah knows what disasters down on us all. I warned you to have a care of Ismail Mohammed, that he loves you to madness, and has the jealousy that goes with such a love. You cannot taunt Ismail Mohammed with safety."

"So you spoke of a girl in Faridkote, hard to woo, and sweeter than honey; no doubt you discovered that in the end."

"There have been many girls."

"It is seen. Then women were likened to birds and horses — delightful. You sounded like an old bannia, telling of his successes in a bazaar brothel."

"What I said at least gave you the opportunity to leave his banquet safely. Now I have more to say. You will listen, Amara." He heard her draw in her breath sharply, but when she spoke her voice was perfectly steady.

"Very well, if we are going to talk the night away, at least let us sit in comfort." She sank down with boneless grace, her unbound hair falling about her shoulders, her soft robe explicit about her body. Dil Bahadur turned and walked away, and stood beside the window. Looking at him, the Begum grew afraid. There was more here than she had thought, some decision had been made, a decision that she feared. She almost cried out to him, almost went over to put her arms about him, longing for the warmth of response that she ached for. But he stood there like a stranger, as if they had never burned a night away in the joyous fires of passion shared with love. Her heart began to beat as if she had been running, as her fear mounted at his first words.

"I must speak of duty, Amara, and the hardships of being, as you are, a member of a princely family. Because you are royal, you are fettered. You cannot choose your life as other, lesser women can, looking here and there for a lover or a husband, influencing your family as I know that girls do. You have no choice. You, married as a child to Pakodi."

Oh, no, no! She wanted to cry out to him, to tell him that she only knew one thing, her lifelong love for him. She wanted to say that she could not listen to anything because of the sound of words that were beating in her heart, the words she wanted him to say. But she was silent, her smooth beautiful face quite without any expression, her eyes watching him.

"I will speak now of Ismail Mohammed. He is a ruthless man, he has fought all his life for power and riches and a position in the world. Life has shown him very little compassion and so he has been hard and cruel himself."

"My father? Did he not show him kindness? And how was he repaid?" She spoke suddenly, with anger she could not control, and then, breathless with the rush of feeling, stopped.

"Your father showed him the same kindness one would show to a homeless dog. He let him come in, and gave him food and a place to sleep. He was not even called by his name. All his life he has been called the 'Nephew' and the title was meant to sound like an insult."

"And so it was right that he took my father's state in return for food and a place to sleep?"

"Your father made no effort to stop him, even in the days when he could have done so. He was too old, and too grieved by Pakodi's death, to do

363

anything. Also — Ismail Mohammed was building the State Forces into a useful army. Your father saw this. Ismail Mohammed took his opportunities when he saw that your father was not going to stop him. Nor was he stopped when he began to recruit young men — and not all of them were reluctant to go with him: he is a leader of men. The villagers came complaining that the young men were being kidnapped into the army. Your father heard them, but seeing how well Ismail Mohammed handled them, he did nothing. And the old men who advised your father did nothing to stop Ismail Mohammed either. In fact, Ismail Mohammed took these young men and gave them a better life, feeding them as they had never been fed before, training them — and making them into a force to be proud of."

"A force to be proud of? An army of fighting animals killing for pay!"

"They are soldiers and they fight and kill. If you like to call your own hill men animals, well, then, that is your pleasure."

"And the women raped and the old

men killed, and the empty houses and barren fields?"

"Yes. But these things are nothing to do with your forces. This is where both your father and Ismail Mohammed did wrong. Ismail Mohammed needed money. He came to your father to ask for payment for the army, and your father sent him away, refusing him. That was foolish. Your father is not a poor man. Then Ismail Mohammed made a terrible mistake. He accepted an offer from the Raja of Sagpur, and took money from him, and allowed the Raja's servants to come in here freely. They are the rapists and the killers. The Raja of Sagpur is an evil man: he will have to be defeated here, and his people will have to be driven out. But I do not know if Ismail Mohammed is strong enough yet. Also — he needs to be made to feel of importance, to know that he has a reason for fighting against these people. He does not have to fight them. He could now take his army out of here, and take employment with the rulers of the far northern states. They are already asking for his services. It would be easy for him. He must be shown that he is needed here — "

He ceased speaking, but only as if he was searching for the right words to tell her something. Watching him she grew as cold as if she was outside in the darkness and the wind instead of in her warm, lamp-lit room. She strove for courage and said, "You forget, Dil Bahadur. What of the deaths of my servants from poison? The poisoned sweets put within reach of my son? What of that?"

"Sagpurna's servants, by his order. Your son was to die to clear the way to two thrones — the guddee of Jungdah, and of Pakodi. Your father was to be poisoned too. You — "

"Yes — what of me? I have been a prisoner, here in my own home, afraid to go out, drugging my child to keep him safely within these walls — what of me?"

"You cannot think of a reason for your captivity? I think you must know of your danger, not from Ismail Mohammed, but from another source, Sagpurna's men. You do know. You told me that Ismail Mohammed would not harm you — remember that? Amara, during the long years of your widowhood here, as you grew from being a child widow into full womanhood, did you not find Ismail Mohammed's admiration, his avowed love, of value? He is a fine looking man. Did he not have sometimes a glance or a word that seemed to give him hope?"

"Never!" But she could not look at him as she spoke, heat rising in her cheeks. He let his glance linger on her down cast face before he said quietly, "Ah, Amara! Well, it is nothing for you to be ashamed about. You have great beauty and beauty demands its due in admiration. Also you must have been lonely here, after the busy courts of Pakodi's Palace in Bombay."

"Lonely? Nay, Lord, how could I be lonely? I was waiting, with certainty, for the day that I knew would come. I knew you would come to me. When my father tried to send me away, I would not go, I kept my son here, saying that his health would not allow him to travel. This is my shame, that I could risk his life and keep him here, because it kept me here.

I knew you would come to me."

"You also knew that I had a wife, and a son — "

"Did you remember them when you took me in love the other night? Did her face come between us; was it her body you entered? Nay. It was mine, and you thought of no one else. Ah, heart's love, do not frown at me. I do not ask to possess you. I am a woman of these hills, we do not own our husbands, they own us. I am your woman; all I ask is to be honoured with your love when it is your wish to hold me. Do not remove yourself from me! Lord of my life, I know of the other one, the English girl. But I was before her! You can help me hold Jungdah, and let my father spend his last days in peace. Come and live here, bring that other if you must, the white woman, live with her in daylight, I will be content to be your second wife and have a smaller share in your life. Love me too, Lord, give me joy and a little of your company. I have waited so long — "

The husky voice, pleading, desperate, broke on a sob and was at last silent.

Dil Bahadur did not turn from where

368

he stood at the window, looking out at the dark night outside. He listened to her, and did not need to see her. She took shape in his mind's eye. Beautiful, moving him to passion with her voice alone, a woman trained as his mother had been trained, to please a man, living only in her husband's love, content with belonging to her husband, asking nothing more than to please him.

He knew that she fitted into his world of hills and valleys, deserts and disasters, dust, gods, devils, flowers and serpents. India. Part of him and part of her. She fitted the life he loved. She would bring him total bodily response, and a mind that would mould itself into anything he wished. There would be no conflicts in his bedroom and no desertions. His first physical love. He knew the wild passion that was waiting behind him, and his body throbbed and ached to take what was so freely offered. Why not?

He turned swiftly, his arguments forgotten — and the speed of his movement shook the chain round his neck free, sending it swinging forward, weighted by the emerald ring hanging from it. He did not see Amara's exultant face: he saw the green fire of the Peacock Ring.

His mother's gift to him; its twin was on Laura's hand. Laura! She seemed so unreal in that moment that it shocked him. Laura, sweet white rose of his heart, and James, his son. They had receded like shadows, like dreams drifting away before they could be properly remembered on waking. Time was running the wrong way for them. With every moment that he spent with Amara, he was losing his identity as Laura's lover, as Laura's husband. He was being taken into another life, a life he might have had if he had never met and married Laura. India was laying her hand on his heart and claiming it for her own. India, his mother's country.

But it was his mother's ring, her gift to him, that now pulled him out of the dream that had been enfolding him.

Laura was clear now in his mind, clearer than the beautiful creature standing before him, her body outlined and emphasised by her thin robe.

The Begum was as much to him then

as any of the girls he had taken before he married Laura. As much, and as little.

Amara looked at him, met the look in his eyes and stood waiting like a sacrifice for the sword to fall.

"You are no junior wife, Amara. For no man, least of all for me. I cannot take another woman. All of my love of heart and mind and body — "

Under her straight, sad look, he hesitated and then nodded.

"Yes, Amara. In spite of our night together in which I had great pleasure, I can still tell you that it is my wife who enthralls my body, and my mind. I took you because I recalled a night in a garden. What man forgets his first girl? And what man could forget you? But there is nothing in my life for you, and you are far from being a woman who would remain content to take second place, living from one visit of your husband every few days — then weeks, then months, with no position and little honour. Listen to your mind, Amara, and you will know that I speak the truth. I think your father has seen this for a long time. To hold Jungdah you must take Ismail Mohammed. You can make him break with Sagpurna. You can, through him, restore this derelict valley to what it was before. You will have children and a husband and you will, I swear to you Amara, be happy."

"And what of Atlar Khan? If I bear Ismail Mohammed a son, where will Atlar Khan go?"

"Where he will be going in the next few months. To England first, where doctors will cure him of the drug addiction he has contracted here. Then to a school. Then, some years later, back to Pakodi, where he will learn to rule his state. It will be hard for you to part with him for so long, and very hard for him, but his mind and his heart and his courage are strong. He will be a fine man, a son any father would be proud of."

"*Any* father?" The tawny velvet of her eyes had no flame in them now.

"A son any man would be proud to own. Ali of Pakodi would have had great pride in him."

She looked away from him, for her eyes were full of tears, and said softly, "Yes. Ali would have been happy to have such

372

a son born to his name."

Dil Bahadur waited for a minute, and then said, "Your next son will be Ruler of Jungdah, in due time. Your father's blood will not be lost. Be content, Amara. Ismail Mohammed, with your presence in his home, will be a different man. You will be happy, be sure of that. In a little while you will find happiness."

He turned away from her and walked to the door. She saw that all he felt was an eagerness to be gone, to be done with a difficult situation, to go out and get on with his life.

Behind her was the open door of her bedroom, and the big bed, and like shadows in her mind she saw all the long nights to come. So many nights, when moonlight would come into that room and the caged bulbul would wake and sing and she would lie alone. For how long? How long before her body ceased to burn and shrivelled instead, like a peach too long on the tree? These thoughts were for later, these thoughts, and the answer to these questions. Now there was one thing she must do.

She stood up, and from some well of

courage she did not know she had, she found the ability to smile.

"Go laughing, Lord. I will remember you, Dil Bahadur, with pleasure, in spite of pain. We will meet again, but not like this." She paused, and her smile trembled and faded.

"Remember me, Lord? Remember me?"

How could she know that her words only reminded him of Laura, leaning in tears from her horse, saying, "Remember me, Robert, remember me . . . "

She could not know. She took comfort from the pain on his face, thinking it was parting from her that brought it there. How could she know?

He went quickly then, shutting the door behind him, and finding Saida in the windy courtyard he said, "Saida, go to the Begum. She needs you."

The old woman nodded, her eyes sad, and went into the room at once. He saw the door close on her frail figure, and, turning, left the fountain court, reaching his room as the pale light of a false dawn rose above the black peaks. What lay ahead of him now seemed easy after what he had lived through that night. He looked at the light on the mountains, and thought of Laura, wondering if she was thinking of him, and if she had decided after all to stay ... and as the light broadened he hurried to Jiwan Khan's room.

24

DIL BAHADUR entered the room saying, "Jiwan, we should go. Ismail Mohammed waits outside the walls with the horses . . . " He stopped, staring with astonishment as Jiwan led Roshanara forward.

"My brother, this is Roshanara, daughter of Jan Mohammed of Panchghar . . . "

Dil Bahadur had recognised the girl as the dancer of the night before, but what was she doing here? As he stared, she said softly, "Lord, you do not remember me? Three days since, I led you to the Bab-i-margh."

Dil Bahadur shook his head. "I do not recall anyone who looked like you — it was a girl called Devi who led me. And yet, I feel I know you."

"There is no time to explain now, Lord. Let us go — a message will be given to you."

Outside the walls, Ismail Mohammed waited with Alam Beg and the horses. Dil

Bahadur swung into the saddle and, as he did so, Alam Beg ran towards him.

"Lord! Wait! Your girth is loose."

Dil Bahadur had just heard the words when he felt his saddle turn under him, and kicking his feet free of the stirrups, he jumped down. The saddle fell, and Dil Bahadur caught the reins of his horse close under its jaw and held it steady. He looked down and saw that the strong webbing of the girth had been cut through. He looked at Alam Beg, saying quietly, "Speak, then."

"No treachery, Lord. I cut your girth. I could not speak with you last night, and had no way of getting close to you this morning. Now, while I change my saddle for yours, I will tell you the message. A woman waits for you beside the great rock that marks the entrance to the Place of the Dead. She is known to you, this woman: she is called the Pahareen. You must go alone."

Dil Bahadur looked at Alam Beg and then, nodding his agreement, mounted again. He saw that the girl was having trouble with her horse and that both Jiwan Khan and Ismail Mohammed were trying to assist her. He kicked his animal into a canter that became a gallop and was quickly well ahead of the others and out of their sight.

The path that led to the Place of the Dead was wider, and this aided his speed, but before he reached the great rock that guarded the entrance to that ghastly place, his horse became almost impossible to control, and he knew that he was closer to his rendezvous than he had thought. He dismounted and tethered his beast, and walked the rest of the way.

She stood beside the rocky path, her camel kneeling behind her. He remembered his last sight of her, standing almost alone in the dusky shadows outside a house in Safed.

Now, still alone, she waited for him again, and he thought suddenly that she carried solitude with her as she carried her tents and her cooking pots; in the brawling hurry of a market place she would still have silence and the air of loneliness about her.

He reached her, was beside her, and heard her remembered voice.

"May you never be tired, son of Muna!"

"May you live long, oh Woman of the Hills."

She smiled, her teeth very white against her sunburned face. It was over eight years since their last meeting, and nothing about her had changed. Robed in her black clothes, she stood as straight as a spear and looked at him out of eyes as grey as his own.

"Eh, a man among men, and the father of fine sons! You bring pleasure to a woman's eyes, Dil Bahadur. One day we will meet beside the blue lake in Lambagh and talk together in peace. But not now. Unless you listen to me now, and move fast, we will be fortunate if any of us see the waters of that blue lake again. Sagpurna is within three days ride of the Palace. Sagpurna, and an army."

He stood beside her, looking down into the barren valley and listened while she gave him her news, setting it out for him as lucidly as one of his own officers would have told it, with no words wasted.

She swept away all doubt about where

Sagpurna was, and what he was doing. He was already in the valley below the Bab-i-margh. Dil Bahadur had seen the army already. What he had not known was that Sagpurna was already with them. The villagers of those parts are all on their way to Dhalli. Dhalli was always a place of refuge in the old days, both the village and the Palace, and in the valley people's minds it was still a refuge. "They are simple trusting people, these valley dwellers. It was good that you sent those men to discover what was taking place. They warned the people."

She shrugged off Dil Bahadur's questions about the number of men Sagpurna had with him.

"But they were swarming like ants when I looked down the ridge and saw them," he protested.

"Yes, they swarm like ants. But they are mostly goondas, sweepings from the slums and streets of the southern towns. They are burning and looting the villages in their way, and Sagpurna finds this an entertainment and does nothing to stop them. He is riding up the valley very slowly, like an advancing conqueror, with a court of singers and silk clad dancing boys around him. Most will flee at the first sign of opposition. But he has some of his senior men with him and four of his personal guard, and *they* are not to be despised."

"If he has more than fifty experienced men with him, then indeed they are not to be despised. My men are good, none better, but they are only fifty — I have sent messages to Lambagh: the Ruler will send more men. I wish I knew for certain what evil Sagpurna intends. I know his main objective is to make mischief in the hills and upset the peace of these regions, but to bring a force here at this time of year! The passes will be closed in a matter of weeks. He stands to be trapped here; what big purpose has he got that he risks this?"

Dil Bahadur was thinking aloud, he had forgotten the woman at his side until she spoke.

"Ach, he is a fool. He has not even thought about the weather. He imagines all places to be alike — hot and steamy, like Sagpur. He has no sense, only evil desires. You know he owns the Jungdah

381

State Forces — he has bought the army for much gold. And Ismail Mohammed with it — so some say."

"Yes — so some say. Perhaps, up until a few days ago, this was true — but now — well, it is my thought that Ismail Mohammed is not so sure of the friendship of the southern Raja as he was — and the army will do as he wishes. They are all men of the hills."

"Who Ismail trusts and who he does not is of little matter compared to what I have to tell you now. Sagpurna wants Jiwan Khan."

"And no doubt he knows, through spies, that Jiwan Khan is here," said Dil Bahadur. "But what will that avail him? He must know that if anything happened to Jiwan Khan at his hands, he would lose his state — and his life too, make no mistake about that."

"A clean death, you think, for Jiwan Khan? Not so, son of Muna. That is not what Sagpurna wants. He wants the heir to Lambagh State alive. Alive and helpless. He plans to take Jiwan Khan, and then — they will drug him."

The plan that the Pahareen then

revealed to Dil Bahadur, speaking in a low voice as if the rocks around them might have ears and the eagle high above might carry news, was so awful that Dil Bahadur felt that he was caught in a nightmare, but a nightmare from which he would not wake. A nightmare that was true.

Jiwan Khan was to be given a strong drug. A week, perhaps less, and he would be unable to be without it. Under its influence he would become a creature, obeying anyone who kept him supplied with it. "A mindless fool," said the Pahareen bitterly. "Then rumours will go up to Delhi that there is trouble here in Jungdah; that Jiwan Khan has been sent by his father to help the old Raja, but that he is helpless and doing nothing, while the state falls to disaster . . . famine and disease stalk the hills . . . and they will, Sagpurna will see to that. The fields are already barren, thanks to the men he sent up here, the flocks are taken, the people are entering winter with little in their grain stores, and when the passes close it will be a long hungry winter. When the men from Delhi come, Jiwan

Khan will be here — in the Palace, sent by his father to help the Raja — and he will have done nothing. They will find a wreck of a man, certainly not a suitable heir for Lambagh State."

The Pahareen paused to draw breath and then continued her tale of treachery.

"They will find Jiwan Khan here, as I say, a debauched man — and it will not only be drugs. They will want to know what the Ruler of Lambagh means by sending such a son to Jungdah, to give aid. There will be those here who will answer these questions. Kassim Khan will be seen as a grasping ruler, bringing up troops, not to rescue his friend of Jungdah, but to take over the state — "

"Ah! Wait a minute. Kassim Khan, a grasping ruler! The British know him too well. They would laugh at that accusation."

"Son of Muna! Not all the British now ruling in Delhi are wise; and there will be Jiwan Khan, shaking and drooling, and almost senseless, and Jungdah in an extremity of famine and disease, and Lambagh troops come up to do what? To take Jiwan Khan back, of course, and give what help they can — you and I know that. But men from Delhi, who do not know everything? They will certainly put a Resident here, and they will say, rightly, that a drug addict cannot inherit the throne of three fine states such as Lambagh. Kassim Khan has not always been civil to the British, even if he has kept order for them in these hills and valleys. They do not all like and admire him."

The Pahareen was a woman who did not know fear, but watching Dil Bahadur's face, she was glad that she was not his enemy. Indeed, a change had come over the young man she remembered, the young man she had helped when he was trying to trap and kill one of Sagpurna's men. Then Dil Bahadur had been a young man of courage and daring, but without the edge of bitterness and hatred that makes a killer. She thought that the man she saw now would kill without thought and without remorse if anything he loved was touched. She waited a few moments, but knew she must make him understand the need for haste. She broke into his thoughts, calling his name, and he turned to her at once. "Yes?"

"Lord, have you a plan?"

"I had a plan, but Jiwan Khan refused to leave me, and my plan with him in danger is going to be much more difficult to carry out. But one thing I tell you, Woman of the Hills. I shall be dead before they touch Jiwan Khan."

"Listen then. I can take him out. I will take him before the others, alone. You know the rooms of the old Rani? I think you must — it is the place where you waited with Alam Beg. Take Jiwan Khan there. It will be made easy for you, the girl Roshanara will aid you. He will be taken out by a way we know. If he refuses, he will be given a drug — nay, son of Muna, it will not harm him! It is only to make him be quiet until we get him to a place of safety. Once he is out, I think you will be able to put your own plan to work. Does this please you, Lord?"

She saw his frowning indecision, and said quietly, "We have no time, son of Muna." Dil Bahadur flung up his hands. "Then, there is nothing else we can do.

It seems good to me. It would be better if you did not have to drug him, but whatever happens, you are right: he must be got out before Sagpurna comes. This girl — is she one of your girls?"

The Pahareen laughed. "That I should be so fortunate as to have her working the routes with me! She is worth her weight in gold. Nay, she is not one of us. She is the daughter of the Khan of Panchghar. She has risked her life to help several of the families of Jungdah, and some of their servants also."

"And now she has caught the heart of Jiwan in a net of love. At such a time!"

"Eh, well, it is good, Lord. She will persuade him to have sense, maybe."

"Maybe. But he has a faithful, stubborn heart, and looks on me as his brother. He is determined that he will not leave me in danger, and cannot be brought to see that his duty lies elsewhere. If this girl can bring him to sense — wah! It will be a wonderful thing. As for you, as always, we owe you too much to ever repay."

"You own me nothing, son of Muna.

As for the Ruler, I too come from Lambagh. Why else am I called Woman of the Hills? I too have taken the oath. My life for his and for those of his blood, now and always. Speak now, Lord, tell me of your plan."

Dil Bahadur hesitated, and she turned to meet his eyes. "Do you doubt me, son of Muna?"

"Never. But the enemies we face here are devils. If by some mischance you were taken — "

"I would never be taken. So do not fear that torture would loosen my tongue. Speak, Dil Bahadur."

Dil Bahadur thought to himself that it was easy to discount the power of torture until you were facing it. Then he looked again into the Pahareen's eyes and saw the strength and purpose of the woman clearly displayed. She was right. She would never be taken.

"Very well. I need your help. I must use tools that you will not care for, but they are all I have at hand. Ismail Mohammed and his trained soldiers are going to assist me in driving Sagpurna's people out of this valley for ever."

"Ismail Mohammed is the hireling of Sagpurna."

"I know that he was. But something has changed. He will come over to me. I am sure of it."

"You trust Ismail Mohammed?"

"Yes. I have a strong persuader."

She shook her head. "If you are paying him to change alliance, he can change again, against you — for more gold."

"There is something stronger than gold."

"What is stronger than gold for Ismail Mohammed?"

"Love."

"Love? I have not thought of love in connection with Ismail Mohammed . . . "

Dil Bahadur told her quickly about the scenes he had witnessed between the Begum and Ismail Mohammed. "He is mad for her, make no mistake. It is not only that he lusts after her, he loves her. He would die to keep her from harm. I am as sure of that as I am sure of my own heart."

"So . . . and the girl? Is she mad for him? I have heard that he is greatly feared and hated by all the family."

Dil Bahadur nodded, frowning. "Yes, it is true. But . . . I think there was a time, when out of loneliness she looked his way and saw him as a handsome man — she *is* very young."

"Indeed, that is true. But it was said, I remember that she had given her heart once before, and that she would look at no one else."

Dil Bahadur looked away from the eyes that seemed to say more than her words could. He said quickly, "She has been a widow too long."

"And if she turns her eyes on Ismail Mohammed, he will become your faithful henchman. Let this be so, Lord. It is a risk, but as you say, you must make use of what tools you can. How may I help you?"

"I need silk, and rich clothing. Can you do this? The sort of clothes that the men from the South wear. I need these things quickly." He forestalled her astonished questions by beginning to explain.

"The senior men of Sagpurna's following are all skilled horsemen. They play polo as we do, and I was told by our risaldar that they were asking if we would care to contend with them on the field on the far side of the village. There will be great interest in the game. The villagers will all come — indeed, they will be ordered to come. We will have music, of course, and the crowds will press close round the field. Among those crowding villagers there will be death waiting for each of the men of Sagpurna's team. But as each man falls, he remounts — or some silken figure remounts. Do you understand?"

The Pahareen nodded. "I understand, Lord, but it is a risk. Will you be playing?"

"Of course. And there is little risk if the crowd is thick enough, the band loud enough . . . And can these villagers ride?" he added. "For I have not enough men to leave it all to them alone."

"Some can ride. They will make shift to ride in any case. You will need drink also — and perhaps some powders to put in it. Men whose wits are scattered see nothing untoward."

For the first time Dil Bahadur looked doubtful.

"How can I persuade the Sagpur teams

to drink before play? I do not think they will do this."

"You are wrong. They drink heavily, these southerners, and will take the field partially drunk in any case. They play well, I must tell you that. Have you seen them?"

"Yes. The first time I left the Palace, on my way to stop Jiwan Khan, they were playing then. As you say, they play well."

The Pahareen took up her things and prepared to leave him. "I will be at the village end of the Maidan at sunset," she said. "I will have the things you require then. The drink I will send in by the usual route, but it will come to the guest court, and your men must not touch it. If you need me sooner, I am camped two kos along the river, where the path turns up towards the chicklet pass. I wish you good fortune, son of Muna. Now I go."

She hauled on the halter rope and the camel, stiff and complaining, unfolded itself and stood up. Dil Bahadur put out a detaining hand.

"And Jiwan Khan — when can you take him?"

"I told you. At any time you tell me. Tonight?"

Dil Bahadur thought of the arguments he was going to have with Jiwan Khan, and his spirit quailed.

"Tomorrow morning — at dawn. Is that possible?"

"It is well. But have a care of him. Bring him to the courts of the old Rani: let him sit there with Roshanara, she will keep him until I come. It would be better if he went there tonight — send me word if you wish that I come then. Otherwise I shall come for him at dawn."

She smiled at him, turned and was gone, as silent as the shadow of a cloud blown by the wind over the rocky path. In the silence that she left behind her he heard the drumming of horses' hoofs.

25

DIL BAHADUR had time to walk back to where he had left his horse and be found sitting at ease, watching two carrion crows swoop and swing above the rocks, before the others arrived. The escort reined up, and the three leaders dismounted, the girl swinging down from her saddle like a boy although Jiwan Khan was waiting to help her. Ismail Mohammed walked over to join Dil Bahadur.

"Dil Bahadur, that was a wild ride you gave us. Why did you leave us so suddenly? I was in fear for my horses when you set us that pace. You have a good beast there — bred in Lambagh?"

"Yes. We too breed good horses. This is a good beast as you say — but once I had a better steed." Dil Bahadur's voice was harsh as he thought of beautiful Shasti and his brutal end. Frowning, he turned away from Ismail Mohammed, saying, "I would speak with you. Let us go aside here, where only the rocks can hear our words."

"If you wish. But why this secrecy? Do you fear an enemy, Dil Bahadur? No one is your enemy here. You should perhaps fear the spirits that must haunt this place — we are near to the Place of the Dead."

"I do not fear an enemy, Ismail. But you have cause to fear one — and to fear for your life. You came here today of your own will, following me. Perhaps next time you will be brought, and will know nothing of the journey. Tell your escort to wait further back." His last words snapped like a whip. Ismail Mohammed was puzzled and angered by Dil Bahadur's tone, but he was also curious. He gave the order, and as the escort fell back he followed Dil Bahadur, climbing with him until they were seated on a great rock, able to see all around them.

Ismail Mohammed looked around him, and then looked down and saw that they were looking directly into the Place of the Dead. He turned to look at Dil Bahadur, and wound the end of his turban over his nose and mouth.

"Why do you choose to come and speak with me here?"

"Because we can see around us clearly, and we cannot be overheard — unless you fear the spirits of your own men calling for justice."

"What — what are you saying?"

"Look yonder, Ismail, where the birds are busy. If there is anything left that you can recognise, I think you will know who those men were — before they were murdered."

Ismail Mohammed leaned over the rocks, staring down, and then turned back to Dil Bahadur. His face was grey, he pulled a flask from his coat pocket and drank deeply before handing the flask to Dil Bahadur, asking, "What happened here — those are my men, ten of my senior and most trusted men. What do you know?"

Dil Bahadur refused the drink, and said quietly, "Unless you ordered their killing, then I am telling you that those men were murdered. They were killed, probably because they knew too much and were going to warn you. They may have overheard some others in the Palace talking. I cannot say more than that, because I do not know why they were killed, but I can tell you who ordered their death: Sagpurna. Your master. You chose badly when you chose to take his money, Ismail."

"I had no choice. I needed money. But never mind that. Tell me what you know."

"I will tell you, and I trust that you will listen to me and then answer some questions." Both men turned so that they faced away from the dreadful scene below, and leaning forward, Dil Bahadur began to talk in a low voice, his eyes on the path that led to where they were sitting.

He told Ismail all that he had discovered, and all that he had been told about Sagpurna's intentions and behaviour, and Ismail Mohammed listened to him in silence, until at last he had finished speaking. Then Ismail Mohammed turned away from him, and sat staring out over the valley, his chin in his hand. With a deep sigh he said, "I have been a fool, as you say, Dil Bahadur. A great fool. But I meant no evil here. I did not come intending to steal the guddee from the Raja. My mother is a woman of these parts, and when there was no place left for me in Pakodi State, I came here, to her. She is a good woman, not as some say, 'a woman of the bazaars'. She was known to the old Rani, who employed her; that is how I came into the Palace. I spoke with the Raja, and he gave me a place in his force, which was then a mere handful of ill-trained, ill-armed old men." He turned to Dil Bahadur, his eyes full of a sudden anger.

"I know there have been slanders put about the place; tales of my evil doings, my killings, my greed — Allah knows where they started, I do not, for they are all lies. I made this army, I have strengthened the force, and now it can stand against anyone in these hills — and beyond! I wish nothing but good here — and I want — I wish — " He spoke with anger and despair that was too great for words, and stammered into silence.

Dil Bahadur nodded and said quietly, "You wanted to rule. Of course you did, trained for the guddee in Pakodi, then turned away because the Begum was carrying a child which turned out to be the son that Pakodi had longed for." He hesitated and looked away, and then said, "The son that Pakodi would have welcomed with joy, but never saw." He spoke firmly, meeting Ismail's eyes with determination. "That boy is the rightful heir to Pakodi, and there is nothing you can do in honesty to change that. Unless your ally kills him for you, and kills the old Raja, and puts you on the guddee by force. That could happen. But of course, the second thing that you wish for would be lost to you then."

He waited, looking at Ismail who looked back at him, and nodded. "Yes. I know what you would say, Dil Bahadur. More to me than life itself is the Begum. I want her, but I want her in love."

"So. To kill her son and her father — that is an ill way to woo."

"There is no talk of them being killed I tell you."

"No? Then what brought you back in such a hurry, Ismail Mohammed? Tell me."

"I had news. Messengers came to tell

me of certain things that were happening here, and I grew afraid for the family . . . Wait — " He stood up and went to lean over the rocks again, looking down into the Place of the Dead. He came back with his face twisted with horror.

"Two of those down there are the men who came over the passes to give me news. Dil Bahadur. I am afraid for Amara. Can we get her away, and the child, and her father? I would leave the others behind, but she will not go without them."

Dil Bahadur drew a great sigh.

"Thanks be to the All Highest. You are not altogether a fool. Do not think about the child. He has been taken out of the Palace already. Now listen to me. This is what we will do."

★ ★ ★

When Dil Bahadur and Ismail had walked out of sight, Jiwan Khan and the girl had watched them go.

"Why do they go up there? That is a dreadful place, the Place of the Dead."

"Dil Bahadur wishes to show the

Nephew something. So it is the Place of the Dead that smells so vile. I thought for one moment . . . I wondered . . . I grew afraid that what I could smell was a permanent part of your person."

Her solemn face struggled with a smile, and she said, "No. I do not like to smell; I never grew used to it. But I had to use the smell as a guard. I was glad to when I saw what could have happened to me, when I saw girls of my age — " She shuddered, and looked away from him. "Some of the girls died after the southerners had taken them. I do not like to smell, but I do not like to be greatly afraid all the time either."

"I, Jiwan Khan, give my solemn promise that you will never live in such conditions again, as long as I am alive and you are with me." He stopped, and then his voice, very low, told her part of what was in his heart.

"Roshanara, if it pleases Allah, you will be with me always from now on."

She looked up at him and away again, quickly changing the subject, suddenly afraid.

"Has Dil Bahadur a plan for the safety

of the Raja and the Begum — and others of the household?"

"Yes."

He was happy to find that he was totally at ease with this companion, that he could say anything to her, discuss anything with her. In the sweet magic of this discovery he forgot what he was saying and looked down at her, smiling, and she, taken suddenly by her own feelings, looked back at him and was unable to look away. There, among rocks and disturbed carrion birds, they looked at their future together and were astonished at their good fortune.

"No flowers, no falling fountains or caged bulbuls," said Jiwan Khan softly. "No moonlight and no heavy headed roses, only — "

"Only what?"

"My heart as a carpet, my love as a covering, a guarding wall about you. My life for yours, and my everlasting love."

"Oh — but is love everlasting?"

"You are how old?"

"I have eighteen years — almost."

"And already you ask if love is everlasting? I am twenty-eight and I have ten years more knowledge than you. Look into my eyes, Roshanara, and speak to me with your heart, and not with your quick, trained mind. Answer your own question for me. Is love everlasting?"

The sun, the pale winter sun, shone on her hair and into eyes that were learning fast. Under his loving gaze her eyes closed and she said very clearly, "I think that love could be everlasting."

And at that time, and in that place, her words made a garden of pleasure for them both.

★ ★ ★

Dil Bahadur and Ismail Mohammed came down from the high rock, and went back to the horses, but Jiwan Khan and the girl were nowhere to be seen. Dil Bahadur turned to Alam Beg.

"Where are they? You know what dangers lie about us. But Allah, if you have let them ride towards the village alone, I will kill you, for we will never get them away if they are captured." Alam Beg was undisturbed. He lifted his hand and pointed, and they saw the two horses standing head to head, and beyond them, a decorous distance apart, sat Jiwan Khan and the girl, perched on a rock overlooking the distant river, the sun seeming to shine only for them. They did not hear the others come up to them; not until Dil Bahadur called Jiwan Khan's name did they turn, startled, torn out of some world of their own, their faces bright with dreams.

"We return to Dhalli Palace now," said Dil Bahadur, and saw the dreams fade from Jiwan Khan's face, and was regretful. But to start a love affair now! This was no time or place for dalliance. In fact — the girl was one more responsibility.

"I think the — " He hesitated. If she was the daughter of the Khan of Panchghar, should he tell Ismail who she really was? He had to trust the man now, and he was fairly certain that he could. But to trust him with someone else's life? "I think the dancer should return to the powindah camp," he said firmly. But Jiwan Khan shook his head.

"The lady goes where I go," he said and lifted her into her saddle, his hands holding her as if she was a small delicate bird and he afraid of ruffling even a feather. Then he mounted himself and they rode back, down the wide easy road to the river, and then onto the steep rough path that led through the village.

The village was alive for once, the rutted main street busy with men and women; even children scattered running before their horses. Dil Bahadur saw that Ismail Mohammed was greeted with dark looks. The people stood back in their doors, catching at their children, their faces sullen and hateful. Both Dil Bahadur and Jiwan Khan had the same thought. When the Ruler of Lambagh rode through his kingdom he was received with tumultuous, joyous welcome. These people had been well doctrinated, and looked cowed and afraid. They watched the riders pass in silence. Only when the girl rode by were there surreptitious smiles, and a hand or two lifted in greeting. Jiwan Khan heard the name Devi whispered, and saw faces that broke into the wide smiles of the hill people who love life and laughter and are not usually given to sullen looks. But the smiles were only for Roshanara. This valley, thought Jiwan, has suffered greatly from misrule and worse, and he wondered if it would ever be possible to return it to prosperity and happiness.

The silent, watching villagers were soon left behind, the party climbed the steep path. They were soon outside the gates of Dhalli Palace. As they dismounted, Dil Bahadur asked Ismail Mohammed if he was sure of the loyalty of the escort. Ismail looked at his men.

"Yesterday I would have been sure. Now — that man there, Dassu. He came with the first detachment of officers from the South, and has been with me, a faithful and honest companion, ever since. I would have trusted him with my life . . . yesterday."

"And now you have doubts? Then, make certain, at once, that he gets no chance to talk to anyone or to leave the Palace. We talked a long time together on the hillside. We may appear to be friendly, but if we are to succeed, Ismail, it might be as well if you were not known as my friend outside these walls . . . "

Ismail Mohammed nodded and spoke aside to one of his guards, a hill man who salaamed and ran from the entry court.

Jiwan Khan lifted the girl from her saddle, and Dil Bahadur, even at such a time, surrounded by dangers and difficulties, had to smother a smile. The girl, who had dismounted so agilely earlier, was learning fast; she had waited like a helpless Palace beauty for Jiwan Khan's assistance.

Jiwan Khan, bringing the girl with him, came over to Dil Bahadur. Robert took the girl's hand and bowed over it.

"I am your servant, Lady." He paused and smiled at Jiwan Khan, and turning back still smiling said quietly to Roshanara, "My life for yours, Lady, now and always."

Jiwan Khan saw that Roshanara knew the vow, and yet did not realise what Dil Bahadur had underlined by saying the words to her. But a moment later she understood and a deep blush stained her clear skin. She joined her hands and bowed over them in salutation and, Jiwan Khan hoped, acceptance. He took

Dil Bahadur's hand in both his, saying, "I have never heard those words with more pleasure, my brother. Now, tell me, where do you suggest I take her for safety?"

Before Dil Bahadur could reply, Roshanara said quickly, "I go to the Rose Court — the court of the Begum. I will be safe there with her. May I take Alam Beg through the passages as my escort?" Robert nodded. "Thank you, Nawab Sahib."

She raised her eyes to Jiwan Khan for a second, her reluctance to go as obvious as if she had spoken it. It was hard for him to see her walk away, and he stood looking after her until she had gone out of sight. Then he was roused from his thoughts by Dil Bahadur's hand on his arm, and Dil Bahadur's voice.

" Oh, Jiwan Khan! To tangle your heart in the strongest net in the world at this time! I need your brain, what is left of it . . . "

"You need me? I am here."

"Good. Now let me speak, and do not question everything that I say to you. If my plan is to succeed, I need you away from here — I wish you to leave tonight with Roshanara, and go to the powindah camp — the Pahareen will get you away in safety — both of you. Jiwan, Roshanara is in danger here, as you know. Sooner or later someone will recognise her as Devi, and then — well, I do not have to put her danger into words. So take her this evening, as soon as it is dark, and go to the Pahareen. I have spoken with her."

"I will not leave you — and I see that you cannot come. The Jungdah family need help. So I stay with you. Do not repeat the oath to me again: I too have taken it, brother, but it is not meant to make me lose my manhood! You did not banish me to my tent when we went in against the rioters in Palampur last year. What has happened to you that you are so anxious for me to leave? Do you want all the glory yourself? I will not go and leave you alone in this nest of serpents. You need me to guard your back — so I will stay." Dil Bahadur took a deep breath, looked at the friend he would die to protect, and gave up arguing.

"Very well. But your spirit and my

spirit will certainly have to spend eternity avoiding your father, if anything happens to us — ”

“Let it happen to us both if it happens at all.”

“You can say that, with love so new? Love is sweet when it first comes to you, Jiwan — ”

“And sours with time? Is that what you would say to me? Is that why you do not go to Laura when she calls to you? Has love soured for you, Dil Bahadur?” Or have you found a new love? he thought, but did not say.

“That is not what I meant, Jiwan.” Dil Bahadur’s voice was hard, with no affection in it. “I do not run to Laura because I am here on the Ruler’s order. And for your information, love does not sour. It grows stronger, with every day that passes — if it is real love. I hope that you discover this for yourself.” Jiwan Khan thought of the Begum Amara’s hungry eyes and passionate mouth, but did not mention her. Instead he spoke of Dil Bahadur’s plan.

“Have we enough men? Will the villagers fight with us?”

"We have enough with Ismail Mohammed's men to back us. But the villagers are needed; we must have them on our side. I will go into Dhalli village now and speak with those that I know, the people who helped me when I was wounded when I first came."

"I will come with you?"

"No. I must go alone — or with Alam Beg, when he returns. You stay here, Jiwan." Jiwan's arguments were interrupted by Ismail Mohammed.

"Dassu was caught leaving by a side door in the old stables. He had one of the southerners with him, and two of my best horses, the villain. He also had a message for Sagpurna, to be handed to him if he could not reach the King himself."

"It is as well that you caught them. Where are they? Well guarded, I trust? We can question them later — "

"Nay. No need of guards or questions. They have made a short journey, and will lie tonight beside men, faithful men, in the Place of the Dead, food for crows and vultures." Such swift justice — but right for this place of treachery. Ismail saw the approval on both Jiwan Khan's and Dil

Bahadur's faces, and grew calmer.

"The games — have you decided when the games will be held?"

"I think tomorrow, at noon. I will give the invitation to the man who commands — under me — the southern soldiers here. There are many . . . "

"How many?"

"Upwards of fifty — but some are music makers and dancers and singers — so say, forty armed men."

"We must have the villagers. Jiwan Khan, will you see our men, and choose the teams? We will need twenty-four of the best riders — including Osman. That will give us four teams. I will play of course."

"And I — of course." Jiwan looked for contradiction and got none. Dil Bahadur had decided what to do, but was not about to tell Jiwan Khan. The Pahareen's plan would have to be followed. Jiwan Khan would have to be given a drug to make him sleep, and then he would be taken out and into safety. There was no question of him joining in the polo matches as they were going to be played the following day. Polo, as it was played in the northern mountain states, was not a gentle game. It was more like a battle than a game. And as it would be played the next day, it was in fact a battle — a fight to the death.

Ismail Mohammed took his leave of them, they would not meet until the following day on the field outside the village where the games would be played. Jiwan Khan renewed his demand to accompany Dil Bahadur to the village and was refused.

"You have your girl here. What would happen to her if we both go out and are killed or captured? I do not know how things will be with the villagers, but I must try. Stay here and guard what you value more than your life. I will, inshallah, return before the sunset gun."

And if you don't? thought Jiwan Khan, and with anxiety in his heart saw Dil Bahadur leave him. He went to the court where the Lambaghi men were, feeling he wanted to be among his own people. He climbed to the tower to watch Dil Bahadur leave — but saw instead a packhorse led out by a mounted man. On the packhorse were two naked

413

bodies, inadequately covered by a horse's back blanket. Ismail Mohammed's swift justice. Well, perhaps it was the best way to act in this terrible place, where it seemed no one could be trusted. He saw that the walls were now guarded by Ismail Mohammed's men, two at every ten paces. He watched a long file of horsemen going up towards the flat ground outside the village. The men of Ismail Mohammed's team going up to view the field? Allah knows, thought Jiwan, filled with doubt and worry.

He did not recognise Dil Bahadur dressed as a pahari, a hill man, with Alam Beg similarly disguised, and, worried, not knowing if Dil Bahadur had left or not, stood in the tower and thought of Roshanara and wished that he was in the Rose Court with her.

26

D IL BAHADUR took Alam Beg with him. The guards on duty at the main gate were all Ismail Mohammed's men, and in any case they paid no attention to the two hill men going out of the crowded entry court. The place was crowded with busy men, the air rang with noise.

The images of the gods were being taken down to the river for their ceremonial bathing. After this ritual cleansing they would be brought back to have their jewels and ornaments polished and refurbished, and if they needed it to have their features repainted. Men, their backs bowed, their legs trembling with effort, staggered through the press, six or eight to a palanquin, heavy with a revered burden, tilting dangerously as the palanquin dipped and swayed in movement.

Against one wall of the courtyard, the painters were already setting out their pots of brilliant, clashing colours, and their precious boxes of gold and silver leaf. Dil Bahadur had never seen anything like this affair.

"How long do they take to bathe the figures?"

"Some are brought back before sunset, but most are kept down by the river while their priests conduct special ceremonies and make offerings to the river goddess, she for whom the river is named, the goddess Chandra."

"The Moon Goddess," said Dil Bahadur, watching a seductive statue of a goddess go reeling past, the bearers sweating already. "Tell me more about this. After the washing and the praying, what then?"

"This running to and fro with the images will go on until the night of the full moon. By that time the images will be returned to their places, and the worshippers will come with their offerings and there will be a great feast, which usually lasts for three or four days. But there is feasting and drinking every night in any case; this is the one big festival of the year for these people."

So at any time, thought Dil Bahadur, all he had to do was provide Jiwan Khan with some loyal companions, and an image, and he could leave the Palace unnoticed. If only he would go. It would be so simple — but he knew his dear friend, and had little hope of this easy way of escape for him.

In Lalaini's house, Dil Bahadur explained his plans to the village elders and asked that as many men as possible should be at the field outside the village on the following day. The house was beginning to fill up as more men came in from the street to listen. With the villagers determined to help Dil Bahadur, the elders — still suspicious — finally gave in. Yes, they would all help.

The men, without hope for so long, now given a vision of coming freedom and the choice to do something about their troubles, were buoyant.

It was an hour before sunset. Time to return to the Palace. Dil Bahadur hoped that the ten men he picked out as leaders would be able to carry out his orders. Lalaini saw the doubt on his face.

"Do not fear, Lord, that they will be

foolish. These men are ready to fight for their homes and their lives. They saw the southerners when they came into the valley. Even Ismail Mohammed is better than those beasts."

"Tell me all that you saw, Lalaini."

"An army comes up the valley, Lord. The men from the fort brought warning, and we ran, calling on the other villages on the way. All the people of Jungdah valley are here now, and all safe. But they burned our houses."

"How close are they? Have you news?"

"Yes. The latecomers say that they are four or five kos away. They move slowly, being greatly encumbered with gear and animals."

"Animals?" Dil Bahadur remembered Sagpurna's state entry into Safed, years before. "Have they brought an elephant by chance?"

"Nay. But they have pack mules and horses, and bullocks, and there are camels carrying great tents, enough to hold fifty men. There are boys with painted eyes and musical instruments, and singing girls in palanquins. Also there are strange animals, large cats with

418

spotted hides — not leopards. They run like dogs at the heels of the southerners, and two of them were set on a herd of our goats for sport."

Cheetahs, thought Dil Bahadur. What a way to come on a campaign. Dancing girls and boys, musicians and hunting cheetahs, and baggage mules and camels. His heart lightened. Such an adversary as Sagpurna appeared to be would surely be easily defeated.

Alam Beg called to him to come, the way was clear for them to leave with safety.

The long procession of images and priests and chelas and monks were still moving on the path and in and out of the Palace gates. Inside the entry court the sunset light was drowned by flaring naptha lamps, while the painters bent, tongues caught between their teeth, already at work on full curved lips or chipped necklaces.

For the first time, as they walked from one courtyard to another, Dil Bahadur saw no southerners. Ismail Mohammed had changed the guards and there were now men from the lower hill towns, and from the villages round Madore and the great plain that stretched from Madore to Safed. Dil Bahadur noted the change, and hoped that Ismail Mohammed had not roused suspicion among the men from the South. But all seemed well, there were loud sounds of music and laughter coming from one of the courts.

"The officers from the South live there," said Alam Beg, and stopped to speak to a guard lounging against the closed gate of the court.

"They celebrate," he said, catching up with Dil Bahadur after a few minutes. "It is, of course, their festival too, they are all unbelievers, worshippers of the gods. Ismail Mohammed has supplied musicians and dancers, and much wine, and has relieved them of duty for the night — so they celebrate."

"That is well done."

The sun had set. The sky was a strange silver-grey, with heavy clouds veiling the mountains. Going down the open colonnade to Jiwan Khan's rooms, Dil Bahadur studied the strange light. This valley appeared to have its own climate, unlike any other. By this time in the winter, the Lambagh valley would have crisp sparkling days and clear skies.

Dil Bahadur sent Alam Beg off, telling him to come back when he had checked round the Raja's courts to be sure that all was well. He found Jiwan Khan, also staring up at the strange sky through his open window. It was the wrong season of the year, yet the clouds, and the damp, heavy atmosphere, spoke of rain.

The two men sat talking, each hearing what the other had done. They had sat like this so often, drinking little and talking much, before many campaigns and border fights, their plans laid, everything ready and only the waiting to be faced until the action started.

"It is strange. There are no southerners to be seen." Dil Bahadur nodded. "No. They celebrate for the next week; the festival is theirs also. Ismail Mohammed has given them leave and they are all carousing in their court, for he has sent them much wine, and musicians and dancers."

Dancers! The word seemed to hang in the air, as if someone was repeating it loudly. The two men looked at each other in silence for as long as it took Jiwan Khan to take a deep breath. Then, with no word spoken he stood up and buckled on his sword, picked up a pistol, and turned, running for the door, Dil Bahadur close behind him.

"Jiwan Khan! Wait, she is safe in the Begum's quarters. Ismail Mohammed knows that she is yours, even if he has not guessed that she is not a dancer. The Begum will protect her. Jiwan Khan, if you go armed into the southerners' court, you will start a riot and jeopardise the whole plan. *Will* you listen to me?"

He took Jiwan Khan by the arms and exerted all his strength to hold him from the door. He saw sweat break out on Jiwan's forehead and was horrified.

"For God's sake, Jiwan! I tell you, she is safe."

"No I am sure that all is not right. I must go because if anything should happen to her — " He had freed one arm, the hand holding the pistol. "I am sorry, brother — I must go — " He spoke the words breathlessly, and then hit Dil Bahadur with all his strength, with the butt of the pistol. Dil Bahadur fell, with a head full of dark sky and shooting stars. His woollen hat saved him from much, but he lost consciousness for a few minutes — not long, but enough.

When he opened his eyes and sat up, the room was empty. Dil Bahadur struggled to his feet and ran unsteadily into the corridor. The old servant who had been sitting outside the door was not there. Had he followed Jiwan Khan? And if so, where were they? Cursing himself for sending Alam Beg away, Dil Bahadur ran down the colonnade and through the empty, ruined court that led to Ismail Mohammed's room. Ismail Mohammed, talking with one of his risaldars, looked up with surprise when Dil Bahadur burst in.

When he heard that Jiwan Khan had gone armed to the southerners' court, and why he had gone, he stood up cursing.

"Young fool! Of course she is not there. The women in there are camp followers, women of no repute, picked up on our journeyings. Some came up from the South with Sagpurna's men. Come, Dil Bahadur, be at ease. I will get him out at once, we know that they will not kill him!"

"But the drugs — what drugs will they give him?"

"It will take more than one dose to do him any harm. I will get him away, saying that I wish the credit of handing him over to Sagpurna myself."

It seemed that Ismail Mohammed took forever to dress and arm himself, and give orders to the risaldar for guards to be placed around the court where the southerners were feasting. No one was to leave that court.

"It will raise suspicions but it is necessary, since Jiwan Khan has behaved so foolishly." Dil Bahadur, tearing off his duffle tunic, pulled on one of Ismail Mohammed's rich robes, and buckling on his sword followed Ismail out, while the risaldar ran for the guards.

There was a different man on duty at the door of the southerners' court. He saluted Ismail Mohammed, who paused to say, "Has the Nawab of Lambagh arrived yet? He came ahead of us."

"I know nothing of any Nawab. People have been coming and going through this door all evening. All have leave to feast but I."

Ismail Mohammed went through the open door and as Dil Bahadur came up beside him he said quietly, "They have changed the guard. I gave orders for my own men to guard that door."

There was no time to say more; in any case, in the roar of the courtyard it was necessary to shout to be heard. The place was blazing with lamps and fires, and in a small cleared space six girls, bare to the waist, gyrated and quivered and stamped to the music of two drums, a veena, a sitar and a flute. A woman sang, with a voice that cut through the noise of the court like a saw through butter. Almost all the words of her song were lost but suddenly some words sounded clearly: "Come soon my love . . . " Dil Bahadur looked at her and saw her eyes alive with a warning, though he did not recognise her. Her song stopped and he shouted applause and tossed her a coin which she caught nimbly, and he turned then and followed Ismail Mohammed, who was greeting the senior man present. He was presented and bowed and coming upright

425

found himself confronting the small dark man who had beheaded Shivnath. There was no sign of recognition on the other's face. He was offering them seats on a cushioned divan. "Where you will have a good view of the dancers. Not of the best quality, but good of their kind." Ismail Mohammed let this insult pass him by.

"Is Jiwan Khan here yet?" he asked, and his host looked in astonishment.

"No, Nawab Sahib — we did not know we were to be honoured . . . This is only the first night of the festival. The night of the full moon, we will have our own entertainers of course. Then we will hope to entertain you suitably."

"Of course," said Ismail Mohammed. The noise in the court was reaching ear damaging heights; the drums were thudding and as far as Dil Bahadur could see most of the men in the court were drunk. Dil Bahadur took a goblet from one of the servants, and, choosing his moment, moved towards the press of men round the dancers. Closer and closer he moved towards the woman who was once more singing, her head thrown back, her eyes closed, one hand held to her ear as if she listened to herself in ecstasy, singing the same words in a drawn-out, quivering stanza: "Come soon my love, Come soon, or who will hear my song?..." She finished, the dancers sank in the usual swooping obeisance, sweat glistening on their bare breasts, and Dil Bahadur caught the singer round the waist and held her close.

"Oh Nightingale of the North — you take my heart. I must have you. Is there a room?"

"The rooms are all empty, Rose of Gold, though they have been full. I must sing again, and then I will come, I will bring you my love, oh tall man of the North — " She was laughing as she spoke, trying to free herself, speaking clearly with practised coquetry. Any paid singer would have behaved like this, trying to avoid an amorous, drunken man. But she had passed her message with skill, and Dil Bahadur knew that there was no need to search the rooms around the courtyard. Jiwan Khan had been here and had been taken out. He clasped the woman closer, then released her and staggered back, repeating, "After

427

this song then. After this song. I promise you gold to fill your slippers!" She slipped back into the centre of the floor, the music grew louder and Dil Bahadur stepped out of the crowd — and found Ismail Mohammed laughing beside him.

"Oho, Dil Bahadur, you did not get your desire! You drank too much before you came! I will take you away now, you must sleep or you will do yourself no credit tomorrow." Protesting and hanging back, Dil Bahadur allowed himself to be dragged to the door. The last thing he saw as they left the rowdy, flaring courtyard were the watchful eyes of the man who had killed Shivnath — Swaraj. Dil Bahadur could never forget his face, and wondered if his own was stirring memories in the man's mind.

27

THE door closed sharply behind them, a babble of voices died away, and Dil Bahadur saw Alam Beg waiting beside the guard. He had to keep up the pretence of being overcome with wine. Supported by Ismail, he staggered, and Alam Beg rushed to take his weight. The three walked away together, Ismail Mohammed deriding Dil Bahadur for becoming drunk so easily, until they were out of sight and sound of the watching sentry. Then Dil Bahadur was released, and Ismail Mohammed said firmly, "He has not been there. Swaraj swore it — and I believe him."

Dil Bahadur had little hope, and now it seemed he had no more strength to argue with Ismail. The thing he dreaded had happened. He followed the others to the Rose Court, and as they came up to it, a flute began to play softly. Ismail knocked on the door, ignoring the two guards, and walked in. The fountain was tossing its plumes of sparkling water, the goddess still stood dreaming beside the pool.

The door on the other side of the court opened and Saida stood there, the lamplight behind her shining on the curved sword she held in her hand. She called over her shoulder, "Amara Begum, it is the Nephew, and the Prince from Lambagh," and stood back as they pushed into the empty room. There were signs that it had been vacated hurriedly: a silk scarf tossed down, cushions that were beginning to regain their shape after weight had been lifted from them; glasses of tea still steamed on the tables.

Dil Bahadur saw none of this. He looked round the empty room and sat down as if he could no longer stand. It was Ismail Mohammed who called Jiwan Khan's name twice, and then turned to Saida and said, "Where is the Nawabzaida Sahib?"

"Why should he be here?"

"Woman, answer my question — "

"I do not know where he is, Ismail Mohammed. One thing I do know. He is not here."

It was then that the girl Roshanara came in. She looked at Dil Bahadur and then at the other two, and her cheeks grew pale.

"What is it? Why do you look for Jiwan Khan here? Oh what has happened to my lord?"

Her voice was as clear and sweet as always but the last words were agonised, as if she already feared their answer.

"Jiwan Khan has been taken by Sagpurna's men — "

Ismail Mohammed faltered into silence as the Begum walked out of her room and came to stand beside Roshanara, an arm about her shoulders.

"What villainy have you caused now, Ismail Mohammed? Why was Jiwan Khan taken by Sagpurna's men? Did you sell him, and now come to act innocent here?"

"Jiwan Khan heard that dancers had been sent to entertain Sagpurna's men, and became convinced that Roshanara was in danger, that she had been taken to dance for the men of the South. He would not listen and has thrown himself into their hands." Dil Bahadur's voice

431

was flat and without strength, the voice of an old man.

"Let us be calm. We know he will not be killed. That is not Sagpurna's plan — "

"No, Ismail. He will not be killed. But perhaps, knowing what Sagpurna's plan for Jiwan Khan is, perhaps it would be better if we wished him dead! Oh, all this talk is wasting time. Where in this place could they take him to keep him hidden?"

Dil Bahadur's desperate words left a silence behind them, and into the silence came the raucous skirl of a horn and the thumping of a drum.

Roshanara and the Begum lifted their heads and looked at each other. Then the girl said softly, "Allah be thanked for he has told us the answer. How would you get a man out and away at this time? There are palanquins and carrying chairs coming and going to and from the river. Even if they have smuggled him through a gate we can find them on the road — "

Before she had finished speaking the three men were running for the outer door. She would have been with them but Saida and the Begum held her back. She swore at them and then, with tears streaming down her face, said, "Amara, would you stay here and sew and wait if it was your love who had been taken?"

"Have patience, Roshanara pyari. We go, but not so that we hinder the men. We go to pray at the river as the Ranis of this court did before. Come, veil yourself. Saida will bring us poshteens and we will take a bag of things we may need."

Veiled, booted, and wrapped and hooded in fur-lined coats, the three women hurried down through the passages and quiet, shadowed courts until they reached the thronged entry court. They passed unnoticed in the chaos through the open gates and began to move swiftly among the many laden men and the swaying, dipping palanquins. Behind their veils their eyes stared and searched, and no palanquin or carrying chair or drunkenly tilted platform escaped their scrutiny.

At the turn, where the path branched down to the river, snaking through the crowds, the women came on the three

men, and saw ahead of them, unwieldy
and rocking, a curtained carrying chair,
the curtains of scarlet and gold pulled
close and fastened, carried by four
staggering bearers.

"*That* one." Dil Bahadur began to run
as he spoke, with Ismail Mohammed
and Alam Beg fast behind him. Their
racketing, banging progress made an
opening in the crowd through which
the women made easy progress, and the
two groups reached their quarry as one.

The chair was lowered and the carriers
stood panting beside it. Alam Beg had
already drawn his sword, and was feeling
for his knife.

"Open that curtain." It was Dil
Bahadur's voice, but not a tone that
any there had heard before. The words
were snarled, not spoken, and Alam Beg
shivered, remembering old stories of men
who became tigers and killed as tigers do.
The front carrier began to whine that he
had been told to take the god veiled to
the river, it was their custom. His Urdu
was broken: he was not a man of the
hills . . . he was a southerner. Alam
Beg looked at the others, bowed with

exhaustion over the poles. All shaven headed, dark skinned. Men from Sagpur, or thereabouts.

"Open the curtains . . . " The carrier still hesitated, his eyes sliding sideways as if he might run. Alam Beg shifted his grip on his sword. If any of them moved, he would have to kill them. It was the right chair . . . He could see sweat starting out on the men's skin, as they stood, bare to the waist in the winter evening. That was the sweat of fear. Ismail Mohammed suddenly cursed, and, stepping forward, ripped the curtain aside with his sword.

Ganesh the Elephant God, with the body of a man and an elephant's head, looked out at them with sad, wise eyes. Ganesh, Son of Shiva the Destroyer, the lord of the cosmic dance, and Parvati his wife. Parvati, who in another manifestation was called Kali.

Ganesh, the God of Beginnings, the Kind God, was the only thing in the curtained chair.

Dil Bahadur stared, unbelieving, like the others. It had been so right — for these carriers were all men of the southern states, dark men, their foreheads marked with Shiva's trident in red dye. If not here, then where? Dil Bahadur repeated his question aloud.

"*Where?*" he said, and Ganesh looked at him sadly as if he would answer if he could.

"Heavenborn, can we now go, we will be late for the ceremonies . . . ?"

The whining voice broke into Dil Bahadur's desperate thoughts. He stepped back, and the carrier who had spoken, and who appeared to be in charge, shouted to his companions to raise the chair, which was securely tied to four poles, one for each man.

Dil Bahadur had turned away to scan the passing crowd when a cry like the scream of a stooping hawk shrilled above the many other sounds.

"No! It is he!"

Ganesh's carriers, swaying and stumbling, were almost on the path as Roshanara, screaming, ran forward and flung her arms about the tallest carrier. The man on the other rear pole turned and Alam Beg, who had moved with the girl, saw the glint of a knife in his hand

and jumped on him, catching his wrist just in time. Saida's voice screamed, "Poison! Have a care of the knife!" and there was a sudden flurry of movement round the chair as the Begum darted forward and snatched up the wickedly sharp knife as small in length as a man's forefinger. Alam Beg dragged his captive away but Dil Bahadur's sword was already bloodstained. He had not bothered to take the two men on the front poles prisoner; they would never move again.

The whole episode was over so quickly that those toiling on the path saw nothing out of the ordinary. To them, if they looked, there was only the usual trouble, carriers who had dropped unconscious from drink or exhaustion and a god who would have to wait until other carriers were brought.

Out of the torch-light the girl Roshanara sat on the stony ground with the third carrier lying supported by her knees and arms. Dil Bahadur knelt beside them.

"Is he — "

"Do not *say* it," said Roshanara, her

voice fierce. "He lives. He *will* live. But oh, my lord, my life, what has been done to you?"

Jiwan Khan stared open-eyed into her face and a slow dribble of saliva ran from his slack mouth and made a snail's track onto his chin and bare, dye-stained chest. His head had been roughly shaved, and cuts showed dark amongst the stubble. The mark of Shiva's trident showed red on his forehead.

The hatred that filled Dil Bahadur when he saw Jiwan Khan in this state made him almost blind for a moment. He stood up, and his sight cleared and he saw the Begum and Saida standing to provide a screen for Ismail Mohammed and Alam Beg, who were swiftly and efficiently gagging the remaining carrier and trussing him into complete immobility. The dead men lay where they had fallen, and as they were in the shadow of the chair the dark blood on their bodies and on the hard ground did not show.

Ismail Mohammed, rising from tying the last firm knot, could not meet Dil Bahadur's eyes. He said, looking aside at

438

the crowded path, "I have taken shame to be my constant companion. I can never forget what has happened while I guarded the Dhalli Palace. Tell me now what I should do."

"You must go back to the Palace, where there is now great danger for you, and behave as if you have never left it and as if you know nothing. If you can, bring your men to the polo field tomorrow as arranged, unless the men from the South refuse to come and prevent you. I will take Jiwan Khan to a safe place. Amara Begum — "

As he turned towards her she stepped forward and stood beside Ismail Mohammed.

"I go back. I know that my son is safe, but my father is still within those walls. So — if Ismail Mohammed will escort me, I will return, and having heard what your plans are for tomorrow I will do my part."

She was veiled, and her voice was calm. Only the wide, tragic eyes showed any feeling. Dil Bahadur did not argue or urge her to come to safety with him. He bowed, and turned back to Roshanara, waiting in the shadows beside Jiwan Khan. The Begum watched him leave and then turned to Ismail Mohammed, and with Saida walking behind them, they began to make their way to the Palace, with haste in their hearts, but no chance of making good speed on the crowded, seething path.

"Alam Beg," said Dil Bahadur. "Is that creature secure? Then roll it behind those rocks and leave it. I may have need of it later."

Furious eyes above a well-gagged mouth, the prisoner glared the curses he could not speak, and was left well-hidden at the side of the road.

"If you are fortunate, we will return before the vultures find you defenceless and pick out your eyes." Alam Beg tested all the man's bands as he spoke, and then left him.

Dil Bahadur had torn off his rich robe and was once more a duffle-dressed hill man, bareheaded in the cold wind. He lifted Jiwan Khan and, putting him across his shoulders, began to walk towards the village.

"If there are any to see us, which

I think is unlikely, we go home from drinking by the river and our friend has drunk very deeply."

With Alam Beg singing quietly in a rich, blurred voice in front, and Roshanara stumbling behind, berating them both with shrill, angry words, they started off for the village.

Jiwan Khan lay on Dil Bahadur's shoulders, silent and inert. The dribble of saliva fell from his mouth as if it would never stop; his eyes, wide and staring, reflected the moon sailing between clouds, but saw nothing.

Lalaini's house was dark like the others, but at their knock they heard movement, the scratch of flint and steel, and saw a lamp bloom as the door was unbarred to Dil Bahadur's cautious whisper.

Once they were all inside, and the door was barred once again, they laid Jiwan Khan on the quilt-covered kang and Lalaini began to examine him.

"His heartbeat is slow, but steady. The drug was given by the mouth: see how he dribbles and his breath is bitter. He must vomit, and it may be that I should purge him also." They heard her pounding and stirring, while they stood, helpless. Roshanara knelt beside Jiwan Khan on the kang, and took his head onto her knees.

Dil Bahadur, who had held Jiwan Khan's head many times after drunken parties, when they had been very young and had not yet learned to hold their liquor, went quickly away, Alam Beg at his heels.

There was silence from the room behind them. They were standing outside the house and the wind was keen, but neither of them felt the cold as they strained their ears, listening for the call they hoped for. Instead, they heard footsteps.

Across the street, in the shadow of the houses, a figure could be dimly seen. Alam Beg, silent as a shadow, melted into the darkness . . . Dil Bahadur heard a gasp, then Alam Beg was back, but not alone. A small figure, his arms held firmly behind his back, was pushed in front of Dil Bahadur.

"If it is a southerner, it is a very small one," said Alam Beg. "The misbegotten bit me: I shall likely die of an evil

442

disease. Be silent, you, or I tear out your tongue . . . "

The child, who had begun to speak, dropped his voice to a furious whisper.

"I am no monkey from the South! I am Halim the Goatherd from the village by the old fort. Can I not enter the house of my father's sister?"

His question ended in a choked snuffle, for his nose was bleeding. The door behind them had opened and Lalaini stood there beckoning.

Dil Bahadur lost all interest in Halim the Goatherd, and hurried inside, followed by Alam Beg, grimly pushing his captive ahead of him.

Roshanara, her face deathly white, said nothing. It was Lalaini who spoke with triumph.

"He sleeps. He is safe."

Dil Bahadur went over to the kang and looked at the drained, sleeping face, but it was the face of a living man. He bent and kissed the damp forehead, and then looked at Roshanara, who was weeping, trying to catch her breath between sobs so as not to wake the man beside her.

"Come, brave and beautiful, and let us

443

give you something to drink. You have a long journey ahead of you now, though not as long as the journey he would have taken if you had not seen him in time. He might have remained alive but not in his right mind."

Lalaini brought bowls of tea, and as they took them she saw the captive.

"Halim! What do you here?"

"I await murder by your friends." Dil Bahadur nodded to Alam Beg who let the boy go.

"Who is this warrior, Lalaini?"

"He is the son of my dead husband's sister. His father was one of the Raja's messengers who did not return. You remember we spoke of a goatherd who was lost? This is he."

"Will you carry a message for me, Halim? Carry a message to a woman who is with a camel caravan four kos along the river road? Ask for the Pahareen, and you will be taken to her . . . "

"I know the Pahareen. What message do you send?"

"I need to get the Prince away from here swiftly. If she could come and take him by camel, with the Lady Roshanara,

444

before dawn, it would be best."

"Before dawn? It lacks but two hours, and I cannot fly. I need a horse!"

It was true. Dil Bahadur groaned his despair. There was no chance that he could get a horse in time from the Palace. In fact, there was no time at all — every second that passed put them in more danger; all of them, but especially Jiwan Khan. He looked at Alam Beg and saw nothing in his face but a matching despair.

"There were three horses stabled at the house where the boy was — " It was Roshanara speaking, all her tears and exhaustion forgotten.

"Three — one was the horse you rode, Dil Bahadur, and two pack ponies . . . We can ride to the Pahareen's camp! We can go to her . . . !" She was transfigured, convinced that everything was possible. Dil Bahadur looked at the man who lay so still beside her.

"Do you think he will be able to ride?"

Lalaini looked doubtful, but Roshanara said firmly, "It is for his life, not for pleasure. I can hold him on the horse, and I know the way. Alam Beg, you know where the animals were stabled — " But Alam Beg had already gone. The two women sat watching Jiwan Khan. After a few minutes Lalaini said firmly, "No. He must sleep. If you can hold him on the horse he can go, but not awake. We will harm him if we drag him from sleep now."

Dil Bahadur looked at the slight body of Roshanara.

"Can you hold him?"

"I can. We will tie him to the saddle and I will hold him as well. We must. You said, Dil Bahadur, that his life would be worth nothing if he falls into their hands. Anything is better than that."

The sound of a horse's hoofs outside seemed to lend point to her words. Alam Beg came in quickly, his face full of anxiety.

"We have little time, Lord. The watchers are about: I met Derva, who warned me. He made a noise and took one of the pack ponies to draw them off . . . He is being followed, but I do not know how many there are."

"Halim!" Roshanara turned to the boy who knew and trusted her as Devi. "Halim, go by the walls and let us have warning." The boy ran out immediately.

Dil Bahadur lifted Jiwan Khan and carried him outside to Alam Beg's horse. They tied him upright in the saddle, and put a roll of quilts in front of him to help to hold him in place. The girl mounted behind him and took up the reins. Dil Bahadur looked at her, and could only say, with a prayer behind the words, "Go in safety, Roshanara," as she kicked the horse into movement. Lalaini watched with them as the horse vanished into darkness. Dil Bahadur turned to her, saying, "I must go at once Lalaini. If any ask, the plan has not changed."

She nodded, and then, as they turned to go, they heard the thud of another horse coming quickly up the beaten earth of the street, and froze. Both men drew their swords, and stood in the shadows waiting. Then Alam Beg sighed deeply and lowered his blade.

"It is the Sparrow . . ."

The boy brought good news. There were, it seemed, only two watchers, and they had followed Derva who had led them down to a lower path which lost itself in a rocky slope below the Palace.

"He will be safe. He carries nothing and goes to look for a lost flock of goats. I brought the pony, Lord, because I can ride after the Prince and guard him from trouble — also Devi, who is Roshanara. Is this good?"

"Very good. Go, and bring back word to Lalaini that they have reached safety — " The boy went without waiting to hear anything more. Dil Bahadur looked at Lalaini and Alam Beg and said desperately, "I have to trust his life to a girl and a child — but it is only four kos. Surely — "

"Surely, Lord. Go and do what you must, and think of nothing else. All is written now and in the hands of the Gods."

Alam Beg said their farewells, for Dil Bahadur was already walking away. Lalaini watched them go, and went into her disordered house and began to set it to rights, and when all trace of their presence had been removed she took up station at the door, and felt the dawn wind already blowing and prayed for the safety of all who had been with her that night.

As she followed Ismail Mohammed back to the Palace, impeded at every step by the crowding people and the conveyances for the statues of the gods, Amara saw that all the men who bent their backs and gave their strength to the carrying of the gods were men of Jungdah, hill men of the villages. She threw back her veil and let them see her face, and heard them say her name. "Amara Begum is here among us, she has been to the ceremonies by the river." She called out to them then, saying, "We need to return to the Palace quickly, help us . . . " Her voice was clear above the hubbub, and immediately men began to make space for her, clearing the path to let her through, smiling their pleasure at seeing her with Saida behind her, and ignoring the man they called the "Nephew".

It was as the path opened for Amara's party and she smiled her thanks, that she saw the four men hurrying down the path towards her. She pulled down her veil quickly. These men were not part of the laughing, celebrating crowd; although they were dressed as priests in orange robes she saw the silks that dragged on the earth beneath them and the glint of jewels forgotten in haste. They were in too much of a hurry to notice her, and did not see Ismail Mohammed walking outside the glare of the torches. He, in his desire to get back to the Palace, had seen nothing. At her gasped words he halted and turned. She told him quickly what she had seen.

"I must stop them," he said in reply. "They will have had news from the watchers that we have found Jiwan Khan. Go, Amara, with Saida, and get into the Palace. These people will do you no harm, and my men are on the gate — "

She interrupted him.

"Your men were on the gate when we left. Who knows what men guard the gate now? No, these men will help us, these men around us. Tell them. They are our people and they hate the dark men from the South. There is no time to be lost, those creatures will know where

Dil Bahadur and Jiwan Khan are and will carry the news to the army by the river. Speak to our people, let them see you need their help . . . "

He looked at her burning eyes, her aroused face, and did exactly as she said, without hope of success. He told the men around him that four murderers, men from the South disguised as priests, were amongst them. "I want them. They must not reach the river or our plans for tomorrow will be overthrown." He saw them look at him without trust, hesitant to do anything he asked of them, and said reluctantly, speaking as he had never spoken to them before, as equals, "If my honesty is in doubt, look for two dead men beside the image of the Elephant God, Ganesh. Those dead men were from the South too; they were abducting the heir to Lambagh's throne. Now they are dead: throw their bodies over the khud. I trust you with my life by telling you this. If you so wished you could earn much gold by running to the Palace people and telling them that I killed those men."

His desire to be believed could be

heard in his voice; but the Begum beside him, her hand on his arm, was all the proof they needed. They did not understand, but if she trusted him, then they did too.

"Do we kill, or take prisoners, Heavenborn?" Ismail Mohammed took a deep breath and relaxed.

"Kill," he said quietly. "Kill. Then there will be four less tomorrow." Then, with the Begum beside him, he turned and began to hurry towards the Palace, the path being cleared before them by willing men running ahead.

From one group to another the word spread. The hunters, unknowing, became the hunted. The order ran swiftly. Far down the path the four men, unprepared, met the death that had been sent and there was the beginning of vengeance at last in Jungdah valley.

28

THE Begum and Ismail Mohammed reached the gates of Dhalli Palace and found all was well. The painters were sleeping, surrounded by a wall of images, cleansed and waiting for adornment. The guard on the gate was composed of Ismail Mohammed's men.

Ismail Mohammed escorted the Begum to the Rose Court, and though went in with her, his face creased with anxieties.

"I am going to put ten men here, outside your court door, and ten more at the back. I ask as a favour that you do not go outside these rooms and your inner court until I come for you in the morning. It is not long now till dawn: try to sleep. I thank you for lending me your power out there. Alone I would not have been obeyed. You are beloved, and because you gave me your trust, or seemed to do so, they believed me and obeyed me."

He looked with his heart in his eyes

at her as he spoke. For the first time she did not turn away from him, or sneer, or rail at him. She lowered her eyes, like a girl before her lover, and agreed that she would stay within her rooms in safety. She asked about her father.

"His courts are closely guarded, by both his own guards, and ten of my men." Ismail was staring at her as he spoke, trying to understand the new softness on her face, the gentle civility in her voice. He longed to stay with her, to find out what had caused this change in her, but there was no time. He took his leave and went to his own quarters, trying to clear his mind of thoughts of her so that he could give his mind to the preparations for the coming day.

After he had gone, Amara bathed and dressed in the clothes put ready for her, rich garments that she seldom wore, and chose jewels to twist in her hair and to put in her ears. She was determined to make a brave showing at the games. The old woman came to comb and arrange her hair.

"But you will not sleep first? Once I have done your hair, with these jewels, you will not be able to rest your head — "

"I have no need of sleep. I have too many things to think about." She tried to avoid the old woman's fixed and purposeful gaze, but finally could not avoid Saida's direct question.

"What game are you playing with Ismail Mohammed, Amara?"

"I play no game."

The comb in her companion's hand grew still, and she leaned to look at the Begum's face reflected in the mirror.

"Then you intend to do as he wishes? You know what he dreams of, Amara, that very dangerous man. He dreams of marriage with you, and a son. Be careful. Such a man, led to believe one thing, and then disappointed . . . "

The Begum turned to her mirror, and spoke bitterly.

"Have you the right to ask me such questions? You should have told me to have a care a long time ago, when you sent me to dance before a prince in a garden. Well, Mother, those days are gone, and the deed was done. Now . . . why should I disappoint Ismail

Mohammed in any way? I am young and strong, fit to bear many sons, ready and experienced in what men call love — and the daughter of kings. What more could a man ask?" She peered closer to the mirror and seemed to be examining her face, but the old woman saw that her cheeks were wet with the tears that she had been unable to hold back.

"Do not weep, child. Any man would be pleased to take you as his wife, of course. But you — how is your heart set? Will you take him?"

"Why not? There is no one else."

There was silence in the room after that, except for the soft sounds that the comb made, pulled through and through the soft fall of Amara's long hair.

Then the old woman put the comb down and said quietly, "That is enough. I will put the jewels in later. Sleep now, child of my heart, and remember that we are leaving here tomorrow, if the gods so will. Then, once out of this imprisoning valley, who knows what may not be made of your life. Sleep, daughter of love, and weep no more."

She went quietly away after that, down

the hidden stair that led from Amara's room into the Raja's bedroom. She walked with dignity, this old woman, the mother of Amara, who had sent a servant out in her place and had elected to stay in the Palace as Saida, the maid of her own daughter, rather than escape and leave her husband and daughter in danger. Saida, Rani of Jungdah.

Amara lay on her bed, convinced she would not sleep, preparing to meet the pain of memories but with no hope for the future to help her bear that pain. But sleep took her, a deep, exhausted sleep. She did not hear the stir at the Palace gates when Dil Bahadur returned with Alam Beg. She did not hear the clatter as Ismail Mohammed's horses were taken out through the entry court, on their way to a field outside the village where the games would be held. Amara lay, lost in sleep, and in that sleep she said farewell to many dreams. In her sleep she heard words of love, burning declarations of passion, all said by the wrong man's voice.

Her mother woke her, alarmed by the depth of her daughter's sleep, relieved when she eventually roused herself and sat up.

Together the two women prepared for the day, speaking very little, each hiding from the other the fears they felt.

When they were ready, it was two hours before noon. The day was clear, only the highest peaks were hidden in cloud, a cloud that drifted and coiled about the mountains, hiding them in thickening veils. "We shall see rain by nightfall," said Saida, the Rani.

There was a hum of sound from the direction of the field. The villagers were already gathering. The gods would be without carriers until the games were over.

The Lambaghi men rode out, two by two, each man leading a spare horse, Osman, his turban tilted over arrogant, resolute eyes, at their head. Dil Bahadur watched them go, pride swelling his heart. His men, his splendid friends, every one of them personally known to him, every one of them a man he could trust to the death. And some of them would die this day, he knew, and the pain this knowledge gave him was added to the bitter hatred he felt for Sagpurna and everything connected with him.

The men from the South made a brave showing, silken and furred with painted eyes and flags fluttering at their lanceheads. The polo players were very richly dressed, their horses glittering with jewelled leather and embroidered saddle cloths.

Dil Bahadur and Ismail Mohammed watched them go. "Very fine," said Dil Bahadur. "Our men will look like beggars beside all that finery."

"Aye. But let us see how they play — and also, think of how easy it will be to grip them with all that loose silk — the women of the village will have rich pickings tonight — inshallah."

"Indeed, God willing. How many are left in the Palace do you think, Ismail?"

"I cannot tell. Some of those were new faces. But I have given orders. The ones that are left are drinking already. Listen . . . "

Behind the sound of the horses going out rose another noise — laughter, and drunken shouting, and clapping hands.

"You see?" said Ismail Mohammed.

459

"There are girls there too. Before another hour, my men will have taken the men that are left. Every swine's son of them. The ravine will receive them."

Alam Beg came clattering up with Dil Bahadur's horse, and Ismail Mohammed turned for the Begum's court.

"Go with joy, Dil Bahadur," he said as he hurried away. "Go laughing. I will see you at the field."

As Alam Beg rode out after Dil Bahadur, he heard the noon gun blaring from the walls. The hour they had waited for was upon them. Dil Bahadur turned and smiled at him, and he returned the smile with his whole heart. This was a leader he was happy to follow.

Like two bridegrooms hurrying to their wedding feasts they kicked their horses into a canter, and saw, far ahead of them, the little flags that fluttered on the lances of the southerners.

29

DIL BAHADUR and Alam Beg rode quickly and caught up with the rear guard.

The field was entirely surrounded by villagers and off-duty soldiers of Ismail Mohammed's army. The hillside was clumped with colour: the emerald, closely-tied turbans of Lambagh, the scarlet caps of the Jungdah troops, and the pink and gold puggorees of Sagpurna's men, loosely wrapped, looking like huge, untidy roses.

At the end of the field that was nearest to the village, the people had left a space and there were cushioned stools and a carpet. The players were sitting on their horses at the far end, opposite the village, each of the contingents keeping a little space between themselves and their opponents. The men from the South had the centre, Lambagh and Jungdah the right and left.

Dil Bahadur rode to the village

end and, looking round, saw that the musicians, inseparable from any hill function, were in place. It was a larger band of players than usual, two men with long curving horns, another with a massive drum, as well as the more usual veena, sitars, and flutes.

Two men were wrestling to entertain the crowd until the match began.

There were other riders coming from the Palace. Armed men rode in front of them and behind them, but the riders so guarded showed no signs of being prisoners. They were talking together, and Dil Bahadur heard a woman's voice say something and then laugh, a rich husky laugh. He had never heard her laugh, but he knew who it was. The Begum was putting on a brave show. She sat before Ismail Mohammed, her body swaying easily to the movement of his horse, his arm lightly supporting her. She was talking to a woman who rode beside her, a woman riding astride, dressed in richly furred and embroidered robes, her head hooded against the cold, but her face unveiled. Saida had gone. This was the Rani, riding beside her daughter, and riding well.

"Who *is* that?" Dil Bahadur was staring, unable to see clearly at that distance. "Is that Saida, that woman?" Alam Beg shook his head.

"It is the Rani, Lord. I kept this thing from you for I swore an oath that on my life I would tell no one. Saida the old servant left the Palace when Roshanara went out. The Rani refused to leave her family and took Saida's place. It was easily done. None of the southerners or the men from the plains had ever seen the Rani. But Ismail Mohammed knew of course — "

There was no more time for explanations. The Raja, waving to his people, had received a wild, shouted welcome. The royal party had come up to the village end of the field, and Dil Bahadur went forward to help the Raja to dismount. The wise old eyes, steadfast and able to smile even at this time of uncertainty, looked into Dil Bahadur's face and each admired the courage of the other. The old man took his place on the largest of the cushioned stools, sitting cross-legged, his beads moving through his fingers. Calmly

463

he looked about him, content, it seemed, to be out in the fresh, sunny day. His Rani took her place a little behind him. Ismail Mohammed, dismounting, lifted the Begum from his saddle and setting her down as if she might break, led her to a stool beside her mother. Dil Bahadur was given the news he wanted by the surwan.

"They arrived safely. The Pahareen is with them, and by this time they will be well on their way. We go by way of the Jalari Pass, which is still open. Word came from a trader coming down last night. The snow is not yet down to the lower ridges of Jalari."

"My thanks. You know what to do here?"

"How not? The Pahareen has told us. We will watch for the right moment, never fear. All is now in the hands of Allah the merciful, and so we are content. Go laughing, brother."

He moved away, and the camels were shortly taken out of sight. Dil Bahadur went back to Alam Beg and the horses and found Ismail Mohammed waiting from him.

"We are ready? The Lambaghis play first, your first team against mine. The airag sellers have been about. Nay, do you think me a fool?" he said in reply to Robert's hurried question. "*Our* teams drank buttermilk."

A trumpet blew a discordant blast, and the teams, six a side for the rough, murderous Gilgit game, rode onto the field, their ponies' unshod hooves tapping on the crisp, frosted ground, the mud rock hard with the winter cold.

There was ten minutes of good, skilled play. This polo was different from the game that was played on English parade grounds in the cantonments. Here every dirty trick was part of the rules: the ball could be lifted and carried by hand and men could use any tactics they liked to unhorse an opponent. After the first ten minutes, it began to appear that the Lambaghi team were not as good as expected. There were many falls, and men had to be replaced. Those who fell took their ponies off with them, and shouted arguments ensued about why the Lambaghi team should have fresh horses *and* fresh men. The villagers jeered at each fall, and the Lambaghis took their diminished pride away from the waiting teams and out of sight behind the villagers. The crowd surged to and fro, altering the size of the field and making it even more cramped. An hour after play started, the Lambaghi teams had all been eliminated, and their leader Osman, publicly scolded by Dil Bahadur, had retreated into the crowd.

Ismail Mohammed, who had played with skill, came sweating off the ground to chose his next team, who were to play against Sagpurna's men. These now rode out, and as if at a signal, the musicians began to play with spirit.

Then play began, but with more confusion than usual. The crowd were pushed back by some of the Lambaghi men who had reappeared. Sagpurna's remaining men, watching their team, conspicuous in their rose and gold puggorees, stared as they saw Swaraj, the best player they had, fall while at full gallop. Fortunately he fell into the crowd, and within seconds, before they could see exactly what had happened, they saw his pony caught and held while, apparently unhurt, Swaraj remounted.

The game continued, but the rose and gold covered heads seemed to be frequently on the ground. True, they were always up again, but the game appeared to be very confused with no score but a great many furious, galloping charges. One of the southerners, watching, said bitterly:

"They have all drunk too deeply of this airag. Look there — another down. Swaraj will have their heads when they come off . . . "

"Well, he fell himself, though he is riding well enough now," said his companion, trying to see through a drifting cloud of smoke that had just swirled over the end of the field. Children were letting off firecrackers, and there was a wild confusion of bucking, kicking, wild-eyed ponies and cursing men, so that the whole ground was convulsed with total disorder. When they had mastered their animals, the Sagpur team were one man short.

"He has gone to piss," said a helpful spectator. "See, there, your Captain calls you . . . "

Swaraj, his clothing disarrayed, his puggoree bound round the lower part of his face was indeed waving furiously. The musicians were still giving their best, and no voices could be heard. This was the last of the Sagpur men, less the one who had not yet returned from relieving himself.

The other team had not yet left the field, which was crowded with shouting men and horses going totally out of control as a fresh batch of firecrackers went off. There was a good deal of movement among the crowd, and the Raja's party left their cushioned stools and moved back.

The men from Sagpur who now took the field were the senior officers, men of Swaraj's own rank, excellent horsemen. Confused but obedient to his frenzied gesturing, they rode down the field towards him, and finally one of them reached him.

"In the name of the great God, Swaraj, we have less than two hours left before we carry out your orders," he was shouting, yelling above the hysterical, mind-shattering din of the field, the crowd and the accursed musicians.

"Less than two hours before sunset — can you *hear* me?"

Swaraj turned, and holding his horse on a tight rein, took a firm grip on — but it was not a polo stick, but a sword. The man found he was gazing into laughing grey eyes beneath the pink and gold silk. Those grey eyes were the last thing the man from Sagpur saw before a sword swept all sight from his eyes and life from his body. He tumbled into the waiting hands in the crowd and his pony cantered away to be caught and held at the far corner of the field.

Ismail Mohammed thundered up to Dil Bahadur.

"That is all. Thirty-eight and all dead."

Dil Bahadur took off the rose and gold folds of silk from his head and dropped them to the ground; they were quickly gathered up. The girls of the villages in the valley would have rich borders to their robes for years to come.

The musicians gave a last defiant skirl on their horns and the drum thundered once — then reverberated into silence.

"The Raja's party?"

"They have gone. One thing — "

"What?"

"The Begum could not go with them. They went very quickly, while she was speaking with a village woman. Alam Beg knows. I was on the field. Speak, Alam Beg."

Alam Beg, his clothes torn and stained, his face bleeding, was troubled by what he had to say.

"She only spoke to the woman as an excuse. The Begum has refused to go, Lord. They could not stay to argue with her: the Raja and the Rani had already gone."

Dil Bahadur looked at Ismail Mohammed, as if to say, "This is *your* trouble." Inwardly, he was furious. If the Begum chose this moment to make trouble it would ruin the final part of the plan. If Ismail Mohammed ever discovered that she had taken Dil Bahadur as a lover he would turn to Sagpurna for vengeance at once.

Ismail Mohammed was also angry, but for other reasons.

"To put herself in danger, to lose her chance of escape — I will have to find a way to get her out. Where is she? With the village women? Then set a guard on her. I will deal with her later. Now is not the time."

Some of Sagpurna's men had had time to fight in the chaos and noise of their killing. Among the bodies laid out like coloured paving stones on the hillside were several Lambaghi men who would never see their beautiful valley in this life again. Some villagers had been killed also and some of Ismail Mohammed's men, but triumph was overcoming grief as the villagers saw their southern tormentors felled.

Obeying orders previously given, the people were streaming swiftly back to the village and some of Ismail Mohammed's men were rolling the dead men into horse blankets and tying them two at a time onto pack ponies. When they had finished several more men from the village came to join them — and an innocent cavalcade of laden ponies and their trading owners moved off.

The field was clear. Only the musicians remained, and now they were leaving too, going down to the river where the last of the ceremonial cleansing of holy objects was still going on. As soon as they had gone, the goats were driven out from the village, the herd augmented by those that had been driven up from the lower villages to take refuge in Dhalli.

The goats were delighted to be free. They strayed about the field, lending an air of pastoral innocence to what had been; in fact, a field of battle. Now there was nothing left to rouse the suspicions of the most alert commander.

"The Begum is coming," said Ismail Mohammed, and Dil Bahadur turned to watch the three women who climbed up from the village, followed by Alam Beg, leading horses.

Ismail Mohammed was severe with the Begum, his voice stern, his eyes belying every word he said. She must go, she must think of her son; by staying here she endangered all their plans. Dil Bahadur looked at her with a face of flint, and dangerous, killer's eyes.

But she did not notice him, or his expression. She did not really hear what Ismail was saying either. Her eyes moved, lifting to the mountains where the clouds had cleared away, leaving the sharp peaks glittering like golden spears. The walls, the mountain walls of her valley. Would she ever see it again? This cold bleak place was her home; she found the pain of homesickness rising in her heart as if she had already left. This fear of never seeing her home again had made her refuse to go to safety this afternoon, even though her son had gone and the rest of her family. She had felt the same when she had first left Jungdah, a bride, a child, frightened and longing to stay.

They stood, the Begum, Ismail Mohammed and Dil Bahadur, beside a ridge of rock masked by thorn bushes.

"How can I go?" She did not know she had spoken aloud, but she heard Ismail Mohammed say, "I cannot bear to see you go from me — but you must. I will not live in happiness until I see you returning. Tell me you will come back, let me have hope while you are gone from me?"

The Begum, looking down at Ismail Mohammed from the high-pommelled hill saddle of her horse, had made no verbal promise. But as they rode away, she looked back, and lifted her hand to the man who watched her. Then the three women kicked their horses into a swift canter, and went out of sight.

Someone was running fast over the field, scudding silently, and waving, and Alam Beg, turning to look, said, "It is Halim the Goatherd — " It was also, thought Dil Bahadur, swinging the breathless boy up in front of him, trouble.

It *was* trouble. Sagpurna had already arrived and was in the Palace. "Ismail Mohammed's men who had guarded the gate?" asked Dil Bahadur.

"They were slaughtered like — like goats at a festival," said the boy, shuddering.

Like a man pulled from sleep in which he was enjoying a pleasant dream, Ismail Mohammed turned from looking in the direction of which the three women had gone, to listen to Dil Bahadur.

"You heard the boy? There is more. Jiwan Khan sent two men to Madore, asking for help, telling them there what troubles there are in Jungdah. I also sent a man. My man, Rabindra, is a prisoner;

Halim knows him and saw him led in. The other two men were slaughtered by Sagpurna's men: a rear guard coming up caught them. There has been fighting in the Palace and Halim does not know how many of your men will still be alive."

Dil Bahadur thanked all the gods he had ever heard of that none of his men had been left in Dhalli Palace. Now there was only himself and Rabindra, who was a prisoner and who must be saved somehow. He began to think aloud, trying to put some confidence back into Ismail Mohammed, who was looking utterly dumbstruck.

"So. The gate is guarded now by Sagpurna's men. But, remember, he does not know what has been happening here. He would have expected to find your men on the gate and slew them at once, which is what we should have known he would do. His own men, his spies and trouble-makers that he sent you as officers, he does not expect to see until moon-rise, for that was the appointed hour. He will imagine that they are out disposing of you, and the Raja's family, as they were ordered to do. The statues

475

of the gods and goddesses are coming up from the river with the priests and the last of the carriers. All is as he expected. He came early because he found the weather colder than he expected. He wanted warm baths and comfort before the festival starts tonight. But Halim watched him arrive and came to tell us. So now we have the advantage."

"Yes, Lord," said the boy eagerly. "The gates are open, even though guarded, for the gods are still returning. Even the painters are undisturbed at their work. I can come and go as I like. I will say I work for one of the painters if I am questioned." He paused and added, his face crinkling in a smile, "They are *very* foolish. They have put the camels in the same court as the pack ponies and there is much confusion."

"Good. In that confusion you can go in easily? You are not afraid?"

For answer, Halim spat. Then Dil Bahadur turned to Ismail Mohammed.

"I go into Dhalli Palace. I will not be alone. Alam Beg comes with me, also this gallant Sparrow. Do not waste time we have not got by arguing, Ismail.

476

Your part is to go and get our men back. Both yours and mine. They are waiting as ordered at the powindah encampment, for long enough to let the Pahareen reach the Jalari Pass. Well, we need them now, and I do not think the Pahareen will be followed. Do not let the Begum stop. She must ride on and join the Pahareen before night falls, for she does not know that road. Send two of your men with her," he said knowing the order to be unnecessary, for Ismail would have done so in any case.

"And when do I attack the Palace? After you are dead?"

"That is foolish talk!" said Dil Bahadur. "You wait until you see a signal fire on the wall on the left of the gate. Then, Ismail Mohammed, come in fighting, for I shall need you. Be ready, but do not come in until I light the fire. If there is no fire, then take all the men and ride for your life, and get my men and yours out of this valley — and return in the spring with an army from Lambagh. For if I do not live to light that fire, it means you will not live to rule this valley with the Begum, for the serpent you allowed in will not let you go alive knowing all that you know."

He turned his horse then, and rode away, followed by Alam Beg.

The sun had dropped behind the mountains and the twilight was silver and the air crackled with cold. Ismail Mohammed lifted his hand in a farewell salute, wondering if he would ever see Dil Bahadur again, and then set spurs to his horse, taking him at a breakneck pace up a narrow goat path that would avoid the crowded river road.

30

WHEN Dil Bahadur and his companions came in sight of the gate they saw that it was open and brightly lit.

The noise, both on the path and inside the entry court, was deafening. The gods had to be back in their places before moon-rise, and some were not yet painted. The new guards had issued orders: the gate would be closed at moon-rise, and the crowd of carriers swayed in, shouting, knowing that if they were locked out with their precious burdens they would be considered to have failed and would have no luck all the coming year. Also the priests would not pay them, and they would be unable to join in the feast that would be part of the celebrations of the night. Desperate, they surged and shouted, and Halim, a bundle on his head, wriggled through without trouble, and came out again shortly afterwards.

Dil Bahadur and Alam Beg had already tethered their horses out of sight, below the overhang of the wall.

"There is a troupe of dancers going in, with their masks. Go in with them, help them with their loads. Now, Lord, quickly."

Dil Bahadur, bareheaded and duffle-coated, seized the leading mask carrier by the arm, and guided him in, shouting encouragement. Alam Beg, looking askance at the leaning statue of a goddess, took time to separate the two fighting men who had been carrying her, and ended up carrying a mask himself, the grateful troupe behind him.

So they entered the Palace, and bedlam closed over them, and no one knew that they were there. They did not speak to each other. Dil Bahadur stayed near the painters, knowing Halim would bring him news there. Alam Beg went to the court of the Lambaghi men, now a dark deserted place, and climbed to the watch tower to wait as patiently as he could.

Dil Bahadur saw a small shadow move and a whisper sounded below the noise of the court.

"Follow, Lord." The shadow was gone, and Dil Bahadur holding the small hand drum he had been given turned and followed the little procession.

The flute player was the Raja's musician, Nathu. They entered the Hall of the Gods, and Dil Bahadur turned his drum so that he could swing the weighted strings and make them tap on the stretched skin. It did not matter what sound he made in that echoing hall.

Nathu did not lower his voice when he turned to speak to Dil Bahadur. There was no need. No one looked at them, no one could hear.

"Sagpurna is in the Rose Court. We go to play and dance before him shortly. Afterwards we will take you out by Kali's shrine. You remember it?"

Dil Bahadur remembered that terrifying place very well. He told Nathu that Alam Beg was waiting to light the signal fire in the watch tower of the Stranger's Court.

"That will be arranged also. Touching another matter, Lord. Rabindra is alive and safe. You will see. Show no surprise, Lord, all our lives are in the hand of the goddess. Now, Lord, make your prayer, for we go soon."

A band of men, staggering, stopped nearby, and began to heave their burden, Ganesh the Elephant God, onto an empty plinth. Something made Dil Bahadur look closer. The bearers were all known to him. Derva sent him a slanted smile. Lalaini's new protector grinned as he sweated to straighten the image. All the others were men of the village.

"They will fight when the signal is given, Lord. They will win, for you have given them hope, and they fight for their valley and the future."

"Come, Lord," said Nathu, and in a close little group they left the hall that was so full of noisy people and walked, the dancing girls who had joined them rustling in their silks, to the Rose Court.

The door was guarded and they had to wait, while the fountain danced in the cold night air and the goddess watched beside it.

The voice that sounded from the room beyond was impatient of interruption.

"If it is not news, then let us be in

peace. Do not come again until you bring news of Jiwan Khan."

"They are dancers, Maharaj, and music makers."

"Dancers? Music makers? In *this* place? It is not possible."

"They are skilled, Heavenborn, I have seen them. They will help to pass the time for you until your men return."

The new voice was soft and persuasive and familiar.

"If you say so, beautiful friend. Let them come then."

They went in and Dil Bahadur's eyes looked at the man lying amongst the cushions of the Begum's divan. A large man, broad-shouldered, dressed in an open, furred robe over tight silk trousers. Thin-faced, handsome. Dil Bahadur remembered the large, hooded eyes and the full, petulant mouth. He looked for, and found, the domed ruby ring that he also remembered.

At first he did not recognise the other person in the room, silk clad and scented, with painted eyes and hair that fell sleekly to his slight shoulders. When Dil Bahadur met the painted eyes it was hard for him to keep his face expressionless.

Rabindra leaning back against the divan, very much at ease, holding a silver cup and wearing a fortune in pearls round his neck and in his ears. He smiled at Dil Bahadur, a charming, knowing smile and said, "Ah, brother. I hoped you would come. I have spoken of you to the honoured one."

Dil Bahadur stood while the dark, imperious eyes studied him, grew interested, and finally warm.

"So you are Gulab, the friend of my friend? Everything he said is true. Come, sit with us, and drink. You, if you are going to dance, dance," he said to some dancing girls. Nathu, feigning a position as a musician raised a flute to his lips and began to play. The girls waited for the hand drum to beat out the time and began a slow, swaying dance, restful and graceful.

Sagpurna paid them little attention. He poured wine for Dil Bahadur himself, and begged him to sit.

"My beautiful friend here has told me much about you. He is right! Such eyes, like snow-filled clouds! Do they

484

ever warm, Gulab?" Sagpurna was either drunk, or drugged, or both. Dil Bahadur tried to think of a suitable reply, and while he did so, he glared at Rabindra who giggled and said archly, "Oh Gulab bhai! Do not be angry. I am sorry I did not meet you as I promised but — well, I had other things to do . . . "

"Jealous is he? You are his boy, lotus face? Well, you should have told me. In fact, if I had seen Gulab first, who knows . . . ?" Rabindra pouted and fiddled with his pearls, and the girls swayed and postured. Sagpurna picked up a fold of Dil Bahadur's rough coat and rubbed it between his fingers.

"Ugh, such harsh cloth! Does it not chafe your skin? We will go to my room in a moment and see what we can find. Though it does give you a sort of splendid *brutal* look. You are watching the girls. Are you a man for girls too? Eh, the best of both worlds! I envy you, Gulab." He drank deeply.

The knife in Dil Bahadur's hand was very sharp. Sagpurna's silks were no barrier. He did not seem to feel anything. He coughed quietly, and fell forward, and the drum continued to beat and the girls danced until Dil Bahadur put his hand out and held the lax wrist for a moment, then let it fall and stood up.

Movement and controlled haste then filled the room. Talking in his affected high voice, asking questions, laughing, Rabindra began to throw off his clothes, while Dil Bahadur followed his lead, laughing loudly and answering questions that no one had asked, clinking bottles and glasses together while the drummer wrapped Sagpurna's body into a neat roll of red velvet snatched from the divan and lifted it to one side. One of the girls had given Rabindra her skirt and her veil. He drew the veil coyly over his face, and turned to the door, walking beside the remaining girl and following the drummer. Nathu stayed, playing his flute to loud applause from Dil Bahadur, while the girl dressed quickly in Rabindra's clothes, her hair bundled into his rose and gold puggoree, and her bosom disguised by the folds of a pushmina shawl draped over her shoulders. Still playing, Nathu walked through to the bed chamber which was empty. The scent of sandalwood and jasmine still lingered here in spite of the new strong smell of musk.

"The girl is safe," said Nathu. "Now we must bring the body away. He must not be found there, not be known to be dead until Ismail's troops and yours are near. I cannot carry him alone, Lord. Will you come?"

Back through the strange, empty rooms and into the painted bedchamber, silent and empty, they lifted the body between them, Dil Bahadur going ahead, carrying the feet.

The place behind the Goddess was empty. Nathu untied the cord that held the body in place, and unrolled the cloth, and Sagpurna lay, sprawled in death, undignified and disordered. As they stood looking down at him, the priest of the shrine came in. He looked at the body in silence, and Dil Bahadur shuddered at the expression on his face.

"Let us go, Nathu. I would not wait any longer, I want to light the signal fire."

"It is lit, Lord, and Ismail Mohammed is coming."

Nathu touched Dil Bahadur's arm, and pointed to a carving on the high plinth on which a figure stood. He pushed and it swung open on darkness. Nathu picked up a small lantern and gestured Dil Bahadur to go through the opening. Bending, he went in, and Nathu followed him. Dil Bahadur heard the panel click into place behind them.

The passage sloped steeply up, and the air grew fresher as the smell of incense was left behind. The lamp flickered wildly in a steady draught, and there was a gleam of light ahead. The light grew stronger, and larger. Nathu stopped and listened and then beckoned Dil Bahadur on.

The passage ended in a clutter of rocks and thick thorn bushes. They emerged into a strange night. The full moon, obscured by clouds, shed a dull leaden light, so that everything was blurred, and a mist drifted over the ground. Gone was the crisp cold air of the day. The wind that gusted round them was damp and Dil Bahadur could smell rain.

"The Goddess is our friend," said a familiar voice and Rabindra came in to meet them, his woman's gear gone, a drawn sword in his hand.

The only clear light went up in a pillar from the wall, red flames and sparks. Alam Beg had lit the signal fire indeed, and they heard shouts and the sound of running feet within the wall. There was also the steady throbbing beat of drums and the high bray of horns. The festival of the Moon Goddess was in full swing in spite of the clouds that hid the moon.

"They will have trouble dousing *that* fire," said Alam Beg, looming out of the mist, his clothes smelling of singed cloth and smoke. "I have used the dry wooden mangers and some old camel saddles with oil from two lamps. There are some sober guards but not many. The villagers took in a skin of airag and the southerners had brought their own toddy. The girls who took the drink round made sure the soldiers got most of it."

"Are the gates barred?"

"There are only four guards on the gate. When I came out, Halim had a girl with him and they were offering bowls of airag. The girl was *very* persuasive, half-drunk herself, it seemed, with her bosom bare and her eyes promising rare delights. By this time I think the gates will be open."

Horses' hoofs sounded suddenly, very close by.

"Alam Beg, go and stop the horses. Tell Ismail Mohammed we go on foot, and put Osman and my men outside, to catch any stragglers." Dil Bahadur did not intend to lose any more of his men. This was Ismail Mohammed's battle, let him fight it with his own men. He, Dil Bahadur, would fight, but only until the battle turned. Then he would take his men off, and go. In the meantime he wanted them as safely placed as possible. He remembered something else.

"Tell them, none of Sagpurna's men are to be taken prisoner. They have brought death here, and will now have it themselves." He felt suddenly tired. Rabindra moved up to him.

"This valley has a curse on it, I think. Even the weather is twisted. Now it is the time for dry cold and snow."

Rain was rolling over the valley like smoke, fine, grey, misting rain that blotted out distances and blurred everything into different shapes. It changed everything. The river that had been almost noiseless raised its voice and rushed and frothed between its banks. Dil Bahadur could hear the horses slipping and sliding as they were reined in.

The noise of the river drowned out the sound of the men taking up their positions around the wall and outside the gate.

Alam Beg was at Dil Bahadur's shoulder as they ran in through the open gate behind a detachment of Ismail Mohammed's men. He saw Halim dancing with excitement on the wall as the swords began to rise and fall, and took time to order him away to safety before he turned to the grim business of clearing the Palace of Ismail Mohammed's folly.

All that night they fought and killed ruthlessly, the villagers fighting beside them. Sagpurna's men rallied after the first shock, and fought bravely, until the news filtered through their ranks that Sagpurna was lying dead on Kali's altar. Superstitious awe fell on them, and the constant beat of the great drum that never stopped and the shrill screaming of the long curved horns blown by the priests completed their discomfort. They broke and tried to run, and were hurled down like dogs.

A yellow dawn found the fighting over, and a heap of bodies in the entry court, the villagers, beady-eyed for bargains, picking among the stained silks and the jewels. Ismail Mohammed made no effort to stop them. They had earned their loot. He posted guards, ordered his precious horses brought in, and went looking for Dil Bahadur, who had fought tirelessly beside him all the night. He had so much to thank him for; so many promises to make.

In the village a cock crowed, a trumpet to wake all the others. The peaks were veiled, and though the rain had stopped, the clouds were still heavy and lowering.

Ismail Mohammed could find no trace of Dil Bahadur, and having searched until he grew alarmed, he sent for Alam Beg.

There was no need for alarm. At dawn, Dil Bahadur had sheathed his sword and ridden away, his work done.

"He will return in the spring, he said.

He said to tell you to remember that a man who rules is a man who serves."

Alam Beg salaamed, and turned back to join the men of Lambagh who were preparing to ride home. He would go with them, for his time in Jungdah was over. He was free to serve a master he had come to love and to trust.

31

THE noise of the night's battle still rang in Dil Bahadur's ears as he rode through the gate of Dhalli Palace just before dawn. Rabindra rode beside him. Dil Bahadur was stiff; his body ached and burned, a sword-cut was run across his face. They were both exhausted. At the second turn in the road, well away from the village, they stopped, and tethering their animals, fell behind the shelter of a ruined wall and slept until the growing light woke them.

Rested, they rode fast.

Dil Bahadur could not understand the deep depression that would not lift from him. Although he felt that all would now be well with Jungdah, he was still haunted by the place; however much he told himself that it was good that Sagpurna was dead, that he had finally killed the Lambagh family's most bitter enemy, he felt that something in him had died too. It was as if he was leaving part

494

of himself behind in that haunted Palace — he felt that he was a changed man. He was riding back to Laura — but as a stranger. Who was he now? He was searching as he rode, hunting in his mind for the memory of the man he had been, Robert Reid, Laura's husband.

It had become urgent for him to find that happy, contented self again. He was afraid to go to Laura so changed that she might be unable to find anything to love in him, that she would see in him only a disagreeable stranger.

His life and his love, the love of mind, spirit and body, belonged to Laura. What he must do now was to try to understand what had come between them, what had made her want to leave him.

Through the misty silence of the mountain passes the two men rode, their horses' hoofs muffled in new fallen snow.

It was sunset when the road dropped below the snow line, and there were trees in full leaf, pine and deodar, cedar and shisham. They rode on in silence and did not see another human being. As night came down they stopped and made their camp beside a deserted shrine, standing amongst trees gnarled and twisted with age. There they lit a fire and made tea, and heated food, then rolled themselves in blankets and lay before the fire.

"Rabindra. Laura Begum. Was she very ill?"

"Yes." Rabindra described to him the events of the journey to Madore, and the women who had helped Laura. Dil Bahadur thought of his wife, his treasured, gentle Laura alone and in pain, being tended by strange women. He remembered James's birth, with Bella, Ayub Khan's Scots wife attending on Laura in their bright, wide windowed room in Lambagh. He remembered Laura's delight when, after a difficult and protracted birth, James was put into her arms. All pain and fear had been forgotten then. But now — after miscarrying in such different conditions, what memories would haunt her? He groaned aloud, and Rabindra said, "Nay, Lord, do not fret so. They were kind women and she was glad of them. She kissed them as if they were her sisters when they left us in the Madore Mahal. The Khanum Bianca was distressed when she saw that your lady was fevered. She did not know that you had gone to Jungdah when she sent me to call you to Madore. Be of quiet mind, Dil Bahadur, Laura Begum is in good hands. Ayub Khan's Bella was there. By this time, no doubt the Begum is recovered and waiting eagerly for your arrival."

"And James — you do not speak of him. Where is he, Rabindra?" This was the first time in all these days that Dil Bahadur had asked for news of his son, Rabindra had already realised, and as a good Moslem, to whom a son was all important, he had been shocked. Now, all seemed well.

"Thanks be to Allah, he is safe and well, in Faridkote with Yar Khan and his Meeta. He will stay there until you send me to bring him to you — unless — " Rabindra paused, and looked sidelong at Dil Bahadur.

"Unless — unless what?"

"Unless you would wish me to take him back to Lambagh, to Kassim Khan, until the woman of your house is ready to travel. Do not look so, Lord. The days of your grief will soon be over."

Dil Bahadur wondered if Rabindra's offer to take James back to Lambagh meant more than it seemed. Had he overheard something said about Laura leaving for England? The people of the valley would disapprove of a wife leaving her husband and taking his son far from him. Had Rabindra heard anything? He could not ask. As for the days of grief being over it seemed to him that they were just beginning. If Laura had decided to continue her journey to England, leaving him, how would he bear it? His resolution wavered for a moment, seemed foolish.

Laying the food out beside the fire Rabindra looked at his master. He prayed silently that the same happiness his master had once felt would be waiting for Dil Bahadur at the end of this long, but hurried journey.

★ ★ ★

Once she had recovered from the misted, time-crooked hours of her fever, the days went slowly for Laura.

The bright cold crescent of a new

moon had hung low in the sky on the night of her arrival. Now that moon had waxed and waned, and it was another curved silver line that she saw in the sky as she looked from her window, out over the lake that reminded her of Lambagh and gave her a sharp pang of homesickness. She longed for Robert's arrival, and yet — sometimes in the heart of the night, when she could not sleep, she wondered if perhaps she should not dread it. Perhaps he would send her away, back to Moxton Park, to his widowed grandmother. After all, that was what she had told him she wanted. She filled her sleepless hours with such suppositions, and rose from her bed in the morning, drained, exhausted and hollow-eyed.

A month dragged by, and Laura, though better, was extremely depressed.

Bianca spoke to Sher Khan when they were alone one night in their bedroom.

"You ask me why he doesn't send a message? Light of my Heart, how can a message be sent from Jungdah at this time of year, at the start of winter?"

Something in his voice, not his words,

made Bianca sit up and look at him.

"Sher Khan, you have heard something? What? Tell me. If we do not quieten that girl's mind, she'll die."

"I trust that girl has not broken their lives to pieces with her foolishness. Going off to England to bear her child, indeed. Look what that has done for her."

Sher Khan loved Laura, but he loved Dil Bahadur more, admiring him and wishing that he was indeed the son that Sher Khan felt he was. He felt anger against Laura for leaving her husband, and it was hard for him to feel any sympathy for her. But the news from Lambagh — well, he felt that it was likely to make Laura worse rather than better. Jiwan Khan abducted and rescued and sent out of Jungdah to save him from another attempt; Dil Bahadur remaining behind to subdue an uprising; rumours of that archfiend and enemy of Lambagh, Sagpurna, attacking Dhalli Palace, and Ismail Mohammed fighting alongside Dil Bahadur, Ismail Mohammed, the contender for Pakodi's guddee . . . a fine collection of terrifying stories to pass on.

500

No, not for Laura, newly risen from a sick bed.

Watching his face, Bianca waited, saying nothing, sitting back against her pillows on their big bed, her eyebrows raised a little as she looked at Sher Khan. He met that look and nodded, and came over to lie on the bed beside her.

"Very well. Yes, I had news from Lambagh, none of it very good, and all very garbled. I think you had better keep it from Laura. Listen . . ."

At the end of his story, Bianca agreed that the news was not anything that would comfort Laura. She herself was very worried by it, but Sher Khan swore that he had no anxieties.

"No doubt Dil Bahadur is now posting down here as fast as horses will bring him. The news is almost twenty-eight days old. But I think we do not tell Laura that either. He may take his time about coming back to a recalcitrant wife, and I cannot say I would blame him."

The following morning Bianca watched Laura going off for a sedate ride along the lake shore, and remembered the first time Laura had come to the Madore

Mahal, and how she had ridden like a reckless boy, and wondered if Laura remembered those days too, with pain and longing. Poor girl. She looked so frail on her return that Bianca was horrified.

"Laura! What am I to do with you. Did you sleep at all last night?"

"A little. Sometimes I like to lie awake and think, you know."

The kind of thoughts that could take the colour and the light from a young woman's face, thought Bianca, and longed to say something comforting, but knew there was nothing to lighten Laura's eyes except the news of Dil Bahadur's coming.

Laura stayed out in the garden all that day, and when it was time to go in and join the family for the evening meal, she excused herself, pleading weariness and went straight to her own rooms. Thus she knew nothing of the man who came riding in with haste with news of travellers on the Grand Trunk Road who were already crossing the plain. When Sher Khan would have sent for her to come and await Dil Bahadur's arrival, Bianca stopped him.

"No, Sher Khan. This meeting between them must be in private. I beg of you, let me speak to him first, and then let him go up to her alone, before you start asking him for the news. Please, Sher Khan. Think, if you and I had been parted . . . "

She could not have thought of a stronger argument. Sher Khan agreed at once and when they heard the horses coming he went out, and watched Dil Bahadur dismount stiffly, and took him into a great bear hug, saying, "Welcome home, boy — eh, what a scar you have! Go and frighten your girl with it. Bianca is waiting to take you to her. I shall take Rabindra and hear your news from him."

Dil Bahadur came up the steps, and Bianca, going to kiss him stopped and stared.

"Robert — is it you?"

"Am I so changed?"

"A little. But it does not matter."

He was looking over her shoulder as if he expected to see Laura there.

"Laura is upstairs. Listen, she does not know you are here — "

But he was gone, taking the stairs two at a time. She did not follow. There had been things she wanted to say, advice she wanted to give, warnings, even — but this changed man — would he take kindly to anything she could say? She wondered if perhaps, after all, there would be no need to say anything.

Laura was watching the moon make silver patterns on the lake as the clouds scudded across the sky in the night wind. It would rain soon, the winter rains — how much longer would she be here to watch the seasons change and no word from Robert?

When the door opened she had no warning. She thought it was the servant come to light the lamps.

"I want no lamps tonight, Ragni. The moonlight is enough." Looking at her, so small and pale, almost evanescent it seemed in that strange half light, Dil Bahadur said softly, "The moonlight is indeed enough. I think the moon is your home — "

"Robert!"

"My love — "

Once he would have been across the room in three strides and she would have been in his arms. Now he stood beside the door, looking at her, and she looked back at him, and a silence grew. Presently she broke it saying softly, "You are Dil Bahadur — Robert has gone. Quite gone."

"It was necessary for him to go, Laura. I could not be two men. Now I am myself — but Dil Bahadur has all Robert's heart — there is no change there."

"No change? Are you going to send me away?"

"Never! But do not tell me again that you wish to go, Laura."

"Why? Will you forbid me?"

"No. But you must understand that if you go, I will not expect you to return. You see, my love, I have learned something — Robert was a fool. I now know that if I gave up my life here, and went with you to live in England, our marriage would die. I know it, and I am sure that if you think for a moment, you

505

will know it too. You would lose respect for me, Laura — I am a whole person here. But if you are determined to go, then you are free. I will not keep James from you."

"You mean — I take James?"

"You take James for the years that he will spend in being educated. Then he returns to me. That is the only condition I will lay on you, if you go."

His voice was so hard, so cold and firm! And he had made no move towards her. It was all her worst imaginings come true. She expected to feel herself supported by anger against this arrogance. But no anger came. Deep in her heart she knew he was right. Their marriage would not be the same if he gave into her wishes and followed her to live in England.

But he was so unloving — could she live with this changed man, this cold-voiced stranger? Laura was used to love and tenderness and companionship. Her heart was heavy as she looked towards her husband.

The wind had strengthened and blew from the lake, tossing the branches of the tree that tapped against her window, blowing aside the creepers that half covered it, so that the moonlight streamed in, clear and cold. Laura saw her husband's face plainly in that light, saw the jagged scar and the marks of pain and exhaustion.

"Oh Robert, what happened! That terrible scar . . . Who wounded you?"

"*That* wound is nothing. I will have a worse scar on my heart, and on my whole life if you leave me. Laura, answer me. Are you going?"

She stood up and moved towards him.

"I told you I was homesick — "

"Yes. You did. Well — " He half turned away from her as if he would leave.

"Wait — I found on my journey that I was indeed very homesick, but not for England. Oh Robert, I cannot call you Dil Bahadur, I never did. But please — I ask you to take me home — back to Lambagh. Forgive my foolishness and let me be with you always, however great the change in you, let there be no change in our love. That did not change for me — did it for you? You said you would love me forever, that your love would never change — "

Her last words were muffled against his shoulder. She was in his arms at last.

THE END

CLOUD OVER MALVERTON
Nancy Buckingham

Dulcie soon realises that something is seriously wrong at Malverton, and when violence strikes she is horrified to find herself under suspicion of murder.

AFTER THOUGHTS
Max Bygraves

The Cockney entertainer tells stories of his East End childhood, of his RAF days, and his post-war showbusiness successes and friendships with fellow comedians.

MOONLIGHT
AND MARCH ROSES
D. Y. Cameron

Lynn's search to trace a missing girl takes her to Spain, where she meets Clive Hendon. While untangling the situation, she untangles her emotions and decides on her own future.

DEATH TRAIN
Robert Byrne

The tale of a freight train out of control and leaking a paralytic nerve gas that turns America's West into a scene of chemical catastrophe in which whole towns are rendered helpless.

THE ADVENTURE OF THE CHRISTMAS PUDDING
Agatha Christie

In the introduction to this short story collection the author wrote "This book of Christmas fare may be described as 'The Chef's Selection'. I am the Chef!"

RETURN TO BALANDRA
Grace Driver

Returning to her Caribbean island home, Suzanne looks forward to being with her parents again, but most of all she longs to see Wim van Branden, a coffee planter she has known all her life.

NURSE ALICE IN LOVE
Theresa Charles

Accepting the post of nurse to little Fernie Sherrod, Alice Everton could not guess at the romance, suspense and danger which lay ahead at the Sherrod's isolated estate.

POIROT INVESTIGATES
Agatha Christie

Two things bind these eleven stories together — the brilliance and uncanny skill of the diminutive Belgian detective, and the stupidity of his Watson-like partner, Captain Hastings.

LET LOOSE THE TIGERS
Josephine Cox

Queenie promised to find the long-lost son of the frail, elderly murderess, Hannah Jason. But her enquiries threatened to unlock the cage where crucial secrets had long been held captive.

THE LISTERDALE MYSTERY
Agatha Christie

Twelve short stories ranging from the light-hearted to the macabre, diverse mysteries ingeniously and plausibly contrived and convincingly unravelled.

TO BE LOVED
Lynne Collins

Andrew married the woman he had always loved despite the knowledge that Sarah married him for reasons of her own. So much heartache could have been avoided if only he had known how vital it was to be loved.

ACCUSED NURSE
Jane Converse

Paula found herself accused of a crime which could cost her her job, her nurse's reputation, and even the man she loved, unless the truth came to light.

DEAD SPIT
Janet Edmonds

Government vet Linus Rintoul attempts to solve a mystery which plunges him into the esoteric world of pedigree dogs, murder and terrorism, and Crufts Dog Show proves to be far more exciting than he had bargained for . . .

A BARROW IN THE BROADWAY
Pamela Evans

Adopted by the Gordillo family, Rosie Goodson watched their business grow from a street barrow to a chain of supermarkets. But passion, bitterness and her unhappy marriage aliented her from them.

THE GOLD AND THE DROSS
Eleanor Farnes

Lorna found it hard to make ends meet for herself and her mother and then by chance she met two men — one a famous author and one a rich banker. But could she really expect to be happy with either man?

A GREAT DELIVERANCE
Elizabeth George

Into the web of old houses and secrets of Keldale Valley comes Scotland Yard Inspector Thomas Lynley and his assistant to solve a particularly savage murder.

'E' IS FOR EVIDENCE
Sue Grafton

Kinsey Millhone was bogged down on a warehouse fire claim. It came as something of a shock when she was accused of being on the take. She'd been set up. Now she had a new client — herself.

A FAMILY OUTING IN AFRICA
Charles Hampton and Janie Hampton

A tale of a young family's journey through Central Africa by bus, train, river boat, lorry, wooden bicycle and foot.

THE TWILIGHT MAN
Frank Gruber

Jim Rand lives alone in the California desert awaiting death. Into his hermit existence comes a teenage girl who blows both his past and his brief future wide open.

DOG IN THE DARK
Gerald Hammond

Jim Cunningham breeds and trains gun dogs, and his antagonism towards the devotees of show spaniels earns him many enemies. So when one of them is found murdered, the police are on his doorstep within hours.

THE RED KNIGHT
Geoffrey Moxon

When he finds himself a pawn on the chessboard of international espionage with his family in constant danger, Guy Trent becomes embroiled in moves and countermoves which may mean life or death for Western scientists.

THE SONG OF THE PINES
Christina Green

Taken to a Greek island as substitute for David Nicholas's secretary, Annie quickly falls prey to the island's charms and to the charms of both Marcus, the Greek, and David himself.

GOODBYE DOCTOR GARLAND
Marjorie Harte

The story of a woman doctor who gave too much to her profession and almost lost her personal happiness.

DIGBY
Pamela Hill

Welcomed at courts throughout Europe, Kenelm Digby was the particular favourite of the Queen of France, who wanted him to be her lover, but the beautiful Venetia was the mainspring of his life.

SKINWALKERS
Tony Hillerman

The peace of the land between the sacred mountains is shattered by three murders. Is a 'skinwalker', one who has rejected the harmony of the Navajo way, the murderer?

A PARTICULAR PLACE
Mary Hocking

How is Michael Hoath, newly arrived vicar of St. Hilary's, to meet the demands of his flock and his strained marriage? Further complications follow when he falls hopelessly in love with a married parishioner.

A MATTER OF MISCHIEF
Evelyn Hood

A saga of the weaving folk in 18th century Scotland. Physician Gavin Knox was desperately seeking a cure for the pox that ravaged the slums of Glasgow and Paisley, but his adored wife, Margaret, stood in the way.

SEASONS OF MY LIFE
Hannah Hauxwell
and Barry Cockcroft

The story of Hannah Hauxwell's struggle to survive on a desolate farm in the Yorkshire Dales with little money, no electricity and no running water.

TAKING OVER
Shirley Lowe and Angela Ince

A witty insight into what happens when women take over in the boardroom and their husbands take over chores, children and chickenpox.

AFTER MIDNIGHT STORIES,
The Fourth Book Of

A collection of sixteen of the best of today's ghost stories, all different in style and approach but all combining to give the reader that special midnight shiver.

DEATH ON A HOT SUMMER NIGHT
Anne Infante

Micky Douglas is either accident-prone or someone is trying to kill him. He finds himself caught in a desperate race to save his ex-wife and others from a ruthless gang.

HOLD DOWN A SHADOW
Geoffrey Jenkins

Maluti Rider, with the help of four of the world's most wanted men, is determined to destroy the Katse Dam and release a killer flood.

THAT NICE MISS SMITH
Nigel Morland

A reconstruction and reassessment of the trial in 1857 of Madeleine Smith, who was acquitted by a verdict of Not Proven of poisoning her lover, Emile L'Angelier.

THE PLEASURES OF AGE
Robert Morley

The author, British stage and screen star, now eighty, is enjoying the pleasures of age. He has drawn on his experiences to write this witty, entertaining and informative book.

THE VINEGAR SEED
Maureen Peters

The first book in a trilogy which follows the exploits of two sisters who leave Ireland in 1861 to seek their fortune in England.

A VERY PAROCHIAL MURDER
John Wainwright

A mugging in the genteel seaside town turned to murder when the victim died. Then the body of a young tearaway is washed ashore and Detective Inspector Lyle is determined that a second killing will not go unpunished.

TIGER TIGER
Frank Ryan

A young man involved in drugs is found murdered. This is the first event which will draw Detective Inspector Sandy Woodings into a whirlpool of murder and deceit.

CAROLINE MINUSCULE
Andrew Taylor

Caroline Minuscule, a medieval script, is the first clue to the whereabouts of a cache of diamonds. The search becomes a deadly kind of fairy story in which several murders have an other-worldly quality.

LONG CHAIN OF DEATH
Sarah Wolf

During the Second World War four American teenagers from the same town join the Army together. Forty-two years later, the son of one of the soldiers realises that someone is systematically wiping out the families of the four men.

DATE DUE

6/98

SE 22			
NO 11 '98			
66 - 7.19			
JY 2 - '99			